Resolutions

Jenn Faulk

Copyright © 2012 Jenn Faulk

All rights reserved.

ISBN:0615784976
ISBN-13:9780615784977

DEDICATION

To Wes, for believing in this and in me.

Because of the Lord's great love

we are not consumed,

for his compassions never fail.

They are new every morning;

great is your faithfulness.

Lamentations 3:22-23

ACKNOWLEDGMENTS

A big, huge thank you to Wes, who valiantly tread into the mysterious world of chick lit by agreeing to read this book for me. This won't be the last "girl book" you read, Pastor! Many thanks to Ana and Emma for being so very patient with Mommy as this project took shape and finally found completion this year. Thank you to Mom, Sandi, and Kerry for reading it early on and being such great encouragers. And finally, THANK YOU to the ladies of Memorial Baptist Church of Pasadena for asking, "When can we read that book?" Your day has finally come, ladies! Hope you enjoy it!

1 NEW YEAR'S EVE

It was ten minutes until midnight on New Year's Eve night, and my mouth was full of wedding cake.

Not my wedding cake, obviously, since I was in my favorite pair of pj pants, a comfy old sweatshirt from high school, and a fabulously tacky pair of leopard print slippers. This cake was our New Year cake, from a vendor who catered most of the weddings I worked and who always had a "sample" available for me once a year. "Because I just love you like that, Emily," he would wink at me as he passed the box across the counter and refused my money. His wife would pat me on the arm and tell me, "You tell all of your brides how wonderful this is!"

And it always was. Tonight's specialty was my favorite – white chocolate with strawberry cream filling, covered with cascading chocolate-dipped strawberries, some of which were decorated to look like little men in tuxedos.

"Exquisite," Sara had said when I lifted it out of the box.

"Kinda creepy," Melissa had noted, pointing to a tuxedo strawberry that looked more headless than his brothers.

"Just wait," I told her. "This will be better than last year's. As if that's even possible."

The three of us were having a party – a party just for us. We had been having these every New Year's Eve since we were ten. Our friendship had started long before then, back when we were the only three babies in attendance at Grace Community Church twenty-eight years ago when my father began his pastorate there. The church had been very small then, but we were blissfully unaware in our crèche department, chewing on the same plastic toys, being diapered by the same volunteers, and babbling incoherent ramblings to one another each and every Sunday morning. As the church grew, we transitioned from the crèche to the preschool, from the preschool to the elementary age wing, from the elementary age wing to the Junior High youth, and from the Junior High youth to the High School group. Along the way there were other friends who came in and out of our lives, but for the most part, it remained the three of us, running to class to meet up and tell one another some silly story during our younger days, coolly meeting up after the service when we were angst-ridden teens who were mortified by our parents, and now, post-college and nearing our thirtieth birthdays, finding time in our busy schedules and lives to continue our friendship.

This New Year's Eve tradition had served us well, even during college. We were fortunate that even though we chose three different universities in different parts of the state, we were all home for the same holidays and could still do our annual countdown of the year.

"This," Sara said, pointing her fork at the layers of strawberry goo wedged so delicately in the cake, "is what I'm getting for my wedding. Think he'll cut me a deal?"

Sara had been planning a wedding for quite a while. Years, in fact. She had met Jon during her last year of college, and although he seemed as committed and focused as she was back then, the six years since had gone on with no move towards marriage. Sara had started working as a kindergarten teacher in Fort Worth after graduation, and Jon had started work on his MBA. Two years later, he took a position with an investment firm in San Antonio, although he had offers nearer to home.

RESOLUTIONS

If you know your Texas geography, you know that Fort Worth and San Antonio aren't exactly in the same neighborhood, and since Jon, two years into the relationship was still no closer to a ring and a date, we all thought it was the beginning of the end. Sara didn't, though. She loved him beyond any valid reason we could see and continued to plan her life with him even though he made no move towards any kind of commitment.

That was Sara, though. Kind and sweet, optimistic and hopeful, perhaps to a fault at times.

Melissa eyed me questioningly for a moment. I gave a slight shake of my head, imperceptible to Sara, or so I thought.

"No, Melissa," she said in a sing-song voice. "He hasn't proposed yet. But there's always Valentine's Day, you know."

"Ugh, Valentine's Day," Melissa groaned. "Hate it, hate it, hate it..." She speared a bite of cake and popped it in her mouth. "This is good," she told me. "And you know I'd tell you if it wasn't."

I knew that she would. Melissa's best trait was her brutal honesty... although at times, it was also her worst trait. I had, on more than one occasion during high school, seen some poor unfortunate and unsuspecting guy shyly ask her out, only to have her look at him dubiously and say, "Me? But you're way too dumb for me." When I would express some amazement about this after the wounded boys would retreat, she'd say, "What?! It's true!" And it was. Melissa was smarter than all of them. She would eventually show some remorse for her harsh treatment of the male gender, saying that perhaps some kindness and tact would have been more honoring to the Lord. But she never apologized for being smart. After racing through a bachelor's degree and a master's degree with high marks, she was now the only female engineer on staff at a secure government location that we couldn't know too much about, even as her closest and oldest friends. "It has to do with missiles," she told us once, very simply, and never spoke another word about it. (I remember Sara's response to this had been to treat her with increased care and gentleness, as she was quite sure Melissa had become a domestic terrorist of some sort.) Melissa's life was her job, and she spent even most of her free time working towards higher achievements there.

As for me, I was also working my dream job, a position that I ironically referred to as "Dream Destroyer." That wasn't the official nomenclature on the door of my office, though, as the truth would have likely scared any and all clients away. The friendlier title assigned to me was Assistant to the Bridal Events Coordinator.

I had applied fresh from college with little hope of getting the position, stepping into the regal downtown hotel for my interview and feeling as though I had shrunk three feet by being in the very presence of such elegance. *Surely*, I thought to myself, *only THE most talented and experienced coordinator could get a job here!* I hadn't counted on being the last of twelve girls hired that year alone, thanks to the gruesome nature of the job. Unbeknownst to me that day, they were fully booked for the season, were in desperate need of some naïve help, and were ready to take just about anyone. My boss, THE Bridal Events Coordinator, greeted me that day in a full pink suit, fresh corsage on her lapel, spike heels on her feet, and hands full of bling. Big, huge, gigantic bling. Her hair was exquisite, her makeup flawless, and her smile so warm and tender.

She had me fooled.

"Dear Miss Fisher," she said, holding out a hand to me delicately. "I'm Evelyn Primrose."

I must confess, I didn't know whether to shake her hand, kiss her 3-carat emerald cut engagement ring, or curtsy. I managed to firmly shake her hand in my own, then on her invitation, followed her to her office, a feminine space dominated by floral furniture and her own amazing bridal portraits. Evelyn had been stunning even then as a debutante set to wed the mysterious Mr. Primrose, whom I had never met. (And whom I suspected was actually a Mr. Butts or Mr. Snarflehock, names that Evelyn would have traded in during office hours for the impossibly feminine and genteel Primrose.) On that fateful day that I interviewed, stars in my eyes, she laid the job out for me with a genuine smile – assist brides in planning their dream weddings, walk alongside the wedding couple as they made decisions for the reception, act as the middle man between vendors and brides, and (she said this with a flourish) exude elegance that befits such a fine venue.

It was perfect. Perfect, perfect, perfect. I would have told Evelyn anything she wanted to hear. Do I know every kind of flower type ever seen under the sun? Absolutely, Mrs. Primrose. Can I sew up twenty layers of silk and tulle in ten minutes? Most certainly, Mrs. Primrose. Was I willing to be a team player in this bridal machine we were running? Without a doubt, Mrs. Primrose!

And so I began, quickly discovering that it was Evelyn's job to dream big with the brides, to suggest the vendors, to show them how extravagant their big day could be, and to fill their heads with impossible fantasies.... before sending them to the face of hard-cash reality, yours truly. I had only wanted to have the fun of planning a wedding without the work of a marriage. What I got was akin to couples' therapy as I broke the news to dazed brides and grooms that while, yes, those peonies that grow naturally in Bali (and nowhere else in known civilization) were exquisite, they did nevertheless cost a fortune. And while, yes, the dance floor we could offer looked like something your Uncle Bubba could set up for you with no problem at all, we would require that our people do it and that it would cost you $300 for set up, $300 for tear down, and, my sincerest apologies, $300 for repair work later at the very least. (Even if you didn't do anything to it!) Oh, and our most efficient meal (Evelyn frowned on my more honest word "cheap") would still cost $50 a head, even though it likely only cost us $2 a plate to make. I was the number cruncher, the business end of the deal, and many times, the great consoler of all manner of hysterical brides.

My dream job was a big nightmare most days. It paid the bills, though, and paid them well enough that I had paid off all of my student loans in record time. With that monkey off my back, I was saving up for a real home... if my little clunker car would just live a little bit longer. I anticipated being the Dream Destroyer for many, many more years, as it was a good job with the opportunity for advancement, for one day being THE Bridal Events Coordinator. And hiring some other poor schmuck to do my job.

It didn't take me long at my job to realize that no one expected me to last very long. All of the other assistants had quit within a month of taking the position, but six years later, I was still there. Evelyn liked my tenacity, and God bless her, I liked Evelyn for just having the guts to be Evelyn. It couldn't have been easy to send the wolves to me every day, but she did it without reservation, noting that even the unpleasant parts of wedding planning were crucial to a truly successful event. When things got really rough for me, she was a shrewd businesswoman who could come to my defense when it looked like I was going to literally be in the middle of a knockdown drag-out between brides and grooms. "Savages!," she told me once, after a particularly belligerent bride had attempted negotiating with me by screaming in my face. "As if they could *ever* have their hootenanny of a wedding *here!*" If for no other reason, I loved her for being able to wear a Chanel suit and Jimmy Choos while saying the word "hootenanny."

The memory made me smile as the seconds ticked by to midnight.

"What?," Melissa asked.

"Oh," I told her, shaking my head and swallowing the last bite of heaven, "just thinking about the perks of the job."

"Amen!," Sara said. "I love cake."

Melissa licked her fork clean and looked at my plate. "Are you done with that?"

I nodded and passed it into her waiting hands. Sara did the same, adding, "Thank you for letting us have our party here."

Melissa waved her away as she walked to her kitchen. "No problem," she said. "I'm still trying to figure out my way around here."

She had bought the house about a month ago, and she still had moving boxes everywhere. The house was, for all intents and purposes, my dream house. Brand new, three bedroom, two baths, extra-spacious kitchen, large living room, and a two car garage. We normally had our sleepover in either Sara's or my cramped little apartments, so this was a treat.

"I would love a house like this some day," I told her. "Just exactly like this."

Sara smiled at me, tucking her legs underneath her on the couch. "What neighborhood would you have it in? Close to work?"

"Oh, if only I could afford something closer to work," I sighed. "Real estate over there is rather astronomical."

"Tell me about it," Melissa said. "It's just better value for your money to buy something or have something built out here in the suburbs rather than right near the heart of the city." She loaded the dishwasher as she spoke, glancing up at us through the open bar window above her sink. "Trust me – the city is growing out, so that by the time I sell this house, it WILL be in the city and will have tripled in value."

"Sell it?," Sara asked incredulously. "You just bought it!"

"Well, I'm not saying that I'll sell it tomorrow," she shrugged. "But I'm just starting out in my career. Plenty of opportunities to move on up, especially at our age. We're not getting any younger, girls. Time we start pursuing the bigger things at work."

Sara winced a tiny bit at the mention of "our age." I'm a firm believer that you can tell a lot about a person based on the way they look at hitting milestone ages. Take us, for example. With our thirtieth birthdays looming on the horizon, Melissa was ecstatic, eager for the added leverage and prestige that being thirty-something would give her in her career. She had confided to us on more than one occasion that she worked with nothing but men in their fifties who not only looked down on her for being a woman but also for being a "kid." The older she got, the better it got, as she reached greater seniority and was getting farther and farther away from the applied assumptions that went with being a twenty-something fresh out of grad school.

Sara, on the other hand, was dreading the leap to thirty. Though she didn't dwell on it with us, it was clear whenever we'd get another wedding invitation in the mail from someone in our singles group or when a young married couple from the church would be back in worship that first Sunday after welcoming home a new baby that Sara wasn't happy with where she was at twenty-eight. Sara's best case scenario was married with children, and with no sign of Jon moving her toward that destination, she wasn't looking forward to aging.

I didn't really care either way. I knew I'd have to be in my forties (or fifties!) before Evelyn retired and promoted me to her position. She was only in what I assumed to be her forties, and with no children, she had plenty of energy and time to devote to many years of working. I didn't really anticipate marriage in my future, so I wasn't worried about my chances becoming more and more slim in that area. Birthdays were just another opportunity to get together with family, blow out some candles, and have leftover cake for breakfast for a week.

Speaking of cake, Melissa was poised with a fork in hand over the tiny sliver left in the cake box. "Can't let this go to waste," she mumbled to me when I looked at her questioningly.

"Well, no, of course not."

Sara, obviously stressed by our mention of age, ran to the kitchen to grab herself a fork. "Em, you want one?," she asked.

"Sure, why not?"

She came back, handed mine to me, and plunged her own into the edge side, taking most of the frosting.

"Hey, hey! That's the best part!," Melissa protested.

"I know," Sara moaned. "I really shouldn't. I'm going to gain so much weight because of this."

"Please," Melissa snorted, and she was right. Sara never seemed to gain or lose weight either way, always effortlessly staying the same size – slim, but not too slim, tall, but not too tall. Just perfect, actually. She made me look like a giant in all of my 5'11 glory. Melissa was only a few inches shorter than me but carried a few extra pounds, so Sara's random mentions of weight while we ate always solicited ungracious comments.

Sara shook her head. "Just watching my waist line," she glared at Melissa, "you know, since we're all getting OLD."

"Well, we're not getting younger. Can't get younger, scientifically speaking," Melissa said. Then, considering the cake, "This probably is a bad idea, though. How many calories?"

I squinted a bit. "Do you want the answer I would give a weight-conscious bride?"

Sara nodded, her mouth full of cake. "Yes."

"Then, nothing at all!"

Melissa considered her fork carefully. "I need to work out more. And more than what I do now would be…. well, anything."

Sara put her own fork down with a sigh. "Is that one of your resolutions?"

"I don't have any resolutions," she said. "How about you?"

She shrugged. "I probably should have some. I just can't ever think of anything good."

"You know," I told them, taking the rest of the cake back to the couch with me, "we should think of some together."

Melissa looked at me questioningly. "Resolutions?"

"Yeah!," Sara said. "If we have some resolutions together, we can help each other! Like having a friend do a diet with you. Accountability, all of that."

"Diet?! Who said anything about a diet?! I was just talking about a little exercise!"

I sat forward, a list already starting to form in my head. "Well, no, they don't all have to be about diet and exercise. Maybe some about... travel? Um... career?"

"Ooooh, I like it," Sara said. "And new hobbies! Getting involved in new ways at church!"

"Wait, wait, wait," Melissa said. "You're making it sound really complicated. That's too much to even remember."

"It could be really easy," I told them. "One resolution a month. Just ten months. Starting in February, and ending in November, before December when everything –"

"Gets crazy," they both finished for me. Seems our careers weren't all that different after all.

"Yeah, Melissa," Sara said. "I think Emily's onto something. Are you in?"

After a pause, Melissa shrugged. "I guess." Then, pointing her finger at each one of us, slowly. "But you're not going to go all Nazi on me with this, are you? Just for fun?"

"Of course, of course," Sara said. "Just for fun."

I pulled my planner out of my purse, turned to a blank page, and asked, "So, what should be on the list?"

We missed the countdown entirely as we threw ourselves into the task and threw out ideas, vetoing some, okaying others, chatting back and forth about what might work for each, and inevitably, arguing over resolutions we had no desire to honor.

"'Amp up my love life?'," Melissa repeated Sara's suggestion, annoyed. "What does that even mean?"

"It means," she began patiently, "that the two of you haven't been on a date since... well, never."

I began to beg to differ, remembering a few guys in college who I went out with a couple of times each and then... well, never went out with again. Maybe she had a point.

Melissa was unwavering. "I'm not going to go out and start dating some doofus guys just because you think I need to."

"They don't have to be doofus guys, Melissa," Sara said in the sweet voice I'm sure she used with her kindergarten students. "There are plenty of nice, normal men out there who you might enjoy getting to know."

Melissa was baffled. "And just how do you propose that I go about meeting them?" She looked to me. "Emily, speak up! How are you going to check this one off your list?"

I shrugged. "I'm sure there's some guy Nick knows that Jessica's been waiting to introduce me to." This was true enough. My sister, Jessica, was always looking out for "potentials" as she called them. Her husband, Nick, ran his own construction business and had a whole crew full of them.

"A blind date?," Melissa asked. "For real? You would really do this?"

I nodded. "I guess. It's not like I have to marry the guy or anything."

"Ridiculous!," Melissa exclaimed, irritated by my lack of opposition to the idea and what it meant for her.

"Well, look," Sara said. "Some of these are going to get me out of my comfort zone, too. Like 'go somewhere exotic.' First of all, I have no money to go somewhere exotic, and second of all, I've never even left the country. If I can do this, you can surely go on one date."

Melissa started to say something, then bit her lip. "Fine," she spat out. "Whatever." She bent her head down over my planner and began scrawling another resolution, while Sara gave me the thumbs up over her. "I see that!," Mel yelled.

Finally, after much discussion, we had it narrowed down to ten resolutions...

February – Get in shape

March – Amp up your love life

April – Volunteer somewhere new in church

May – Go somewhere exotic

June – Begin attending a weekly Bible study

July – Help someone who is truly in need

August – Improve your home

September – Start a new hobby

RESOLUTIONS

October – Move forward in your career

November – Improve your social life

"That all sounds great!," Sara said, clapping her hands enthusiastically. "This is going to be so much fun!"

Melissa shook her head. "I don't much like that last one. I love our social life! Occasional outings and dinners with the singles group, our New Year party every year…. I don't know that I want anything to change!"

"Mmm," I said with a smile. "I wonder what next year will be like… will we all be together again, eating cake?"

"I hope so," Sara said.

"Me, too," Melissa agreed.

"To us," I said, as we all three tapped our Diet Cokes together in a toast.

2 JANUARY

Sundays, for a pastor's family, are a cross between family time and show time.

My childhood, for example, was full of Sundays with just too much family and not a whole lot to show for it.

I remember racing my older sister, Jessica, to the bathroom every Sunday morning so that I would get at least five minutes to shower and brush my teeth before we had to leave for church. Unfortunately, her petite build made her quicker than me, and she always seemed to get there first, where she proceeded to hog the space until we had three minutes to go before we had to leave. My mother would come into our bedroom just as Jess sauntered out of the bathroom, looking beautiful. The two of them would stand there together, two perfectly put together versions of the same woman, and stare at me, my hair going in all directions, my pajamas still on, and my teeth unbrushed.

"Well, Emily?," my mother would ask. "Are you planning on getting ready? Ever?"

I would sprint past them and rush through a quick shower, brushing my teeth while I was in there to save time, then throwing on whatever my hands grabbed first from the closet, snatching up a pair of flip flops and my purse just as my younger brother, Matthew, shut the door to the garage.

"Hey, hey!," I'd yell, flinging it back, then sprinting past him to the van, where my mother was already sitting in the driver's seat, Jessica sitting smugly next to her in the passenger seat.

"I'm ready," I'd grumble, as Matthew would edge past me, throw himself into the seat next to me, and sigh. I would search through my purse for a brush and do what I could to the wet mess on my head.

"I tell you kids," my mother would begin, as she backed the van out of the driveway, "one of these days I'm going to leave early with your father and just let you all hitchhike to church! Why, if I had a nickel for every time..." On and on she'd rant, until we would pull into the church parking lot where she'd slide into the space next to the pastor's, shut off the engine, and smile at us, clapping her hands and saying, "It's church time!"

She wasn't a hypocrite. By that time, we were all finally awake, okay with one another, and ready to go. It was "show time" in a real way, a good way. Church was a living and active experience every week, meeting with God and learning from Him, and we were fortunate to do it as a family.

Sundays as an adult weren't much different. Thankfully, I no longer had to fight my sister for time in the shower, but old habits die hard, which meant that I was almost always late for worship. That first Sunday of the year was no different and found me pulling into the parking lot just as the very last spot was being taken... by my sister, in her giant mommy van.

"Great," I muttered. Then honking the horn and rolling down my window, I yelled, "Way to take the last spot!"

"Aunt Emmy!" My oldest nephew, Sean, waved to me, jumping up and down. He was almost six and into a superhero phase. Jessica had actually let him wear a Superman cape to church today, which must have prompted his three younger brothers to request their own strange church clothes, as evidenced by four year old Sam in fatigues, three year old Scott in boots and a Stetson hat, and even one year old Stuart in footy pjs. Well, maybe Stuart's get up was more for comfort than anything else, what with the chilly weather that had blown in over the weekend.

"Hey, you!," Jessica yelled back as she flung a huge diaper bag over her shoulder and handed Stuart in his carrier to my brother-in-law, Nick, who waved hello to me. "There are plenty of spots still left!"

"Where?"

"Over there," Nick said, pointing to the outlying lot across the street.

"Fan-tastic," I said. "I'll see you inside... you know after I trek halfway across from my parking space on the other side of the world and –"

"SEAN NICHOLAS HUNTINGTON! If I see you even THINK about running across the parking lot without holding my hand, I swear I will snatch you COMPLETELY bald-headed!" Jessica was in fine form today, her tiny little frame already clicking away in high heels, as she bid me adieu with a toss of her head, a little boy's hand in each of hers.

I rolled up my window and turned around, crossed the street and parked, then began the long trek into the building, wishing for warmer weather as I did so. She didn't keep me from the shower anymore, but in some ways, this was worse.

She was waiting inside for me when I got there, looking slightly apologetic. "Sorry that I didn't let you have that spot," she said. I noticed the dark circles under her eyes and the way her curly hair fell in her face. Suddenly I realized that now SHE was the one who didn't have time to get ready in the morning, and I felt guilty for begrudging her a parking spot.

I waved her apology away. "You have your hands full. You needed it more than me." I blew warm air into my cupped hands. "Where are the boys?"

"I sent those wild monkeys off with Nick. Told him he could take them to the nursery and preschool departments. My nerves are just ALL shot after this morning."

"Tough morning at home, huh?" I couldn't even imagine, to be quite honest. Jessica and Nick had met right here at the church eight years ago through our singles ministry. The Pinnacle, it was called. I had to hide a smirk even now, remembering how Jessica, who had no other dream in life than to be a wife and a mother, had set her sights on finding a man at The Pinnacle. "The odds are good," she told me, which I followed up with, "but the goods are odd." Sure enough, there was a string of odd ducks that she brought through our home as she sifted through them all, dating and then dismissing, in a fashion that was almost cruel. Finally, she seemed to just completely give up as the possibilities ran low. She began leading a ladies' study through Pinnacle and became so immersed in her service that she didn't hardly notice when a new believer named Nick, won to the Lord through one of Pinnacle's men's ministries, started coming to church. He finally caught her attention by getting her women's group involved in a construction project he was organizing for the twenty-something singles. They fell in love practically overnight, were married a little under a year later, and had been having babies ever since. Jessica was living her dream, staying at home while Nick ran his construction company, and loving her life, despite her insistence that her progeny were tree-climbing primates. Which they indeed were, if you wanted to get all technical about it.

She let a smile play smugly on her lips. "Well... I wouldn't call this morning tough," she said as we began walking to the sanctuary. "It was quite good, actually."

"Okay, if this is going to become another TMI conversation about how you and Nick wake each other up, then I would just rather we –"

She rolled her eyes. "NO. That's not it. Geez, grow up, Emily." She paused, with a mischievous glance my direction. "But it's kind of related."

I stopped walking and put my hands on her shoulders, leaning close to her to whisper, "Are you… are you pregnant?" I refrained from adding, AGAIN?!

She smiled triumphantly. "Yes. I took the test this morning." She was practically beaming.

"Another nephew!," I whispered, excited for us both.

"OR NIECE," she said severely. "Please, Lord, PLEASE…"

I smiled at her. "Oh, but it's great either way. A blessing no matter what." I hugged her. "Congratulations!"

She hugged me back. "Don't say anything to Mom. Wouldn't want her knowing that I told you first or anything."

"Of course not. My lips are sealed. How far along are you?"

"Oh, only six weeks, probably. Not really sure. I'll probably be due in August. Again."

Three of Jessica's four boys had been born in August. She and Nick were apparently most fertile in the brief few weeks between Thanksgiving and Christmas, and as she had confided to me once, "you would think that eating all of that food would really put a man on the outs as far as that kind of thing goes, but I swear to you, I think it makes Nick even MORE touchy-feely and –"

I closed my eyes to stop this memory from playing any further and ruining my Sunday. "That's great news," I told her. "Let me know when you start feeling sick in the mornings, and I'll try to move my schedule around to help out when I can."

"You're the best," she said, as we continued walking. Then, changing the subject, "How was your New Year party?"

"It was great," I told her. "Made some resolutions, ate some cake, watched the countdown. You know, that kind of thing." I smiled.

"Did Sara get a..." She looked at me questioningly.

"No," I said, repeating what Sara herself had said about it, "but there's always Valentine's Day."

Jessica looked sympathetic. I wondered how big of a conversation point this was with people who knew Jon and Sara both, and I hoped that, for Sara's sake, people would just mind their own business. Including my nosy sister. She opened her mouth to say something about the topic, but I cut her off.

"How was your New Year?"

"Oh, fine," she said, suppressing a yawn. "I'm just so tired these days. I only made it to ten o'clock, but that was just so I could call Matt."

I closed my eyes and cringed. "Ohhhh..."

"Did you not call him over the holidays?"

I shook my head. Our younger brother, Matthew, was a US Marine. He had enlisted straight out of high school despite my mother's histrionics that she would DIE if he joined the military and went into combat. I was shocked when she didn't drive him back up to the recruiter and tell him to undo it all, but I credit even that rare moment of self-control to Matthew, who calmly told her that he was a "freakin' adult, Mother" and that "this is the best choice for me." He was right. Seven years later, he was still in active duty, had done two tours in Iraq, and was now stationed in Okinawa, Japan. I made it a point to call him on holidays and his birthday especially, but I had completely forgotten in the insanity that had been my work schedule this year. All those Christmas brides...

"I'm such a dunce," I told Jessica.

"No, you're not. Call him tonight."

I nodded. "I will. Don't tell Mom I didn't call him!"

And right on cue, there was our mother, stepping out of the "powder room" just outside the sanctuary.

"Well, THERE you girls are!," she said, hugging Jessica first, then looking up at my hair and commenting, "Emily, is it fashionable to let your roots show like that?"

"Good morning to you, too, Mom," I said, giving her a hug, as Jessica rolled her eyes at me behind Mom's back.

"I'm not trying to be ugly," Mom protested, obviously sensing Jessica's eye-rolling chastisement. "It's just that I really don't know what's fashionable. I'm not nearly as connected and on the 'up and up' as you young people."

It was a complete lie. My mother was more connected and modern than I was. She spent half of every day on Facebook, maintaining twice-removed friendships with people who were my acquaintances in college, people I hadn't heard from in years. "Emily," she would say from time to time, "did you know that dear Marianne finally had her little boy last week? Looks like she and her husband just bought a HUGE house." She knew everything about everyone as long as they posted their information online, and for this very reason, I only kept a minimal presence on any and all social networking sites, half convinced that my mother would totally be all up in my business if I ever completely ventured into the wild, wild, west of the Internet.

"Oh, I know my roots are showing," I told her, touching the crown of my head. "I just haven't been able to get in to see the stylist." I sighed. "I'm half tempted to just go gray naturally to save myself the trouble of trying to book an appointment."

My mother looked aghast at this. "You're... gray?!" Please, like her own hair hadn't turned white when she was two years younger than me. "Must be your father's genes."

Jessica tried to hide a smirk. "Must be, Mom. We better get inside – the service is about to start." The two of them continued chatting as we walked in together through the back door of the sanctuary.

The church always took my breath away. Grace had grown in my father's long tenure there. When we first arrived, we had been in an older building with school cafeteria type acoustics, wood paneling, low ceilings, and bright red carpet. I had loved the seventies feel of the building as a child, not knowing that all churches weren't so dated, forming in my mind the idea that this was just what church was supposed to look like. By the time I was in junior high, we were having a hard time fitting everyone into our sanctuary, and rather than splitting into more than one service, my father insisted that the church body needed to stay together as a whole to worship. The only option that left us with was a building project. It took us three years from start to finish to build the traditional, cathedral-style sanctuary we were now in, and as soon as the loan was paid off a year later, construction went up for the activities building, then the singles annex, and on and on until our little one building church had become a complex facility. I wondered at times if my father's vision of one church body in tight community and fellowship had been lost in the growth and if we weren't now just functioning as several groups within the same building. I looked around, as I did every week when I made my way to my seat, and found the faces of the people I had grown up knowing, alongside many more faces of those I had yet to meet.

Then, my eyes found an all-too familiar face. One that offered an awkward smile as he caught my eye. Pastor Stephen Hayes, my father's associate pastor. I sighed as I waved, just as awkwardly, as he began making his way over to me.

Pastor Stephen had come on staff fresh from seminary. I was in college when he became "associate pastor to young adults and singles," and I well remembered the hype that had surrounded him when he arrived. He was the "young blood" that was going to revitalize the church, in my father's opinion, bringing new and edgy ways of reaching the next generation that older pastors like my father just weren't able to duplicate, try though they might. Pastor Stephen had come with these expectations already placed upon him, and while he did a lot to grow the percentage of young people and young families that we had in the church, he was more intent on Biblical teaching than catchy gimmicks. The result was real spiritual growth and not the astronomical exponential growth of fad members, who would fall away after the newness of the programs wore off. Some people loved Pastor Stephen for his "sola Scriptura" approach, and some people hated Pastor Stephen for not being more program-driven.

And most were just plain confused at how odd it was that such an attractive man would still be single at his age.

That, of course, is where I and all of the awkwardness came into play. There had been a rush of eligible bachelorettes who threw themselves at him in the beginning of his pastorate, but he had successfully dodged them all. For a while, it seemed that every woman in the church was intent on making that man her man, but much to the shock and dismay of every one of them, Pastor Stephen had no intention of marrying any of them and was actually more focused on – gasp! – ministry. Those who didn't get married to other men eventually gave up on Pastor Stephen, and over time, he became less of a sex symbol in the church – praise the Lord for that – and more of an actual pastor to his people. People had very nearly forgotten all about the fact that he was single... until he started seeking my help with projects, one-on-one.

My theory on his recent interest? I was in the singles department. I actually kept attendance records for the group and did follow up with our visitors, so I knew everyone, at least in that ministry area of our membership. Being the senior pastor's daughter and an events coordinator was also helpful, as I understood better than most how to protect Pastor Stephen's time and how to structure our events as to have them run the most efficiently. Programs and events were my forte, and with his guidance, we had increased the number of fun activities to supplement the real spiritual growth going on in our group. We weren't just growing spiritually – we were growing in numbers, too.

But more than that, I think Pastor Stephen sought me out because I was perfectly happy being single. I didn't date around, had no real interest in finding anyone, and sincerely believed that I had the gift of singleness . And I was thankful for it. I wasn't giving off a needy, want-a-man vibe. And for Pastor Stephen, who had spent the first several years of his ministerial career stepping gingerly through a minefield of women with itchy engagement ring fingers, this was a refreshing change.

People still talked, though, and I'm sure he had heard the rumors just as I had. Stephen and Emily, sitting in a tree, k-i-s-s-i-n-g and all that. There was no kissing going on, of course, but the implication was there still – that we would be well matched, an obvious coupling that would make sense for us and for the church. This was the source of awkwardness. And just recently, over the last few months, I had started wondering if perhaps there wasn't more to what was going on, if perhaps I didn't want more than what was going on, if maybe all that people were saying didn't have some semblance or shade of truth to it. To my great shame, I had to be honest with myself every now and then when he asked me to do something and admit to myself (if never to another living soul!) that I had a little crush on him. Just like every other single woman who had walked through the doors at Grace during the last decade.

So, sue me.

But I had to hold it together at all times. Because everyone was watching. Even now, as Pastor Stephen made his way across the sanctuary to speak with me, I could feel the eyes boring into us, the whispered gossip, and, heaven help me, the audible creak of the pew as a whole section of senior adult ladies leaned forward to hear what we were going to say to one another.

"Good morning, Pastor Stephen," I said brightly, offering my hand and sparing him the hug quandary. My father was a hugger – a loud, boisterous, grab-you-up-out-of-the-pew hugger – but Stephen, for obvious reasons, was more reserved.

He seemed grateful for the handshake. "Hey, Emily," he said. For an illogical second, as I looked up into his face (he was one of the only men I knew who was actually taller than I was in my heels), I fell into the blueness of his eyes, let my gaze drift over his brownish-blonde locks, and felt my heart speed up when he smiled his dimpled smile at me. I cursed myself silently while Pastor Stephen went on obliviously. "I know this is far in advance," he said to me, "but I wanted to know if you had plans for Valentine's Day...???"

I blinked, thinking that surely, I hadn't just heard what I thought I heard. Sure enough, though, he had said it, as evidenced by the reactions around me. My mother and my sister, both sitting next to me and chitter-chattering away, couldn't keep their heads from shooting up and all out staring in our direction as they fell into silence. I turned my head to the side, gave them a look, and turned back to him as soon as they looked back down at their laps.

"Um, well," I said, pulling my planner out of my purse and mentally shaking my head free of its crazy wanderings, "let me see." February 14th -- not a Saturday this year but still a popular choice for some brides. Sure enough, there was an early evening wedding on my schedule.

"I have a wedding and a dessert reception at seven that evening," I told him, pulling out my pen and getting ready to write down whatever instructions he had. I was sure there was some event he was wanting to have for the singles department.

His face fell slightly. "Oh...seven that evening?"

"Well, yeah, but I still have the rest of the day free. I won't need to be up there until two in the afternoon." I looked at him questioningly. "Were you wanting to plan an evening banquet for Pinnacle again this year? I could get a team together and have it all set up the night before, or that morning even."

He smiled a little as he shook his head. "No, it wasn't that... it's just that..." He seemed flustered. Which made me a bit flustered. Without turning around, I knew that those senior adult ladies were practically falling out of the pew with as far as they were leaning forward. God bless them, I could even hear some of their hearing aids buzzing from being turned up so loud in an effort to catch this awkward little episode of my life.

Mercifully, the praise band began their opening set, and Stephen, who needed to be at the podium to give the welcome after their first song, had to go. "I'll talk to you later about it, okay?," he offered. I nodded. "Sure." He turned and began walking to the front, wiping his brow as he went.

I sat down, considering this strange exchange. Jessica elbowed me, grinning madly. "Emily!," she said. "Pastor Stephen was about to ASK YOU OUT!" My mother shushed her, but she kept right on going. "I told you so!" Nick, looking quite worn down from depositing all of his children in their different classrooms, made his way into the pew, where my mother scooted over to make room for him. "Nick," Jessica said, turning to him, "didn't I tell you that Pastor Stephen TOTALLY has the hots for Emily?" He looked at me rather doubtfully. Gee, thanks.

"You are NOT having this conversation with me in the middle of church," I whispered fiercely to Jessica. There had to be some other explanation for Pastor Stephen's interest this morning. All of the other times, it had been about events, classes, and other church business. Surely it was this time, too, right? Because he didn't want anything else, right? And because I didn't want anything else, right? Right?!

I slugged her. "Thanks a lot!," I said, as she winced. "Way to put all of these weird unholy thoughts in my head," I gestured wildly, indicating the swirling confusing things that I was thinking. Then, remembering that she was expecting, "Oh, I'm so sorry! I shouldn't have hit you in your condition."

She opened her mouth to tell me to forget about it, but before she could get the words out, my mother leaned over Nick, grabbed Jessica's knee, and hissed, "Condition?! Please tell me that you're not expecting AGAIN?!" Ah, Mom. Gotta love that tact!

Jessica put on her pout face and hissed right back, "Well, yes I am! And the way you asked me makes you a shoe-in for grandmother of the year!"

"Stuart is barely a year old!"

"He's almost a year AND A HALF old, Mother!"

"Do you want your uterus to just COMPLETELY fall out of your body?!"

"MOTHER! How DARE you say something that crass!"

"Oh, Jessica –"

"Oh, Mother –"

Back and forth they went for a few minutes, two of the exact same personalities in different bodies, neither one of them even listening to the other's tirade, taking the attention completely off of my enigmatic conversation with Pastor Stephen. Nick looked at me and shrugged, not bothered in the least by the way my mother was beginning to hyperventilate and by the way Jessica was spitting as she sped-talked. Pastor Stephen could have been telling all of us that the church building was on fire from the podium, and my family wouldn't have heard a single word.

Then, my father took to the pulpit to pray. And our pew fell silent. I smiled a little to myself as I bowed my head, thinking of how often this scenario had played itself out in our history. Fights, bickering, hysterical crying fits, all of the hazards of growing up – and my father's calm insistence that we all stop, whether at home or at church, and pray it out. As he prayed over the morning service, over the membership gathered there with us, his words were calming, empowered, and led us all to focus, each in our own way.

We sang songs about God's faithfulness. I could see Sara from her place at the microphone singing lead vocals in the praise band and Melissa, sitting near the back of the sanctuary with some of the other singles, and I thought about all the resolutions we had committed to the Lord together. As my father preached from Lamentations about how God is faithful in season and out, in the good and the bad, in our times of trouble and our times of joy, I thought about the year ahead and how I could better serve Him as faithfully as He loved me. I reached over and squeezed my sister's hand, knowing that she was fighting back tears. I saw God's faithfulness to her, day in and day out, with her van full of boys and the neverending energy the Lord supplied to her. She smiled at me appreciatively.

We sang at the conclusion of the service, all holding hands, then prayed once more. As we were dismissed, my mother took my sister's hands, and with tears in her eyes, said, "I'm sorry. Congratulations." My sister began to cry as well, and they collapsed into one another's arms, weeping uncontrollably. Nick and I shrugged at one another again, and my father, who had made his way to our side rather quickly this week, surveyed the scene, and said, without even asking for confirmation, "Congratulations, Nick. I'm assuming God has blessed me with another grandchild." He gathered him up in his arms and gave him a huge hug.

"Thanks, Thomas," Nick said. "Jessica was just telling Lydia."

"Oh, Thomas!," my mother exclaimed, pulling my father up to her by the lapels of his suit jacket to hug him. "Another grandson!" Her trilling voice betrayed her a little as she said, "So soon!"

Jessica didn't seem to notice as she allowed herself to be embraced by my father. "It could be a granddaughter! It could!"

"Have you told Matthew yet?," my mother asked.

Jessica shook her head. "No, I talked with him over New Year's, but I just found out this morning. I'll probably call him tonight."

My mother got a gleam in her eyes. "Maybe he'll take some leave and come home for the birth!" She was always itching to find reasons for Matthew to come home. Although he hadn't been able to come out for any of the births since joining the Corps, she still held onto hope with each pregnancy announcement that she could wrangle a visit out of her youngest and have all three of her kids at home at the same time.

"How are you this morning, pumpkin?," my father asked as he picked me up in a hug. "Big wedding last night?"

I nodded. "Always."

"Thomas," my mother said, "I think we should all go out to lunch together to celebrate."

"Great idea," my father boomed. "I've got to catch a few hands on my way out, though, so I'll meet you at the car." He turned to leave, shaking several hands as he parted through the crowds.

"We've got to go get the boys," Jessica told my mother. "Emily, do you want to ride with us?"

I shook my head. "No, actually, I've got to go catch Sara and Melissa first. Can I just meet you all there?"

We made arrangements, said our goodbyes, and I darted through the crowds towards the spacious lobby, knowing just which couch I would find Melissa and Sara already sitting on. We'd met at church many times, so there wasn't much guesswork involved. Sara had told us before we all left on New Year's morning that we needed to meet at church on Sunday, several days away, to discuss what our plans were for our first resolution – get in shape. "Accountability needs to start early with this, ladies," she had told us. I already had a plan in place and was looking forward to starting it during that first week of February. I took my planner out as I was walking and marked February 1st with a star, and as I was doing so, ran right into Pastor Stephen.

Had he not caught my arms in his hands, I would have flung my planner about ten feet up in the air, throwing business cards and scribbled-on scraps of paper everywhere. I should have been thankful about this, but as I looked up into his eyes again, this time only about two inches from my own face, I could only think about how red my face must have been.

"I'm so sorry," he said, backing away. "Are you okay?"

I laughed a little too loudly. "Yeah, I'm fine, I just need to watch where I'm going."

He smiled. And the angels sang. I closed my eyes to block this thought out and opened them to find him staring at me, an unasked question in his expression. "Yes?," I prompted.

"Oh, well, I was just going to say that... I'm... I'm glad to see that you have your calendar out," he said, indicating the planner, which I was still holding, pen poised like an idiot.

"Oh, yeah!," I said breathlessly, as though I hadn't been thinking about February 14th all along. "You wanted to know about Valentine's Day, right?," I expertly hedged, while thinking, "please don't ask me out, please don't ask me out, please don't ask me out." I blinked and looked at him, confirming for about the millionth time since I had met him that he was indeed hot and that there wasn't any reason to NOT go out with him, but... oh, I just hadn't thought through it enough, and who knew what this would do to our church family if things didn't work out, and what if –

"Yes," he said. "I think a banquet of some sort on Valentine's Day would be wonderful."

Whew. So, THAT'S what he'd been getting at earlier.

(Of course, he had said that WASN'T what he had intended to ask, and he HAD seemed disappointed that I had other plans, BUT if he was willing to pretend like none of that ever happened, I was super happy to play along and not wonder about the "what ifs" until a much, much, much later date.)

"I agree," I said, calm and poised, and we launched into a spirited discussion about the program, the plans, and the details as I jotted down ideas, both of us seemingly much more relaxed with this kind of relationship than whatever he had hinted at earlier.

"Great," I said, smiling up at him and capping my pen, my mind temporarily removed from the awkwardness. "I'll get right on it."

He smiled. "You're the best, Emily," he said, squeezing my shoulder for just a second longer than was necessary, then walking back towards the offices.

Well, that was weird. But that was our relationship these days.

I sighed and continued walking towards the lobby, where Melissa and Sara were standing near the door. Melissa kept glancing down at her watch, while Sara saw me and started waving.

"There you are!," Melissa practically shouted across the room. "Some of us are starving to death over here!"

"Sorry, sorry, sorry," I told them. "I was..." I shook my head. "Nothing. I'm here now."

Sara looked at me with a hint of a smile of her face. "Okaaay," she said slowly. "I didn't want to keep either of you for a long time or anything, I just wanted to hear what the plans are for February." She looked at Melissa. "What are you going to do to get into shape?"

"Well," Melissa said, "I joined a gym."

"A gym?," Sara asked, impressed. "Do you even know what to do on gym equipment?"

This was probably a long shot, as Melissa had never, in all of our years of knowing her, ever aspired to any kind of athleticism. She looked at us disdainfully, though, and said, "Well, of course not. Which is why I signed up with a personal trainer." She said the last two words as if she had just signed a lease on a fancy European car.

"Wow!," Sara said, smiling. "You've got me beat. I'm just taking a yoga class at the Y."

"They offer yoga at the Y?," I asked, doubtful.

"Hey, I'm as surprised as you," she said. "It's all I can afford, though, so I'm giving it a shot."

"How about you, Em?," Melissa asked. "Synchronized swimming? Rhythmic dance? Archery?"

"Ha, ha," I managed drily. "Actually, I'm joining a running group."

"What's that?," Melissa scrunched up her nose.

"People. Running. In a group." I wasn't being flippant – I honestly didn't know all that much about it, but the hours and days they met worked with my crazy schedule.

Melissa nodded. "Well, that sounds good." She looked to Sara. "Happy now? We've done our homework. Can I go eat?"

Sara patted her on the back. "Good job! And yes." Then to me, "We're going to that new restaurant on 3rd and Main. Do you want to come with us?"

I shook my head. "No, I'm meeting up with the family. We're celebrating the good news that my sister is expecting."

"Again?!," Melissa asked, as a shadow of longing passed over Sara's face.

"Yes, again," I said.

"Ugh," Melissa said, "I can't imagine."

"Can't imagine what?," Sara asked.

"I can't imagine being pregnant every year!" A pause. "Or being pregnant at all, for that matter. Yeesh. Are they ever going to take a break?!"

I shrugged. "They're happy. Outnumbered but happy."

"Well, to each her own," Sara said. "Tell Jessica I send my congratulations."

"Will do," I said.

Melissa shrugged. "Me, too. Are we all still on for dinner next Thursday?"

After coordinating our schedules, we said goodbye, and I made my way out to my car, pulling my coat even closer around me as the temperature continued to drop.

Lunch with the family was as it always was – crowded, hectic, and drawn out about an hour too long. Jessica and my mother couldn't help themselves when they got together, though, and talked ceaselessly the entire time. The younger boys were all draped over shoulders by the time we finally got up to leave, well into their afternoon naps. I kissed them all goodbye, drove home, and settled into my comfortable clothes, where I curled up on the couch and read a book. I only stopped for dinner, which was warmed up leftovers from lunch, and then returned to the couch. This was one of the best parts of being single, of not being married, of not having children. So much time for me, to do the things I enjoyed doing, without worrying about someone else's preferences or someone else's needs. And with friends and family so close by, it didn't get lonely much at all.

I stayed up until late that evening, laying out my clothes for work, writing out my schedule for the week on a dry-erase board I kept on the fridge, and crunching some numbers for the Valentine's Day event. Finally, at 11pm, I called my brother on his cell phone. I never could remember the time difference, but I figured he was on his way to lunch. Or just returning. Or maybe it was seven o'clock in the morning. Who knew?

"Matthew Fisher," he answered, all business.

"Hey, Matt, it's Emily," I said.

"Well, well, well," his voice changed to the kidding tone I knew well. "You're calling a few weeks late."

"You know, there's no rule that says I have to call you at all."

He laughed. "I know, I know." I heard him cover up the receiver and whisper, "it's my sister" to someone. A female someone, who laughed at some joke he made that I couldn't hear.

"Well, well, well," I said, imitating him, "Who's that?"

"What are you talking about?"

"I hear a Guuu-rrrrl!," I said in an annoying sing-song voice.

"That, big sister, is none of your beeswax," he said. Then casually trying to change the subject, "How were your holidays?"

"Oh, no, you don't!," I said. "Who is that?"

He groaned. "Emily, please..."

"Fine," I said, "I don't have to know right now."

"Good. Thank you."

"But I'm going to find out soon enough. When I'm there!" I had figured early on that I could take a break from saving for a house and afford to go out and visit Matt for my exotic travel resolution. Since I hadn't seen him in two years, I thought it was well past time anyway.

Back on the telephone, there was a pause slightly longer than the normal delay. Thinking he hadn't heard, I took a breath to say it again, but he stopped me with, "What? When you're where?"

"I'm coming to Okinawa!"

Another pause. "Why?"

Well, that was a little insulting. "Well, I'm coming to visit YOU, you twit."

"When?"

"I'm looking at May. Is that a good time?"

There was a pause on the line. More whispering. The female voice shrilled excitedly.

"Okay, clearly there is someone there with you. Who is she?!," I demanded.

"I'm not telling you anything!"

I could picture her in my mind as clearly as though someone had taken a picture of her and laid it in front of me. A female Marine, dressed in her fatigues, eating a bento box next to my brother in some off-base little sushi shop, smiling at him adoringly for who knows what reason. I mean, I have trouble imagining him as anything but the kid who ran over my Barbies with his toy army tanks.

"Fine, fine, fine," I said. "Is it okay if I come in May?"

"Um... well, yeah, I guess."

"Don't sound so enthusiastic," I said.

He laughed. "I just don't get the sudden interest. You've never visited me before. "

I sighed. "Well, before now you've been stationed in combat zones. Not a lot of freedom for civilians to visit you there."

"True that," he said.

"And I guess I should have made more of an effort this fall, but work was insane."

"And it won't be that way in May? Before the summer wedding rush?"

I shook my head. "No, it will be. Which is exactly why I need to take my well deserved vacation right then. I need to get out of town before the June brides make me crazy. Crazier than they're already making me."

"You already have June brides?!"

Oh, how little he knew. I was already working with brides who had wedding dates three years out. I was even planning weddings with brides who didn't even have potential grooms. Never underestimate the insanity of a woman who is intent on having a dream wedding.

"Yeah," I said. Then, talking faster, "Look, I don't want to waste all of your minutes, but I just wanted to call and say merry Christmas, happy holidays, etc and let you know that I'll be sending you some emails about travel plans for May."

"Cool. I'll still be here."

"Great," I said with a smile. "I really miss you, kid."

"Yeah, I miss you, too," he said.

"And I can't wait to meet your little girlfriend," I said quickly, before he could hang up on me.

3 FEBRUARY

We were only five minutes into the first run, and I had already lost sight of all the other runners. As I neared the top of a hill, I surveyed the horizon, shocked that everyone had seemingly vanished before my very eyes. Where were they? And how fast were these crazy people running?

I hadn't expected that first inhalation of cold air to so pain my chest. I hadn't expected that my muscles would scream their defiance at me after only a couple of minutes of light jogging. I hadn't expected that I would be so thoroughly reminded that I was completely out of shape.

I lumbered down the hill, thankful that the incline did eventually have an end after all, and saw another runner, bent over, one hand on a fence post, the other clutching his stomach. I jogged closer to him, digging in the pockets of my new workout pants, checking for my cell phone, thinking that I might have to call an ambulance.

"Hey," I called, jogging right up to him. "Are you o— HEY!"

I narrowly avoided running right through a pile of what appeared to be vomit.

He looked up at me, embarrassment clearly etched all over his face. "Yeah..." Indicating the pile of vomit with one hand, he smiled slightly.

"Much better now, actually."

We were still in the middle of flu season, and while the profuse sweating he was doing made me wonder if he wasn't perhaps just starting the virus, I made a split minute assessment that this was the result of running and nothing contagious. "Do you need something to drink?," I asked, holding out my unopened bottle of water to him.

He shook his head, still gasping for breath.

I tightened my grip on the cell phone, eager to dial 9-1-1. "No," I said, "really, take it. I don't think I'm going to need it."

"That in shape, huh?," he asked, taking the bottle, adding a "thanks." He took a drink, exhaled deeply, and looked at me curiously.

"Oh, no," I said. "I mean, I think I'm done running. Everyone else has completely disappeared. "

He stood up and stretched, running his hand through his dark black hair as he studied me with his dark brown eyes. At his full height, he was exactly as tall as me, which, you know, wasn't short. "Wow. You're like the tallest woman I've ever seen," he managed.

I had heard this before. "Yeah, I've heard that before," I nodded.

He took a deep breath, smiling. "I feel much better. Thank you." He held out his hand to me. "Josh Morales."

"Emily Fisher," I said, shaking his hand.

"You want to walk and see if we can find the others?," he asked, indicating the road ahead.

I didn't think he'd be okay on his own, so I agreed. "Sure."

We started walking at a slow pace, and eventually Josh began breathing normally again. He looked at me sideways, a grin on his face. "So," he paused, saying it properly, "Emily Fisher," grinning even wider, "I have to tell you that I'm kind of ashamed that you had to come to my rescue back there."

I loosened my grip on the phone as a normal shade of pink came back to his face, and he began speaking in full sentences without growing winded. "Ashamed how?"

"Well, you're a woman! A woman younger than me." I looked at his face, noting the youthful way his eyes sparkled and the shape of the smile that never left his lips.

"Likely not. How old are you?"

"Thirty-one." He pronounced it as though delivering a verdict in a crowded courtroom.

"Ahh," I smiled. "An ancient."

"Oh," he clutched his heart, mockingly, "that hurts worse than the running."

"It's not that old," I conceded. "Besides, I'm a fossilized twenty-eight myself."

"See! Younger! And you had to rescue me like I was an old grandpa."

"Yeah, but technically YOU were ahead of ME on that little jog."

He laughed out loud. "And doing a fine job of it!" He ran his hand over his face. "I had no idea it would be this hard!" He slowed his pace slightly, looking over at me for affirmation.

I shook my head. "Me either. I thought this would be an easy way to get back in shape, but I should have just taken a water aerobics class."

"Hey!," he said. "I know of a good one! All the senior ladies from my church take it at the Y."

I made a face at him, while he laughed good-naturedly. "Might be just my speed, actually. Maybe you should look into it, too, huh?" Then, more seriously, "What church do you go to?"

He nodded. "Iglesia Redeemer. I'm the pastor, actually."

I had passed the church often on my way to and from work. It was a small building, but the cars were lined up outside of it every Sunday and Wednesday, so much so that I was certain they must be in violation of several traffic laws.

"Really?," I asked. "You're young to be a pastor."

He grinned. "Well, actually, I'm ancient, like you said. And the position is bi-vocational."

I smiled. "My dad was a bi-vocational pastor while he went to seminary. There's a definite calling for that."

He nodded. "Your dad still a pastor?"

"Yeah." I was surprised that as we walked the wind seemed less chilling and that as I breathed in more and more of the frigid air, it felt warmer in my lungs. "What else do you do? For fulltime work, I mean."

"I teach," he said. Then for clarification, "High school chemistry."

"Wow," I told him. "High school. That takes some guts."

He smiled. "It's not all that bad. They actually enjoy my class, since you know, we spend a good portion of our time in there mixing things together that will explode."

We began picking up our pace as we laughed together over his stories and warnings about which chemicals should NEVER go together.

"How about you?," he asked. "Do you blow up anything at work?"

I thought about this for a moment, thinking about the exploding brides in my office who literally self-destructed when I gave them that first price quote. "Ah, no. I plan weddings for a living."

He gave me a funny look. "Plan weddings? What's there to plan?"

"What do you mean?"

He spoke with his hands as we walked. "Boy meets girl, boy proposes, they meet with the preacher, say some vows, and her parents have cake and punch waiting for everyone in the fellowship hall." He looked at me, a silly smile on his face. "What is there to plan?"

I pointed a finger at him. "Oh, I'd hate to be the girl who has to explain to you how it REALLY works." I took a breath, thinking of all the details and extravagances that come with a modern wedding. "Though there is something special about what you describe, most girls have something different in mind when they envision a wedding. Had one at my church just last week with over three days of festivities."

Josh balked at this. "That's a whole lot of celebrating. Which church is that?"

"Grace Community."

"Oh, that place is huge!"

I smiled. "It feels like home to me."

"The pastor there," Josh said, admiringly, "he's just incredible! I listen to his sermons on the radio on Sunday afternoons, just gleaning what I can from what he's teaching, how he teaches, and," in a lower voice, almost conspiratorially, "sometimes, I even steal some of his illustrations. Shh! Don't tell!" He winked at me. "Of course, you probably never even talk with him face to face with as big as that place is, so my secret is safe, right?"

"Well, he's pretty good about getting around to interact with everyone. Me especially, since you know, I'm his daughter."

Josh stopped walking and looked at me. "Emily FISHER. Well, if that doesn't make me feel like the biggest idiot!" He laughed out loud. "You're Thomas Fisher's daughter?"

I nodded, smiling.

He had a great laugh, full and loud, and it made me smile to hear it. I looked out in front of us, and miraculously enough, saw a few stragglers running about half a mile in front of us. "Hey, Josh!," I pointed. "More runners!"

He peered in the direction I pointed, his smile growing bigger. "Hey, hey!" He looked at me. "Want to try and catch up?"

"I'll settle for just jogging," I told him, and we began running alongside one another. The sun began to tentatively rise above us, as the city started coming back to life. We ran through the park listed on the trail, over the railroad tracks, and nearby the zoo. I would glance over at Josh periodically to make sure that he was still okay, and he would catch my eye and wave a fist triumphantly in the air to indicate that he was still, as he huffed out once, "alive and kicking!"

Two miles later, we were both unable to speak, our clothes sweaty and our faces red, as our feet continued plodding down the street. By the time we reached the time keeper, it was obvious that they had stopped keeping time long ago. The poor girl looked at us apologetically, but Josh waved her concern away with a, "S'okay."

We stood there for a moment, catching our breaths. Then, Josh told me, "Emily, please let me get you something to drink since I... well, since I drank all of your water before the running even really started." He laughed out loud at this.

I reached for my keys, glancing at my watch and thinking of how I had to now shower halfway across town before making my way to the office. "Maybe next time. I've gotta run, or I'll be late for work."

"Next time?," he asked, surprise on his face. "You're going to try this again?"

I nodded, rolling my eyes. "Yeah, I kinda have a deal going with some friends. Gotta see this through, at least until the end of the month."

He looked at me, wordless for a moment. "Well, then," he said, seeming to make up his mind, "I gotta come back, too. Just so you won't be the slowest man on the track." He smiled his great smile again.

"Slowest WOMAN, Josh," I corrected.

"Oh, well, you'll still be the slowest woman." He smiled. "But you'll have me running, oh, a mile or two behind you the whole way to make you feel better about that."

I nodded. "Okay," I said. "I guess I'll see you Wednesday morning, then."

We waved good-bye, and I walked to my car with a smile.

I barely made it to the office before Evelyn. I had been stuck in traffic which delayed my arrival home. My shower had been half as long as I would have preferred, and when I got out, frantically trying to save time, I discovered that my hair dryer was broken. I had thrown on clothes, done my makeup, and jumped in the car, resolving to hang my head out in the cool air to settle my hair down.

That had been a supremely bad idea, as I now sat in the office with a runny nose and hair three times its normal size. BIG hair, as my mother would have criticized soundly. *Did you INTEND to have giant Texas hair this morning, Emily?*

Evelyn sauntered in, looking perfect as normal. "Emily," she said, making my name three distinct syllables. "We have FOUR appointments before lunch this morning." She clutched her hand to her heart, dreamily. "All of those New Year proposals, I suppose." Her expression froze as she saw my hair, then flourished into a beautiful smile. "I like what you've done with your hair. Very elegant."

I patted it, noting that with this hairdo and my one pink suit, I looked like Evelyn's mini-me. "Thank you, Evelyn. Just something different I was trying."

"Well, it's just gorgeous," she trilled. Then, switching to her business mode, she handed me a ream of paper. "Here is a complete list of our elegance upgrades," she said. Elegance upgrades was the Evelyn way to say price increases. We did this every year, once a year, which made it simpler to explain our pricing code to brides. "The Donovan wedding couple will be here at 10am to discuss their final arrangements with you. I want you to make them aware of the upgrades at that time," she finished hastily, making her way to the door.

"Hold up, Evelyn," I said. She stopped mid-stride, a painted look of surprise on her face. Oh, she knew what I was going to say. The Donovan couple had been a headache and a half for the past year. Stacy Donovan, who I quickly renamed Circus Bride in my mental files, had sauntered into our offices in March with a solitaire the size of Texas on her left hand and a groom, God bless his heart, who was barely fluent in English, trailing behind her. I renamed him Dancing Bear, as he never said anything, only followed his bride around as though he was on a leash, grunting responses in between cleaning his fingernails and (heaven help us all) picking his nose. He was money. Some far off, old European money. As Stacy had told me when we first met to discuss her lavish wedding and reception, her mother's family – not Donovan, which was her father's side, of course – but her mother's family had co-owned a vineyard in some tiny European nation YEARS ago, and had worked alongside a PRECIOUS family and her great-grandmother fell hopelessly in love with the son of the other vineyard owner, and they would have wed had the war not happened and had her grandmother not fled the country with a – shudder here on Stacy's part – an

American GI, and now, all these years later, relatives had found the family back in Europe and had done some matchmaking (likely because Stacy had demanded it when she learned how wealthy they were) and now she was in love and they were getting married and she was, in fact, super excited about having a villa of her very own across the Atlantic for the summers. (I had worn a pasted on smile for the duration of Stacy's run-on monologue. At this point, I had opened my mouth to discuss prices, but before I could, she was off and running again.) And the wedding! Would be so outrageous and ostentatious that ALL of Stacy's sorority sisters would be able to see how fabulously rich she was going to be, and she would stop at nothing short of a virtual circus to make it happen and --

I shook my head, trying to end the neverending Circus Bride rambling that had plagued me for an entire year.

Evelyn took my shaking as a dismissal. "Well, if that's all, Emily, I shall be on my way."

I watched her leave the office, sighing in every inch of my being, imagining Stacy's reaction to the price changes. She was marrying money, true, but she hadn't been born into money and could see a rip-off for what it was. I had no doubt, even without looking, that Evelyn had so increased prices, as she did every year, that there would be more than one set of tears shed in my office today. As much as I disliked the pompous and arrogant way that Circus Bride went about things and the way that she almost talked down to her Dancing Bear in her heavily twanged Italian (or whatever it was she was speaking to him) when she wasn't dragging him around on his invisible leash... well, I felt sorry for her. She had signed the contract over a year ago, had paid everything down, and now, two weeks before her wedding, we were going to charge her a few thousand dollars more.

I sighed, running my hands over my face. It would be okay. She would be able to pay it. But not all of them would. And I would have to watch them cry. My heart always wanted to minister to these hopeless women, who hung every bit of their worth and significance on a three-hour event, oftentimes which they couldn't even afford. But as it currently stood, my hands were tied, and I couldn't minister to them when I was the one who was bulldogging the money right out of their bank accounts.

I put down the ream of paper and counted to ten. Then one hundred.

It was going to be a long, long day.

The morning had, surprisingly enough, flown by with only a few tears. Circus Bride was so stressed out about fitting into the designer size six dress she had ordered (she was a size ten, if not a size twelve), that the price changes didn't even faze her. At one point, she clutched my hands frantically and said, "Emily, do you know if there are some pills or something that I could take to lose just a few tiny little pounds?" Few tiny, my foot, I thought. But then, looking at her helpless expression and the way even her Dancing Bear seemed concerned for her as he placed his grubby paw on her shoulder, I felt the way I always felt at the end of the wedding preparation road. I wouldn't be seeing her again until the wedding, and despite all the drama that she had brought into my life, I could almost feel myself tearing up along with her, as we discussed how beautiful she would look and how her fairy tale day was going to be perfect. Sigh. The best part of the job.

As she wiped away tears, imagining her wedding, I patted her hand and gave her the card of a doctor who specialized in colon cleansing treatments. Ew, I know, but several of my brides, smug in their impossibly tiny dresses, had sworn by it. I would just have to take their word for it, but Circus Bride started crying all over again, hugging me profusely, telling me that she would try ANYTHING at this point.

Despite this conversation and the unhelpful visuals that my mind couldn't expel (pardon the pun) afterwards, I was still starving hungry by one o'clock. As she did most days, Evelyn had taken an extended lunch break, courting an especially wealthy potential client in the hotel's premiere restaurant. I had finished my 12:30 consult with a very sweet bride who wanted "simple" (Evelyn had rolled her eyes when presenting me with the folder for the relatively inexpensive celebration) and checked both ways before speed-walking across the lobby and out to the street, straight towards the hot dog vendor who knew me by name, hoping that Evelyn wouldn't notice my absence.

Ten minutes later, she was still gone, and I was settled into my chair, taking a huge bite of my lunch when the phone rang. I chewed at lightning speed, swallowed, and picked up the phone on the third ring, annunciating past the bread that remained on my lips, "Evelyn Primrose's office. This is Emily Fisher speaking. How may I make your celebration extraordinary?" Yes, this is how Evelyn wanted the phone answered.

I heard a faint groan on the other end. "Hello?," I prompted. Silence. Then, "Emmy?"

The only people who called me Emmy were immediate family members. "Jess? Is that you?"

Then, "SCOTT! SCOTT! Put that baseball bat down in the house!!! You're going to KILL your brothers!"

Yes, it was Jessica.

"Hey," I said. "You sound awful."

"I FEEL awful," she moaned. "This baby is killing me from the inside out."

She said this every pregnancy. I couldn't sympathize from experience, but the thought of throwing up daily for fourteen weeks was something you wouldn't wish on your worst enemy. I felt truly sorry for her, literally hearing the nausea in her voice.

"Can I do anything to help out?," I asked, pulling out my schedule for the rest of the week. "I only have afternoon appointments tomorrow... then, a small reception tomorrow night. I have the morning off."

"You do?," I could hear the hope in her voice, and I smiled. It was nice to be needed.

"I sure do," I said. "Can I come over and play with the boys tomorrow morning? Be there when they wake up, and let you sleep in?"

Jessica started crying. Oh, pregnancy hormones. "CAN you?! You're an angel. You're MY angel, Emmy! I'm going to name this baby after you!"

"Can't do that," I said. "Would ruin the whole S name thing you've got going."

"Well, maybe a middle name, then," she said, still sniffling.

"Okay," I said soothingly. "I'll be there at six o'clock, okay? I've got my key, so don't wake up to let me in." Then, after a pause, "Just please make sure Nick knows I'll be there and that he won't wander out of the bedroom naked or anything."

"I'll tell him. Thank you, Emmy."

"No problem."

Lunch was over approximately two minutes later when Evelyn noisily made her way across the lobby, laughing with a group of people and heralding the hotel's finer qualities as she sauntered. Her volume gave me all the warning I needed to sweep what was left of lunch into the trash, to tidy up my suit, and to be standing by my desk to greet her visitors.

She came in with a flourish, as always, and held the door open for a well-dressed middle aged man and woman who were followed by a beautiful young woman and an equally attractive young man. Mother of the bride, father of the bride, bride, and groom. I didn't need an introduction, but I still smiled in anticipation of receiving it.

"Emily, dear," Evelyn said, grasping my hands and kissing the air on either side of my cheeks. Oh, well, this had to be an important couple, since Evelyn was being so formal and put-on with her introductions.

"Mrs. Primrose," I smiled sweetly, then looked to her guests eagerly. I turned to the mother of the bride. "Are you planning a wedding here, young lady?"

She laughed daintily. "Oh, you're about thirty years too late, dear." We all shared a polite laugh.

"Emily, this is Dr. and Mrs. Evans," she began.

"Dorothy and Stan," the mother of the bride said, extending her hand. Her husband did likewise.

"And this," Evelyn indicated with a grand sweeping motion, displaying her largest diamonds in the process, "is Lauren Evans and her fiancé, Justin Bennett."

Lauren was practically beaming, as was Justin, as she shook my hand, a gargantuan three-stone princess cut ring winking out to me.

"Mr. Bennett," I said, and smiling sweetly, "and the soon-to-be Mrs. Bennett." Lauren giggled, as Justin sighed contentedly, Stan gave her a thumbs up, and Dorothy – aww – wiped away a tear. This was going to be one of those sweet weddings that I actually looked forward to working. Adoring parents, adoring fiancé, and adorable bride.

Evelyn clasped her hands together. "The Evans have selected December 18th as the wedding date." Then, shifting into professional detail mode, "Rehearsal dinner in the crystal ballroom. Full-service meal. Bridesmaid brunch the morning of the ceremony in the arboretum. Ceremony downtown at the Presbyterian church in the evening. Cocktail hour in the garden room. Then, dinner, dance, and reception in the grand ballroom. Full service, sit-down meal."

"Nothing big," Dorothy added, "just the very simple basics."

If you're royalty, perhaps. But I refrained from saying this and diplomatically stated, "Well, elegance can most often be found in the absence of excess, can it not?"

Lauren looked at me in admiring wonder, as Justin nodded the truth of this statement, and Dorothy squeezed Evelyn's hand. "Oh, I think Emily said it perfectly."

Of course I did. Evelyn had taught me well.

Evelyn led the Evans family on to her office where they began some preliminary paperwork, which would be passed over to me by the end of the day. I would, as was our custom, take it home that night with me, crunch the numbers, and write up a proposal and summary sheet to give to the bride during our second meeting, which would be scheduled for some time over the next two weeks.

After an hour, I said goodbye to the Evans entourage as they left the office with Evelyn, who slid the paperwork onto my desk inconspicuously. It was longer than normal, and I sighed heavily as I mentally calculated how much of my time this would take up tonight.

I was elbow-deep in it when the phone rang at a quarter till eight.

"Yes, yes, yes," I picked up the phone, knowing instinctively that it was my stressed-out sister on the other end. "I'll be there tomorrow morning. I didn't forget."

There was a pause on the line. "Is this Emily Fisher?" It was a man's voice. I closed my eyes and paused in my writing. Way to go, Emily.

"Yes, it is. So sorry about that, I thought this was —" I stopped myself from divulging my life's story about my hormonal, pregnant sister and how I was her angel, realizing that the man on the other end of the line could be a total stranger. "Who am I speaking to?," I finally managed to ask.

"Oh, it's Stephen." A pause. "Um, Pastor Stephen. From the church."

"Pastor Stephen!," I practically shouted at him, shifting the paperwork from my lap to the couch, picking my planner out of my purse as I did so. "How are you?"

"Good, good," he said. "Just going over some of the details for the party on the 14th. Has the committee run into any problems?"

I shook my head. Then realizing that he couldn't see this, I added, "No, not that I'm aware of. They bought all of the stuff to decorate with last week, and we came up with a tentative schedule for the day of the party. For set-up, catering, working the tables, teardown, all of that."

"Great," he said. "So..."

A giant pause. This was what unnerved me about Stephen. Long silences. Which were not bad in and of themselves, but they were always followed by something ambiguous. Ambiguous and awkward.

Sure enough, he cleared his throat, and said, half-laughing, "Well, then I guess we don't need to meet up for lunch this week to discuss the details."

Ambiguous. Did he WANT to meet up? Or was he relieved that we wouldn't be meeting up? Was he looking for me to say, "Oh, darn, and I really wanted to go out with you, Stephen," or was he looking for me to say, "Oh, praise the Lord, we don't have to go out and make the rumors true, Stephen!" What was he expecting?

I opened and shut my mouth a few times before settling on an ambiguous line of my own. "Well, okay."

"Okay?," he asked. "So you can meet up for lunch?"

I wanted to say, "Wait, did you ask me?" But instead I said, "Sure." As soon as it was out of my mouth, I felt exposed and added, "If we need to go over the details again. I guess." I rolled my eyes. Really smooth, Em.

"Oh… well, great," he said, actually sounding relieved. "How about Friday, around noon?"

Friday was his day off, just as it was my father's day off. Did this put our meeting in a non-church business category? I pushed the thought aside for the moment and answered with, "Sounds good. Where would you like me to meet you?"

He hesitated, then said, "Well, I can pick you up. I know where the hotel is, and I'm assuming your office is… well, somewhere in the hotel, right?" He laughed nervously.

My breath caught in my throat a little. Picking me up. On his day off. "Um… yeah. First floor, opposite side of the lobby from the coffee shop." I exhaled.

"Great!," he said. "I'll see you then. Thank you so much, Emily."

"You, too," I said. "Bye."

"Bye."

I clicked off the phone and stared at the date… the date of THE DATE, in my calendar. I had a date with Pastor Stephen.

Wait a minute. Did I even WANT a date with Pastor Stephen?

Five thirty came early the next morning. And it came with immense soreness. I didn't even remember my running group until I sat up to turn my alarm clock off and noted that my arms were screaming at me.

Why in the world were my arms hurting when I had been running? It wasn't like I was doing the bear crawl out there or anything.

I got ready quickly, feeling the pain over every inch of my body. I didn't know how this was helpful in getting me more fit, as it had only seemed to make me more frozen, like the Tin Man. I stretched the soreness out until I felt like I could walk again without hobbling, then climbed into my car a few minutes later.

Jessica lived fifteen miles away from my apartment exactly. She had clocked it on numerous occasions, when she had to drive all the way out to meet me with the boys, telling me that there were so many houses out where she lived within my budget. Places that she didn't have to endure a whiny thirty minute round trip car ride to get to. I loved my sister, but I loved the distance. Just close enough… but not so close that she would be running next door every afternoon to borrow a cup of sugar. Or drop off a baby with stinky pants.

I arrived five minutes before six, let myself in with my key, and made my way into the kitchen, stepping over numerous toys and baby clothing items on my tip-toe through the living room. I started a pot of coffee for Nick, who would be getting up soon, and started searching the cabinets for some decaf ginger tea for Jessica. I was preparing a plate of saltine crackers to go with the tea (the only things that seemed to help Jess with the morning sickness) when a little man in stocking feet padded into the kitchen, rubbing his eyes.

"Aunt Emmy!," Sean said with a bright smile.

"Hey, buddy," I whispered, kneeling and gathering him into my arms.

"Are you gonna make pancakes?"

"Well," I said, patting his head. "I guess I could." As he climbed up into his booster chair, I searched for a skillet, finally finding one in the sink, along with approximately eight thousand other dirty dishes. "Think your mommy would mind if I washed her dishes first?"

"Likely not," Nick responded, walking into the kitchen, already dressed. "Hey, coffee."

"Actually, the name is Emily," I said, handing him a mug.

"Har, har, har," he muttered, rubbing his eyes.

"You're up early. And didn't get much sleep, apparently."

He rolled his eyes. "Your sister is a pregnant mess. Dreams all night long. And TALKS in her sleep. Last night, she was telling an invisible baby that the moon was going to fall out of the sky and we were going to eat it like it was cheese."

Hmm. Strange.

"Anyway," he said, "I've got a big project starting this morning. Have to be there early every day for the next month." He took a sip of the coffee, wincing at the heat. "Mmm, this is good. Thanks."

As I scrubbed pots and pans, he looked to Sean. "Good morning, son," he said, rubbing his thumb on Sean's tiny little chin.

"Morning, Daddy," he chirped, smiling up at Nick.

I glanced away from them, wanting to give them their privacy. These moments, watched as a bystander to my sister's happiness, felt stolen at times, as I relished in the sweetness and imagined what life would look like for Jessica five years, ten years, thirty years from now. Would she always treasure every time period of their lives as a family, saying and meaning every time that it was THE BEST time of their lives? Each season would only grow sweeter. I was sure of it.

"Uggggghhh."

Jessica was slumped in the doorway, green faced. Well, maybe it wouldn't take much to be sweeter than this season.

"Jess," Nick scolded. "You shouldn't have gotten out of bed. Emily's got it all under control."

I nodded to her, drying my hands off with a dish towel. "Here are your crackers and the ginger tea. I wish you would have let me bring them to you while you were still in bed. It's supposed to help with the sickness if you —"

"If I eat them before I sit up," she finished for me, turning away from my offering with mild disgust on her face. "Yeah, that's another lie that they tell you about pregnancy. Eating before you get out of bed will make the morning sickness better. LIE! Almost as wrong about the whole pregnancy is only nine months long spiel. LIE! It's ten months if it's a day." She kissed Sean on the head and slipped her arms around Nick. "I want to die, you know."

"You're glowing," he deadpanned, making me turn my attention back to the sink to hide the smirk that came to my face.

"Mommy, is the baby making your tummy hurt?," Sean asked.

"Yes, sweetie," Jessica answered. "She sure is."

"Or he," Nick said.

"Don't even start this morning," she said, plopping down into the chair next to Sean.

"Would you like some pancakes?," I asked her, turning on the stove. "I'm making some for the boys."

"Ugh," Jess sighed. "If I eat those now, I'll forever associate pancakes with morning sickness. I can't even stand to cook anything when I feel like this, much less eat."

"Exactly," Nick said. "Which is why I tend to lose weight during the first trimester."

"Yeah, you really suffer," Jessica muttered. He passed behind her on his way out the door, pausing to kiss her head and squeeze her shoulder, rubbing Sean's back as he walked by. "Gonna go peek in at the others before I leave. See you ladies later."

The first pancake was cooking, so I turned to Jess. "Please," I said. "I've got it under control. Go lie back down for a few hours. Get your rest while you can."

She shook her head. "I'm resting right here. Sitting at the table, talking to you."

I sighed and flipped the pancake over. "Hey, Sean," I said, "do you want syrup on this?"

"Yes!"

I looked in the fridge. "Um…. well…" Things were going moldy in there, but that didn't shock me as much as the small amount of food in the fridge. "Looks like it's going to have to be just butter until I can get to the grocery store."

Sean bowed his head sadly. "Okay."

Jessica rubbed his shoulder and looked at me. "You don't have to go shopping for me," she said. "I'll get around to it. Soon, maybe even –" She stopped, throwing a hand over her mouth and sprinting out of the kitchen. I heard Nick protest as she blew past him and into the guest bathroom down the hall.

Nick came in, Stuart in his arms. "Sorry about all of this, Emily," he said, handing him over to me. I pulled the pacifier out of my adorable nephew's mouth, while he stared at me in wonder.

"No problem," I told him, giving Stu's head a smooch. "I'm happy to help."

Nick picked up his keys and gave the two boys in the kitchen one last kiss good-bye. Before he could navigate through the toy mess on his way to the front door, it opened on its own. My mother stood in the doorway, a puzzled expression on her face.

"Emily!," she said. "I thought that was your car out there. What are you doing here?"

Jessica slumped back into the kitchen. "She came to help out. What are you doing here?"

Nick waved to me, slid past my mother, and went outside. A few moments later, I heard his truck start up, over my mother's long drawn out story. Some cancellation in her busy schedule, free morning, knew it in advance, and –

"I told your father yesterday morning, and he said he would tell you," she said, taking off her coat, "you know, when he called to tell you about the leak in our roof."

"Leak in your roof?," Jessica asked. "He didn't call about that."

"He didn't? Are you sure? Maybe he talked to Nick," she said.

"Mom, he didn't call. Not about a leak, not about you coming, none of it."

"Oh." Mom stopped hanging up her coat, midway. "Well... do you even need me here?"

Jessica began to say "no," with a rather exasperated look on her face, but I stopped her with a "Yes, Mom. I'll need to run and get some groceries in a bit if you can stay with the boys. Or you can go get the groceries, and I'll stay with the boys. Whatever." Jessica shot me a look, but I ignored her, settling Stuart into his high chair, then pouring another circle of pancake batter.

"Well, I would LOVE to stay with the boys," she said, kissing Sean's cheek.

"Morning, Grammy," he spoke through a mouth full of pancake.

"Morning, sweetheart," she cooed. Then, looking at Stuart, "Where are your brothers?" Stuart banged his fists on the tray in response, and my mother was back on her feet. "I'll go wake them up."

Jessica opened her mouth to protest, then snapped it shut. "See?," she hissed at me. "This is why it's more stressful to have her HERE. She wakes them up, forgets their naptimes, gets them ALL off schedule, and creates more work for me!" She walked right up to me. "Just wait! Just wait until you have babies and she goes all Grammy-psychotic on your children!"

"I think you're exaggerating a bit," I scolded.

She sighed and leaned back against the counter.

"Are you feeling better, at least, after that last…" I motioned in the general direction of the bathroom.

She rolled her eyes. "Oh, it never gets better. Not –"

"—until week fourteen," my mother said, walking back into the kitchen, a sleepy Sam holding one hand and a smiling Scott holding the other. "It's always the same, isn't it?" She settled the boys into their seats and pointed a finger at Jessica's still-flat tummy. "I'm telling you – it's another boy."

"Oh, Mom," Jess groaned.

"I'm telling you," she said, "my Matthew pregnancy and my pregnancy with you were TOTALLY different. Sick as a dog with him, healthy as a horse with you. Strangest thing."

"What about me?," I asked.

"Oh, with you I was fine, too, BUT," she said, fanning herself with her hand, even though it had to be sixty degrees in the house, "your

FATHER was sick. Has Nick been sick?"

Jessica shook her head.

"Oh, well, then, who knows." She walked to the fridge and opened the freezer, standing right in front of it turning her head from side to side.

"Mother," Jessica said, "what are you doing?"

"Hot flash," she panted. "Nothing helps. But thought I'd give this a try anyway."

Pregnancy hormones, menopausal hormones – no wonder Nick had left so quickly. I finished the last pancake and served the boys.

"Mom, can you get the milk out of the fridge?," I asked, taking two extra sippy cups out of the cabinet for the newcomers.

"Well, since I'm right here and all," she said, pulling out the carton for me. "You know, it's really odd that your father just completely forgot to call." She bit her lip for a moment. "He seems to be forgetting a lot lately."

"Or maybe he's just pretending to forget," Jessica mused, nibbling at one of the saltines I had laid out for her.

"Now what is that supposed to mean?," Mom said, putting her hands on her hips.

"Oh, nothing," I said, smoothing over the crankiness of both of them. "Jess," I barked the command at her. "Go lie down."

She didn't hesitate this time, no longer interested in sitting around and chatting with our mother giving commentary to all of our conversations.

Mom watched her leave. "Is it just me, or does she get grouchier with each pregnancy?," she asked.

I smiled. "No, I just think she's really tired today."

"Hmm," Mom thought this over, sitting down next to the boys. She smoothed down Stuart's hair as he held up a piece of pancake for her to see. "I was just looking online the other day at pictures of Ethan's children. You remember Ethan, don't you?"

Ethan. The name wasn't ringing any bells. Maybe someone I had known in the third grade whom my mom had friended on Facebook. I nodded as though I knew just exactly who she was talking about.

"Well, he has three girls." She smiled at her own grandsons. "Just gorgeous! Made me wish for a granddaughter. Not that I don't love the boys, but a girl would be nice. Your sister won't be having any more babies after this one, and your brother doesn't even know any young women over there, so it looks like it's up to you."

I glanced up at her. "Is it now?" I wasn't sure which part of this was most erroneous. That she assumed (wrongly) that my sister was going to stop at five children, that she assumed (wrongly) that my brother wasn't meeting any women in Japan, or that she assumed (wrongly) that I would be the first to bring a girl into the family, though I was clearly the most unlikely candidate.

"Oh, yes," she said. Then, more quietly, "It's not like we don't all see what's going on with you and Pastor Stephen." She looked at me coyly.

I rolled my eyes. "Oh, Mom, I'm just going out to lunch with him."

Her eyes widened. "What?! Lunch?!"

I mentally slapped a hand to my forehead. Of course, she didn't know that. No one knew that. My brain wasn't working up to speed this early in the morning, and I had just blurted out that which I never intended to tell another living soul. At least not until I knew what it all meant.

I groaned. "Just to discuss church stuff." This didn't dissuade her. "Just forget you heard that."

"What part – the church business part or the DATE part?," she practically sang.

"ALL of it, Mom."

She smiled. "Well, it's just a DATE. Just one DATE. Not like you have to marry him or anything when it's only a DATE —"

"Mom!" This was so NOT what I needed.

She smoothed out the sleeves of her shirt, which had started riding up in her arm-flinging excitement. "You know, that's how your father first asked me out. Church business and all," she said, making large quotation marks with her hands when she said "church business." She laughed a little smugly. "But it didn't take long for us to figure out that there was more there. It never takes love a long time."

I refrained from rolling my eyes. "I should probably go and get those groceries," I told her. "Can you handle the boys for an hour?"

She nodded and began shooing me away with her hand. "Grammy's got it under control!," she sang to the boys. "You go on out and shop. We'll be here when you get back."

I spent about forty minutes at the grocery store, loading up the cart with the regular staples my sister kept stocked in her pantry when she was feeling like herself, plus a few Aunt Emmy extra surprises for the boys. I got back to the house, where the noise was four decibels higher than it had been when I left. I wondered how Jess could sleep through this. After I unloaded the groceries, my mother assured me that she had it all under control, so I left the boys with her and drove back to my apartment. I had nothing on the schedule until two and planned on making the most of it with a nap. A long nap to sustain me through the next few days when I would be working later than usual to make up for this morning I had taken off to help my ailing sister, who didn't need my help after all, thanks to my mother.

Just as I began drifting off into a comfortable snooze, my cell phone chirped at me. Groaning, I pulled it up to my face – Melissa. This was likely not at all important, but you never could tell.

"Hello?," I said.

"Hey," she answered, all business-like. "It's Melissa."

"No kidding," I yawned.

"Are you napping at work?," she accused.

"No," I said, propping myself up on my elbow. "I'm napping at HOME."

"Home? Why are you at home?" A pause. "You have the flu, don't you?"

"I don't have the flu."

"Oh." Melissa was a big advocate for any/all vaccines and immunizations. She had insisted that we all march right down to the public health center the day that the flu vaccine became available, but Sara protested, saying that she was more likely to get the flu by going to get the vaccine than she was working with kindergarten students every day. Melissa went without us and had sworn every day since that we would get sick. So far we hadn't, but she continued to almost anticipate it.

I sighed. "I went over to help Jessica this morning. Then my mom showed up, so I figured I would come home and get some sleep."

"Ah," she said.

"What are you doing?"

"Just taking my break at work," she said. "Did you know that they're now MAKING us take breaks? I could work right through the day, straight through, without a break, but now the HR people are really big on making sure everyone gets a break, a lunch hour, blah, blah, blah." I could hear the frustration in her voice. "Really cuts down on my productivity. And I'm BORED."

"Bored at work," I said. "That's a first for you."

"Yeah," she huffed. "So, what are you doing this weekend?"

"Valentine's Day weekend?"

"Yeah," she said. "Sara has plans with Jon."

I sat up. "Plans? Like, special plans?"

"Yeah," Melissa lowered her voice, as though Sara was sitting next to her. "Though not Jon's doing, the little weasel. She told me that he hadn't even planned on coming up until she called and ASKED HIM to please make the trip. What kind of loser boyfriend is he when he can't even think to –"

"Oh, Melissa," I said, warning, "but she loves him."

"WHY?!"

I thought about this for a moment. And I couldn't come up with an answer. Sara did all the work in the relationship, believing in Jon too much, and never seeing any kind of move towards real commitment on his part.

"I tell you, Em," Melissa said, anger in her voice, "he HAS to have some other girl down there in San Antonio. He barely comes into town once every two months. And I know he's not calling Sara like he used to. And she's expecting him to show up with a RING this weekend, and there's no way on God's green earth that –"

I heard a buzzing in the background.

"Oh, hallelujah," she breathed. "The break is over, and I can get back to work."

"Hey," I said, before she could hang up on me, "don't forget that there's a singles' event at the church on Sunday. Valentine's Day, you know. "

"Are you going?"

"No," I sighed. "Wedding that night. I'm going to set up the room that morning before church, though."

"Well, I imagine I'll be there if it's on Sunday night. Not like I have anything else to do."

"That's the spirit," I said.

"Hey, I'll talk with you later," she said, eager to get back to whatever it was that she did.

"See you," I said, clicking the phone shut and snuggling back under the covers.

Wednesday and Thursday were beyond crazy at work. It seemed that Evelyn had brides coming into my office via a conveyor belt, assembly-line style. Brides at all different stages in planning, brides with vastly different styles and price ranges, brides in tears, giddy brides, brides paying down deposits, brides signing final contracts, on and on and on. I was making calls to photographers, to florists, to jewelers, to dress designers, to limousine companies, to bakeries – even to skywriting companies. I ran back and forth from the catering office all week long, so much so that Stella, the secretary over there, finally noted that she and I should just use our walkie talkies to save me all the miles I had trod through the hotel lobby.

Friday proved to be the same, with just a bit of added craziness that always came with Fridays, "the rehearsal day" as Evelyn called it. I had four weddings on Saturday, with two of their rehearsals that evening in our hotel. I was working the set up with our moving crew, when my pager went off. Evelyn.

I made my way quickly to our office, smoothing my suit down in the likely event that she had a client waiting to meet with me in her office. When I opened the door, I stopped breathing at the sight of Evelyn... and Pastor Stephen. Noon. I had completely forgotten.

"Emily, dear," Evelyn began. "I paged you because your... friend, here... was it Stephen, darling?" She appraised him with fondness.

"Yes, ma'am," he said politely.

"Yes, Stephen is here to meet with you." Evelyn smiled at me slyly, no doubt wondering when her mousy assistant had snagged such a hottie.

"Thank you, Evelyn," I said. "I'm going to take my lunch break now. We're setting up the crystal ballroom right now for the Malone rehearsal dinner, the arboretum for the Getz rehearsal dinner, and the garden room for the Smith wedding tomorrow morning. We're waiting on the Elin wedding set up since –"

"Since they're using the crystal ballroom for their evening wedding tomorrow," she finished for me. "Oh, dear, I have it all up here," she pointed to her bouffant. "No need to remind me." She glanced over to Stephen. "Emily always keeps this place running, Stephen. She's quite the catch, don't you know."

Stephen looked at me awkwardly. I could feel the blush rising on my cheeks. "Well, then, we'll be going," I said.

"Oh, take your time," Evelyn graciously sang to us. "All the time you need."

"Thanks," I mumbled as I led Stephen out of the office and through the lobby.

"Nice boss," he said to me.

I didn't comment as we walked into the bright sunshine.

We were seated at a booth in one of my favorite downtown restaurants after waiting only a few minutes. Stephen waited to sit until I was seated, then leaned across the table to ask me, "What's good here?" He was wearing just a hint of cologne, and the brief sniff I got clouded my thinking. More so than usual.

I looked down at the menu, blushing. "Um... well, I always get the penne pasta. But anything off the lunch selections menu is a good bet."

He nodded. After a few moments of contemplative silence, with deafening noise all around us from the lunch crowd, a bubbly waitress took our orders while practically drooling over an oblivious Stephen. I watched him as he ordered. He was wearing khakis and a nice blue sweater that made his eyes seem lighter in color. His summer tan, gleaned from all of those outdoor events the church had during the hotter months, was all but faded, leaving a clear complexion that looked creamy next to his light hair. Everything about him was attractive, right down to the adorable smile he gave as he laughed at himself for mispronouncing the name of the entrée.

Oh, be still my heart.

He caught me looking at him as the waitress left us to ourselves. Fumbling for something to explain my gaze, I dumbly said, "You got a haircut."

He put his hand up to his hair. "Yeah... day off, you know. Time to do all of the things that just don't get done while I'm at the office."

"How are the preparations for the party?," I asked, already knowing that the set-up schedule would swing into motion early Sunday morning with the help of the decorating committee. I had called the head of the committee to check on things earlier that morning.

"Great, actually," he said. "It looks like it'll run really smoothly with all of the planning you've done. Thank you."

I waved his words away. "No problem."

"It's a shame," he said, with a tentative smile, "that you're going to miss the party that you planned."

I smiled. "Well, that's my life. Although, I'm there for most of the receptions I work on, I don't exactly get to enjoy the cake and shake my stuff on the dance floor." I paused, reflecting on the wisdom of offering up the mental image of me "shaking my stuff."

Stephen didn't even seem to notice. "Hmm. Kind of like doing a wedding ceremony, too. I did one last summer for one of my cousins and ended up coordinating so much that I don't remember enjoying any of it." I imagined Stephen at a wedding ceremony, counseling the engaged couple, giving a beautiful exposition of the Scripture, shaking hands with all of the guests, and just being his dreamy, dreamy self.

This thought process wasn't helping anything. "It's a shame that more churches don't have planners on staff," I said, jabbering on over the mental fawning I was doing. "I know my dad, especially in the early part of his ministry days, spent so much time in administrative tasks that had nothing to do what he was actually qualified to do – teaching the Bible, obviously – that he was worn out when it came time to lead the church spiritually."

Stephen nodded at me. "And now," he said, grinning, "your dad has an 'associate' to do all of that for him, right?"

My mind flicked through several responses to this before finally settling on, "Well, that's why they pay you the big bucks, right?"

"Right," he said, laughing. "Yeah, it can all get exhausting, doing all those administrative things." He hesitated before adding, "Which is why it's a good thing you're around. I mean, with all you do in that area, freeing up so much of my time to do what I know I can do." He smiled. "Can you imagine how crappy this party would be if I had been the one to plan it?"

Pastor Stephen had said "crappy." Like a real, live person. I smiled at him, relaxing a bit. "Well, it would've been different."

He laughed out loud. "Yeah, that's a way to describe it." Then, hesitating again, "Thank you. You know, for all that you do."

I dismissed his words with a simple, "Well... thanks."

Mercifully, our drinks came soon. Then, the entrees. We continued chatting, dancing back and forth from playful, to hesitant, to laughing, to blushing. It was like being on a first date. With someone you knew well enough... but in such an entirely different context that it felt like dining with a stranger. Still, though, the conversation was good, the atmosphere was fun, and the eye candy – oh, my – the eye candy was very appealing to me. The hour clicked by rapidly, and before I knew it, the check came. Stephen picked it up before I could offer to, and a few moments later, we were walking back to my office.

"Well," he said, stopping just within the lobby, "thanks for coming with me."

"Well, no problem," I said. "Thanks for taking me away from the craziness here for a while."

He smiled. "I had a... a good time." And there it was, that awkwardness we'd been dancing around all afternoon, that awkwardness that defined my relationship with Pastor Stephen. Why was I so socially inept around him? Should I hug him? Should I shake his hand? Why was this such a weird deal?

He squeezed my shoulder and bent down, almost as if to kiss my cheek, then stopped and said, "See you around, Emily."

I waved weakly. Then, after he was out of view, I groaned over the wild beating of my heart and trudged back to the salt mines.

RESOLUTIONS

Once again, Josh and I were the last runners in the pack. This was true of every run we had done so far with our "running group," which I believed was some sort of code name for the US Olympic Field and Track team.

Of course, I didn't know if being in the back of the pack was because we were just that slow or because we spent the majority of our three mile jogs chatting. On that particular day, he had been telling me about a Valentine's dance he had chaperoned at the high school where he taught, I had been telling him about the Valentine's Day weekend weddings, and we had both concluded that it was a rather stupid holiday.

"I've never seen so much red and pink in all my life," I told him, huffing and puffing as we rounded a corner and finally started descending down what appeared to be a neverending hill. "I mean, to each her own when it comes to color preferences for a wedding, but I've been in this business since college, and I have NEVER seen so much red and pink. The groom was even wearing a PINK suit – can you imagine?"

Josh laughed out loud, which was surprising, given how red his face was from the run. I couldn't imagine where he had found the lung capacity to speak, much less to chuckle. "I'll bet you anything that wasn't his idea."

"Not at all," I said. "But he was a good sport about it. As were all those groomsmen they had. Ten, Josh. TEN!"

He shook his head. "I'm not sure I even have ten friends," he said thoughtfully, with a sideways smile at me.

"Sure you don't," I said sarcastically. "You're probably one of these guys who's going to end up with a thirty-member bridal party."

"Well, I can guarantee you that I won't be wearing pink," he said.

Saturday had been a full day, trailing into an even fuller night. I ran from event to reception, correcting things, giving directions, and checking that nothing was out of place or off schedule. Stella and I had worn the batteries on our walkie talkies completely down by the time two am rolled around and the last guests of the Malone wedding had left. She had come into the ballroom a moment later, and she and the entire wait staff threw themselves into chairs and started eating the leftovers on the buffet. Evelyn would have had a fit, but since she had taken the weekend off to celebrate the "most romantic of all holidays" with the mysterious Mr. Primrose, I was in charge. And I filled a plate right alongside them, laughing and chatting even later into the evening, until we finally got everything cleared away for the janitorial staff. I had run to church the next morning to check on the set-up for the party, getting there so late that I had to sit in the very back of the sanctuary during the service. Then, I was off and running again to the hotel, where the red and pink extravaganza later took place.

And now, barely hours after I had laid my head on my pillow the night before, I was nearing a heart attack (I was sure) with this insane running group. Where had they all gone?

"Can we..." Josh sputtered. "Can we walk... for a little while?"

I slowed down to a brisk walk, wiping the sweat from my forehead as I did so. "I was about to ask you the same thing." We continued on in silence for a minute, catching our breaths. "I think I'm out of my league here."

"Yeah," Josh said. "Me, too. I even ran on Saturday morning, just to see if it would make this week easier."

"Did it?"

He gave me a look and gestured to the sweat stains forming on his shirt. "Does it look like it helped at all?"

I smiled. "No, unfortunately not. But think of all the extra calories you burned."

"That's actually a good thing," he said. "There were a lot of refreshments at that dance on Saturday night."

We kept walking and chatting, me pulling my jacket tighter around me as the wind picked up. I wondered when the weather would finally start to change, giving us those two brief weeks of spring before the sweltering hot summer temperatures took up residence until October. Surely the running would be easier when it wasn't so cold outside. Blazing hot seemed preferable to frigid cold.

Josh seemed to be thinking the same thing. "I'm having a bad thought," he whispered.

"What is it?," I whispered back.

"See that coffee shop over there?" He pointed to one across the busy street from the park.

"Yeah?"

"I think a huge hot chocolate sounds a whole lot better than finishing up the next two miles," he said with a smile.

I shook my head at him, playfully "tsk-tsking" his thought.

"Oh, I know," he said. "Haven't even really started this running thing, and I'm already wimping out."

"No," I told him. "I'm more disappointed by the fact that you're going to get hot chocolate instead of coffee." I smiled at his surprised expression. "Come on, let's go."

We spent the next fifteen minutes chatting in the warm shop, Josh drinking a hot chocolate with double whipped cream and me attempting to be good with a regular coffee... then going with the triple-fudge mocha instead, while Josh nodded approvingly. He told me about the finer points of the high school dance, like when he broke up a drinking party in the boys' bathroom, when he stood in the middle of a fight between two girls near the concessions, and when he, to the applause of all the students (or at least he claimed it was to the applause of all the students), "busted a move" on the dance floor.

"Hmm," I said. "I'm trying to imagine that... but I just can't." I smiled at him.

"Well, it's hard to imagine true greatness, I know," he said, quite humbly, with a smile of his own. "But I was awesome. Just take my word for it."

I was surprised by how much we were able to talk about in such a short amount of time, how there were no lapses in conversation, and how I was almost disappointed when, at the end of the hour, he said, "We should probably, um, cross the finish line. Like the champions that we are."

I raised my cup to him. "We should definitely take these with us."

We left the coffee shop and cut across the running route, eliminating those extra miles and crossing the finish line with the last of the runners. There were a few curious glances towards our cups, but for the most part, everyone was entirely focused on finishing with a good time. They all circled up, and we joined their ranks, looking at one another questioningly. Were we about to do a victory chant or something? We had missed this part every time, likely because we were always so far behind.

"Great run, everyone!," an emaciated but perky blonde said, entering the middle of the circle. "Now that we have a couple of warm up weeks under our belts, we'll be increasing our distance to prepare for the marathon."

This was a marathon training group? This was very bad news to me, and as I looked sideways at Josh, I could tell that it was to him as well.

"Next week, instead of five miles, we'll be running ten and meeting an hour earlier."

What? They had just run FIVE miles? And next week, they were going to do TEN? I mentally calculated how early I would have to get up to make this happen. There was no way. As if I could even run ten miles at all, much less in that brief amount of time!

"So," she concluded, happily, "be here on time next week. And make sure that you're getting your miles in during your long runs on Sunday!"

Another surprise. We were supposed to be running on the weekend? And what exactly constituted a LONG run if ten miles was a short run?!

The crowd of hyper runners dispersed, leaving Josh and me standing alone with our empty cups. Suddenly, I felt the weight of all the sugar in my drink.

"Are they for real?," Josh asked.

"A marathon!," I hissed. "Where was that in their promotional material?"

He shook his head. "And I can't get up another hour early. This is too early as it is. The sun isn't even up yet!"

"Josh," I told him, "it's been nice knowing you, but I think I'm done with this running group."

He seemed at a loss for words for a moment, then seemed to get an idea. "Well, we can keep running. Monday, Wednesday, Friday, just like we've been doing, and just not worry about the group. Just pretend like we're still running with them. How different will it be from what we've been doing, since they leave us in their dust anyway?"

I considered this for a minute. I had resolved to get in better shape, and this was cheaper than joining a gym or hiring a trainer since running outside was completely free. (Even with the expense of mochas, it was still cheaper.)

And I enjoyed the company. I wasn't putting much stock in this reason since Josh and I had spent a combined total of only a few hours together. I didn't know him that well... but I knew him well enough to know that I looked forward to talking to him.

I shrugged. "Sure, why not?"

The last two weeks of the month passed by in a blur. We had a slight lull in our work pace, working only a few weddings each weekend. The spring rush would soon be on hand, though, and with the summer brides in the final stages of their preparations and Evelyn spending her days courting and romancing the fall and winter brides, we were guaranteed that things would pick up significantly in the months ahead.

Circus Bride had her wedding extravaganza during the last weekend of the month. It was gorgeous, if not totally over the top, and she was beautiful. So much so that even I teared up as she walked down the makeshift aisle we had set up in the grand ballroom. Evelyn discreetly handed me a Kleenex, making the general "isn't this gloooorious?!" hand motion that she was prone to making at every six-figure celebration.

Circus Bride found me in between the first dance and the cake cutting and squeezed me tightly in a hug. "Thank you," she whispered. "For that doctor's referral!" She winked at me, motioning to her dress.

"Size six suits you, Stacy," I said, smiling.

"Size eight, actually," she confided. "He had it shipped from Italy last week and altered at the last minute." She gazed adoringly at the Dancing Bear who was, appropriately enough, dancing with a group of his European groomsmen on the dance floor.

"Well, you look fabulous," I said. "I can tell you've lost a lot of weight."

"All thanks to your miracle worker!," she said. "You've been so great this whole year. I just can't thank you enough for making this the wedding of my dreams." She leaned closer to whisper, "My sorority sisters are practically green with envy. I've passed your information along to all of them."

I smiled at this. "Well, we do our best here at the hotel."

She shook her head. "No, it was YOU, Emily! Apart from the hotel and the amenities, you made this wedding. Listening to all of my stress, talking me through it all -- thank you."

I was touched by this. I prided myself on being a good worker under Evelyn's rules and regulations, but my heart was to minister to these brides as they prepared to make such a big commitment. It was good to hear that I had been appreciated as more than an event coordinator's assistant.

She got a mischievous look on her face. "In fact, I'm so thankful that I have half a mind to hook you up with Michael's --" she gestured to the Dancing Bear "—cousin, Javier. If I wasn't a married woman," she said with a twinkle in her eye, "I would so totally be going there."

I hesitated, thinking how to kindly decline the offer, but before I could come up with an excuse, Stella indicated that it was time to cut the cake, and Circus Bride started that way, calling over her shoulder that, "You have my number, Emily! Give me a call about it after the honeymoon, okay?"

The wedding concluded three hours later with fanfare. Despite the frigid temperatures, Circus Bride and her Dancing Bear (or Stacy and Michael, as I had been careful to call them all evening) had opted to leave in a horse drawn carriage, circling downtown a few times until most of the guests had cleared out and they could return to the hotel where they had reserved the honeymoon suite for the night. Evelyn left early (of course), but I was there with a jacket for Stacy when she came back in, her lips practically blue from the frost. I enjoyed taking care of my brides like this, being mindful of the details that no one seemed to consider when planning a wedding.

I stayed until the clean-up was complete, checking my planner for the next day. No weddings. Only church. And lunch out with the girls.

The three of us decided on pizza. Well, Melissa and I did, much to Sara's frustration.

She frowned at the cheesy concoction that the waitress brought to our table. Supreme and meat lovers combined – everything on it but the kitchen sink.

"You know," she said after we prayed, looking at her slice critically, "this kind of works against what we were trying to accomplish with the whole getting in shape resolution this month."

Melissa, her mouth already full of pepperoni and sausage, gave a short laugh. "Just one meal! Not like this is going to cancel out any of the pain and torture I went through."

"Was it that bad?," I asked, thinking of the few times I had talked to her since she began meeting with a personal trainer at the gym four days a week.

She gave me a look. "That personal trainer? She's THE DEVIL."

Sara shook her head. "That's not a very nice thing to say."

"It's the truth, though! I'd tell her that I was done – DONE – and she'd get all up in my face and yell that I still had ten more reps to do. Just about killed my arms every day." She gestured towards her bicep for emphasis, "I mean, seriously... how much flab is there on an arm anyway?"

Sara poked her arm. "She's helping you to develop muscles, after you get past the flab."

"I don't want muscles!," Melissa shouted. Then, seeing the gazes of other lunchers darting over our table, she lowered her voice. "Not huge muscles anyway. I feel like I'm going to be one of those scary-looking bodybuilder types if I keep this up. You know the ones I'm talking about. So buff that they don't even look like women anymore?"

Sara didn't even acknowledge the last part of her statement. "How about you, Emily? How did the running group go?"

I nodded, chewing, then responded with, "Good. I think I'm going to stick with it. Well, not the group, but the running definitely." Then, thinking over the miles Josh and I were now able to cover comfortably without feeling like dying, "Maybe do a 5K or something later on in the year."

Melissa looked at me thoughtfully. "You know, if you work with my trainer, she can have you ready for a marathon."

"Now, you see, you say all of these bad things about her and then suggest that I start working with her, too. Why would I want to work with the devil?"

She shrugged. "Well, she'll get the job done. That's all I'm saying." She nodded to Sara. "What about you? How did the yoga go?"

"Well, I don't think I'm going to stick with it."

"Hurt too much, huh?," Melissa said.

"Yes, and I'm not nearly coordinated enough for it. I think I might just start swimming laps. Not much coordination needed for that. And it's not as expensive as a class or a trainer."

I looked to Melissa. "How about you? Are you going to stick with the trainer?"

She picked up another slice, causing Sara to shake her head disapprovingly and prompting her to take a huge first bite. "You know," she said around her chewing, "common sense tells me that I shouldn't, but I don't like the smug way that woman acted like I SHOULD quit after the first month."

"She didn't!" Sara said, mock-shocked, then put her hand over her mouth to conceal her smile.

"Oh, she did. And I'm going to keep with it just to show her that she can't scare me off," Melissa said.

We ate in silence for a while, the pizza quickly disappearing. Melissa, finishing her last bite with a flourish, pushed her plate away from her place and looked at us. "So. What was the next one? The resolution for March?"

I pulled out my ever-present planner, flipped to the beginning and read the entry aloud – "Amp up your love life."

Melissa groaned, while Sara clapped her hands together, delighted.

I considered my options. There was always letting Jessica fix me up with someone, but that would mean enduring weeks of endless questions and much butting in from my mother, who Jessica wouldn't be able to keep from telling. I wasn't looking forward to the possibility of the drama that would ensue. There was always meeting someone on my own and going out with him once or twice... but all of the men I met were prospective grooms, and though some of them had flirted behind their brides' backs, I didn't think taking any of them up on their offers would be ethical. (Or wise, since – hello! – they were already being unfaithful to women they had promised to marry. Quality men, you know.)

And then... there was the obvious. That I had already gone on that one lunch date with Pastor Stephen. Maybe that would count, and I'd be done with the resolution. But did I want to share this information with anyone?

Fortunately, Sara directed her attention to Melissa. "How are you going to amp up your love life, Mel?" Patting her arm, she added, "I mean, it won't take much to upgrade from total inactivity."

"Well, thank you very much," Melissa sighed. "Um... I guess I'll do one of those internet dating things."

"Oh no, you don't," Sara said.

"Why not?," Melissa rolled her eyes in exasperation.

"I know you! You'll sign up, sift through all those men, and NOT GO ON A DATE."

Melissa closed her lips tightly. "Darn it."

"Found you out, didn't I?," Sara said, self-satisfied. "Of course, I don't have a problem with it, if you'll agree to go on AT LEAST one date with someone."

"Just one?"

"Just one."

Melissa nodded. "Fine. But that's it."

Sara turned her attention to me, but before she could ask, I blurted out, "Sara, how are you going to complete this one? You know, since you already have Jon?" There had been no ring at Valentine's Day, and Sara had said very little else about Jon in the weeks that followed. We had left the subject alone, not knowing what had happened between them or where they stood.

Sara smiled an unsure smile. "Well, I was thinking that... that I'm going to finally give him an ultimatum about getting married."

Melissa and I both took in a deep breath, neither one of us daring to exhale in the silence that ensued. After a moment of Sara looking at us timidly, Melissa breathed out a, "For real?"

Sara nodded, looking at the half-eaten slice of pizza left on her plate. "Well, we've been together a while now," she began.

"Six years," I confirmed.

"Well, yes," she said, "but it's not like he could have proposed back when we first met or anything. I mean, he was still in school and everything."

I didn't see how this was a real reason for delaying marriage when you were madly in love, but Sara seemed to. Or was determined to pretend that she did.

"So I don't count those years," she continued. "Not when it comes to this, at least." She began playing with her fork, not meeting our eyes. "But, you know, we're not getting any younger, Jon is settled in his career, I could move, and... well, just continuing on with long distance at our age just seems..." She trailed off, not wanting to say the word.

"Ridiculous?," Melissa offered.

Sara nodded. "Yeah. I don't know what the hold-up is. And I'm tired of waiting." She looked at us, real uncertainty on her face. "Does that make me awful?"

We rushed over one another's words, trying to reassure her that she wasn't awful, that any other woman would have done the same thing a long time ago, and that she was well within her rights as his long, long, LONG term girlfriend. Still, though, I could see the obvious question on Melissa's face as she glanced at me, and I knew that we were both thinking the same thing. Could Sara REALLY go through with an ultimatum? If Jon said he wouldn't marry her, would she leave him or stay with him? Surely she had, at some point in their six years, talked about a greater commitment, and SURELY he had put her off once before. It hadn't ended their relationship then – why should we believe that it would now?

And more importantly, why should he?

Sara seemed to discern our thoughts. "I mean, we've talked about it... you know, as in us still being together years from now. Well, I've talked about it at least. But we've never actually talked about making it official, and I just..." She looked out over the restaurant, trying to find the right way to say it. "... I just need to know. You know, where this is going."

Melissa nodded. "You sure do. Should've known long before now! He owes you that."

Sara shook her head. "It'll all work out. I'm sure it will."

I looked down, thinking about the improbability of this, hoping that I was wrong and that Jon would sweep in with a huge diamond and roses and a candlelit dinner and all of the other over-the-top clichés that Sara had been pinning her hopes on since she was a little girl. I was still lost in thought when Sara's perky voice demanded, "What about you, Emily?"

Well...

"Oh, well," I began, not looking at them, "I'm actually kind of seeing someone. So that's taken care of for me."

Silence. Deafening silence. I glanced up to make sure they had heard me, only to find them both staring, Melissa with an open mouth and Sara with a gleeful smile.

"Who?," Melissa barked.

"No one you need to know personally," I hedged.

"Who?"

"I think it's enough that I'm dating someone, and —"

"I don't believe you."

I looked at Melissa, her arms crossed over her chest. "You're just trying to get out of this." I opened my mouth to protest, but she cut me off with, "Oh, trust me — I considered saying the same thing to get out of it! Making up some pretend man!"

I frowned at her. "He's not a pretend man."

"Sure he is."

"He is NOT!"

"Whatever."

Agitated by her haughtiness, I blurted out, "It's Pastor Stephen!" Then kicked myself mentally. Why did I keep telling people this?

Sara laughed out loud, bouncing in her seat. "Pastor Stephen! Oh, Emily! I knew it! I see you two talking together at church all the time!"

And she likely had. The weeks following the ambiguous lunch date had probably fueled even more rumors as Pastor Stephen and I had spent more time chatting in the hallways at church, singling one another out at the singles' events, and getting to know one another better... if you can call our nervous, awkward encounters meaningful conversations. What no one seemed to discern, though, was that the handful of interactions they saw at church was the extent of our "relationship." Honestly, I hadn't even seen Pastor Stephen outside of church since our lunch date.

Sara didn't know any of this, of course. "This is perfect!," she continued on. "When did it happen? How many times have you gone out?"

I exhaled sharply. "Well, just once, and we have another... date, I guess... coming up soon." Maybe. Not like he had asked me yet or anything, but the small fib made me sound more legit. "It's no big deal, really."

"Of course not," Melissa said.

"Well, what does that mean?," I said crossly, assuming that she still didn't believe any of it. "Do you want me to call him and have him confirm it for you?"

"No," she said, rather smugly. "I'm sure you've gone out with him. I'm sure you'll go out with him again. Shoot. I'm sure he'll propose in no time at all."

Sara gasped. "You really think so? Oh, Em – you'll have the most beautiful children! So tall! And your wedding! It'll be so amazing and so beautiful and --"

"BUT," Melissa practically shouted, "it doesn't matter because –" she fixed me with a steely gaze "—you don't feel that way about him."

My breath caught in my throat. What had she been seeing? What had I been missing?

"You don't know that," I said softly. "I don't even know that. I don't know how I feel." And this was true. I thought back to the times we had seen one another, the awkwardness and the stolen glances when I was sure he didn't notice me staring at him. Couldn't that – nervous butterflies and crazy confusion – be that elusive "something more"? Or at least lead to it?

"Yeah, Mel," Sara said. "It's all so new. Give her time to figure it out."

"Well, I think it's only fair," she said, "that you should go out with someone ELSE this month, too, just so we're all on even footing here. Right, Sara?"

Darn it. Not only had they dragged the Pastor Stephen news out of me, but I would also have to go on a date with whatever Joe Schmoe my sister scrounged up.

Sara shrugged, "Well, I'd be happy with Pastor Stephen and Emily." She caught a glare from Melissa. "But it would be good support for Melissa, you know. Both of you going on blind dates and all."

I waved my hand at them. "Fine, fine. I'll get Jessica to fix me up with someone." And I guess this was fair, after all, since I had no guarantee of going out with Stephen again. Or really any knowledge about whether or not I wanted to.

We finished up lunch, chatting about work and our families. After an hour of visiting, we left the restaurant together, then went our separate ways. I ran by my office, wrote down Stacy's number from my files, and wondered who would be the worst of two evils… Stacy's cousin-in-law, Javier, or someone my sister could find? I tucked the number into my planner, resolving to just not think about it until the middle of March.

Or maybe even the END of March.

.

4 MARCH

I learned something interesting during the first week of March. International flights are expensive.

I told Josh about it after we successfully ran the entire five miles one Monday morning and decided to celebrate with a breakfast buffet. My attempts to explain how this cancelled out what we had just done fell on deaf ears as Josh, who had the whole week off for spring break, insisted that it was his treat.

Our plates were full of omelets, pancakes, and bacon. Josh had covered all of his in blueberry syrup, which I had never seen done on eggs. I did little to disguise my look of disgust, but Josh didn't even seem to notice as he thoughtfully took a bite.

"I have a friend from the church," he said. "Works at a travel agency downtown. Bet he could find a deal for you, especially since you're visiting a member of the military."

"Why would that make a difference?," I asked, taking a bite of my own pancakes.

"He's retired military himself," he said. "Semper Fi and all of that, you know. Always wants to make a deal for Marines and their families."

He called his friend on his cell phone as we were finishing up our meal, and after a few minutes of asking questions about connecting flights, confirming my preferences with him, and laughing over something that had happened on Sunday morning in the youth department, he gestured for my phone, took it as I passed it to him, and typed in a number on my notepad to show me.

"Are you serious?," I mouthed at him.

He nodded, his eyes twinkling. "Told you he'd have a deal," he mouthed back.

"I'll take it. Does he need my credit card info?"

Josh shook his head, asked his friend about office hours, then asked me if I could go by later on that day. I didn't have any appointments until the afternoon, so I told him I'd be on my way within the hour.

"Great!," Josh said, to me and his friend both. "Hey, man, she'll be by later on this morning. Thanks a lot. Her brother sure will be glad to see her."

Likely not. But I would be glad to see him anyway.

Josh hung up and took one last sip of his orange juice.

"That was amazing," I told him. "Thank you so much."

He smiled. "No problem. Of course, now you know what you have to do, right?"

"Yeah, go down there and pay for the tickets before he changes his mind and charges me fair value!"

Josh laughed. "No," he said. Then, with a mock air of seriousness, "Now, you have to at least try the blueberry syrup on your eggs."

I looked at him in horror.

"Oh," he pointed his fork at me, "don't pretend like you weren't secretly coveting mine. I saw you."

"That's disgusting," I told him.

"Have you ever tried it?"

"No!"

"Then how do you know it's disgusting?"

I frowned at him. "Because I'm around food all the time at work, enough to know what goes together and what doesn't. And this —" I indicated his syrupy eggs "—does NOT go together."

"Try it," he said, holding up a small bite from his own plate. "Come on. You owe me for the tickets."

"I don't want to try it."

"Try it, try it, try it, try it..." He smiled. "I'm going to keep on until you try it."

I sighed dramatically, then leaned across the table to take the bite that he offered. He watched me with raised eyebrows as I chewed, grinning when he saw my expression change from apprehensive to thoughtful to... well, pleased.

"Josh Morales," I said. "That was actually quite good. Very surprising."

"Oh, Emily," he said. "Life with me always is."

The Evans family was in my office later on that week. December 18th was a long way away, but there were so many things to be done in the meantime, especially with a celebration of this magnitude. I went over the financials for all that Evelyn and Lauren had discussed and planned. The numbers were alarmingly huge, but Dr. and Mrs. Evans (excuse me,

Stan and Dorothy, as they had insisted numerous times that I call them) didn't seem to think that they were beyond reasonable. We discussed color schemes, design styles for the linens, and all of the other particulars that Evelyn would have glossed over in her initial assessment.

"Now, all of this can change," I assured Lauren, who was beginning to look overwhelmed by all of the choices. "If you or Justin change your minds on these details, up until October, we can change it. What we won't be able to change, obviously, are the things that take longer to order and have ready. Like your dress. And some of your flowers. And the groom."

They all laughed politely at my joke. Then, Lauren, in all seriousness said, "Well, I won't be changing the groom, obviously. But my dress... I..." She looked helplessly at her mother, who encouraged her to go on. "I just don't have any idea what to pick."

I had fielded this type of anxiety many times before and knew just what to suggest. "I don't recommend beginning with bridal magazines," I told her. "They give you too much selection on too many types of dresses. If you spend too much time browsing those, you'll get to your first bridal shop and not even know where to begin."

Lauren looked at her mother, panicked. Then, she whispered to me, "I've been subscribed to Brides magazine for four years now."

Ahh. Well, that would explain the confusion.

"What I would recommend now, then," I told her, "is going to an upscale shop. I know of one in the area that does great work. Ask them to let you try on one dress each from the basic dress styles. Once you narrow down what you don't like in lengths, necklines, cuts, and fabric types, you can focus in on one that you do like."

Lauren nodded enthusiastically with each word I said. I handed her the business card of the bridal shop, suggesting that she make an appointment with them for the best service. She took it eagerly, then asked, "Could you come with me?"

I didn't generally get this involved with brides. And by "generally," I mean that I never got this involved with brides. There was no time to do tasks like this, and since we made no direct profit on dress sales (although I had managed to get a percentage from a few smaller bridal shops a couple of years ago when I started referring brides who were looking for lower-end dresses), we didn't waste our time on that part. I had been disappointed in this when I first started working for Evelyn but quickly got over it, telling myself that most brides had no trouble picking out a dress, even if it didn't fit the theme they were going for with the rest of the event.

But I liked this family. And I was reminded of Stacy's words, about how I had been more than a coordinator to her, and I saw this as a chance to minister to a young bride who was already very stressed out about all the details. So, I made a decision, reasoning with myself that if Evelyn had a problem with it... well she would just have a problem with it. Which would make it my problem. Which meant that I should probably say no --

"I would love to."

Why don't I ever listen to myself?

My tickets to Okinawa arrived two days later, via courier. As I was shutting the door in the UPS guy's face, he stopped me with, "I have another one here, too."

He handed me an envelope without a return address. I signed for it, then after I had gone back inside, broke the seal and pulled out a cashier's check for over half the amount of my ticket.

I knew just who to call.

"Hello?," she said, sounding a bit stressed out.

"Mom, are you okay?"

A pause. "Oh, yeah, I'm fine. How are you doing, dear? Are you at the office?"

"No," I told her. "I came home for lunch. Save some money, you know."

"Great idea," she said.

"Yeah, and speaking of money, something was delivered to me today."

"Oh?"

"Mom," I chided.

"What?," she chided right back.

"I can't take this money."

She sighed. "Emily, it's not even half the cost of a ticket, and –"

"But, Mom," I began, "it is, and I had the money to pay for the flight, and –"

"You should go right ahead and put that money back in your house fund! We want to help you go and see Matthew. I would go with you myself..." I held my breath in horror, imagining how much crazier a foreign country would be with my exceptionally loud mother providing commentary on everything. Oh, please, no...

"... but I just can't." Whew.

But then, I heard it in her voice. She sounded upset. The springtime and early summer season were busy at our church. Easter was a big part of the church's year, then summer programs for the children, revival services in the summer, convention meetings, and the list just went on and on. With all of the activities that started up over that stretch of time, my parents rarely got any kind of a break until September, when they took a tiny breather to prepare for the holiday season.

"Maybe you and Dad can take a trip in the fall," I said. "You know, when things slow down around the church."

She sighed. "Emily, I'm going to tell you something. And I want it to stay between us for now. It's about your father."

I felt a cold panic set in. Was he leaving Grace? Were they relocating? I couldn't imagine having my parents anywhere but here, in the city I grew up in, at the church I had always been a part of, in our comfortable lives. Were they moving on?

"Can you keep it between us, for now?," she asked.

"Yes," I barely whispered.

"I... I think your father may be... sick."

Sick. This wasn't something I had expected.

"Sick? Like a cold or something?," I asked. "Melissa kept warning us about the flu. Did Dad get his shot?"

She sighed again. "Yes, dear. I'm not talking about that kind of sick. He's... he's forgetting things."

He had been forgetting things. In the past year, he would stumble over names of church members and forget stories halfway through telling them. But we all did that from time to time, and he was in his sixties. It was bound to get worse with age. We had even made it into a joke, talking about how all those hours at Grace were making him senile.

"Oh, Mom," I said, reassuringly. "It's probably just stress. The church has been really busy lately, and —"

"Emily," she said with some authority, "he couldn't remember the way back home the other night."

This sounded very bad. "He couldn't remember... how to get home?"

"No," she said, her voice slightly trembling. "He left the church and called to tell me like he always does. You know, so I could have our dinner ready, like I try to every night. Two hours passed, and he still wasn't home. I thought maybe he had made a side trip or something, had gotten caught up with someone leaving the building, gotten a call on his phone about a member needing a visit... so I waited. His cell phone was turned off when I tried to call, and in between being so agitated with him and so worried, I almost jumped in the car to go and find him. I finally decided to call the OnStar people – and, by the way, we are so glad that you suggested we get that for his car! Anyway, they located his car for me, got him talking to them, and called the police to come and help him. He was sitting in a McDonald's parking lot twenty miles away. He went in and ordered a Big Mac, took it back out to the car, and just sat there eating it! When the police arrived, he didn't even remember how he had gotten there."

I sat down on my couch, running my hand over my face. "Wow... that's..." I was at a loss for words.

"It was scary. VERY scary," she said. "And the next morning, he was back to normal. Couldn't remember the episode at all. Thought I was making it all up!"

"How often has this happened?," I asked.

"Well, that was the first time it involved a car and him getting lost. But he's had other moments, where things just don't seem to connect anymore, and I... I'm just worried."

I struggled to find the right words to say. "Is there... is there some doctor you can take him to?"

I could hear her blowing her nose. "I want to wait. Just wait a little while and see if it's the stress. I mean, like you said, he's been really busy."

"He has," I confirmed, wanting this to be all that there was to the story.

"And maybe once he gets a break this summer, it will all just... fix itself."

"I think it will," I said.

"I'm finding reasons to go up to the church with him most days, to spend most of my time with him. Just to make sure he's okay." She sighed. "I didn't intend to worry you with it. Just wanted to let you know – and just you – what was going on with him."

I took a deep breath. "I'll be praying for both of you, Mom. Let me know what I can do to help."

"Thanks, sweetie. You just give Matthew a big hug for me in May," she said, crying all over again.

"Will do..."

The situation consumed most of my thoughts the rest of the week. I tried, in vain, to hear every detail Evelyn gave in her dramatic monologues on the weddings that were up ahead for the week but seemed to miss a great majority of the important ones, as evidenced by the look she gave me halfway through her endless droning.

"You seem a bit... frazzled, Emily."

Frazzled wasn't an endearing term with Evelyn. I patted down my hair and straightened out my clothes, almost subconsciously, as I explained it away with, "Just a headache this morning."

"Well, please," she said, exasperated and yet still so mannerly all at the same time, "take something before your eleven o'clock appointment."

I nodded. "Any details on the couple?"

"None at all," she said, waving her bling in the air thoughtfully, avoiding my eyes.

This coolness meant that Evelyn DID have details on the couple but was choosing not to share them with me. Likely, this was a train wreck just waiting to happen, and she was letting me deal with it from start to finish, expecting that I would do my best to monopolize on the couple's cash flow and make their prelude to a disaster of a marriage as ostentatious as possible. Which went against everything I believed.

Sure enough, my eleven o'clock appointment walked in ten minutes late... and about seven months pregnant. And dragging a three year old behind her.

"Hi!," the bride said to me, thrusting her hand out to me. "Ashley Smith."

The groom did likewise, stating, "Bobby Billings."

"Pleasure to meet you both," I said, indicating the seats in front of my desk. I bent over to be at face-level with the toddler and asked, "What's your name?"

"Oh, he doesn't talk much," Ashley said. "But he'll sit here and be real good." The little boy looked at me, shyness etched over every inch of his little face.

I started to tell her that I wasn't concerned about his behavior, but she launched into her story before I could say another word.

"We're wanting to get married in a few months. The baby's due in May, and we would do it now, but I don't want to wear a maternity wedding dress."

I nodded. "Were you looking to do the ceremony, reception, or both here?"

"Honey?," she asked, looking at her betrothed. He looked at me curiously as he said, "Well, it really depends on the price."

"Completely understandable," I said, as I brought out a laminated copy of our basic prices. "Here are our base prices, which just includes the rental of the space. It doesn't include chairs, tables, linens, flowers, or any of the services, such as music, sound, catering, and the like."

Bobby's eyes seemed to almost pop out of his head. Ashley looked at him, then glanced at me, concern on her face.

"We're not cheap," she said. "It's just that with the first kid —" she jerked her finger over at him, "—I'm only getting so much child support from my first husband, and with my second kid —" she jerked her finger toward her bump – "I'm not getting ANY child support from my second husband." She rolled her eyes. "He won't even give me the divorce I've been demanding now for three whole months!"

"Two months, baby," Bobby said, still glancing over the prices. "We've only been together two months."

"Yeah," she said to me, with an expression of sheer incredulity. "I mean, I told him that it's over and that he doesn't need to be involved, and he just needs to give me the divorce, so I can go on with my life, and OW---"

She clutched her stomach.

"Are you okay?," I asked, my hand on the phone, ready to call an ambulance. If there's anything I had learned from my sister's multiple pregnancies, it's that a woman that far along needs to be taken very seriously in all of her aches and pains.

"Yeah, yeah," she said, breathing slowly through her mouth.

"Baby, it's just talking about him that's got you upset," Bobby said to her.

"I know, I know," she said. Then, after a moment, she looked up at me and smiled. "Anyway, what was I saying?"

"Well," I began, not knowing what part of this story to concentrate on, "finances are tight."

"Sure are," she said.

Against my better judgment, I decided to ask a question. Oh, I could almost see Evelyn in my mind, shaking her head at me, pushing the price sheet towards me and indicating that I should sell them the biggest wedding of the year. But I just couldn't do it. Not in good conscience, with things so unresolved in her past (excuse me, current) marriage and with children involved. The little boy looked up at me, and I just couldn't help myself.

"May I ask a question?," I asked Ashley.

"Well, of course," she said.

"Is this the best time to get married?"

She looked at me, confused. "Well, NO... not with me pregnant and all. Which is why we want to wait a few months."

"Yes, I understand that and all. But is it even LEGAL to get married right now? Or, let's say in a few months when you still haven't gotten your divorce?"

Bobby looked at her, and she looked at him. "Well," he began, "it's just the ceremony. We can get a license later on after the divorce is finalized."

I stopped myself from adding, "Yes, and by then, she will likely be pregnant with YOUR child and divorcing YOU. Except she won't because you won't really be married, and I will have played a part in this charade of a spiritual union between two people!" Instead, I pulled the price sheet away and took a deep breath.

I was no expert on relationships. But this marriage? (Or whatever it was, because they were basically telling me that they wanted a wedding without a legal marriage.) Had failure written all over it. I could not and WOULD not be any part in the break-up of this woman's still-alive marriage with the father of the child she carried. I knew I would catch grief from Evelyn about the lost commissions and percentages, but I didn't care.

Choosing my words carefully, I spoke softly. "It is my professional opinion as a wedding coordinator that until you have resolved things in your previous marriage, a move in any direction towards planning a ceremony of this magnitude would be ill-advised."

Ashley couldn't hide her disappointment, and Bobby sneered at me. "So, we're not GOOD enough to get married here?"

I had to stop myself from screaming, "YOU'RE TRYING TO MARRY A WOMAN WHO IS ALREADY MARRIED, YOU FOOL!!!" Instead, I diplomatically said, "No, that's not what I'm saying. What I'm saying is that there are legal ramifications for our staff in performing a remarriage for someone who is still married." (Likely so, as I was very nearly certain that our on-call Justice of the Peace who we brought in for couples who requested one wouldn't be able to do anything in this instance.)

Bobby pushed his chair back. "Come on, baby," he spat at Ashley. "Let's go."

She looked at me sadly. I wanted to reach out, take her hands, and ask her about the man who was refusing to divorce her, to see if there was any way things could be worked out, to encourage her to think about the choices she was making and what effect this would have on her children... but I couldn't say any of them. Because this was a business and not a ministry.

She picked up her purse, hefted herself up out of the chair, and led her three year old out the door.

Evelyn was in the middle of her lecture on how we never turn away ANY business when the Evans family arrived. She caught herself mid-soliloquy and said, "Well, what a wonderful surprise!" Grasping their hands in turn, she cooed, "Dr. and Mrs. Evans. And the lovely Lauren. How are all of you?"

"Just peachy," Stan chuckled. "Gonna see our girl try on some wedding dresses today!"

"I have my tissues ready," Dorothy said with a giggle, wiping a tear away with one even as she said it.

"Mrs. Primrose," I said, standing, "at Lauren's request, I will be escorting the Evans to the Elegance Dream bridal shop this afternoon. I thought it best that we give our very important clients all the assistance that they require in planning their event."

Evelyn's mouth was frozen in an O shape, no doubt amazed that she hadn't caught wind of this little friendship between her wealthiest clients and her mousy assistant. "Well, that sounds lovely, dear," she said to me. "Emily has an eye for fashion."

This was said for their benefit, as Evelyn had, on more than one occasion, chastised me for my poor clothing choices. I smiled sweetly at her.

"I hope you don't mind, Emily," Stan began, "but we rented a limo for the shopping trip. Have to have our little girl feeling like a princess before she tries on all those dresses!" Lauren beamed at me, as Evelyn clasped her hands together.

"That sounds perfect," I said. "If you'll just allow me to gather Lauren and Justin's information, I'll be with you in a moment."

As soon as they exited the office, Evelyn turned to me. "You...," she hissed.

I held up a hand, "Yes, I know you're still frustrated that I wouldn't do a ceremony for a woman who's ALREADY MARRIED and that you're likely unhappy that I'm spending an afternoon at a bridal shop that doesn't give us a dime, but —"

"Frustrated with you?," Evelyn gasped. Then, conceding, "Okay, well, yes, I'm frustrated about your ethical concerns with the married client." She took a breath, "But I'm THRILLED that you were invited along for the dress shopping!"

I couldn't help my ineloquent response. "Huh?"

"Think about it, Emily," Evelyn crossed her arms over her chest with a huge smile. "You hold little Lauren's hand and give her all this caring attention, and her parents who are RICH and so very well connected all around this city, will SING our praises from here to the other side of the world! We're going to have so much business!"

I sighed. It was always about the money. "I better go. They're waiting."

"Oh, yes, don't keep them waiting." She was practically beaming. Before I could leave, she said, quite thoughtfully, "By the way, make sure and refrain from telling her she looks ghastly in any of the dresses she tries on. Wouldn't want to offend them."

"Of course not," I said, rolling my eyes as I left the office.

Evelyn had no need to worry about the ghastly part. Lauren, in all of her youthful beauty, was gorgeous in every single dress she tried on. She insisted that I come back to the dressing room with the seamstress, and as I helped with each dress, my breath caught again and again. Just beautiful. Lauren saw my stare each time and asked, "What?" so self-consciously.

"You're going to be such a beautiful bride," I would smile at her, as she beamed.

Dorothy went through her own box of tissues and half of the store's tissues before Lauren stepped out in her final dress – a strapless Reem Acra ballgown. The seamstress placed the matching veil in her hair, and I placed the tiara her own mother had worn for her wedding on Lauren's head.

"Oh my stars," Stan breathed.

"It's just perfect," Dorothy wept into a tissue.

Lauren looked to me, a smile on her face. I nodded, giving her the thumbs up.

"I'll take it," she told the seamstress who immediately began taking measurements and filling out the order forms.

Stan poured us all champagne once we got back in the limo, telling Lauren again that she was "just peachy" in that dress. I was liking Stan more and more every day, with all of his sayings and the precious way Dorothy would look at him adoringly as he said them. Lauren smiled at them both as she sipped, looking down at my notes, making choices, and sighing contentedly now that she had her dress.

When we pulled up to the hotel, I told them that we'd arrange another meeting for the month of April and that I had a lovely time shopping for dresses.

"Emily," Lauren said, "can I walk you in?"

"Oh, I'll be fine –"

"Peachy idea, princess," Stan said. "You can't be too careful these days, Emily. It's dark outside after all, and we are downtown."

I wanted to point out that his own daughter would be walking back out by herself if she walked me in, but I refrained. They were such a sweet family.

"That'd be great, Lauren," I said, and she smiled.

As soon as we were out of the limo, she whispered to me, "I need to talk to you."

"Okay," I whispered back. Perhaps there were changes she wanted to make to choices her mother had made, doubts she was having about how the planning was going, or just general venting that some brides – even brides with amazing parents like hers – sometimes needed to do.

We made our way through the lobby and into the offices. Evelyn had already left for the day (of course), leaving the office empty.

"What did you need to talk about?," I asked Lauren.

"Well," she said, smiling, "I just wanted some... advice."

I nodded. "Was it on the ceremony or the reception?"

"Um... both, actually," she laughed a little. "I'm having a little... problem. With my parents."

I couldn't imagine anyone having a problem with those two, much less their perfect only child having a problem with them. But the stress of a wedding sometimes brought out unexpected family conflicts.

"Tell me about it."

"Well," she began, "It's already... getting out of hand."

The planning was indeed extravagant. Dr. Stan and Dorothy had a lot of friends, colleagues, and connections, and Justin's parents had even more. I could remember only a few weddings in my years of working for Evelyn that were this large, and for each of those, the brides had been thrilled with the glitz and glamour of every step in the process.

Lauren was looking decidedly less than thrilled as she twisted her engagement ring around her finger.

"Out of hand how?," I asked.

"Oh, just the guest list alone, actually," she sighed. "Five hundred people. Five HUNDRED!"

"Lots of people to be included, for sure," I began, diplomatically, "but a large guest list shouldn't make things more stressful for you. "

"Well, it's not just that, though," she said, turning her ring faster as she continued. "It's the flowers and the food and the pictures and the decorations and the cakes and the music and the attendants and –"

"Hey," I stopped her, placing my hand on her shoulder. "Those are just simple decisions. No big deal. And once you make the decisions, you're done. You don't have to do the work of getting it all put together for the big day. Just tell us what you want, trust that we'll do it, and don't stress out. Just enjoy the wedding that you want."

She closed her eyes for a moment. "That's exactly it, you see." She looked at me, tears in her eyes and a small smile on her face. "What I want, the wedding that I want, is not this. Not ALL of this."

"What do you want? What does your dream wedding look like?," I asked, afraid that the answer was going to cut down on her costs and obliterate our company's profits. Not that I was out for the money, mind you, but I did work for someone who WAS. And seeing as how I wasn't her favorite person at the moment, I was hoping to avoid any major upsets.

Lauren was oblivious to my quandary. "What I want is just a few friends and family. A simple, outdoor ceremony. Like in my own backyard simple. Walking down the aisle barefoot. That kind of thing."

In my mind, I could so clearly see and hear Evelyn gasp at the thought of wearing that Reem Acra ballgown outside with bare feet. Hey, I wasn't superficial, but it was bothering me a little, too.

"Have you... have you told your parents this is what you want?," I asked.

She laughed. "Oh, I've tried! But... but my mother is SO excited. And my dad is just... he's just as excited. And I don't want to hurt them. I know they have obligations, you know, or at least feel like they do, to include everyone they know. So, I see why it's gotten out of hand so quickly, and I just... I haven't had the heart to tell them."

I could understand this. "Have I ever told you," I told her, knowing full well that I hadn't, "that my father is the pastor of Grace Community Church?"

Surprise shown on her face. "No, I didn't know that. That's a big church!"

"Exactly," I said. "And when my sister got married, her wedding was, quite frankly, way over the top. Not because she knew everyone in the free world, mind you, but because my parents have so many connections and are so loved by so many people. Her reception was like a denominational convention."

"Was she upset about that?," Lauren asked quietly.

I thought back to how Jessica wasn't at ALL upset by it, how she relished standing in a receiving line for hours – literally – to greet whole hordes of people who meant something to our family. Nick, however, had been very uncomfortable with it at first, but as the day drew near and he fully accepted who he was marrying and the kind of family he was marrying into, he stood next to her and shook just as many hands as she did, knowing that sometimes you do things for your family, just because.

"Well, it was challenging," I said simply. "But it was just part of being in our family, letting our whole community celebrate with us." I thought I should probably leave it at that, letting her make her own decision and figure out what she and Justin needed to do without anyone else deciding things for her... but, heaven help me, I could almost feel Evelyn's perfectly manicured finger, poking me in the back repeatedly, prodding me to "seal the deal" and stop this talk of a barefooted, backyard wedding right this very minute.

So, against my better judgment, I took Lauren's hand, looked into her eyes, and said, "I think it would be a real blessing to your family if you let them do this. For you."

She nodded slowly, breathed a sigh, and smiled. "Yeah, I guess you're right. It'll be great, right? Just like we've been planning?"

I nodded. "Absolutely."

"Thanks, Emily," she said, giving me a hug. "You're a great planner... and a good friend."

Well, that last part remained to be seen. I sure didn't feel like such a good friend as I watched her walk back to her waiting parents.

March was flying by. It always did, what with all of the weddings we had planned around different spring breaks and spring holidays. Dates were taken up quickly during this time of the year, and the rush didn't end until well into the fall.

Knowing how rushed and busy I was going to be for the remainder of the month had NOT inspired me to pick up the phone and arrange a blind date for myself. If there was anything I didn't have time for, it was a meal out with a stranger.

"You have to do it," Melissa demanded, when I whined to her on the phone one afternoon.

"You know, you and I can tell Sara to shove this resolution, and we can just forget this month, and —"

"It's TOO LATE," she groaned. "If you had told me this at the beginning of the month, I would have totally been onboard. But now, I've been on Contemporary Christian Match and Meet for two whole weeks, and I have a," she practically growled, "- date."

I sat in silence for a moment. "What was it called?," I asked, not wanting to mention the d-a-t-e and incur her wrath but wanting so desperately to hear more.

"Contemporary Christian Match and Meet. It even sounds stupid, doesn't it?"

It did kind of sound cheesy, but before I could agree with her, she was moaning and groaning again.

"I mean, seriously, it's like throwing my money down a toilet. Looking through those profiles, just knowing that way over half of those men are dimwits and that the only reason that they put Jesus as their best friend is because they have no real friends."

"Well," I told her, "that's kind of mean-spirited."

"It's the truth!," she yelled at me. "I'm not impressed by it. Doesn't make me think they're more spiritual. Not at all."

"So," I said. "Do you… are you…" How to approach this d-a-t-e information without seeming too nosy…

"What?"

"Well, did you find someone?"

She sighed dramatically. "There was one guy who didn't look too stupid. He sent me a message before I could send him one, and I agreed to meet him next Friday. On my lunch break. In a public place. With lots of people. In broad daylight. While I'm carrying pepper spray."

I laughed at this.

"What's so funny?," she asked.

"What you just said!"

"Well, that's what I told him."

"You told him you'd have pepper spray?"

"Well, duh," she spat out. "Yeah! And I also told him that I'm a black belt in karate, which is totally a lie, but he doesn't have to know any different."

I could hear her work buzzer go off in the background and knew our conversation was coming to a close.

Sure enough, she said, "Good deal, that's the end of my break, and I can get on with my life."

"Tell me how your date goes," I said quickly.

"Yeah, yeah, yeah," she answered while hanging up.

After my Monday morning run with Josh (which included another trip to our coffee shop), I came home to get ready for work, then called my sister en route to the hotel.

"Are you driving?," she asked. Apparently she had heard that horn honking at me while we were making pleasant small talk.

"Yes, I am," I admitted.

"You know how dangerous that is, don't you?"

I rolled my eyes. "Well, I'm glad to know you're feeling better."

"How do you know I'm feeling better?," she asked.

"You're feeling good enough to treat me like one of your kids, so you must be over the morning sickness," I said.

She laughed a little. "Well, as a matter of fact, I have been barf-free for five whole days. And I'm eating Froot Loops three times a day."

It was always like this. Fourteen weeks of puking, then twenty-six weeks of cereal cravings. With Sean it was Cap'n Crunch, then Cheerios with Sam, Trix with Scott, and, of all things, healthy Raisin Nut Bran with Stuart.

"Mmm, Froot Loops," I murmured.

"You have no idea," she said. "I dream of that stupid toucan."

"Well, listen," I said, switching lanes as I did so, "I'm calling to ask a favor."

"Sure."

I took a deep breath, knowing that this would not end well, knowing that my mother would catch wind of it. Hey, with all that was stressing her out right now with my dad, this might actually be a good distraction.

"Will you fix me up with someone?"

Silence. Then, a, "I'm sorry, what?"

"Jessica," I warned.

"Seriously?"

"Yes, seriously," I said, already sorry that I had done this.

"Why?"

I rolled my eyes again. My big sister tended to bring this out in me. "Just because I might want to meet someone."

"Okay, well, I think you need to get your head checked, because you

NEVER want to meet anyone."

This was true. "Well, things change," I lied.

"Darn it!," she said. "And I don't even KNOW anyone right now! All of the guys on Nick's crew are married. Or, like, too old for you."

Hey, I wasn't going to be picky. "How old is too old?"

"TOO old," she said. "I'm sorry, but... I just don't know anyone."

I sighed. This would normally be sweet music to my ears, but right now? When I needed a date? This wasn't what I wanted to hear.

"No problem," I said.

"Well, I feel just awful! Maybe Mom knows someone —"

"NO!"

"Touchy, touchy," she said. "I'm really sorry that I can't help."

"Oh, I'm sure I'll figure out something." I would give Stacy a call when I got to the office. I was already crossing my fingers that Javier spoke English. Or, even better, no English at all, so that we wouldn't have to worry about mindless small talk on our date. "No big deal, you kn—"

And with that, I hit the car in front of me.

"Shouldn't have been talking on your cell phone, young lady," the officer, who was writing out the accident report, said to me.

"No, sir," I said, hanging up my cell phone, having just called Evelyn to let her know why I was running late. "It's a good lesson learned the hard way, I suppose."

As far as I could tell, the driver in front of me had also been talking on his cell phone and had hit his brakes too quickly at a stop light in an effort to avoid hitting the car in front of him. I had done the same without the same success. Clearly, I was the one at fault and would be seeing a jump in my insurance premiums. Lovely.

My car was... well, not much worse for the wear. That was the good thing about driving a piece of junk. It wasn't ever going to look spectacular, so a few more dents were inconsequential.

The other car, however, had some serious cosmetic problems. I didn't know much about cars, but just the sound of this one's name "Lexus" brought up visions of dollars quickly exiting my bank account. As I listened to the officer continue to berate my irresponsibility, I thought about the cost of repairing a flawless car that was now wearing my own car's red paint and sporting a crumpled left bumper.

Not good.

Fortunately, before I could dwell on these thoughts too much longer, my phone rang. Assuming it was Jessica, calling to freak out about the fact that I had actually gotten into a wreck while talking to her, I moved to shut it off but stopped when I saw the church's number.

"Hey, Dad," I said.

"Um... no, it's not him," a familiar voice answered.

My throat tightened. Pastor Stephen. Like an idiot, I held my blazing cheeks in my hands and stood there in the middle of traffic, while the officer continued writing his report and talking about defensive driving.

"Hey, Pastor Stephen," I said, going for an air of casualness.

"Sorry to call you on your cell phone. I hope I didn't catch you at a bad time?"

"Well, actually," I said, finding the humor in the situation. "I just hit a Lexus."

The officer shot me a look, as Stephen laughed.

"Are you serious?" Then, more composed, "Oh, wow, you ARE serious. You got in an accident? That's not funny at all."

"Oh, no," I said, "it's hilarious. Because what else did I have to do during the biggest wedding week of the spring except deal with the insurance company and get all this fixed?"

"I'm so sorry," he murmured. "You're not hurt, are you?"

"No," I said. "Don't worry about it."

We sat in silence for a few moments, as I began to wonder why exactly he called. Before I could ask, he explained himself.

"Well, I just wanted to call and thank you again for all of your help last week with the game night. Everything was so well prepared and put together. I think we may try to do it again in another couple of months."

I smiled. "It was a hit. Sara said everyone really enjoyed themselves." I, of course, had been at a rehearsal dinner that night and hadn't been able to attend.

"I was hoping," Stephen began, "that we could have dinner together sometime this week."

Another date. Maybe I could take care of the resolution this way. Surely, Sara and Melissa wouldn't demand a blind date if I was starting a serious relationship with Pastor Stephen, and I could just –

"Emily?" Apparently, I had lost focus there.

"Oh, sorry," I said. "I was answering a question for the officer." The office looked up at me and rolled his eyes. How very unprofessional. "What were you asking?," I said again, wanting to make sure that Stephen had said what I thought he said.

"I wanted to know if you would let me make dinner for you this week," he said. "Any day that works for you."

Making dinner for me? Well, surely that had to beat a blind date. The extent of my own kitchen skills was opening up a can of Spaghetti-Os. With an electric can opener. So a real homecooked meal sounded great.

"That sounds wonderful," I said. "I'm free Thursday night." Miraculously.

"Great," he said. "I'll email you directions to my place. Is seven o'clock okay?"

"Sure," I said.

"Well, then, it's a date."

A date. God bless that man for finally defining it for me!

"See you then," I added before we hung up.

The officer walked over to me and with a flourish handed me my copy of the accident report. "Stay off the cell phone," he warned again, likely doubting my ability to do so since I hadn't been able to keep off of it since he stopped me.

"Will do," I said, before slipping in the car and driving away.

The very next day, I got an email at work from my sister.

"Em,

I would call, but I know you're busy. And I can't seem to find your office number in the mess of papers on my desk. And your CELL PHONE IS TURNED OFF! I don't understand why you do that in the middle of the day.

Anyhoo, I wanted you to know that I did manage to finally find someone to fix you up with. Well, that makes it sound like I really had to get to the bottom of the barrel to find a real catch, didn't it? Honestly, Em, this guy is fantastic. Just started working with Nick's brother's father-in-law's company as their accountant. Really smart, apparently. Now, I haven't seen him in person or anything, but I've talked to him on the phone, and he's just hilarious! I think you'll like him. He was very eager to meet you.

So, I set it up for next Monday night. I know you and your horrific wedding schedule, so I figured that was the best time, although it so obviously sucks for the rest of the working world. I know this guy is a great catch, though, because he didn't complain AT ALL. I think he could be the one, Emily!

Okay, so he's meeting you at Frank's Fried Chicken Bucket on 4th and Pine at 6:00 on Monday. You have to call me and tell me what you're wearing!

Love,

Jessica"

I groaned audibly, putting my head in my hands. I should have known she'd figure out something. Two dates in one week. While the quantity of dates was certainly on the rise, I couldn't say that the quality was improving. Frank's Fried Chicken Bucket? Lovely. Because we all know there are so many dainty and feminine ways to eat greasy, fried chicken. I would likely be wearing a large bib.

And what was this mystery accountant's name anyway?

I picked up the phone to give Jessica a piece of my mind, but when her answering machine picked up, I hung up without leaving a message. I would deal with it all later.

RESOLUTIONS

The rest of the day was filled with paperwork, Wednesday included four – count them, FOUR – bridal meltdowns in my office, and Thursday was spent from sunrise till sunset supervising the set up for our ten weekend weddings. I kept looking at my watch, nervously waiting for 6:30, when I would need to leave in order to get to Pastor Stephen's house on time.

I had never been to his house before. No one I knew had ever been to his house before. I had, against my better judgment, let Sara know about my plans. She was leaving for San Antonio and "the talk" with Jon, taking the last days of her spring break to do so, and she had needed a motivational talk the night before. During our conversation, it slipped out (again!) that I had a date with Pastor Stephen. She shrieked, asked about twenty questions, and then chattered on for thirty minutes about what I should wear, what we should talk about, how early I should get there, and on and on and on until I was even more nervous than I had been.

Nervous enough that at 6:28, I could hardly go back to my office, get my purse, and head out to the parking garage where my car was parked.

I arrived five minutes early, checking my hair and make-up in the mirror, wishing that I had worn something more casual than my pink suit. There had been no time to go home and change, so this was it. I gave myself a nod in the mirror and started making my way towards the front door.

Pastor Stephen opened it before I could even knock. Apparently, he had been waiting for me. He was in jeans and a sweatshirt, having obviously been home long enough to get comfortable while cooking. Wow – he really looked gorgeous in anything. Suits, business casual, formal, and totally and completely casual. He could have come out in a giant cow costume like they have at Chick Fil A and still looked hot.

As my eyes bore holes into his clothing, I was even more aware of just how painfully overdressed I was.

"Hey," he said with a smile, having no idea what I was thinking. Praise God for that.

"Hi," I said. "Sorry about the way I'm dressed. Came straight from work." And yet there I went, like a total moron, telling him what I thought anyway.

"You look nice," he said. Then, we stood there awkwardly for a minute. "Come in, please. No need for you to stand outside in the cold."

I went in, taking in the surroundings of the mysterious Pastor Stephen's house. As far as I knew, no one else from the church had ever been here before. Probably some of the guys, of course, but the women all talked and none of them had ever mentioned Pastor Stephen's home. I drank in the ambience, trying to record everything to memory. Brown furnishings... everywhere. Neutral walls. Natural wood bookshelves. Bland. Well, this would be easy to remember, simplicity and all. No hint of any female input in this decorating scheme, no splash of color, no –

"AHHH!!!" I screamed, as a full-size bear jumped right on top of me, knocking me on my knees.

"Tasha, DOWN. Sit." I immediately sat, like an idiot. The bear, mercifully, took its claws off me and sat on its haunches, still a good two inches taller than me on my knees. I looked into the bear's eyes and realized that it wasn't a bear. It was a...

"What is that?," I asked Stephen, staring intently into the brown and black beast's eyes.

"I'm so sorry about that, Emily. I don't have much company. I guess Tasha is a little territorial."

"What's a Tasha?," I said, attempting to get up, never taking my eyes off the beast.

He held out his hand to help me up, then continued holding it reassuringly. The Tasha seemed irritated by this and let out a low moan of agony.

"Tasha, in your bed," Stephen barked.

"In MY bed?," I asked.

"No," he said with a smile. "It's a command for…" He noticed that we were still holding hands and dropped mine awkwardly. "I'm just trying to get her to lie down. Tasha, get in your bed."

The Tasha hung her head, then rose up on her legs, gave me one good sniff, then turned on her heels and sauntered off.

"Good grief," I managed. "Is that a dog?"

Stephen nodded. "Yeah. An English Mastiff, actually. My parents breed them. Tasha was the runt of one of their litters and just took to me. She's not the purest expression of the breed, obviously, being too small and all."

"That dog is too small?" I reached down to straighten my skirt and felt… drool? Good grief…

"Yeah, if you can believe it. She was supposed to be a lot bigger."

Tasha continued shooting me evil looks from her bed, so I looked down at my hands, covered in… yes, that was drool.

Stephen looked at my hands, too. "Oh, wow. I'm so sorry. Did she lick you?"

"No, she drooled on me, but who can blame her? I was in and out of catering all day, so she must smell the food." That day, they had been smoking brisket. I'm sure I smelled just heavenly, especially to a three thousand pound dog.

"Speaking of food," Stephen said, wanting to move our conversation away from his dog and her hatred of me, "there was a…. problem with dinner. And by that I mean, I almost set the kitchen on fire trying to cook dinner."

"Oh, no," I said, biting back a laugh.

"Yeah," he smiled. "I'm... well, hopeless. I can't even boil water, frankly."

"Me neither, actually," I said, looking down at my hands, which were now sticky. Eww.

"Emily, there's a bathroom down the hall, first door on your left if you want to... well, clean that up." He smiled apologetically.

"I think I will."

I cleaned up in the bathroom, using every bit of self-restraint I had to keep from going through the bathroom cabinets. The bathroom – what I could see – was nice and neat. But I know, just like any rational person, that you can tell more about someone by going through their cabinets than you can by just looking around the rooms as they've been prepared for visitors. As mysterious as Stephen was to me, it felt like the cabinets were calling to me, "Emily! Open us! Open us!" My mother would definitely have done so and made itemized lists of her findings. The temptation was strong for me to be equally obsessive compulsive, but I refrained.

I rounded the corner in the kitchen, where Stephen was opening up a pizza box.

"Now, THAT?," I said. "Is how I cook."

He smiled. "Well, good. This beats what ended up in the trash."

"I love your house," I said to him, taking in the – again – neutral colors of the small kitchen. As bland as the colors were, everything was neat and organized. Unexpected for most bachelors, but characteristic for the always put together Stephen.

He turned around to smile nervously. "Thanks. It's home... even if I don't spend much time here, thanks to work."

We sat down a few moments later and dug into dinner.

"This is great, Pastor St... I mean, Stephen," I said, embarrassed.

"Still calling me Pastor after knowing me all this time," he shook his head, a small smile on his face. "And thank you. I'm on a first name basis with the delivery guy."

That seemed to ring true with the rest of his surroundings. Take out dinner, under-decorated home, large bear-like dog... normal, stereotypical single guy stuff. As we sat in silence, a very loud clock in the living room counted the minutes for us. My apartment, cramped though it was, felt cozy and far less lonely than this cavernous, silent home. I wondered how often Pastor Stephen got lonely, how those lonely moments might make him more prone to call up mousy girls from church, ask them on dates, and –

"Emily?"

I looked up to see him staring at me. Oh, no, he had just asked something, and I totally hadn't heard it. "I'm so sorry," I said. "Long day, brain mushy... what did you say?"

"Just asking about how your work is going."

I sighed, thinking about my last meeting with Lauren, post-dress expedition. She had sat in my office alongside her mother, seemingly shrinking smaller and smaller under the weight of Dorothy's big plans, until it was like she wasn't even there at all. I had felt horrible about the upgrades and changes I had affirmed and encouraged, even as Evelyn praised my work.

"Well," I started, "it's hard when people expect so much, you know?" Evelyn was expecting many things from me, Lauren's parents were expecting many more from her, and all of their colleagues and friends were expecting even more from them.

"Tell me about it," Stephen said.

I sat back and considered his words for a moment, wondering what expectations fell on him. I knew what a pastoral load looked like for my father, but I wondered how it differed for Stephen.

"Does the church have some pretty high expectations for your ministry?," I asked, taking a drink.

"I think," he said, crossing his arms and leaning his elbows on the table, "that they have more expectations for my personal life than my professional life, to be honest with you."

And with that, my drink went down the wrong way, and I began choking. Because that's classy.

"Are you okay?," Stephen asked, clearly concerned.

"Yeah," I sputtered out. "Just peachy." Oh, I was a mess. Always a big, huge embarrassing mess. A few more coughs, and I dabbed my eyes with my napkin. "All better now."

"You sure?," he looked at me doubtfully.

"Oh, yeah. Just great." I put down my napkin. "Now, what were you saying about your personal life?"

"Well," he tried again, "it's no secret that people like to try and fix me up at the church, right?"

Actually this WAS a secret. I had no idea. Apart from the rush of single ladies at the beginning of his ministry and now whatever was going on with me, I thought the church had given up.

"For real?," I said.

He looked at me as though I was joking. "You haven't noticed? It happens all the time. Has been happening since I came to Grace. It just really bothers people to see a single man in ministry. They begin to make all kinds of crazy assumptions, and they try to 'fix' a problem that's not even there."

I thought about this for a moment. And I couldn't resist asking. "Who've you been fixed up with?"

"Why do you want to know?," he asked, a slow smile building on his face.

I shrugged. "A girl can be curious and all, right?" I was dying to know which of the Pinnacle girls had arranged to have themselves on dates with him...

He shook his head. "No one you know," he said. "Just nieces and granddaughters of members, girls outside of our church. I've been really clear and firm on not dating within the church. You know, because being on staff would make it odd if things didn't work out... or if they did. It would likely be awkward either way."

Awkward. Well, that was the word du jour with Pastor Stephen and me, but tonight, for some reason, I felt free to talk about even this.

And surprisingly enough, so did he.

"You know," he said, relaxing, "people talk about us."

"Yes," I answered back, smiling myself. "I hear them."

A moment passed in silence. Just as I begin to wonder at the wisdom of having said what I said, he spoke softly.

"I think," he began looking down at his hands for a moment, "that people love Thomas and Lydia so much, that they love you so much, that they have... hopes." He looked at me for a moment. "Do you know what I mean?"

"Hopes?," I asked, not getting it.

"Hopes maybe that you'll... be a bigger part of the church. Than you already are now. And, well, they have expectations of me to... settle down and look like what a pastor should look like... in their minds, at least. Does that make sense?"

Was Pastor Stephen saying that Grace was already planning our wedding? He was probably right, but still. I wasn't sure how to respond to this.

"Well," I said, "that makes sense. Kind of. Not really." Brilliant.

He laughed. "Well, I enjoy spending time with you. I think you probably understand me better than most, thanks to your father. Not that it means I understand you at all, of course," he finished with a smile.

I was pretty much an open book. "I'm pretty much an open book," I offered.

"Not so much," he said, shaking his head. What was this? Was *I* as confusing to Pastor Stephen as he was to me? Did *I* leave things awkward and ambiguous with *him*?

We continued eating as I thought all of this through. We chatted about our families, about our friends, about what our work schedules looked like for the week, until I could tell it was getting late.

I looked at my watch and sighed. "Well, I should probably get home."

"All those rehearsal dinners tomorrow night," he said, shaking his head. "Do you ever get tired of it?"

"Some of it," I said, honestly. "But for the most part... no. I really love being there for people, helping their big nights go well."

He smiled at this. "Well, let me walk you out."

Tasha eyed me from her bed as I made my way out, and when she saw that Stephen was going with me, rose to her feet.

"Whoa," I said lightly.

Stephen gave her a simple hand motion, and she retreated with a grunt.

"Wow," I said. "Well trained."

He shrugged. "Some of the time, at least."

It was still slightly cold outside, but the temperatures were definitely on an upward change. In another week or two, we would finally have springtime weather. No more cold running days, and no more shivering as I walked brides out to the garden while I gave them the grand tour of the hotel. I sighed contentedly at the thought of this.

At my car, I turned to Pastor Stephen and smiled. "Thanks for dinner," I said sincerely. "It was good to get to talk with you for a while."

He nodded. "Yeah, you, too. It gets lonely around here, you know, so I thought it would be nice to have someone over for dinner."

Just "someone," not me. Or maybe he did mean me. I was too tired at this point to try and figure it out, to be honest.

I slid into the driver's seat, waved good-bye, and started the car, jumping slightly when he crouched down near my window and tapped on the glass. I rolled down the window, just in time to hear him say, "Would you like to go out again sometime?"

The night had been enjoyable enough, and he – well, he was just about perfect by everyone else's estimation, so I didn't consider his offer long before saying, "Okay."

And with that, we had another date... or just the assumption of a date, since neither of us hammered out any details and we would likely pass one another in the halls at church for weeks without making things any clearer, and...

Oh, well. It was something, at least.

I was in the middle of the Mulligan/Ingles reception when my cell phone started ringing.

This particular bride had an affinity for rap music, which was fine, of course. We had heard everything from reggae to tejano to country to pop to classical to polka to even Afrikaans music in the grand ballroom before, but this particular DJ wasn't one with whom I had ever worked before. He seemed to be under the impression that louder was always better, and in no time at all the walls were literally shaking with each beat and the chandeliers were moving (just enough for me to notice) with each beat. The bride had emerged in her "reception attire," and I was pretty sure that after just a few songs, all of her guests and the staff would have seen her panties from the way she was grinding in a dress that was no longer than a pair of hot pants. (Or perhaps not, since she could very well have not been wearing panties at all. Ugh…)

Evelyn had excused herself from the reception (of course), telling me that it was a "young people event" and that the bride much preferred me anyway. Which she did – it was true. Cecilia and I, style differences aside, had a smooth working relationship, and I had loved how certain she was with her plans, how she had done her homework, and how she could confidently make decisions without any trouble. And because of that, it was a fabulous event. Ghetto-fabulous, but that was just what the bride had wanted.

Cecilia saw me checking on the cakes from her position on the dance floor and smoothly motioned for me to join her and her group of gyrating friends on the floor. Mercifully, my cell phone started buzzing, and I held it up, indicating that I would have to go outside to hear anything at all.

One step outside the doors, and it was like I had entered another world. My head still throbbed with the beat, and my hearing wasn't entirely all there, as evidenced by the way that I practically shouted, "HELLO?!" into the cell phone. It seemed as though every head at the check-in desk turned to face me.

Nice.

I couldn't hear anything but crying for a moment. Holding the phone closer to my ear, I tried again, this time more gently. "Hello?"

"Emily?," I heard through gasping breaths. The crying was so mangled that I couldn't even recognize the voice. I held the phone away from my ear, checking the number. Sara. Sara, who was supposed to be in San Antonio right now, giving Jon an ultimatum...

Oh, no.

"Sara?," I asked, cautiously. "What's wrong?"

She continued crying. "It's over. It's all over."

"What?," I asked, hoping that I hadn't heard her say it. Don't get me wrong – Jon was certainly not my favorite guy in the whole world, but Sara cared for him. I had wanted things to work out, for Jon to do the right thing, and for Sara to call with good news.

"It's over," she whispered. "And I don't know what I'm going to do."

She began crying again. "Sara," I said. "Where are you? Are you still in San Antonio?"

"No," she blubbered. "I couldn't stay. I've been driving for about two hours now. I'm in.... well, the middle of freakin' nowhere!," she screamed.

I was surprised to hear that she had been able to make it that far with the hysterical tears. And that, well, she had said "freakin'" and was now screaming. None of these things were characteristic of our sweet, mild-mannered Sara, which meant she was not doing well at all.

"Can you make it home by yourself? Does someone need to come and meet you?," I asked, concerned.

"I tried calling Melissa, but she's out."

Out on a Saturday night? That didn't sound like Melissa.

Sara continued on. "But I'm fine. I'll be there in a couple of hours. I just... I just... I need someone to talk to!"

And so we sat on the phone for the next ten minutes, not really discussing the details. I just let her cry, calculating the time it would take her to get back to Fort Worth, how late I would be here, and if we could track down Melissa and meet up.

"Sara," I said, in the midst of her tirade about speed traps in little towns along the freeway, "when you get into Fort Worth, come up to the hotel, okay?"

"Okay," she said, still crying. I hung up with her and began trying to reach Melissa. No answer at home, and her cell phone sent me to voicemail. Surely she wasn't screening her calls. I kept trying her cell, as I went back in to check on the party (which was really shaking the walls by this point) and as I tried to confirm with Cecilia (who was feeling pretty good after a few too many drinks) that the party would be wrapping up in another hour, so that the younger guests could go and hit the clubs.

Finally, after my tenth call, Melissa answered, obviously quite irritated with me.

"Yeswhatdoyouwant?!," she spat into the phone, her teeth clenched and her voice surprisingly low.

"Where are you?," I said.

"Why are you calling?"

I sighed. "Sara is on the freeway between here and San Antonio, crying hysterically, and neither one of us could reach you."

Melissa's voice lightened considerably. "Is everyone okay?"

"No," I said, "she and Jon broke up."

Melissa gasped. "NO!"

"Yeah," I said, holding my now aching head (thanks to the music and the drama of the evening). "I don't know the details yet, but she's really upset." Then, trying again, "Where are you?"

A pause. "Out."

"Well, duh," I said, "but where are –"

"So, where is she going? Your place, her place –"

"The hotel," I said. "Can you meet us at the hotel in about two hours?"

Another pause. "Yeah, I should be able to do that."

"Where are you?!"

"Gotta run, Em. See you then!"

Dial tone. Was the whole world going crazy around me?

Two hours later, I was helping with the tear down of the black and red lights the couple had paid for in the grand ballroom. It had taken our crew nearly an hour's worth of work after I escorted out the last heavily inebriated groomsman (and called a cab for him, which I pushed him into rather roughly after he managed to grab my butt, I might add), but minute by minute the grandeur of the grand ballroom came back. Stella's crew took out the last of their trays and dishes just as I was doing my final walk-through, and we both broke out in applause at the fine job done in record time.

Sara was waiting in the lobby when I got there. Her eyes looked hollow and empty, but otherwise, I couldn't tell that she had been so desperately upset two hours earlier. Either the drive had been therapeutic or she had managed to get into one of the restrooms on the lobby floor and reapply her makeup.

"Hey," I said, grabbing her up in a hug.

"Oh, wow," she said. "You smell like beer. And sweat."

"Do I?," I asked, sniffing my own little black dress, thinking of how I had all but hefted that groomsman onto my back to get him out on his shaky legs. His aroma was obviously still with me. (The sweat was probably mine, though. Well, most of it.)

I released her and held her hand. "Are you okay?"

She nodded, biting her lip. "Yes... no..." She shrugged, struggling not to let the tears in her eyes fall.

"Here's what we're going to do," I said, patting her hand. "I'm going to figure out where in the world Melissa is —" ten minutes late, not like her "—and we're going to go to that little coffee shop on Main. We'll even walk since it's such a nice night out. That'll help, right?"

Sara looked as doubtful as I felt. I had no experience with this type of thing, having never been in a relationship deeper than a few dates with guys who always felt more like brothers than potential marriage partners. Melissa was just as clueless as I was, but I thought one more supportive friend might make up for our inadequate ignorance at such a time as this. I dialed Melissa's number on my cell phone.

She answered on the first ring. "Hey," she said, out of breath, "sorry that I'm late, I'm two blocks over, hold on."

Dial tone. What was with her tonight?

Before I could even explain the situation to Sara, Melissa's Hummer sped into the driveway, she tossed her keys to a valet, and she was rushing into the hotel.

"Sorry, sorry, sorry," she said again, rushing up to us.

"Did you just use the valet service?," I asked, surprised because she NEVER used that, insisting that the free parking a few blocks over was a much better deal than pricey parking.

"Yes! What about it?," she said, turning her attention to Sara. "Hey, Emily told me what happened." She put her hand on Sara's shoulder. "That really sucks."

Classy... except, she actually looked VERY classy. Melissa, shock of all shocks, was in a dress. A little black dress, only slightly more formal than my own. And heels!

She caught my shocked expression and gave me a look.

"You look nice," I said, ignoring it. "Where were you?"

"Out."

Sara, despite her grief, noticed the outfit as well. "Where to?"

"Just out," she said, rolling her eyes. "Why are you two so nosy?"

"Because we can be. Where were you?," I asked again.

She sighed dramatically. "Okay, fine. I was on a," she began mumbling, "date."

"A what?," Sara asked.

"A date, okay!," she shouted, causing several of the people at the front desk to turn our way.

"Okay, we need to hustle out of here before I get kicked out of my own building," I said, ushering them to the offices, where I picked up my purse from my desk. Shutting off the lights, I asked, "Wasn't your date yesterday at lunch?"

"What date?!," Sara said, having missed this all while visiting Jon.

"You two are going to make me scream!," Melissa said. "Look. Tonight is NOT about me. It's about Sara. So, can we just drop ALL the conversation about me?"

I nodded. She was right. Sara nodded.

But I couldn't help myself. "You found TWO guys on that site?" Maybe I should check it out.

"NO, Emily. ONE guy."

I opened my mouth to note that two dates in two days with the same guy (and to such a formal location, judging by her attire) sounded intriguing, but when I caught the glare she was shooting my way, I snapped it shut again.

"Where to, ladies?," Melissa asked, relieved.

The three of us made our way to the coffee shop a few blocks away, mindlessly chatting about the nicer spring weather, about how we were so thankful that the cold temperatures were gone for good, and about how we were looking forward to the summer. Meaningless chatter, while all of us were clearly only thinking about Sara and Jon and wondering what could have happened.

When we got there, I sent Sara to get the table in the far corner, where our conversation could be private, and Melissa and I ordered drinks for the three of us. We brought them to the table, along with a stack of napkins (because you never have Kleenex when you need them), and looked at Sara cautiously.

She was silent for a few minutes, then sighed.

"Well, I'm not even sure where to start."

Melissa looked at me. "Well, I guess, you can start with what you talked about. What led up to the…"

She didn't want to say "break up," and Sara certainly didn't seem like she could hear it without another breakdown, so we all sat in silence.

Sara sighed again. "It started earlier than that. I got down there, and he just… seemed like he was somewhere else. Worse than before. I mean," she said, seeming to build up some strength in the telling, "he's been distant for a while, but this was worse. Far worse."

Melissa and I nodded, afraid to say anything to deter her from letting it all out.

"Anyway," she said, "I noticed he kept getting a lot of calls on his cell phone that he wasn't picking up." She rolled her eyes. "And I'm not stupid, you know. You probably think I'm naïve, but I know enough to know that it wasn't his mother on the line."

"Sara," I said, diplomatically. "You don't know that it was… another woman or anything." I nudged Melissa.

"Yeah!," she said, a bit too enthusiastically. "Could've been work or friends."

"No," she said, looking at both of us. "It was her." She exhaled a very shaky breath. "Katie."

"Who's Katie?," Melissa asked me, certain that we had missed a part of the story.

I had no idea and shrugged my shoulders in response. Sara put her hands to her head and moaned, "See, there's so much more to the story! I don't even know where to begin…"

"Who's Katie?," Melissa asked again, since this was as good a starting point as any.

Sara looked at her cup without any emotion on her face. "A woman he works with. A woman he's likely sleeping with."

Well, this was a bit shocking. Jon wasn't one for commitments, but he wasn't unfaithful. And as far as we knew, he had always shared the same convictions we shared, so the idea of him sleeping with anyone was surprising. I glanced over at Melissa, who seemed equally shocked.

"I've met her before," Sara said. "And it was obvious that Jon was attracted to her. And, you know, a few months ago, he started acting distant the more time he spent working with her. It's not hard to figure out. I had it figured out months ago, but I kept hoping I was wrong and that he was going to be faithful and that he was still committed to me."

She paused and didn't seem to want to say anything else.

Melissa encouraged her along with, "There might not be anything there. With her, I mean. Maybe she's just a really good friend."

"Oh, no," Sara said, taking a sip of her coffee. "He admitted it when I confronted him."

I frowned. "He did?"

Sara nodded. "Said it had been going on for a while, that our relationship was just too long distance to really work out, and that it would be best if I just moved on."

Melissa shook her head. "Hold it," she said. "The whole reason the relationship was long distance was because HE kept you from moving down there! You could have fixed that before all this other nonsense began if he hadn't been so hard-headed about it."

Sara ran her hand over her face. "You know, I only told everyone that it was Jon who wouldn't let me move away. The truth is... I just couldn't be in the same town with him all the time, while we weren't married."

"What?," I couldn't help but ask. I was so confused.

She looked down at her drink. "Y'all..." she began softly. "I was sleeping with him before he moved."

For a minute, we didn't say anything. I could only assume what Melissa was thinking, but it was likely along the same lines as my own thoughts. While I was surprised that our friend had been struggling in this way for who knows how long, I was more surprised that she hadn't been MORE forceful with Jon when it came to their relationship as a result. If they had been this close, surely she had expected, even more than in the most chaste circumstances, that marriage was ahead, given that they both believed like we all believed. We had all taken the True Love Waits pledge together, believing fully that we would honor that commitment. But we had gone to college, seen what a minority we were, and understood that people are people and that even Christ-loving people made mistakes. The Christian friends I had who had done so, though, had ended up marrying those guys. I couldn't imagine the desperation of making yourself that vulnerable to someone else with absolutely no guarantee of any kind of lifelong commitment.

I looked to Melissa. She seemed at a loss for words.

"I don't blame you guys for being shocked," Sara said. "I'm sure you think badly of me."

"No," Melissa said, taking Sara's hand across the table. "We're not thinking badly of you at all. I'm just more worried for you now, knowing... well, actually NOT knowing, since I have no idea how much more serious sex can make you feel about someone. Sara, I wish we would have known. Maybe it would've helped if you had... I don't know..." She looked at me helplessly.

"Yeah," I said, "if you had us to talk to, to help you work through what you were feeling about him. All this time, waiting for him to propose..."

She shook her head. "We were only together like that for a little while.

Just a few months before he moved. Then, he left, and I knew it had been wrong. I didn't go to live down there, knowing the temptation would be too strong, especially in a town where he was the only person I knew. I made sure that when I visited him that I had a hotel room, that we didn't spend a lot of time alone together, and that we were working hard on being pure. He understood – he agreed with me. I thought we were on the same page. I thought, you know after all that, that he would have the same sense of urgency about getting married that I did... and then..." Her eyes started tearing up again. "I just lost him."

Melissa and I glanced at one another, our expressions as dejected as Sara's as she cried.

"And you know what?," she managed to snuffle out through the napkin she was blowing her nose in. "I know it wasn't about the sex. Or lack of sex or whatever. It wasn't about that. He didn't break up with me because of that. I think it was just... just ending. Because it was supposed to end. We aren't the same people we were. We have different plans for our lives. And it's not like we were married or anything, so what sense did it make to stay together? What sense did it make for us to try to fit our lives together when we weren't really as committed as I thought or hoped we were?"

"But it FELT that serious, Sara," Melissa said. "And you're allowed to grieve like it was that serious. Six years is a long time."

"Yeah," she managed a bitter laugh. "That's what gets me most of all, what convinces me more than anything that this wasn't really love. I'm more upset about those six years that I lost than I am about having lost him!" She clasped a hand to her mouth, shocked that she had actually articulated this out loud. Surely she had been thinking about it on her long drive.

"Is that awful that I feel that way?," she whispered.

"I think you're allowed to feel whatever way you're feeling," Melissa said. "I'm in foreign territory with all this anyway, since you know I never date."

"Yeah," I added, "me, too, since my last relationship was... well, never."

Sara managed a smile at this.

"So, you're the expert on love and loss, honey," Melissa said. "You tell us if it's normal to mourn the time lost over the guy lost."

She looked at her drink for a while, thinking. "You know, I don't know if it's normal... but it's the truth." Then, after a pause, "I just wish I could reach back a few years and slap some sense into myself! It didn't matter even if we HAD ended up married! I should never have slept with him, or even planned a life around him, because it gave me some emotional claim to him that wasn't mine to have. And it just completely colored the way I looked at the whole relationship. I think I could've let him go a lot sooner without hurting so much if I just hadn't..."

We sat in silence for a moment, no one knowing what to say. Sara took another drink of coffee, put it down again, and said, "Do I sound like an afterschool special or what?"

I couldn't help it. I started to laugh.

Melissa looked at me in horror, but Sara grinned just a tiny bit.

"Really, Emily," Melissa began scolding, "I think this is a little too serious to be laughing about."

"Oh, you're right," I wheezed out. "I just think about all of those talks we heard at church all those years. And how they were right! And how... wow, them being right still doesn't change how difficult it is to do the right thing!"

"And you obviously know all about this since you've become an alcoholic," Melissa said.

"What?," Sara asked.

"Have you SMELLED her tonight?," she looked my direction with a pinched up face. "It's like you took a beer bath or something."

This made Sara laugh out loud, which made me start laughing all over again.

Melissa looked at us both, then finished her drink, grabbing her purse off the back of her chair, shaking her head at us. "Honestly, you two are crazy. Just crazy." She made a move to leave, but Sara, obviously feeling better when the attention was off of her, asked, "Hey, who's the guy?"

"What guy?," Melissa shot back.

"The guy you've had TWO dates with in TWO days!," I said.

"Is this really the best time for this?," Melissa asked, seriously.

Again, she was right. Right until Sara said, "Please, guys. This helps. Talking about something else. Please. Dish, dish!"

Melissa sighed. "I really don't want to," she said.

"Then, I'll dish first," I said, surprising myself. "Pastor Stephen cooked me dinner the other night. At his house."

Sara perked up considerably. "I forgot all about it! Tell us how it went!"

"Oh, it went fine, I guess," I said. "I have no idea what it means, of course, but he did mention taking me out. Eventually, I guess."

"He didn't tell you when?," Sara asked, her forehead crinkling in confusion.

"Nope," I said. "I can't figure the guy out. He's professional, he's flirty, he's shy, he's forward... it's like he's got multiple personalities, and I can't figure out if I really like any of them." This made me burst out laughing again. Seeing how this was doing Sara a world of good as a smile spread even wider on her face, I continued discussing my nutty love life. "And I have a date on Monday. With an accountant. We're going to have fried chicken."

"What?," Melissa asked. "You're just making up stuff now."

"Oh, if only! It's ALL Jessica's doing. And you two, of course, with the whole 'amp up your love life' thing." I noticed that Melissa was looking at the table thoughtfully. Maybe I could get her to talk. "I mean seriously, right, Melissa? That was the most worthless resolution ever! How could any good ever come from that?"

"Well," she said quietly, "I've met someone."

Sara gasped again. "You HAVE?!"

"Oh, don't act all shocked," Melissa said, once again her brash self. "You both know! And you've forced me into telling you about it, which I'm totally not happy about, so don't interrupt me and make me repeat myself."

Sara and I exchanged a happy glance, knowing that if Melissa was protesting this much it was because she REALLY wanted to tell us about her mystery man.

"His name is Beau."

"A beau named Beau, you say," I said.

She shot me a look. "Do you want me to tell you about him or not?"

Sara shook her head at me. "Let her talk!"

"Anyway," Melissa continued on, trying very hard not to smile, "he's 35, never married. Great Christian guy, very involved in his last church." She nodded very matter-of-factly. "And I didn't take his word for it. I called the church myself."

"You didn't!," I said.

"Oh, I did. Took me forever before I could finally get to a staff member. I think the church is bigger than Grace."

Sara shook her head. "You said last church... is he new in town?"

"Yeah," Melissa said. "Just moved here. He told me that, but I already knew, thanks to my background check from..." She chose her words carefully. "Connections I have at work. You know."

I didn't. But I couldn't believe her. She saw it on my face.

"Well, good grief, Emily," she said. "You can't be too safe these days!" Then, turning to Sara, "But to answer your question, yes, he's still relatively new to the DFW area."

I smiled. "He sounds great! And obviously safe, if you've had him run through the FBI files."

"I didn't say FBI," Melissa covered her tracks.

I waved her away. "Please. Where's he from?"

"Louisiana, originally. But he's been in Houston for the past ten years, working at..." she couldn't hide her smile, "NASA."

"Doing what?," Sara asked.

"Astrophysics engineering."

We were all silent for a minute. "You're dating a rocket scientist?"

She finally allowed herself a smug grin. "Well, he's not stupid, that's for sure."

And I could totally imagine it. Because the only man smart enough for Melissa would have to be nothing short of a rocket scientist.

"Why's he in Fort Worth if he works for NASA?," Sara asked.

"Oh, well, he's doing a five year contract with a company here," she said. "Something about jets and drafting new parts. I don't really understand that side of the engineering world as well as..." Her face became unreadable, thanks to the mysterious nature of her job. "Well, you know." Lowering her voice, she whispered, "missiles."

"When do we get to meet him?," I asked.

"Please! I've only been on two dates with the guy," Melissa said. "It's not like it's serious or anything."

Sara smiled knowingly at me, and I raised my eyebrows. We all sat for a moment, finishing our drinks. Melissa looked over at Sara and asked, "Are you going to be okay?"

Sara paused for a minute, thinking through the question, then said, "Yeah. Yeah, I think I'm going to be okay."

By the end of March, the weather was so pleasant that Josh and I spent our time together actually running instead of sitting around the coffee shop. I suspected that Josh had been running more than our normal routine because not only was he looking a whole lot trimmer, but he was running much faster than I was. So much so that I struggled to keep up at times, especially when we were talking, like we were that last Monday of the month.

"Let me get this straight," he said, barely breaking a sweat, while I could feel the perspiration starting to slide down my back. "You don't want to lead our youth choir?"

I had been telling him about the resolutions, about how this next month, I was supposed to volunteer at church. This sparked some interest on his part, and he was quick to offer me a position leading the youth choir at his church. I carefully explained that it was supposed to be at MY church and that I couldn't read music, sing, or carry a rhythm. He had said that none of that was necessary to lead the youth choir.

Scary. I had declined.

"It's not that they're not talented, I'm sure," I said diplomatically, "but it really does have to be at my church. And besides, I have the perfect way to get involved."

"What's that?," he asked.

"My dad is finally joining the rest of the century and converting all of his taped sermons to digital files. The IT guys are ready to get it done, but his office is in such a mess that he can hardly begin to find thirty-five years' worth of sermons," I explained.

"He has recordings of sermons that far back?"

"I wouldn't be surprised if we found sermons on 8-tracks," I said.

Josh laughed at this. "So, your new ministry is going to be getting the pastor's life in order?"

I nodded. Part of my reasoning behind this had been to keep an eye on my father, to see what my mother was seeing, and to draw my own conclusions. Every time I had seen him, he was fine – acting like himself, remembering everything, and being the man he always had been. I didn't doubt my mother, but I wanted to spend more time with him, to understand where he was at and what he was going through. "Maybe I'll start my own business. 'Getting Pastors' Lives in Order.' I'd be rich!"

"Yeah," Josh snorted. "If pastors actually made enough to pay you anything. I'd hire you, though."

"What's out of order in your life?," I asked.

He sighed. "Oh, for starters, I have a stack of chemistry homework to grade every night. Lesson plans, quizzes, tests, papers, and grades to report. It might be manageable if, you know, I didn't have a church to pastor as well."

"Yeah, that bi-vocational position is more like fulltime, isn't it?"

"And then some," he agreed, as we neared the bottom of the largest hill on our jog. "You look a little worn out," he smiled.

"Me?" I wiped the sweat off my forehead and noticed pit stains already forming under my arms. Lovely. "Yeah, maybe."

"Want to walk this hill, then run the other side?," he asked, clearly just for my benefit, as he looked like he could sprint his way up it.

"That'd be great," I said. And we began walking up at a leisurely pace.

"What other resolutions have you done so far?," he asked.

I thought about the past two months and all that had been accomplished... or not accomplished, as the case had been this month.

"Well, the first one was to get in shape. Which I'm doing a swell job of right now," I said, indicating how slowly I was walking.

He laughed out loud. "It's a start!"

"The second was to," and I blushed to even say this, "amp up my love life."

He laughed even louder. "What does that mean?"

"I think it was just my friend, Sara's, way of getting my friend, Melissa, and me to actually go out on dates."

He nodded, choosing his words carefully. "Oh, I thought it meant to, you know, get the guy you're dating to commit or something."

"Well, I'm not dating anyone."

This seemed to lighten his countenance, even more than normal. "Then you're not doing a very good job of completing the resolution, are you?," he said, smiling at me.

"No, not really," I smiled back. "I have a date tonight with someone."

His face registered... something that I couldn't process. But his expression quickly became playful again as he said, "And who is the lucky guy?"

"Some accountant," I said. "My sister fixed me up with a friend of a friend... or maybe he was a relative of her husband's co-worker? Oh, wow, I don't even know, but I'm meeting him tonight at Frank's Fried Chicken Bucket."

"Oh, I LOVE that place," Josh said, patting his disappearing belly.

I looked at him dubiously. "Fried chicken on a blind date, though? GREASY fried chicken?"

"Well I didn't say that it was a good place for a date. Just that it was good food." He looked over at me again, that mysterious something that had been on his face earlier crossing his expression again. "You know, if you were really that desperate to tell your friends that you had completed their resolution, you could have gone out with me."

"You would have done that for me?"

He shrugged. "Well, it would have been a huge sacrifice on my part, of course," he said, winking, "but sure. I would've taken you out on a date."

"Well, that would have been a whole lot more enjoyable than tonight is going to be," I said.

"Oh, well," he said, smiling. "Maybe next time." He stopped and peered over the top of the hill, then turned to me with a gleam in his eye. "Race you to the bottom!"

And we were off running.

RESOLUTIONS

My date was... interesting.

The accountant's name was Stuart, and heaven help me, from the moment I heard that, my mind couldn't get past the mental image of my darling little nephew Stuart in his footy pjs. Then, I tried to picture this somewhat nerdish, balding, clearly fortysomething accountant in – that's right – footy pjs. Something was obviously wrong with me, not him, as we sat down and tried to have a civilized dinner. From a bucket, of course.

Stuart didn't have much to say about himself personally but had everything in the world to say about the latest in his business. We "discussed" spread sheets, budgeting, line items, and the like for a good two hours. At some points, I found myself actually listening to what he had to say, but for the most part, I just ate my chicken and waited for the clock to run out. It's amazing how time spent with some people – like Josh – could be so effortless, so easy, and time spent with others – like Stuart – took all the power within me just to stay awake.

The comparison was not lost on me.

After we finished, Stuart informed me, in a very brisk and efficient manner, that he didn't see this relationship going anywhere and that it was probably best to go our separate ways. It was the first "define the relationship" talk I had ever had on a first date, and I'd be lying if I said it didn't sting just a little... until I remembered that I wouldn't have to endure another date with him. Then, it was all good.

He gave me his business card in case I ever had use for a good accountant (not likely), then said goodbye in his curt, precise way.

I spent the rest of March trying to convince Jessica that I didn't need her to "try again."

5 APRIL

My father met me in the lobby of the church on that first free afternoon I had set aside to help him.

He was the only pastor I knew who wore a suit to the office every day of the week. Most younger pastors had gone much more casual, even in the pulpit on Sunday mornings, but my father was part of a generation that couldn't bring themselves to wear even a pair of khakis in the church building. I had often wondered if this made him less approachable to younger church members, but they seemed to regard it as just part of his age. He didn't have a problem with them wearing whatever they grabbed out of their closets first, and so a "clothing war" within the church had been avoided, along with so many other generational conflicts that other churches experienced.

My dad had been the only son of a traveling evangelist, which meant, for the most part, that he had been raised by my grandmother. Not that my grandfather was a bad husband or father, but he had a hard time staying put in one place when the call to share Christ was so urgent. Dad had reaped some hard lessons from the sowing his own father did, the biggest of which was that you only got once chance to be a father to your children, so when he felt a similar urgent call to Gospel ministry in his youth, he did everything he could to live a life that would allow him to effectively minister and still raise a family. He paid his own way through school, working odd jobs and becoming an associate pastor under a wonderful senior pastor named Paul Witter, who quickly became his mentor and friend...

... and in time his father-in-law. My grandfather had four older daughters that were of marriageable age, but my father only had eyes for seventeen year old, Lydia, who soon proclaimed to her father in her typical dramatic fashion that she would just DIE if she couldn't marry her Tommy, even though she was just barely out of high school. And so she had, even though it must have been quite the scandal. She had sworn to us years later that it wasn't nearly as scandalous as we imagined because, in her words, "It just made sense, me marrying right into the ministry of the church, when I had been raised in the big middle of it."

Maybe this had a little something to do with how much my mother wanted to pair me up with Pastor Stephen.

Anyway, my parents had certainly made a go of life together and ministry together. There's a statistic out there that says only one out of ten young men in seminary will actually still find themselves in ministry ten years after graduation, and my dad had been the one in ten. He had been in an even smaller percentage with where he found himself now, planting himself in one church for the majority of his career and being able to adapt through three decades of change in that same church. Dynamic and charismatic, shrewd in his leadership and confident in his position, sensitive and devoted to the Lord, and best of all, a father who had always been there, no matter what.

He was and is, in a word, awesome. But I'm biased, you know.

Dad was chatting with one of the janitors when I came in, asking her about how her kids were enjoying the last few months of school, if they had plans for the summer, calling them each by name. I smiled to hear the conversation, knowing how much of his time he spent relating to all the people God put in his life, from the most influential deacon to this sweet woman who had been on staff only a couple of years.

"Emily," he said, as I approached them. He said his good-byes, took my arm in his, and started walking to the offices. "Did you have lunch yet?," he asked.

"Yeah, I stopped by the apartment," I said, stifling a yawn.

"Tough morning at work?"

It had been a wild morning at work. Evelyn, in atypical fashion, had accidentally booked two weddings for the same venue on the same day only an hour apart. She discovered her mistake (not calling it a "mistake," per se but an "oversight of the most unfortunate type") approximately fifteen minutes before the consult with the second bride who had been booked. Thus had ensued a brainstorming bonanza between the two of us about how we could make another venue in the building sound that much better. We had agreed to give her a discount – totally unheard of – on the alternate venue, hoping that would keep her business since she had quite a sizeable quote. It had, thankfully.

"Oh," I replied, smiling up at my father. "Just busy as usual."

He squeezed my arm. "We're so proud of how hard you work," he said. "All those years at that job, working such crazy hours and never complaining about it!"

Well, I did complain, but I was careful not to do it with them. Parents tend to want to fix problems that just can't be fixed, so when I was particularly exhausted or acutely frustrated with Evelyn, I made sure to tell my woes to someone else. It was a great job overall, and that's what I wanted my parents to know.

Dad took a breath as we approached the main offices. "Well, I can't figure out why you would want to help an old guy like me out with this stuff, but I sure am glad we'll have some time to spend together!"

I had told my parents that I had some extra time and wanted to help out, not explaining the resolutions. My mother knew that I had other reasons for wanting to spend time with my father, but he didn't and just seemed glad for the help and the company. When the girls and I had met to discuss what we were doing for the month ahead, Melissa had informed a somewhat shocked us that she was volunteering in the singles' hospitality ministry. "Totally not me," she said, "but this whole resolution business is about trying new things, right?" Sara had also picked something new to her, volunteering to fill the spot left over on the missions committee when one of the members left to, as you might imagine, pursue a fulltime missionary appointment in East Asia. Sara hadn't ever expressed any interest in any missions – domestic or foreign – so this was a stretch for her.

"Here we are," Dad announced, opening the door to his office and revealing… my mother, sitting at his desk, peering at his computer.

"Mom?"

She looked around the screen for a moment and smiled. "Hi! Did you already eat lunch?"

"Already asked her, dear," Dad said, leaning over and kissing the top of her head. "Looks like we're on our own."

"Mom, what are you doing here?," I asked.

She shrugged. "Oh, it gets lonely around the house, you know. So, I come up to the office with your father every now and then."

"Won't leave me alone for a second," Dad said with a wink.

Mom and I exchanged a discreet look. She had never been lonely at home in all of the years Dad had been in the pastorate. This was likely her way of explaining how terrified she was to leave him alone, expecting that to do so would guarantee a call from the police hours later when he was found, confused and disoriented.

She went right back to her computer. "Em, did you know that Shelly, you know, from your dorm? She's getting married!" Ahh, Facebook. I'm not sure I had spoken to Shelly at any point since graduation, but apparently, my mother was keeping in touch.

"That's nice," I said.

As I was trying to find a place to leave my purse, there was a knock on the door. "Come in," Dad said, as he continued bringing in boxes of tapes. Boxes and boxes and boxes...

The door opened to reveal Pastor Stephen, who seemed surprised to see me. "Emily," he smiled. "I didn't know there was going to be a family reunion today."

My mother laughed a little too loudly and came around the desk to put her arm around me. "You boys are going to be seeing Emily a lot more often! She's volunteered to help Thomas get all of his sermons organized so that the media team can put them all online." She grinned at him. "Isn't it going to be great to have her around?" I could've killed her.

Stephen nodded politely. "Thomas," he said, "the vision committee is meeting tonight, and we still need to go over the agenda."

Dad looked up, surprised. "Tonight?"

"Yes," Stephen said patiently. "It snuck up on me, too."

"Well," Dad took a breath, glancing at his watch. He looked to Mom, "Can we delay lunch for a little while longer?"

"No problem," she smiled at him. "In fact, Em and I can go and pick something up if it would make things easier. Stephen, would you like anything?"

Stephen shook his head. "No, I already ate." He smiled at me. "A sandwich."

Well, that *was* an entrée that required no cooking skills.

Dad put the lid on the box he was looking through. "Those tapes are circa 1981." He looked at Stephen. "Were you even alive in 1981, Stephen?"

He thought about that for a moment. "Yes, but I'm fairly certain that I wasn't preaching back then. Or even reading."

My father burst into laughter at this. "Oh, to be so young," he said. "Okay, girls, I'll see you in a bit." Then, to Stephen, "Let's go to the boardroom to look at that agenda."

Stephen waved to me with a smile, and with that, he and my father were out the door.

As soon as they were out of hearing distance (or maybe not, given how loud she is), my mother turned to me and practically shouted, "WELL! You and Pastor Stephen!"

"Oh, mother," I muttered.

"I saw the little smiles, the little jokes you two lovebirds have that no one else gets. SANDWICHES! Ooh, la, la!"

"Mom, it's nothing. It's —" But I stopped myself. I didn't need to explain anything, especially when there were more important things to discuss. "How has Dad been doing?"

All merriment left her face, and worry swept in. "Well," she said, "today, you'd never know that anything had ever happened. He did forget that meeting, but that's... slight. You know compared to other days."

"What's he been doing?"

She shook her head. "He just doesn't respond when I ask him questions some days. Seems confused." She looked concerned, then smiled at me. "But those are small things. And just on bad days. Most days are GOOD days. Like today."

I started to ask more questions, but my mother seemed to want the conversation to end. She smiled at me brightly and said, "Why don't we pick up some Chinese food?"

Despite my best efforts the rest of the afternoon and on several subsequent afternoons that I spent with her in the office, I couldn't get my mother to revisit the conversation without having her reassure me that the mishaps were "little things" and that, she finally said in a warning voice, "we would all do well to forget about it, Emily."

Thankfully, I had so much work that conversation was sparse after that. My father had a few decades worth of tapes, some CDs, and, heaven help me, reams and reams of typed out sermon manuscripts that some poor secretary in the early seventies had kept color coded and filed for him. Of course, she didn't leave instructions on exactly what the colors meant, so her filing system was lost on me. A few weeks into the month, I was elbow deep in it all when Pastor Stephen came by and asked (in my mother's hearing, no less) if I was free for dinner on Thursday night. When I told him I was and he left, I shot my mother a warning look across the boxes I was working on, and she didn't say a word. Just smiled and went on with her work.

I had very nearly forgotten all about the look until my phone rang that evening.

"Hello?," I asked, while folding my laundry.

"So, Mom tells me that you have a DATE with Pastor Stephen."

I put down the shirt I was folding. "Are you calling me all the way from Japan to talk about this?"

Matthew laughed out loud. "Yeah! You have a date! It's like the world's stopped turning or something!"

I sighed. "When did you talk to Mom?"

"An hour ago," he said. "She just went on and on and on about your love life. Which would normally be really annoying, but at least being fixated on you keeps her out of my business."

"Yeah," I said, "speaking of YOUR business, I'm going to be there in two more weeks, you know?"

"I know," he said. "I have your flight information right here." A pause. "You know, I don't really mind that you're dating Pastor Stephen."

Oy. "Well, thank you very much, but I can do without your interest in who I'm seeing or NOT seeing, as the case may be –"

"No, I'm being serious!," he insisted, even through his laughter. "Stephen seems like a stand-up kind of guy... I guess. I've only met him a couple of times."

This was true. Matthew had been gone so long that we often found ourselves talking about people new to the church – or a few years "new" to the church – with him, only to have him tell us that he had no idea who we were talking about. This must be how my mother felt about her Facebook friends when their names no longer sounded familiar to me.

Matthew went on. "Maybe it's not a bad thing that you're getting out and seeing people... you know, you're not getting any younger." He started laughing all over again.

"Okay, you've had your fun now, and I'm going to hang up."

"Okay, okay," he said hurriedly. "See you in a few weeks!"

"TWO weeks, Matthew –" But the line was already dead.

I went back to my folding, pausing when the phone rang again.

"Look here, you little turkey," I said as soon as I picked up the phone, "I'm glad that you're so amused by my –"

"Um, excuse me?"

Jessica. Well, great. She was probably calling to make fun of me, too. Mom must have been going crazy on the speed dial this afternoon.

"Oh, hi, Jess," I breathed out.

"Who's the turkey?," she said, over loud squeals of delight in the background.

"Matthew, of course." The boys' screams reached ear-splitting level. "What's all the excitement?"

"Well, I had a doctor's appointment today!"

I nodded. "Everything okay?"

"It most certainly WASN'T, when I got there."

My heart froze. The baby wasn't okay? Before I could even verbalize the fears, Jessica continued on.

"Nick was supposed to keep the boys, but he ran into some delays at work, called me, and said that I'd have to take them with me." She groaned. "Because an OB's office is just the PERFECT place for little boys to be running around, right?" She continued on, not waiting for a response. "Anyway, I took them in with me, sat them down, and then had to go and get a URINE sample done. Eish! Four little boys running around like monkeys while I'm trying to pee into a tiny cup, which is NOT easy, especially when you're as huge as I am, and —"

I decided this was a good time to switch ears. I moved the phone from my right ear to my left.

"—and then, the doctor came in to do the routine Doppler scan. And he couldn't find a heartbeat. Just about scared me to death. Told me that the baby was likely in a strange position and that he'd need to do a sonogram. So, he took us all back to the sonographer, and we got a good look at the baby's heart, everything was fine, and so on and so forth."

I mentally checked back through the story for any reason why my nephews would be screaming so loudly. "I don't understand," I said. "Why are the boys so excited? Are they wanting to pee in cups, too?"

"WELL," she said, ignoring me, a smile apparent in her voice, "I asked if they could tell the gender of the little one, since you know, we're getting close to that time. The sonographer said she couldn't on the regular view, but that if I'd be okay with a" she lowered her voice to a whisper "*different* angle, she could probably check out the goods." She raised her voice again, which was a good thing, since I was having trouble hearing her over the calamity. "Anyway, I herded the boys all up by my head, so there would be at least SOME propriety, the sonographer did her thing, and tada – the baby's butt was showcased larger than life on the screen."

"And?," I asked, certain that it was a girl based on the excitement in her voice.

"As soon as we got a good look, Sean yelled, 'What's THAT, Mommy?' And sure enough, the sonographer smiled at me, and I smiled at the boys and told them that they're getting a BROTHER!"

I waited. A boy?

"Well, didn't you hear me?," she said. "It's a BOY!"

"Yeah," I said, "I heard, it's just... I thought you were hoping for a girl?"

She blew out a breath. "Well, I kinda was, but the more I think about it now, I wouldn't even know what to do with a girl. And how crazy would it be for her anyway, growing up with FOUR older brothers?"

I tried to imagine this... and couldn't. As feminine as Jessica herself was, I had never been able to picture her with anything but boys. "I guess so. Well, congratulations! Have you told Mom and Dad yet?"

"I haven't even told Nick yet," she said. "That's what the boys are so excited about. They're working on a picture of themselves with the little brother to show him. Sean's actually... well, it's a little graphic."

"That's what you get for letting him be there to see his brother's backside."

She laughed. "I guess so. But, anyway, the REAL reason I called was to see if you were free this weekend. Nick has this friend that —"

"I don't want to be fixed up anymore," I began, politely.

"Well, I know that the accountant wasn't what you were looking for, and I TOTALLY wouldn't have set you up had I known what a bore he was, but of course, I didn't KNOW him myself, and I just had to go by what Nick's secretary's assistant's friend said about him, and—"

"It's fine, it's fine," I interrupted, trying to figure out a way to get off the phone. "No harm done. But I'm done with being fixed up."

A pause. "Are you sure? Because I think you'd really like Wyatt."

"Wyatt?"

"Yes!," she exclaimed. "Good friend of Nick's cousin's wife's sister's husband. He's in between jobs right now, but he's TOTALLY hot, and —"

"You haven't met him, have you?"

A pause. "Well, no. But I have it on good authority that —"

"Don't worry about it, Jess. I think I'm done with romance."

After an especially long Saturday evening, spent with a mother of the bride and a bride who could hardly keep from engaging in an all-out fist fight during the reception (I had, thankfully, seen worse between them in my office and made sure to keep them as far away from one another as possible), Sunday morning seemed to come earlier than normal. I managed to take a shower, throw on the first thing I grabbed from the closet, throw my hair up into a ponytail, and put on my glasses, not even bothering with my contacts. It took me three tries to get my car to start, but even then, I'm certain that it was the prayers, mingled with the violent beating I did on the dashboard, that finally kicked it back to life. I filed the experience under "Reason #793 why I'm still in a crappy apartment instead of a house." Honestly, I'd been driving the car for over ten years, so I couldn't really complain. I just didn't want to think what a monthly payment on an inevitable new car would do to diminish the efforts I was making towards home ownership.

Oh, well. At least I had a job.

I pulled up to the church ten minutes before the service was set to start and began speed walking towards the sanctuary. How long had it even been since I had made it early enough for Sunday school? Saying hellos and waving to those I hadn't yet met, I nearly ran into Pastor Stephen, who was heading away from the sanctuary.

"Hey," he said, a nervous smile on his face.

"Hey," I said back. I wondered if his look had anything to do with Thursday and the awkward conversations we had over dinner, during a stroll through the zoo, and finally, through the last handful of tedious minutes together over ice cream. Not that I hadn't had a great evening, but it took so much effort, finding things to discuss with him, worrying over how he took my responses, each of us choosing our words so carefully... unlike here in the hallway at church, where I felt totally free to blurt out, "Aren't you heading the wrong way?"

He raised his eyebrows. "Well, yes, actually. Your father thought he grabbed the Bible with his sermon notes and grabbed this by accident." He held up a book of illustrations with – for real – comic book characters on the neon colored cover.

"Hmm... doesn't look like a Bible," I said, mulling this over, wondering what my father had been thinking, wondering if he had been having any clarity at all...

"No, it doesn't," Stephen said, slowly, glancing at me. He seemed to be weighing his words carefully, but wasn't that normal for us? "I should probably go and get his Bible before the service starts."

"Sounds good," I told him and started walking away.

"Hey, Emily?," he called out after me.

"Yeah?"

"Are you free for dinner again on Thursday?"

I nodded and smiled. "Sure."

I had about half a minute of solitude to think about my father's mistake and what it meant about his general health. I had another half a minute of solitude to wonder how many dates with Pastor Stephen I would have to go on before I had some idea of how I felt. I only had a full minute to consider this all because I was all but assaulted by Melissa at the door to the sanctuary.

"HEY!," she yelled at me.

"Hey yourself," I said, noticing that she was more dressed up than usual... and that she wore a very peculiar smile. "Don't you look nice?"

"Why, thank you... is something wrong with your contacts?"

I touched my very outdated glasses and said, with all the self assurance in the world, "I'm considering switching back to glasses. Contacts are just too much trouble on my schedule."

"That's what I told her," said a severe-looking man who came up with a group from the singles' department and stopped by Melissa's side. Even though he was smiling, his tone was all seriousness, even as he took Melissa's hand in his. She beamed up at him, then looked away nonchalantly as he looked down at her.

Hello, Beau.

Sure enough, he held out his hand to me. "Beau Thibideaux," he said. Oh, well, that was an unfortunate name. "You must be Sara."

"Actually, Beau, this is Emily."

"Emily!," he exclaimed, his expression still unchanging. "I just spoke with your father this morning."

I thought about asking him if my father had said anything out of the ordinary, perhaps about why he intended to preach out of an illustration book that looked as though it belonged in a twelve year old's locker, but I stopped short. "Oh?"

Melissa smiled at me. "Beau's joining the church today."

"Really?"

"Yes," he said, nodding. "The singles' department here is VERY hospitable." A glance at Melissa, then a small smile that didn't make his expression any less severe.

Oh, my. Melissa swatted his arm, then looked at me. "Not really, of course. But Beau appreciates that I've made some order in the absolute chaos that was the singles' hospitality ministry." She lowered her voice. "Did you know that they didn't even have a rotation system going for greeters at the door, name tag sign-in, and coffee/donut pickup? It was like a CIRCUS."

"That it was," Beau said. "Melissa and I put together a policies and procedures manual, put a rotation system in place, and posted it all online. Now, everyone has a schedule, knows where to be, and knows what to do." He looked at her again, then glanced back at me, all business. "She's brilliant, you know."

And alarmingly OCD. But that fit Melissa, and it seemed as though Beau fit her as well.

"Well, welcome to Grace," I told him. "I hope you'll be happy here."

"I think I will," he said. "I've been looking for a church here for a while now, so I'm really glad to finally be at home somewhere."

The three of us made our way into the sanctuary, Melissa chatting with a group of girls from the singles' department while Beau asked me about the church. As I was telling him about how Grace had grown over the years, I noticed that Sara wasn't onstage with the rest of the praise and worship team.

"Where's Sara?," I asked Melissa, who had said good bye to one group of singles and had begun chatting with another group. Apparently, getting involved in a ministry at church had been a great thing for Melissa, who seemed to have a new camaraderie with people I thought were just mere acquaintances.

"She's with the missions committee this morning," she explained. "They're visiting an apartment church over on the east side of town, trying to figure out how we can get volunteers from Grace to do recreation ministry in the area."

I tried to picture sweet, kind Sara in the midst of a shady part of town. "Is it... safe?"

Melissa gave me a face. "Well, is that really important? Those kids living in those houses don't have much of anything, not even decent food half the time. I think the need far outweighs the risks."

I thought about this as we all filed into a pew, catching my mother's eye as she glanced around for Stephen. Surely, then, she knew about the mix-up as well and would be wondering what to do, questioning what was going on with my father, looking for me to help her find some answers...

... and so I sat by myself that morning, not at all prepared to hear the questions and help her with what I couldn't yet understand myself.

Monday found me back at work, again, earlier than normal. Josh and I had cut our run short that morning so that I could be in my office at 8am to greet the steady stream of brides and grooms that flowed in throughout the day. I had talked so much and listened to so much more that I was having trouble keeping all of them straight and found myself looking at my notes in between consultations so that I wouldn't call confuse the Chambers groom for the Morrison groom, the Anderson bride for the Duncan bride, and so on and so forth.

After a meeting with one bride who insisted that her four miniature dachshunds walk her down the aisle (in the Grand Ballroom where three other weddings were scheduled for that day, no less), I was about to pull all of my hair out and scream when Evelyn sauntered in, looking fresh and rested. Which she should have been, seeing as how she had taken a late morning to brunch with her "sweetie bear." Ugh.

"You have the Evans family coming in today," she said, clicking through the appointments in her planner, not even offering me a hello. "Then, an Alyssa Star." She looked up at me. "Nice name, don't you think? Alyssa Star. I met with them for an initial consult last week."

Oh, great, then this was the dream killing appointment where I got to put a dollar sign on all of her girlhood dreams. "Star... yes," I muttered still writing notes from my last nightmare of a consultation. *Four dogs. Pooper scooper on hand.* "Evelyn, is it against some sort of rule to have dogs in the building?"

"Excuse me?"

"Is there some rule about having dogs in the building?"

She gave me a look as though she smelled something distasteful. Which is probably what the guests of this wedding would be doing as well.

"Who in the world wants to bring DOGS into the building?"

"Miss..." I scanned the haphazard notes I had made... "Carson. She's marrying a Nealy."

"Oh, well," Evelyn said, her demeanor instantly changing. "If she's marrying a NEALY, she can bring a whole herd of cows into the building if she wants to."

Money. Always about money.

I gave Evelyn a curt smile and wrote, *FOUR pooper scoopers* in my notes.

The highlight of my afternoon was most definitely Stan Evans, who came in by himself.

"Dr. Evans," I greeted him with a handshake. "How are you today?"

"Oh, just peachy," he said, rolling back on his heels.

"Will Mrs. Evans and Lauren be joining us today?," I asked, showing him to the seat in front of my desk.

He sat down and steepled his fingers together, putting them to his lips. "Oh, no, I sent the ladies on for pedicures and some spa wrap thing or whatever. I don't ask the questions, Emily, just pay the bills!"

I smiled at this.

"You know," he said, leaning forward, "Lauren has been having just an awful time of it lately."

"An awful time? With the wedding plans?" My mind flittered over my conversations with her about scaling down the festivities. I was beholden to do what she wanted, if Stan had finally gotten a clue. Sure, Evelyn was going to kill me, but…

Stan sighed. "Yes!" He looked at me. "Did you know that she was stressed out about the wedding plans?"

I smiled through a shrug. "Well, I think that's fairly normal. Most of the brides who come through here have some stress about their weddings. That's completely understandable."

"I'm sure it is, but I'd like to do something about it. You know, reduce the stress."

And here it came. Stan was going to cancel events, scale down the guest list, and cut my commission in half.

Oh, yeah. Evelyn was going to kill me.

"Emily," he said, looking me in the eye, "I think we should bring it up a level."

Well, that was unexpected. "Pardon?"

"Step it up a little," he explained. "You know, more flowers, more people, more food, more everything. Make it a really big to-do."

I paused, choosing my words carefully. "How would making the wedding larger reduce Lauren's stress?"

He leaned back, crossing his legs at the ankles. "Well, I think part of the stress is that it's just not what she always dreamt it would be. I know I've been a little bit conservative when it comes to finances, but after seeing how that's stressing out my Laurie, I think we should just go all out. Give her what she really wants!"

Stan was the polar opposite of cheap, and his plans had been anything but conservative. I was mystified by how greatly he could have missed what his daughter really wanted. But what was I supposed to do?

"Think you can do that?," he asked with a smile.

I nodded my head. "I'll try my very best."

"Just peachy, Emily. Just peachy."

Whereas Stan Evans was the picture of illogical generosity and exuberant riches, Alyssa Star came in with a father who... well, wasn't.

I can't say that I blamed him, though. Alyssa was a very beautiful girl with a very beautiful diamond on her hand. She had come in with her father who, as she explained to me, would be paying for the wedding. This was the way most brides handled the finances – the parents covered the big expenses, never involving the groom's family. As we began discussing Alyssa's plans as had been laid out by Evelyn in elegant script, then later typed out by me, I learned that Alyssa was the oldest of three, that her mother had passed away years ago, and that her father was indeed paying for everything on an installation payment plan. I didn't think any of these things boded well for the reaction that was to come when I unveiled the big number, and sure enough, as soon as I showed the figure to them, it was like curtains were drawn on his face and panic set in on Alyssa's.

"This... it's just..." He looked at her. "Can't do it."

"But this is where Trevor's parents wanted the wedding, and I'm sure they'd be willing to help out with some of –"

"Don't you think I can pay for my own daughter's wedding? Haven't I done alright paying for your college, for your sisters' college, for everything?" He stopped, seeming to remember my presence. He turned to me. "I just don't think this is the place for our wedding."

"Well, Mr. Star," I began in my most diplomatic voice, "this is a working number. We can adjust some of the choices to lower the overall cost."

RESOLUTIONS

I began working with the numbers, showing them how cutting down on flowers, how switching to a deejay instead of a band, how downgrading from china at the reception – how all of these changes decreased the cost.

Alyssa looked to her father hopefully, but he shook his head. "Bottom line, ma'am," he said to me. "What's it going to cost to have the wedding here, no frills, nothing special?"

I wrote the price down, slid it over to him, and watched as he deflated in front of my eyes. "I can't do it," he said quietly to Alyssa. "I just can't."

Alyssa nodded, biting her lip to hold back the tears that had obviously started pooling in her eyes. "It's okay. Trevor's parents will get over it," she said, her voice breaking. She looked at me and managed a smile. "I was just so excited about having it here because of all the help. I don't… I don't know the first thing about planning a wedding, and my mom is gone, and…"

Her father held her hand as she took the Kleenex I offered and began dabbing her eyes.

I hated this part of the job. Absolutely hated it. I looked at our ridiculous prices, trying to find a loophole, a way to work things out, ANYTHING. There was nothing.

Alyssa let out a sad laugh. "It's okay. Emily, thank you for your time. I guess we'll just…" She looked at her father. "Have some sort of wedding. Somewhere."

They stood to leave, and against my better judgment, I told them, "Wait, please." I had a thought, a very wrong thought, and Evelyn was going to kill me.

I took one of my business cards and scribbled my cell phone number on the back. "Here," I said, putting it into Alyssa's hand. "Sir," I said to her father, "you wanted to know how much it would cost to have a wedding with nothing special. It will be impossible to have a wedding with nothing special because this BRIDE is special."

They looked at me like I was insane, so I kept right on going.

"Now, you can have an ECONOMICAL wedding, but don't ever say that your own daughter's wedding could be anything less than supremely and extravagantly SPECIAL. Because it's HER wedding, and SHE is special."

Alyssa looked down at the card. "We can't afford this place," she said.

"I know," I told her, "which is why I'm going to help you find a place – and vendors – that you can afford. A place just as great as this place." I paused. "If you want my help, of course." Oh, yeah. Evelyn was going to kill me.

Alyssa and her father exchanged hopeful looks. He cleared his throat. "And what will you charge for your services?," he asked.

Well, I hadn't thought that far ahead. Before I could figure out what was fair, calculate what my time was worth, or even dream up a reasonable number, I blurted out, "I really like you two. I'll do it for free."

And with that, I had just secured my first ever independent client. I made a mental note to come up with my own net worth and fix a price on my services before offering them up again. Then, I made a mental note to NEVER offer my services up again, lest I lose my sole source of income at the hotel.

Was it really robbing Evelyn if I took a client who wasn't going to use her venue? I didn't know, but I still felt that somehow, in some way, I had betrayed her.

She was SO going to fire me if she ever found out!

Josh had betrayed me. Or so I told him when I caught him running by himself along our trail on that Thursday afternoon, which was NOT one of our days to run. I had to loop back once before I was certain that it was him, then glanced at my clock to see how much time I had before I needed to meet up with Pastor Stephen. Deciding that even a little bit of time was enough, I pulled into the lot beside our coffee shop, parked, and began speedwalking (because I was in heels) as fast as I could to catch him as he rounded one of the curves on the trail.

He saw me a few moments later, gave me a surprised look, and then turned around to run the other direction.

"Josh!," I yelled. "What are you doing?"

His shoulders slumped as he turned and gave me a guilty look. "Trying to run away from you," he said, as he quickly closed the space between us. Then, looking at me, in my heels, of course, "Geez, you're tall!"

"You've mentioned that before," I said. "What you didn't mention is that you're now... what, running EVERY day?"

He gave me a guilty little smile. "I didn't mention it because I didn't want you feeling like you had to come out and run on my crazy schedule, and... well, I'm training."

I could feel my eyebrows furrowing. "Training for what?"

He took a breath. "Well, I'm going to TRY, heavy emphasis on the word try, to run a marathon this fall." He cringed. "Don't hate me for going over to the dark side!"

I smiled. "I'm actually quite impressed."

"Really?"

"Yeah!," I said enthusiastically, then with lowered voice, "Of course, I feel supremely betrayed that you've been doing all this running by yourself, leaving me to feel like I'm completely and hopelessly out of shape when we run together."

"Well, you're in great shape. Better shape than I would be if I was only running three times a week like you. Slacker."

I moved to swat his arm, just as he dodged my fist. "Hey!," he protested. "I would invite you to finish the mile with me, but you're obviously not dressed for it."

I looked down at my little black dress, worn for a particularly important meeting with a "more prominent client," as Evelyn called them. I shook my head. "Yeah, I probably look like an idiot, standing out here on the jogging trail wearing this."

"No," he said sincerely, "you look amazing."

This gave me pause. Then, the fact that it gave me pause gave me even MORE pause. Why did this small compliment seem like such a HUGE compliment, simply because of who it came from?

Before I could even formulate a response, Josh looked at his watch. "You know, I think it's time to have some dinner. Do you... do you want to come with me? I mean, I know I'm all sweaty and gross, but I'd love the company." He looked at me, waiting for my response. "Or if, you know, I'm THAT gross, I could go and get cleaned up and we could meet later tonight...???"

I considered this, thought about spending the evening with Josh, and almost said yes... before I remembered that I already had plans.

"Can't," I said sadly. "I've got... something I've got to be at."

"Another wedding thing?," he asked, smiling. We had spent so many hours together talking about the all-hours meetings I had with brides, with grooms, with florists, with caterers, with anyone and everyone even remotely connected to the bridal world. He knew what my days looked like. Or as much as he possibly could without living the trauma of wedding coordinating himself.

"Yeah, something like that," I said. "But I'll take a rain check. And who knows? Maybe I'll start running every day, too!"

He rolled his eyes good naturedly. "Well, of course, you will. How else will you run the marathon with me and leave me looking pathetic trailing your dust?"

"Exactly," I said with a wink, turning to leave... wondering and knowing at the same time that his eyes followed me as I went.

"So, what's the deal already?" Melissa had positioned herself in front of the television, where neither Sara nor I could see around her. We were having our new weekly date, watching The Bachelor over pizza and making bets on who would be sent home, who would get a rose, and who would be the unfortunate girl at the end of the season to get a ring and have to watch her new fiancé kiss all the other women when the show finally aired. The "winner," as they ironically called her.

Sara had been coping with the breakup. There were bad days and good days, many nights spent on the phone with three way calling, and many more lunches and dinners met up around town. We had been spending Monday evenings together for the past month, and slowly but surely, Sara seemed to get better and better.

She didn't seem to appreciate the television being blocked, though, as it hindered us from hearing how the blonde with ample assets really felt as though she and the Bachelor had a real connection as they went on this journey together. (The connection seemed to be completely in their tongues, as they spent half of all their time together making out for all of the cameras.)

"What are you talking about?," Sara asked.

Melissa waved a hand my direction. "I'm talking about Emily!" She turned around and flipped the television off.

"Hey!," Sara and I both protested at the same moment.

"Hey, nothing," Melissa said. "We're getting to the bottom of this."

I sighed. "The bottom of what?"

Melissa sat down, studied me for a moment, and then leaned forward on her knees, counselor and interrogator all rolled up into one. "You and Pastor Stephen."

Oh. This. I had told them during one of our lunches that I had gone on yet another date with him. It was becoming a normal thing, and I had given them my bland summary of the most recent one. He picked me up, we went out to dinner to see the newest romantic comedy, and then, he dropped me off at my front door, sans kiss, hug, or even handshake. It was a bland summary because, frankly, it was a bland date.

"Well, what do you want to know?," I asked, as Sara also leaned forward on her knees, the same glint in her eyes. Oh, great.

Melissa looked at me like I was holding something back on her. "How about we start with how you feel."

I rolled my eyes. "Well, right now I feel like my friends are ganging up on me, and –"

"Do you like him?," Sara asked.

I gave her a look, then sighed. "Well... I guess." I shrugged. "I don't know." And this? Was the truth. And the problem, all at the same time. I respected Stephen, found him attractive, and saw that he would logically be a good match for me. On a totally superficial level, I was proud to be seen with him and found myself imagining what life would be like if we ended up together, making our way to a life of high profile ministry.

But still. There was something very sterile about our conversations, our interactions... our very existence in close proximity to one another. Oh, the awkwardness had improved over time, as had the unexplainable tension that had always existed between us, but at the same time, the thrill of being near him had dulled for me, calmed down, and all but disappeared.

Wasn't love supposed to be like that, though? Respect, admiration, commonality, over time providing more substance than initial feelings and mush and gush?

Oh, who knew.

"Does he give you butterflies? When he looks at you, does he make you feel like there's no one else in the world but him?" Sara rested her head on her hands.

It was Melissa's turn to look at her. "Um... barf."

I leaned back on the couch and sipped my Diet Coke, confident that the conversation was veering away from me and my situation, as Sara's face reddened. This was one of the healthiest changes we had seen in her since the break-up – she felt free to be annoyed by people and wasn't afraid to tell them about it. Much healthier than the passive attitude she had about everything back when Jon was in the picture.

Sara looked offended. "What? I don't think it's wrong to want those kind of feelings." She shrugged. "I don't know that Jon and I would have stayed together so long without those feelings. And I'm not saying that things were perfect, obviously, but... I think I'll want those feelings the next time around. What's wrong with feeling that way?"

Melissa shook her head. "Well, nothing, but I don't think that's REAL love."

"Oh," Sara shot back, "what's REAL love, then, Melissa, since you seem to be the expert?"

"It's..." Melissa paused, choosing her words carefully. "It's being with someone else, and almost forgetting that they're there, because being with them is so natural and so right and so... so much like home."

No one said anything for a moment. Finally Sara said, "Then, I'm in love with Ginger, my dachshund. What kind of description is that?"

Melissa put her hands on her hips. "Well, that's the way I feel about Beau. Like...," she moved her hands around, searching for the right words, "... like, he's home. Just home. Like anywhere in the world that I find myself, if Beau's there, I'm home."

Sara and I watched her for a moment, the deep, wordless feelings she had developed for him in such a short time evident on her face. She looked up, seeing us stare at her and scolded, "Well, this isn't about me!"

"Well, it SHOULD be, since you're talking about Beau like you want to MARRY him or someth—"

I interrupted Sara, sensing that the argument would just explode further if I didn't cut in. "But we're talking about me and Pastor Stephen."

Sara glanced at me. "Do you still call him Pastor Stephen?"

I nodded. "Not to him. But in my head... yes. And I know that's weird."

Melissa nodded her agreement. "Sure is."

"It's just the only thing I can think of when I see him now," I said. "I mean, there are butterflies... there WERE butterflies, back before all of this began, and now? I don't know. There's just nothing beyond how he looks and how perfect everyone thinks we would be together. Is that horrible?"

Sara shook her head. "I don't guess so... wow, though. That's so disappointing."

"How so?," Melissa asked.

"I thought they were going to end up together," she said, sadly.

"Well, maybe," I told her. "I don't know. I haven't figured it all out." I paused. "I actually feel bad for him. I think it's harder for him to find the right person, being in the position he's in, and..." The thought that had crossed my mind before crossed it again, and I told them, very bluntly, "Well, maybe we both on some level thought that we were worth a try since everyone else seemed to think it was such a great idea. And maybe we are, and we should, and..." I sighed. "Maybe I need therapy."

Sara sighed right back. "No more than the rest of us." She glanced at Melissa. "Well, maybe not as much as Melissa. So at home that you FORGET HE'S THERE?!"

Melissa scowled at her. "Just forget I said anything, then."

I switched the television back on, and we all directed our attention back to the screen and the most dramatic rose ceremony ever.... well, the most dramatic this episode.

My mind was still working, though, thinking over the dates with Pastor Stephen, the anticlimactic, platonic vibe that had been steadily replacing the gushy tweeny feelings, the way Melissa described love as being home with someone, home BEING someone...

And I was only mildly surprised to find that my thoughts drifted easily and quite naturally to Josh Morales.

The last weekend in April was INSANE. At one point during the seven weddings and twelve (twelve!) receptions that we were working, I mentioned Japan, and Evelyn, panic evident in her ceaselessly calm voice practically screamed, "What?! You're going on vacation?!"

Once the festivities calmed down, I patiently explained, back in our offices, that I had cleared my trip with her months ago.

"See?," I pointed to the marked off week in my planner. "You said this would be the best time of the year, given that the real rush doesn't start until mid-May."

She peered at my planner. "Hmm..." Then, consulting her own planner, which seemed to carry more authority than mine, "Oh, well, there it is. A whole week." She shook her head, then sighed. "Well, what's done is done, my dear. I expect you to close out everything tonight and handle the three events tomorrow, before you leave. Oh, and set up on Monday for Tuesday's brunch." She smiled at me tightly. And a few minutes later, she was gone, with two hours of work ahead of me.

I had told Dad that I would be able to work in his office that Monday, but with the added responsibility flung so sweetly onto me, I was going to have to cancel. I dialed their home number on my phone and slid my heels off while it rang.

Dad picked up on the third ring. "Hello?"

"Hey, Dad."

"Hi, Jess."

I smiled. "Dad, it's Emily. You hear that?" Silence. "If this was Jess, you'd be hearing a whole horde of little boys screaming."

He laughed loudly. "Hey, Emily! Are you at home?"

"Nope," I said. "Still at the hotel."

"Long night?"

"Yeah, and it just got a little longer." I rubbed my eyes tiredly. "I'm not going to be able to make it on Monday. Evelyn has me working before my flight."

"Flight?"

"Yeah," I said. "Remember? I'm flying out to visit Matthew on Monday."

A long pause. "Who's Matthew?"

"Ha, ha, Dad," I said. "Very funny."

Another pause. "I'm serious, Emily. I don't like the idea of you flying out to meet some young man. Especially one I don't know!"

A cold feeling of dread began to wash over me. All month, I had been watching him. And all month, he had been clear and focused, seemingly as strong and present as he had ever been, so much so that I had, like my mother, pushed aside any thoughts that something was wrong.

"Dad," I said weakly. "Do you not remember Matthew?"

"I said I didn't," he scoffed at me, "and I don't." Then a hint of warning in his voice. "This isn't a good idea, Emily."

I couldn't keep my voice from trembling as I said, "Dad, can you get Mom on the phone? I need to tell her something."

He was better the next day, the same man I had always known, preaching from the pulpit during the early service. He caught me on my way out, kissed my head, and told me, "We'll pick you up for the airport at noon tomorrow," with no apparent idea of what had happened the day before. My mother, who stood by his side, gave me a brave smile and desperately squeezed my hand.

6 MAY

Twenty-four hazy hours, a stop in Taiwan, and airline seafood and noodles for breakfast (ugh) later, my plane landed in Okinawa.

I had a lot to think about as we flew. My father and his condition ranked at the top of the list, the conclusions my mother and I had drawn after the troubling phone conversation I had with him all but voided by how well he seemed to be doing in the days following. "Good days and bad days," my mother had said, sharing with me what she had found out in her online research on memory loss in older age and the different illnesses they might indicate. I had urged her to take him to the doctor, but as he continued to have good days, she put it off, assuring me that it couldn't be as bad as all of that and that we would simply "wait it out."

"Wait it out" was a fitting theme for so many areas of my life, it seemed. After talking with Melissa and Sara about Pastor Stephen, I was pretty sure that it was time to let that relationship (or whatever it was) taper out. Of course, we hadn't had any time to talk since our last date. Or rather, he hadn't sought me out or made any move to spend any more time with me which made it seem... well, like it was going to end on its own anyway. I was surprised to find that this left me feeling relieved.

Relieved and just a tiny bit anxious as I thought about how different that relationship was when compared to my friendship with Josh. I hadn't had a chance to run with him again before leaving, thanks to Evelyn and all the work she heaped on me at the last moment, but he had called and asked if he could take me to breakfast the morning of my flight. Explaining that they likely wouldn't have decent bacon in Japan, he insisted that I eat more than my fair share so as not to feel deprived while gone. We had talked and laughed for such a long time together that we were still at the restaurant as the lunch crowd moved in, putting me at the airport later than I had planned.

Of course, I was thankful about that now, given that my late arrival had spared me at least a few minutes of sitting on a crowded airplane.

To my relief, the announcement that we would be landing soon came on over the intercom as I was once again calculating how many hours I had spent sitting in one position. I looked out the window at a whole lot of nothing but water as the plane began its descent, and I kept watching until we had landed and were clear to move again. I moved my creaking old body out of the last seat, grabbed my carry-on, and headed for the terminal. After going through passport control, baggage, and exiting into the arrival lounge, I finally looked up to take in the scenery of my first overseas destination. Exotic land, Japan, and all I could see around me were US Marines.

Not in uniform. Just so obviously military with their haircuts, thin frames, and curt, clipped manner. Marines everywhere! Was I just really jet lagged, or did all these men look exactly the same?

"Emily!"

I turned at the sound of my name. Ah. There was one that looked like me. Matthew made his way over from the edge of the crowd, looking very much like a younger version of my father, a male version of me --

"Get out of the way, Emily. Standing there like you don't know what planet you're on, geez."

With my mother's winning personality, of course.

"Good to see you, too," I reached up to hug him. "So, this is Japan?" I surveyed the area around me, stretching and trying to loosen up all the muscles that had painfully frozen on the long flight.

"No," he said, as he began briskly walking me outside, taking my bags and carrying them himself, "this is the airport. Out here is Japan."

As soon as we exited the building, a great wave of heat blew in on me from every angle and direction. Oh, wow. "I thought it snowed in parts of Japan," I told him. "And that it was cool all year long."

He gave me a dubious look, as though I should have known better. "Not here. We don't even get cold in the winter time – too far south. It's more like Houston than the rest of Japan. And it's MAY, Emily."

"But aren't the seasons switched? Like, summer in winter, winter in summer?"

He stared at me for a minute. "Are you being serious?"

"It's science. Yes."

"This is the northern hemisphere. You LIVE in the northern hemisphere. You're not switching seasons!"

Did I think changing time zones meant changing hemispheres, thereby changing seasons? I'm not stupid, but...

"Wow." Matthew shook his head at me.

I gave him an icy glare. "You know, I've been really busy at work."

"And that's made your brain mushy?," he asked. "Come on, the car's over here."

We got to his car (which was like a clown car, much to my amusement and Matthew's chagrin), got in, and thus began the most horrifying ride of my life. Ever. I had prepared myself for driving on the other side of the street. What I had not prepared myself for were hordes of motorcycles jumping in and out of lanes effortlessly, and Matthew's car almost clipping each one of them, while huge trucks vibrated past us, so close that I could roll down the window and touch them with my hand, as if I even dared. Every time I winced or couldn't stop myself from shouting, Matthew laughed even harder, as he told me all about the island, about his church, and his friend, Shoko.

Yes, Shoko. He just kept talking about "Shoko this" and "Shoko that," telling me about all of these crazy adventures and thrilling times and hours and hours spent with Shoko. That place over there? Oh, Shoko and I went there a few months ago. Terrible food. Great atmosphere. Oh, and that festival advertised on that sign? Yeah, Shoko and I went. Great food. Kinda crowded, though. Oh, and that random guy riding a bike in that dark alley over the hill there? Reminds me of something that Shoko once told me about Okinawa. On and on and on. I felt like I knew Shoko personally after our long drive to the on base hotel where Matthew had booked a room for me.

"Hey," I told him before he left me for the night. "When am I going to meet the girlfriend?"

He looked at me, feigning confusion. "What?"

"The girlfriend, you twit," I said. "The one I could hear whispering with you on the phone. So far, I've not heard a word about her. Only some Japanese guy named Shoko." A pause. "You do still have a girlfriend, right?"

He just shook his head at me and gave a terse, "Good night, Emily."

Which is why I was completely shocked the next morning at Matthew's church when I met Shoko. Matthew entered Central Baptist Church, an older red brick building along the busiest highway on island, shaking hands with everyone in sight and introducing me as we went. He practically ran up the stairs to the third floor fellowship hall, telling me that Shoko would be up here, getting ready to teach the youth Sunday school class. As soon as we got there, Matthew beaming and me panting from the rather steep stairs, he breathed a soft, "Shoko," with stars in his eyes, and I followed his gaze to a young and beautiful Japanese… woman. Who, as she gazed on my goofy kid brother, also had stars in her eyes.

"Matthew," she whispered, glancing over nervously as she walked towards me, then pausing, putting her feet together, placing her delicate hands in her lap, and bowing slightly. "Emily," she said, "it is my pleasure to meet you."

Having no idea how to top that introduction, I extended my hand, which she took, and said, "Nice to meet you, Shoko. My brother has told me…" I looked at him, accusingly, "… well, a lot about you." But not everything, obviously.

She smiled and snuck a glance over at him, where he remained, glued to the floor, a sappy look on his face. Oh, brother.

Shoko studied my bulky sweater and wool pants for a moment. "You have beautiful clothes," she remarked kindly. How nice of her, leaving out the "it's a hundred degrees outside, you idiot."

"Thank you. Although it's a little hot." I lowered my voice, confiding in her since she seemed so sweet. "I had no idea it was going to be so warm here!"

She lowered her voice, too. "Matthew did not tell you?"

I shook my head. "He wears the same thing to work every day, so I guess he doesn't think about these things, huh?"

She smiled and laughed a little. Then, an idea struck her. "I would like to take you shopping. For clothes that are not so warm!"

I looked to Matthew, who had shaken himself out of his stupor long enough to nod at me. Well, I needed more appropriate clothes, and

Shoko would likely be a better hostess than my workaholic brother. "I would love that," I answered her.

"Wonderful!," she exclaimed, holding my hands.

Matthew stepped over to us as teenagers began to enter the fellowship hall, and with a brush of his hand on Shoko's slim shoulders, softly said, "We will see you at worship."

She smiled at him, he smiled at her, and I felt so completely in the way. This happens every once in a while in my business, when a bride and groom come into the office, so consumed in one another that I feel merely like I'm taking notes on their great love conversation with one another, scarcely daring to breathe or move so as not to interrupt the delight and intensity they find together. I much prefer these couples to the ones who sit in my office yelling at one another.

But that's beside the point.

I cleared my throat softly, needing to break the moment so that I could find a bathroom. Shoko smiled at me once more, bowed again, and turned to her youth group. Matthew patted me on the back, as I whispered, "Shoko, huh?" to his beet red face as we exited into the hallway. "Hmm..."

"Don't start with me," he warned.

"I'm not starting anything," I protested. "I'm only wondering why you never even mentioned her before. Mentioned ANYTHING about her. Mom doesn't even know you're dating anyone, much less... well, a civilian." But "civilian" didn't really make my point, so I added, "A Japanese civilian."

He made a face. "Yes, and you see, this is the reason why I didn't say anything before. Mom and Dad are pretty progressive and all, but there are a lot of wrong conclusions they could have made since they've never been here. I mean, you concluded that it was going to be snowing in

May, so –"

"Ha, ha," I muttered.

"Anyway," he interrupted me. "I'll tell them when I tell them. Like when I bring her to the States for the first time, so that they can meet her in person instead of imagining all kinds of crazy things an ocean away about how she wears kimonos and spends all of her time doing tea ceremonies and how her father is a samurai warrior."

I missed everything else he said, still caught up on the "bring her to the States" part. I gave him a sidelong glance, keeping my voice low. "Is it that serious?"

"We'll talk later," he said, leaving me at the restroom.

After the worship service, the entire congregation gathered in the fellowship hall for a potluck. Yes, a potluck. In Japan. How very Baptistic of them! At the insistence of a large group of older Japanese women, I loaded up a plate full of food that I couldn't easily identify, all situated just right over a bed of steamed rice. When I took a set of chopsticks to use instead of a fork, they all found this very amusing and praised my elementary efforts again and again as I ate and they all chatted in Japanese around me.

Matthew and Shoko sat on my other side, almost whispering to one another, smiling and laughing the entire time. I kept trying to catch what they were saying, but between the laughing on my right, the children running around the hall, and the loud crunchiness of one of the unidentified meats (um, chicken?), I couldn't pick up on much.

Afterwards, I shook everyone's hands again and headed out to Matthew's car with him. Before I could even start in, the jet lag hit me full force, and I nodded off while we were still driving.

We resumed our conversation the next day.

"You're what!?!" Surely I didn't hear that right.

"I'm going to ask Shoko to marry me." Well, I DID hear that right. I studied my brother as he squirmed in his seat. He had picked me up for his lunch break, along with some fabulous pork and rice from a place called Hoka Hoka Tei, which we were eating at a park in the neighborhood.

He looked at me sheepishly. "Mom's going to be upset, isn't she?"

It's not that our mother would have a problem with Matthew getting married. It's not that our mother would have a problem with Matthew moving halfway across the world and marrying a girl. (Well, not too much of a problem, at least.) It's not that our mother would have a problem with anything that her precious, perfect, only son and baby Matthew would do. It's just that she would have a problem with not knowing about it until after the fact. She's a good woman, but she does have her vices. And over-protecting and being over-involved in her son's life? Is the greatest. Mom's kryptonite, if you will.

"Oh, Mom's going to be upset. In fact, I think she'll have a cow."

Matthew shook his head at me. "You're being too dramatic."

"No," I stated, firmly. "She will lie down and literally give birth to livestock if you propose to a woman she has never met. Or even heard of! Think what you will about our wrong perceptions of things, but it is just plain BIZARRE that you never mentioned Shoko to us before now."

He grimaced. "You think?"

"Yes! You HAVE to let them know about her. Sooner than later. Especially if you're going to propose." I paused for a moment. "I can't even believe I have to explain that to you!"

Matthew took a deep breath. "My life here is a lot different than it was back in the States, you know."

I studied his face for a moment. "Different, how?"

He sighed and looked out over the playground. He had aged since I saw him last. He had enlisted at eighteen and had been almost immediately deployed to a tour in Iraq. He was thrilled; my mother was not. It was a rough nine months – not for Matthew, who thrived on the hard work and stressful circumstances – but for those of us who had to live with my mother in the meantime. Since then, Matthew had been stationed in the States for a short while, had done another tour in Iraq (this one he volunteered for – oh, yeah, Mom was steamed), and had ended up here in Japan for a three year stay. This August would mark his two year anniversary here, which I assume meant that he had been seeing Shoko for as long. The last time I had seen him was when he packed up for Okinawa, still silly in his own right, but so consumed with work and all of his physical training that his face was becoming hard, prematurely, with the age and stress of it all.

Today, though, there was a new softness to his features. He ran his hand through his barely-there hair and shrugged. "I've been really focused for the past few years on work."

I had seen it in him. I nodded, waiting for him to go on.

"I've really enjoyed being in hard places. Just being forced to do nothing but work. Then, they sent me here, to Okinawa, where it wasn't the same. I mean, there's work... but it's an office job, without the excitement or thrills, you know? Unless, of course, they deploy me again. Which isn't likely, given the last two tours."

It wasn't. Which was the ONLY reason my mother was glad that Matthew was going to Japan. At least it wasn't The Sandbox.

He continued. "I became discontent. Just with where I was in life, what I was doing. Kinda felt like I had no purpose doing this new work, and it made me wonder... where was my worth, really? Because if it's in my job, then it's likely in the wrong place. I thought about Dad and how he's always told us that Grace is where he's supposed to be right now, but if God called him out of ministry tomorrow, he would go. That his worth isn't tied to his job but to Christ." I had heard Dad say this a million times. I felt a strange hollow in my stomach, holding in secrets about what was happening with him now. But I brushed them away when I saw a new light in Matthew's eyes.

"And I knew, just had to confess it to myself, that I had been leaving God out of my career, out of my life, out of all of it. Not maliciously, or anything. He just wasn't a priority. Which probably meant that He had never really been Lord at all."

He smiled at me as he continued his story, maturity showing itself in his calm and careful explanation. "So, I re-committed myself to following God with ALL of me. To live for Him instead of for my work. I found Central and joined the first Sunday I visited. The pastor asked me what kind of ministry I could see myself serving in. I asked him what kind of needs they had, not having any idea what I could do. He introduced me to Ms. Kinjo, who was in charge of ESL."

I stopped him with, "But you don't know Japanese."

He looked at me like I was a moron. Ah, there was my old Matthew. "Yes, I know that, Emily. Apparently, it didn't matter. They grouped the students into different classes, depending on their English fluency. The students who didn't know English at all went with teachers who are fluent Japanese speakers. And those who knew a little English went with a teacher who knew some Japanese. And so on and so forth, until they formed the 'advanced' class, with students who knew English fluently but wanted practice with native English speakers who didn't know Japanese at all."

"Ah," I said. "Which you were qualified to teach."

He smiled brilliantly, "Exactly! Who knew that speaking your own language would be a skill, huh?"

I laughed at him. "And then...?"

"Well," he said, "our first class was right after work one night. I barely had time to shower and get dressed in civilian clothes before running up here. Once I arrived, all the students were lingering around the lobby. And I was totally out of place. There were no other Americans teaching! And all of the students? Women. ALL middle-aged and older Japanese women." He shook his head at the memory. "Ms. Kinjo had given all of the students their classroom numbers, and the group broke up and headed to the rooms. I walked as slowly as possible to the fellowship hall, where I was assigned, imagining a room full of senior adult ladies, and I practically fell over myself when I opened the door and saw... her."

I nodded. "It was Shoko, huh?"

"Yeah," he sighed. "Just Shoko. We introduced ourselves, started talking through the subjects that the curriculum gave, and before I knew it, the two hours were up. She was so easy to talk with – the time just flew by! The next week, we talked without the curriculum for a while longer. I found out that she was born in Okinawa, grew up in Yomitan, went to the Christian school there, and was now teaching Japanese at one of the primary schools in Naha. She was an amazing Christian woman, had been going to the Japanese speaking church that shared a building with ours, and decided to come for help with English, so she could – get this," he held his hands up to prepare me, "—so she could better share the Gospel with Americans on island."

I smiled at the spark in his eye. "Wow. She sounds incredible."

"Tell me about it," he said. "I was so convicted. Here I was, a native speaker who knew all about Christ, and I wasn't sharing my faith at all. I mean, AT ALL. And there she was, a Japanese woman, so burdened for men and women like me that she was using her free time to better learn a language that would help her communicate so that she could share Christ. It was so easy for me to do, so difficult for her. And yet, SHE was the one who was more faithful to do it!"

He sighed, then continued. "I thought I had recommitted myself before that point. But after meeting her and spending those weeks with her? I was changed again. I covenanted to be serious, to not just keep blindly living a routine anymore. To live a routine with HIM as the center and purpose. Do you know what that's like? To live with everything – friendships, relationships, work, life – glorifying Him?"

I smiled wistfully. No, but I wanted to. How often had I felt the same, chatting with brides over tulle and flowers when my heart really longed to chat with them about Christ, the foundation of their marriages? How often had I felt so run down lately, with all the relationships in my life, trying to figure out so many of them, trying not to spread myself thin with others? When was the last time I had honestly let the Word of God change me?

Matthew continued on, even as my mind kept turning through these thoughts.

"At the end of our three month study, we weren't even using the curriculum. Her English had long since breezed past its level of difficulty. I apologized to her on the last night, telling her that she hadn't gotten her time and effort's worth with such a pitiful teacher, who was more intent on hearing her stories than on really teaching her anything about English. But she told me, so sweetly and kindly, that I had been a wonderful 'sensei' and that just talking to me had improved her English more than she had hoped for at the beginning of our study. I couldn't imagine not seeing her again, so I asked her if I could take her to dinner. She agreed." He smiled at me, as if this was the end of the story.

"And?"

"And what?" He grabbed another bite of rice with his chopsticks.

"Well," I prodded. "How did we go from 'your English is good' to 'will you marry me'?"

He grinned at me. "Well, I haven't asked her yet. But we've been dating for a year and a half now. Her parents aren't so thrilled. I don't think it's me. Just that I'm not Japanese." His brow furrowed. "Which means that it IS me. But not my character or anything." He shook his head. "She switched churches about six months ago, which her parents couldn't understand. She told them that I couldn't understand the sermons, the music, any of it in her church, so me joining them would have been silly. So, she joined Central. At just the right time, too, since she's now teaching the youth and getting really involved with the young ladies' fellowship group. I think it's been good for her to be around the other Americans, to... you know. Get used to how we are, how life might be for those times that we're stationed back in the US. You know..." He smiled at the thought. "When she's married to me."

"Oh my. Oh my! Matthew, this is all too much. You're getting married. MARRIED! To a woman who is much too good for you." I punched him playfully across the table.

He smiled back. "I know, Emily. I know."

I spent the rest of the afternoon that Matthew was at work doing what any good American will do while traveling overseas. I went shopping for tacky souvenirs.

My mother and Jessica had sent me with lists of things they wanted me to buy (silk robes, pearls, china), and Matthew, good sport that he was, dropped me off on Gate 2 street, which was full of shops that did frequent business with non-Japanese speaking Americans.

"Have fun," he told me before he drove off with instructions on where to meet him in a few hours.

While I was browsing, I thought about Sara and Melissa and how their own little exotic vacations were going. Sara had been roped into going on a one week trip to Costa Rica with a missions team to do medical aid.

She wasn't a doctor or a nurse, obviously, but because she was serving on the missions committee at church and she hadn't taken any sick leave from school all year, she was the first they asked to handle administrative concerns for the team. She had been nervous but excited all at the same time, spending her days studying a Spanish phrasebook, trying to remember all of those hours spent in Spanish class in high school. Melissa, despite our protests that it was NOT exotic, had gone to New Orleans to meet Beau's family. They were still dating, still seeing one another every day, and still spending more time together than she spent with either of us. We had all talked about how serious it was getting, and though Melissa denied it, Sara and I knew that this introduction to his family was likely a precursor to an engagement.

With requested pearls in hand, I picked out a couple of strands of multicolored seed pearl necklaces for gifts for the girls and paid for them all. I found the robes and some cute pjs for all four (well, almost five) nephews at the next store and was headed towards China Pete's (Pete? Really?) when I stopped in front of a shop full of samurai swords. They were displayed on elaborate stands with kanji and depictions of temples and dragons on them. When I went in, I found an understated set with carved wooden handles, edges stitched in black ribbon, and blade covers with simple kanji letters, almost hidden back in the store, yet clearly more valuable and authentic than its more obvious brothers in the front window. Thinking of Josh, I paid for the set and had it gift wrapped.

"Shoko!" I shouted. "HELP!!! Oh, no, I – HELP!!!"

I could hear her outside the dressing room, timidly asking, "Emily, what seems to be the problem?"

Well, I couldn't see anything, mainly because there was a much-too-small dress wrapped around my head, so tight that I couldn't get it off.

My arms were hung straight in the air, and I was stuck. I leaned over slightly, trying unsuccessfully to unlock the door. "Oh, man! This is why we leave a big space at the bottom of American dressing rooms, Shoko! There's no space here for you to crawl under and unlock the door!"

Silence. "I do not think that I should be crawling on the floor, Emily." A pause, then disbelief. "There's space under the doors in America? Really?"

"Just in dressing rooms and restrooms."

A sharp inhale. "Restrooms?! Aren't you afraid that someone will... will hear you or see you going?"

I sighed. "Actually, no, right now, I'm more concerned that I'm going to have to go through the rest of my life with this dress on my head. I can't get out!" Bending over once more, I finally, successfully – hallelujah! – managed to unlock the door. I swung it open to a gasping Shoko and pleaded, "A little help, please?"

She scurried in, shutting the door behind her to preserve what little modesty I had left, and with a grunt and a tug, she mercifully pulled the offensive dress off of my head. "There," she stated, handing me my own shirt with her eyes averted. As soon as I was covered again and she had hung the impossibly tiny dress on the hanger, she spoke as she swept her hand over the fabric. "Well, this is not your size."

"Yeah, no kidding." I eyed her tiny frame, so petite and trim, so like most of the Japanese women I had met so far... and caught a glimpse of my gargantuan girth and broadness in the unforgiving dressing room mirror. "I'm not sure there are clothes in Okinawa that will fit me, honestly."

Shoko clasped her hands together, a new idea springing into her mind. She looked at me and exclaimed, "We are looking for the wrong kinds of clothes! Come with me, and we will find a wonderful outfit. Very Japanese."

I followed her through the rows and rows of the Jusco department store, half expecting her to lead me to a rack of kimonos and tiny little slippers, which most certainly would not fit my size ten feet, which were killing me at this point.

It had been a long day. I was woken up at 6am by the ringing phone. A very enthusiastic military mom was on the line, re-introducing herself from Sunday, telling me that today was the PERFECT day for visiting a long, long list of sites on the island. Oh, yes, we could do it ALL today, if I would be ready in thirty minutes. I jumped up and rushed through my routine and was ready, waiting by the curb outside when a fleet of three mini-vans, all packed with children and sailed by energetic mommies in baseball caps, tank tops, capris, and Nikes, pulled up. They all practically squealed in delight as we stopped over at the donut shop on base so that their combined thirteen children between them could load up on sugar for our full day. As we chatted, they filled me in – whose husband was deployed, whose husband had just come back from deployment, who was due to PCS first, who was doing her second tour on Okinawa, etc. They gave me their children's names, ages, and birth places – Germany, Virginia, California ("Oh! We were there at that time, too!"), Korea ("Oh, were y'all stationed there, too?! When?!"), Hawaii, Guam... just a veritable United Nations kindergarten running around us as we ate.

We had blown through the entire island in one morning and afternoon, and I had barely managed to get three words in edgewise. Even with the noise and bustle, though, I felt as though I had actually seen Okinawa, and with all the pictures I had taken, I was sure my mother would feel like she had seen it for herself as well. We concluded the day at a little shopping center called American Village, where Shoko had made plans to meet with me. It was a little piece of Americana right there in Okinawa.

It had been very thoughtful of Shoko to have me come to a department store that felt so much like home. I had noticed the large numbers of Americans in the store already and appreciated how sensitive Shoko must also be to these things with my brother.

"Here we are," Shoko said, breaking me free from my thoughts. And there we were. Not in front of kimonos, like I had thought, but in front of a rack full of leggings and oversized shirts. Very cute. And loose enough that I could probably pull off a large. I smiled at Shoko, who, noting my pleasure, smiled as well.

After trying on several matching sets and finding a couple that would work well for the remainder of my trip, I cracked the door to give her a thumbs up, which I had to explain, before she thrust a pair of stiletto heels into my hands.

"What are these?" I asked.

"You'll need shoes for your new outfits."

"These!?!"

"Well, what were you planning on wearing?"

"Um…" Well, what would look right with these? All the Japanese girls were wearing… stiletto heels… with theirs. I sighed in resignation.

Shoko must have heard. "I got the biggest size. Those are the only pair in the whole store that size. I hope they fit." I could almost visualize her on the other side of the door, crossing her fingers.

And like Cinderella and the glass slipper, my huge foot fit perfectly into that strappy stiletto heel. "Perfect," I said, uncertainly. And the whole look was nice. A very modern Japanese me.

After I paid for my purchases, we left the store and stepped out into the balmy night. "Are you hungry?," she asked, as my stomach growled so quietly that only I could hear it. "Most definitely," I said, and we headed across the street, past the cinema, the Starbucks, the countless little shops and the massive ferris wheel, which advertised Coca Cola on its side, to a sushi bar.

"Sushi? Whole plates for five dollars?!" I couldn't contain my shock.

Shoko smiled. "Well, five hundred yen for that plate. Which is... kind of like five dollars. Yes."

After we had both pulled plates from the revolving bar and had prayed over our meal, I studied Shoko for a moment as she filled her tea cup up with hot water from the tableside dispenser. "Tell me, Shoko," I began. "What is it like living in two cultures all the time?"

She shook her head. "What do you mean?"

"Your life... teaching Japanese at the primary school, having been born here in Okinawa, going to church with so many Americans...." I spoke the last softly, so as not to embarrass her, "... dating my brother."

She blushed slightly. "It is... different. Different from what I expected my life would be like."

"I imagine," I said to her, as the waitress brought the bottle of Coke Shoko had requested for me.

"I did not intend to have anything to do with the Americans, you see. My parents put me in OCSI, the Christian school, so I would learn English better than if I was in Japanese school. And in doing so, they unknowingly gave me the chance to hear about Jesus." A light in her eye began to sparkle at this turn in her story. "I came to really understand who He was and what that meant for my life very late. I was sixteen."

I laughed. "That's very young!"

She nodded. "Yes, but very late for the number of years I had been in the school, you see. I had wonderful teachers, who loved me very much and were patient with me, as God Himself has been patient with me in all the years that I have not lived for Him but lived for my parents' approval. When I became a believer, they told me about Makiminato Church, which is in the same building as Central."

I took a bite of sushi (oh, heaven on earth!) as she swallowed her second piece of sashimi. "My parents would not have it, me going all the way down to Urasoe City by myself. But they saw that this was very important and took me themselves. I'll never forget it, those difficult months of tears and prayer, while their hard hearts remained closed to the Gospel, Sunday after Sunday."

She folded her hands for a moment. "For my parents, it's not just about a belief in God. It's a change in culture, in identity. It's very difficult. There will be ridicule, shunning, a great bit of shame, in coming to Christ, especially here with such an American presence on island... such a disputed American presence."

I had heard whispers of this, that not all were happy about the military here on island. It was safe, but there were still tremors of discontent about the situation among some of the Japanese.

She smiled at me. "But Christ was Lord. He overcame it all on the cross... what were two hardened hearts in Okinawa compared to the weight of the world He carried during His time on Calvary? Absolutely nothing. They became believers."

I couldn't help but smile. "WOW."

She nodded. "And we all became burdened, together as a family, for the lost around us. Many of our extended family put their faith in Christ. We saw the church grow. I finished school, went on to university in Tokyo, and came back here, to teach in Okinawa, mainly so that I could be near family and our wonderful church."

I sipped a little bit of Coke. "And enter my brother."

She smiled a different smile now. "Yes. Matthew." She covered her face with her hands, embarrassed, then looked at me shyly. "You will think I'm silly if I tell you that the first time I met him, I was so flustered that I could hardly remember any English at all!"

"Oh, I find that very hard to believe," I said. "Your English is great! Shoot… it's better than mine!"

She shook her head slightly. "You are kind for saying so but certainly not. And that first day, oh, Matthew doesn't remember it correctly, but my English was horrible, and he was so handsome that I could not concentrate. I had almost decided that I would not be back, I was so embarrassed you see, but he seemed so pleased at the end of the session that he had been able to 'teach' and do something for the Lord, that… well, I couldn't let him come the next week and not have a class to teach."

I laughed, picturing the smug expression on Matthew's face, thinking that he must have done a superb job even while his lone student was trying to figure out a way to never come back. "It must have gotten better."

"Oh, yes," she said, fondly remembering. "I spent a lot of time praying before the next session, and while he was still just as handsome, I could remember my English."

I studied her for a second. "You're happy with him?"

She nodded and looked at me very seriously. "I'm more than happy with him. I love him."

On cue, the door to the sushi bar swung open, and Matthew stepped in, still wearing his fatigues, snatching his hat off his head. He scanned the crowd, while I waved to him, not noticing us until Shoko turned around and caught his eye.

"Hey," he breathed out, sliding into the booth next to her and kissing her softly. "What have you girls been up to?"

"Your sister has some very beautiful, truly Okinawan clothes now." Shoko smiled at me in delight.

And I just nodded my head with a smile, looking at my brother, who had not taken his eyes off the beautiful girl next to him since he had entered the room.

I took some time for myself the next day.

As my jet lag had finally disappeared and I felt coherent enough to make sense of where I was (the northern hemisphere, apparently), I felt brave enough to take a taxi by myself to a beach that one of the military wives had recommended. I had packed my ever-present planner, some notes from work, a journal, and my Bible, and as I laid out my beach towel, took a seat, and surveyed the ocean in front of me, I thought about changes.

There was so much that was changing. My father, of course, was at the front of my mind. Would his health continue to decline? Would we need medical answers? Would this change Grace and our family forever? And my brother. He was clearly changed from who he had been just a year earlier. How would the changes in his life change our lives back in the US?

And me. I thought about work and the growing level of discontent I felt with how I wasn't who I wanted to be, doing Evelyn's bidding. I thought about how Matthew had realized his work was his entire life, and I wondered if I wasn't guilty of the same. How often did late nights at work keep me from spending any time in God's Word the next morning? How often was my mind completely filled with so many details and so many frustrations that I was left with no attention to really seek what the Lord wanted me to do with my life? Sure, I had to make a living, but did I have to make my job my ENTIRE life?

I wasn't sure. And what was more troubling was that I couldn't remember when I had last asked myself these questions... or if I ever had.

My plane was leaving on Sunday after church. Matthew had arranged to take me out on Saturday morning for us to spend some time together during my last full day on the island. He quizzed me on what I had seen, what I still wanted to see, and after thinking for a moment, he and I were driving through the city streets of Naha in his car. We toured Shuri Castle and the Prayer Peace Gardens, sites where I shot lots of video and even more pictures, making sure to get reluctant and fussy shots of Matthew in every few. My mother would thank me. After a lunch of Soba noodles, we hit some tourist shops, then headed back to the base. I collapsed in the hotel room as soon as he dropped me off, exhausted by all the walking in – you got it – those stiletto heels. I blended in with the crowd (well, as much as I could being twice as tall as everyone else) in my new rags, but Matthew just about burst out laughing every time he looked over at me, prompting several, "oh, shut up"s, which I'm sure were caught on videotape. I had to bite my tongue several times during the day to keep from asking him when he planned on proposing. It wasn't my business. And I sure didn't want to explain any of those sound bites that might have found their way onto camera, so I just didn't bring it up.

All of the questions I couldn't ask were answered at church, when Matthew and I arrived to find Shoko surrounded by a horde of military wives. Her eye caught mine, prompting her to smile and hold up her left hand... which boasted a flawless diamond ring.

"You putz," I whispered to Matt, smiling myself. "You proposed last night and didn't even tell me on the drive over here!"

He just shrugged and grinned, looking over at Shoko. Oh, sappy, sappy love.

Shoko made her way over to us quickly, hugged me, and whispered, "We will be sisters now, won't we?"

I nodded, a lump in my throat, and smiled over at Matthew, who reached for his bride, pulled her to himself, and caused a blush to spread over her beautiful face. "Matthew," she said, "my parents are here."

He let go of her and straightened up quickly, glancing towards the far corner of the lobby, where a rather severe looking older Japanese couple stood. He was balding, stocky, and she… well, my goodness. Shoko was going to age very well. This woman could have passed for her very uptight older sister.

I watched as Matthew strode over to them and greeted them politely. Shoko's father looked at him skeptically, as her mother gave a guarded smile. This was new to them, so much of one foreigner. I could just imagine the wedding now, my boisterous mother scaring the skin right off of them with her chattiness.

Shoko took my hand and led me to them, saying, "This is Emily, Matthew's sister." I bowed slightly and couldn't miss the small gasp that Shoko's mother gave, no doubt imagining granddaughters of Amazonian proportion.

"So nice to meet you both," I said, smiling.

We stood around awkwardly for a moment, before Shoko laughed nervously, bid us farewell for the moment, and ushered her parents upstairs. I glanced at Matthew once they were out of view, and he sighed.

"It'll take a while." Yeah, that was an understatement. But then, he shook his head. "But I can't blame them. There are so many unknowns about our future, about her future when she marries me. Where will we be, how will I take care of her, what will our lives be like? I understand how hesitant they are."

"Well," I offered, non-helpfully, "I'm sure they know you'll do your best. And I wouldn't worry about Shoko. She can take care of herself."

I spent the service stealing glances at Matthew, who was stealing glances at Shoko, who was stealing glances at her ring, while her parents leaned slightly forward in their seats, trying to understand the more difficult English words in the sermon. I doubted that they would leave their own church for this international congregation, but the fact that they were there for the announcement of the engagement spoke volumes.

Matthew and Shoko were both there for the long drive back to the airport, the check-in, one last souvenir rummage through the shops, and last hugs at the check-in gate.

And, as I always had with Matthew, since my scrappy little scrawny eighteen year old brother took off on his own for basic training, I couldn't stop from crying. So many miles between us... and this beautiful girl beside him. It didn't make it easier to leave. Now there were two of them to leave behind, not just one. I clung to his neck even tighter as Shoko looked away.

"Hey," he whispered in my ear, hugging me, "it won't be that long until we see you again. Another year or so. Right here, back in Okinawa."

I pulled away, my expression surprised. "You're getting married... here?"

His brow furrowed, and a tightness came to his face. "Of course. This is Shoko's home. It will be OUR home."

My mind raced with the finality of it. Home. "But, you'll be stationed in the US sometimes, and other parts of the world, and –"

"Yes, yes," he said calmly. "But we'll always request to be stationed here in Okinawa. Shoko has family here, she has her career here, she... she wants to have our babies here." I could see Shoko flush at the thought of her tiny perfect babies, as she looked away, trying not to hear us. "You can understand that, can't you? It's her home."

I fought back another rush of tears, thinking of my baby brother gone from home. Not like before but in a much different way now. I watched him look at Shoko with unreserved devotion and love, caught my breath as she glanced back to lavish admiration on him with her smile, and realized... Shoko's home was in Okinawa. And for my brother, Shoko had become home.

"I'm proud of you," I whispered back to Matthew, kissing him on the cheek. He smiled as I kissed Shoko one more time, bowed to her, and told her, "I'll see you soon, sister."

How was it possible that the flight back to the US, following the exact same route, seemed ten hours longer? I don't know, but it did. When I finally landed in DFW, I pressed my lips to the filthy airplane window, mentally kissing American soil.

I had resolved to change some things. Next month was going to be a big one. I was going to become more involved in the ministry of our church by attending a Bible study, which was actually part of our resolutions anyway. It was time to invest in the lives of other ladies, study the Word with a group, and learn from a woman farther down the road of faith than I was. I was excited to talk this through with Sara and Melissa, who were both on their way back to Dallas as well.

After a long trip through passport control, I could see the doors leading out of the airport. Hallelujah. My parents were standing by the baggage carousel, my mother waving to me enthusiastically, her face already full of questions. I could almost hear her, even from a hundred yards away, behind security glass. *How is he? Oh, I know he must miss me. Does he look too thin? Oh, he should really eat more. Did he get a tattoo? Oh, I'll kill him! Did he find that shop that sells the pearls that Julia Stanley's son found while he was stationed there? Oh, you know, she goes ON and ON about those pearls and her "perfect" son, and I just can't EVEN stand to –*

"Emily?" Oh. Well, there she was. Right in front of me. I hadn't noticed that my feet had carried me the distance to her while her imagined inner monologue rattled on in my head. "My goodness. Don't you look awful!"

I smiled. "Thanks, mom."

"Well, I don't mean that YOU look awful. In fact," she glanced down at my Japanese stilettos and followed my figure up my Shoko-selected ensemble, "you look very feminine. I like it!" She smiled at me brilliantly, then, put on a worried expression. "You do look tired, though."

I nodded. "Long flight. Longest flight ever."

She grinned. "Worth it, though."

I thought over all the many moments that had made this trip "worth it." Shoko's beautiful smile, my brother's gaze in response to her every word, the love, love, love, so sappy sweet that I wouldn't need to pick up another romance novel for ten years, at least. Maybe more. And all these moments? I was sworn to secrecy regarding every last one and couldn't tell my mother anything. Until Matthew called to deliver the happy news himself, which he promised to do as soon as my plane was due to land. I had finally convinced him that the news would be easier to process, even if it included wrong presumptions, if he would do it now, rather than when Shoko made her first visit to the US. I had even snapped a picture of the happy couple, Shoko's engagement ring visible, to show my mother once she stopped hyperventilating.

"Totally worth it," I told her as I gave her a hug. I smiled over at my father. "Hey, Dad."

He put an arm around my shoulder and squeezed, one of my bags in his other hand. I wondered if there had been any episodes while I was gone. I bit my lip and shot a furtive glance at my mother, whose face mirrored my own. She would tell me later.

"Well," she said. "You'll have to tell us all about it!" The three of us turned to exit and began maneuvering our way out of the airport, when my mother's cell phone chirped at her.

"Oh!," she said, surprised. "It's Matthew! Probably checking to make sure you got in safe. How thoughtful!" She pressed a button. "Matthew! She's here!"

He said something, which she laughed at. "Yes, she still has the high heels on!"

Oh, ha, ha. Glad she was laughing, though… at least for now.

"Well, we're on our way to –" She paused, mid-stride. "Well, yes, dear. I'm just fine." A pause. "Well, now, why would I need to sit down?" She put her hand to her heart, a troubled expression on her face, while my father glanced at me nervously. "Matthew Caleb Fisher! Did you get a tattoo!?!" Oh, wow. She was completely off. "Oh. Well, no, of course, I didn't *really* think that you had gotten a – well, it's just that Julia Stanley's son—" oy " – well, *he* came back from Japan with this awful, huge *dragon* on his back, and I just couldn't EVEN imagine if you –" She stopped speaking entirely. Took a deep breath. Then, said, extra-politely, "Would you please repeat that?" A pause. Then, in a voice so loud that it seemed every set of eyes in the arrival lounge of the DFW International Airport found her open, gaping mouth…

"WHAT!?!"

Jet lag was worse returning than it had been going. I had been cautioned by everyone who had ever done any overseas travel to give myself a few days to readjust, rather than jumping right back into work. Gradual transitions made for easier adjustments, they said.

Which was good and well for them, but they didn't work for Evelyn, who was all but shoulder deep in May weddings and was already calling my cell phone an hour after the plane landed. So I returned, rather unceremoniously, to work the very next day, where Evelyn met me at the door with a stack of files.

"Consultations!," she trilled. "So many consultations while you were gone, dear!" She cut her eyes at me. "It's almost like you KNEW that every Christmas bride in the Metroplex would pick the first week of May to begin planning their weddings, and you LEFT because of it!" She snapped her mouth shut.

I had worked with Evelyn long enough to know that this sour attitude was a pre-cursor to the summer. If I had stayed in the States and gone on vacation in September, when we weren't so busy, she still would have been rude to me. If I had been by her side during the most horrific week of the year EVER (so far, at least, it was going to get much worse), she still would have been furious. If I had done all of the work for her and raised revenue by twenty percent (which I had done one year when she took the time off to cruise the Mediterranean with Mr. Primrose, if that was indeed his real name), she still would have shot me a look that could have withered every overpriced flower that we were set to bring in, arrange, and display that spring.

In other words, I was prepared for this.

"Evelyn," I said sweetly, fighting back a yawn. (It felt like 3am in the morning because it WAS 3am in the morning in Japan.) "I'm planning on having all of this," I said, indicating the stack of files, "done by the time we open the office tomorrow morning. Now, however, I think my time would be best spent helping you with the meetings and with set up for this weekend's weddings. Friedman, Yoast, Matthis, Hawkins, Rose, Gain, Romer, and Boyd... those are the eight receptions on Saturday, correct?"

She sighed, obviously relaxing a bit. "Yes." She looked over her planner. "Although today, I would rather have you concentrate on meetings than on setup."

I put the files out of sight behind my desk, hoping to hide their bothersome presence from Evelyn's sensitive eyes. I didn't need a day full of blow-ups and recriminations for – hello?! – actually taking the vacation legally due to me. Especially not with jet lag.

"So many appointments today!," Evelyn trilled. "Summer is upon us, and the LOVELIEST weddings happen during this season, wouldn't you agree?"

I agreed but could only manage a "Sure," absentmindedly, my brain still flying somewhere over the Pacific.

"Today, you'll be meeting with Evans, Greene, and Bennett," she finished, "and then lunch."

I was getting a lunch break today? Glory to –

"Which, of course, you'll spend assisting in set up for the Grand Ballroom because I was MORTIFIED—" she rolled her eyes at this, "— with the ATROCIOUS job they did for the Johnson reception. Which you didn't see, of course, since you were off jet-setting around the world and all." She jabbed this little dig in with a mutter. Then, she looked at me with sunshine in her face and said, "I'll be meeting with a HUGE potential client this afternoon to book a wedding for next spring. I can't drop any names just yet... but let's just say that half of the buildings in town are named for this bride's great-grandfather."

I nodded, yawning.

"Wake up, Emily. We've got a busy week ahead of us!"

Her heels clicked out of the office, leaving me there with only one thought... I had a busy week ahead of me.

The day just kept getting better and better.

RESOLUTIONS

After dealing with yet another bride who spent the entire meeting screeching at both her groom and her mother (and me – hello!), a fairly chirpy looking couple sat down across from me. Dawn and Cliff, planning a late October wedding ceremony and reception in one of our smaller rooms, and –

"We REALLY wanted to do this at Walt Disney World."

I looked up from our plans to see Dawn looking a bit somber. "Disney World?"

"Actually, it's WALT Disney World," Cliff corrected me.

"Yeah," Dawn continued on, lost in her apparent gloom, "we REALLY wanted to have a big wedding at the Magic Kingdom. You know, right outside the castle at sunset, with 'When You Wish Upon A Star' playing in the background, with MICKEY officiating..."

I couldn't tell if she was being serious or not. "Well, that would have been memorable," I offered.

"We're Disney people, Emily," Cliff explained. "I myself have been there twenty-nine times, and Dawn has been there –"

"Thirty-two! Got him beat by a few," she giggled.

Oh, so they WERE being serious.

"The thing about Disney," Cliff said to me, "is that they're in the business of making dreams come true. And this woman, right here?" He pointed to Dawn. "She is MY dream come true. My Cinderella, if you will."

"Oh, Cliff," she cooed. "You're the Prince Charming to my Cinderella."

"The Mickey to your Minnie," Cliff added.

"The Philip to my Aurora," she said.

"The Eric to your Ariel," he added.

"The Robin Hood to your Maid Marian," I interrupted.

They turned to me with stunned expressions. "Vintage, 1970s Disney," Cliff breathed. "I'm WAY impressed."

Hey, I was impressed with myself. I was actually really good at this part of the job – finding a commonality even with the nuttiest people. And these Disney folks? Were just a few nuts short of a praline. Nutty but sickeningly sweet, somehow.

"Well, I can understand how this," I indicated our hotel, "is a far cry from Disney World. I mean, WALT Disney World."

"Yes," Dawn cooed. "But it's just too much to expect our grandparents to travel all the way out to Florida. I mean, they're really getting up there in age."

"I understand that," I said. "How about if we do our best to make this," again, indicating our hotel, "as close to the real thing as possible?"

As we began to chat, I looked at what Evelyn had planned for them... and I made big changes. From the elegant soiree that Evelyn had talked them into to the kitschy Disney-themed celebration that they wanted. It was a gamble, since this was cutting costs and not making us nearly the profits we would have made, but the look of glee on Mickey and Minnie's (I mean, Cliff and Dawn's) faces was worth it.

Could my job, my work, be more than just a hustle and grab for more money?

The next morning was a running morning, and I woke earlier than normal, excited to see Josh for the first time in two weeks. I had missed his company, more than I knew I would.

He had been eager to hear about Japan, about Matthew, about how work was going now that I was back, about... everything, actually.

"Sushi, for five dollars? Wow!" He marveled over every detail that I could give, all that I was still processing, as we finished up the first mile and headed into the second. "Of course, I hate sushi, so that still would have been too expensive for me." He smiled at this.

"You would have enjoyed the teppanyaki. You know, where the chefs come out and cook your meal right in front of you," I clarified, trying to catch my breath. The brief break from running was having an effect on my endurance. Or maybe Josh was getting in shape that quickly.

"Oh, yeah," he said, not even winded in the slightest. "I'd probably love that."

We talked about the beach, about the sites, about all that I had seen and done while I was there.

"Who is Shoko?," he asked, his brow slightly furrowed.

"My brother's fiancée," I said, with a smile.

We were nearing the end of the fifth mile, so Josh began walking, much to my gasping relief.

"Your brother's engaged? You never told me that," he said.

"Well, it happened while I was there," I said. "Honestly, we didn't even know he was seeing anyone, much less serious enough to be considering marriage."

Josh shook his head. "There's no way anyone in my family could keep a secret like that. We can't keep quiet about anything – none of us!"

I looked at him, considering this. "You tell each other everything?"

"Yeah, and it gets us all in plenty of trouble," he said. "We're a really close-knit group. Like," he said, looking over at me cautiously, "for example, they all know that I have this really hot girl I run with every week."

This made me blush. "Are you running with someone else on my off days?"

He laughed out loud. "No, no, no... anyway, they know all about that, and they are NOSY about it. About my life, about everything, actually. You know, I'm the only one in my family who's still single, and I catch an earful about it every time we all get together. Especially from the women. Eesh!"

I held my breath as we walked, waiting for him to talk more about his life, about being single, about maybe possibly wanting to date the hot girl walking next to him...

But he didn't.

"So, your brother has a mysterious fiancée," he said. "What do you think about that?"

I sighed. "I think it's great. I think she's great. And I'm excited that he's found someone to spend his life with, you know?"

Josh looked over at me. "Yeah, I do."

A moment of silence passed between us as we, regrettably, neared our cars. I glanced down at my watch, knowing that I had very little time to go home and get ready for another busy day at the office. But before I could do that, there was something I had to do.

"Hey," I told him, moving to unlock my trunk (which on my old clunker involved turning the key then beating the lid in just the right spot and in just the right way), "I have something for you."

I pulled out the wrapped swords and put them into his outstretched arms. I suddenly felt awkward, as the surprise shown on his face, but the awkwardness was quickly replaced with joy, as he tore away the paper and laughed out loud at the gift.

"Samurai swords!," he bellowed. "These are awesome!"

"They just… called your name, I guess. Made me think of you while I was gone," I said, smiling at his enthusiasm.

He looked at me, a surprising, wistful expression on his face. "Well, the gift is great, but… knowing that you thought of me while you were gone? Even better."

And it felt so right when he reached out and embraced me in a warm hug.

"OH MY WORD! WHAT IS THAT?!"

Sara and I had arrived at the restaurant a few minutes earlier than Melissa had. I had commented on her amazing Costa Rican tan, and just as she was about to tell me all about her mission trip, Melissa walked in.

With a wedding band on her finger.

Sara's screaming had directed the entire restaurant's attention to us. Still, though, that didn't stop me from screaming as well.

"IS THAT A WEDDING BAND?!"

Melissa looked mortified and horrified, if not just a little smug, as she excused herself past all the staring hordes and sat across from us.

"Well, welcome back to you, too," she said, picking up the Coke we had ordered for her and taking a sip.

"Did you get engaged?," Sara gasped.

"Engaged?! That's a wedding band!," I shrieked, my tone lowered by Melissa's look, even as I grabbed her left hand to study the evidence.

"Actually, NO, Emily, this is indeed an engagement ring. I told Beau I didn't need some fussy engagement ring with a big diamond. Just a simple band, I told him. Of course, he didn't listen entirely and gave me this thing, which while technically a band, has diamonds all the way around, but whatever. Not like I was going to tell him to take it back or anything because THAT would have been stupid."

We sat there staring at her for a moment, shocked.

Then, like a wave cresting over our table, Sara and I began talking louder than we should have. "You're getting MARRIED!," I yelled.

"Oh my WORD, Emily," Melissa said, a smile escaping her scolding expression. "You're going to make me deaf. But, yes." She paused and looked down at her hand. "I'm engaged. Beau and I are getting married."

Then began the story. As we ordered our entrees and began eating our meals, Melissa told us about how she had gone to New Orleans to meet the Thibideaux clan and how we were wrong about the whole trip not being exotic enough.

"I'm telling you," she said conspiratorially, "it's like a different world down there. Some of Beau's relatives, for real, need a closed captioning system for me to understand what they're saying. I'm not even sure what kind of accents those were or that they weren't just speaking French and trying to pass it off to me as English."

"Did you meet the whole family?," Sara asked.

"Every one of them," she said. "But I spent the most time with his parents and his sisters." She gasped. "His sisters, y'all! Sophie is, like, brilliant, and Chloe is so sweet. I so seriously thought I was going to hate them because they're so perfect and rich, but... we all clicked from the moment we met." She stared at us, shocked. "Who would've ever BELIEVED, right?"

"How about Beau's parents?," I asked.

"Well," Melissa began. "I'm not so sure about his mother. She didn't seem so sure about me either, though. Guess I can't fault her for that, since this is all really quick. "

"How did it happen? How did he do it?," Sara squealed.

"He took me out to dinner, right down in the French Quarter," she said, lowering her voice, "which, again, is like some other world down there. Seriously." Raising her voice again, "Anyway, he took me out to dinner, then we walked along the water, where he got down on one knee, told me that I was a good choice for him, he was a good choice for me, and that we should get married."

Sara and I looked at one another. "Those were his sweet nothings?," I asked.

"Well, they were plenty sweet," she said. "Sweet because they were right on. And I wouldn't call it nothing," she said, wriggling her exquisite eternity band at me.

"I would say not," Sara concluded, smiling. "That sounds just exactly like the kind of proposal, the kind of family, God had for you."

"So," I asked, smiling, "do you know when you want to have the wedding? Any plans on where? Any bridesmaids, perhaps?" Sara and I leaned our heads together and gave her matching smiles.

"New Year's Eve. Grace. I'm surprised you haven't heard it from your dad, Emily. Beau and I already met with him."

I made a mental note to check and see if any of this had made it to my father's schedule. He would have surely told my mother, and she would have surely told me. Another sign of the trouble he was having, or just an oversight?

"And, OF COURSE, I already have two of my bridesmaids sitting right here," she said, shaking me out of my thoughts.

"Yay! A wedding!," Sara shouted, her voice not showing any signs of jealousy or envy. This was a marked difference from all the conversations we'd had in the past. Sara seemed to be acting different, not just since the breakup with Jon, but different even now, just a few weeks since we had last seen her.

Melissa seemed to note the change as well, and pushing away her empty plate pointed her question towards Sara. "So, how was that exotic vacation?"

Sara's eyes shone. "Costa Rica was... amazing. The work we did, the people there... just all of it, amazing!"

She went on to tell us about their daily work, some of the challenges, the kindness of the people, and most importantly, how life affirming and life changing it had been for her to be able to share the Gospel with others in need.

"I've been home for a week, you know, and I've just caught myself again and again wondering how I can get back there.... how quickly I can get back there. I just... I really don't think I'll ever be the same."

As we finished up our visit, my mind kept returning to her words and my suspicion that this was the beginning of something really big in both of my friends' lives.

7 JUNE

June was, traditionally, the worst month of my life.

My mother likes to say that I exaggerate when it comes to June brides, but as I stood in the bridal room with a screeching woman surrounded by twelve attendants, I found little exaggeration in the statement. June was, traditionally, the worst month of my life.

"WHAT IS THIS THING?!," the "genteel Southern" bride (as Evelyn called her) continued to holler at everyone. They had just gotten her in her impossibly giant dress, despite the fact that the hoop skirt gave none of them any room to lace up the bodice for her. It had been nothing short of a gymnastic feat to do that job, and a few of her girls or "precious flowers" as she called them were looking downright wilted from the exertion. Those that weren't gasping for breath were gaping at one another as she continued screeching at them.

The issue at hand? A spot on her dress. Barely a pinpoint sized spot on her dress.

"AIEEEEEEE!!!!," she screeched as her meltdown continued.

They had called me in to do damage control. Upon surveying the scene, I was tempted to light a match and let the whole mess go up in flames. That was the only damage control that could right this situation, likely.

"What seems to be the problem?," I asked pleasantly.

The bridesmaids audibly exhaled, relived to see me. I smiled at the bride.

"What seems to be the PROBLEM?!," she shouted. She had never been more than pleasant to me, but this was her breaking point. "Do you SEE the SPOT?!"

I came as close as I could with all that tulle in the way and squinted. Ah, there it was.

"Hmm," I said. "Can't see a thing."

"What?!" She looked at me doubtfully. "It's RIGHT HERE!," she yelled, jabbing her finger at it.

I looked again. Yeah, there it was.

"There's nothing there," I confirmed. I looked at her, concerned. "Are you seeing spots?"

The bridesmaids all looked to one another worriedly as the bride took a breath to start screeching at me again... before stopping, putting her hand to her forehead, and saying, pitifully, "Well, now that you mention it... I AM feeling kind of dizzy."

Well, this was working out better than I had hoped. "I think we need to help her sit down. Get her some water, put her head between her knees, and get her cooled off before the ceremony," I told her attendants, who moved quickly into action.

As she lowered herself (with much assistance) into a chair, she looked at me. "Thank you, Emily. I'm just... I'm having a hard day, you know."

Weren't we all?

I left the room, after confirming for the millionth time that I would be back to usher her right to the grand ballroom for her grand entrance, irritated by drama brides. More than that, though, I found myself irritated by the friends of drama brides who couldn't bring themselves to slap some sense into their brides and tell them that a spot wasn't worth all the fuss. Or, failing that, just LIE to them like I had. What was a little white lie anyway when it came to angst-ridden, melodramatic brides with too much time on their –

My phone cut me off mid-thought. I looked at my watch. I didn't have time for whoever was calling...

"Hello?," I answered curtly.

"SHE IS KILLING ME!"

Ahh, speaking of melodramatic brides. "Melissa, who is killing you?," I asked, noting the concerned looks I got from the caterers as I asked this.

"Beau's mother! OH MY WORD! You would think this is the wedding of the century or something, the way she's overplanning it all!"

I had already met Beau's mother once, and to be honest, she wasn't at all over the top. Sure, she was money, and she had opinions, but I had watched her defer to Melissa along every step of the way. I didn't know a whole lot about mother-in-law and daughter-in-law dynamics, but Melissa's attitude going into it wasn't making things easy. It seemed as if she almost wanted to antagonize this generally pleasant woman whose son she was marrying.

"Look, I think you need to dial it down a few notches, crazy," I said, before thinking better of it.

A gasp. "Excuse me?" Irritating an already explosive bride-to-be? Maybe not the best idea. At least not if I wanted to get off the phone anytime this evening.

"Oh," I told her, "not you, just someone I was talking to." I shrugged at the caterers. I was no better than those wimpy bridesmaids.

"Oh, well," she said, "I just don't know what to do! I didn't want a big to-do for this, you know!"

"I know," I said calmly, walking through the reception room, checking items off my list. "But you have to understand that Beau is her son, and she has expectations, too. What does Beau think about it all?"

"No opinion at all!," she shouted. "It's like he wants his mother and me to have a cage match fight on all of this. Which is weird on SO many levels, right?"

I continued checking items off. "I think you need to calm down and not do any wedding related activities until all three of us – you, me, and Mrs. Thibideaux – can get together. Okay?" I had been roped into more of the planning that I really had time for, but Melissa was my friend and no one knew Grace better than I did, at least when it came to event planning there.

"Okay, okay," she muttered, then hung up.

Two crazy brides down... countless others to go.

Welcome to June.

Pastor Stephen gave me a call early that Monday morning from youth camp.

This was one of my father's favorite parts of his job. Even as the pastor of a large church, he managed to spend a couple of the five nights at youth camp with the church kids. In his earlier days, when he wasn't shepherding a congregation of over a thousand people, he went as an adult sponsor, at the same time amusing campers with cannonball plunges in the river and horrifying his mortified offspring.

In recent years, though, Dad's schedule had permitted him to only do night visits to the camp, and Stephen took his place as the pastoral adult sponsor. I was pretty certain that Stephen didn't specialize in cannonball antics and that camp was a little different now than it had been in my youth. It had grown from a rustic camp atmosphere to a multi-building campus, from a few counselors to a whole staff of college aged ministry students, all working throughout the summer months. If anything, the changes meant that the churches worked less than they had in those early days, back when each church did everything for their campers and basically ran the program themselves.

That's why I was surprised to get the call from Stephen, asking if I could come up for the evening service to help out. They had taken a large number of girls to camp, and after the services, they were scrambling to find enough volunteers and counselors to work with all of them. Sara, who had been ravenously hungry for any and all ministry opportunities since coming back from Costa Rica, had gone as one of the female sponsors, and she had suggested that Stephen call me to see if I could make the drive out for at least one of the nights to help out. I agreed, went home to change into more comfortable clothes after work, and drove the hour out of town to get there as quickly as I could.

As soon as I arrived on campus, the night session was concluding and hordes of students were flooding out of the main auditorium. Pushing against the steady current of sweaty, loud teenagers (and as tall as I was, I was still only at armpit level with a few of the sweatiest of the boys – ugh), I made my way to Grace's meeting point – a large oak tree that had been there for literally decades, expecting to see Sara, Pastor Stephen, and the other adult sponsors surrounded by students.

What I found instead was Pastor Stephen, standing by himself.

"Hey," I waved to him, as I pushed past the last throngs of teens heading away from the auditorium.

"Hey, Emily," he said, hands in his pockets, looking almost bored.

"Sara said you might need some help," I offered, looking around.

He shrugged, scanning the crowd to see if any of our students would be making their way over to us. "I thought we might, but so far... not so much." He smiled at me. "I'm so sorry you made the long drive out here."

I exhaled and continued surveying the area. I had so many great memories of our times here, as a family and as a teenager taking part in the activities myself. My parents had taken the three of us along when we were still tiny children, and I had spent so many evenings just like this running around on the grass outside with Jessica and Matthew, steps away from where my both of my parents counseled young people as they made decisions. Then, there had been my own decisions made in response to the messages during my teenage years, decisions to follow Christ more nearly, to know Him better in the year to come. It was a place for eternal, significant meetings. And it was a wonderfully significant place to me.

"Oh, it's okay," I said to Stephen, "I love this place."

We waited in comfortable silence for a few more minutes as the crowds cleared out. When it became obvious that there weren't any students coming for counseling, Stephen turned to me.

"Do you want to take a walk?"

"Sure," I said, following him down the main road.

After a few moments of silence, he sighed. "I have to apologize to you," he said softly.

"Apologize? For what?"

"I haven't... well, I haven't done such a great job of communicating with you lately."

Lately? We had never done a very good job of communicating with one another, at least not on a personal level. True, I hadn't spoken but a handful of words with him over the past few weeks since returning home from Okinawa, but given our history together, this wasn't unusual.

"It's okay," I reassured him. "Honestly, I hadn't even thought much of it until you... well, until you mentioned it." I looked at him, and he looked at me... and after untold months of wondering what was going on, what we wanted to go on, we both figured it out.

I hadn't given it much thought because... well, because, honestly, Stephen didn't occupy my thoughts. He hadn't for a while. Oh, he was gorgeous. And kind and compassionate. And warm and godly and... nothing. I felt absolutely nothing, despite all of the logical prodding from my mind, unable to find any reason to feel something more for him than this – respect and admiration. Totally platonic respect and admiration. When I had told Sara and Melissa that the butterflies had disappeared, I had half expected that a truer, richer feeling would replace them. I had figured that something more solid would be built between us as we spent time together, but the time together, or rather lack of time together, had just shown me that it wasn't what we thought it might be. It wasn't this great romance that everyone at the church seemed to hope that it would be. It wasn't this great romance that we had been trying to have. Without us even acknowledging it, perhaps because it didn't bother us to NOT acknowledge it, it was done. This quasi-romantic, are they, aren't they relationship? Was done.

And that? That was okay.

"Yeah," he said.

"Yeah," I said.

He exhaled sharply and laughed out loud. "Are we thinking the same thing?"

"I think so," I said. "I'm thinking you're a... great pastor. Right?" I looked intently at him, maybe for the first time ever, without feeling awkward or anxious.

"Yeah," he said, sharing my look. "I'm thinking... well, that's okay."

I smiled at him. "Wow, you're telling me!"

And every bit of awkwardness we had been experiencing was replaced by ease and familiarity. Stephen probably actually COULD be my friend now. It would be so great at Grace now, being able to relate to him and speak with him and be a real friend to him without everyone wondering what was going on, and –

"I have to tell you something," he said. "I... haven't even told anyone yet. Except your father, of course."

I stopped walking, turning to him at the serious tone in his voice.

"What is it?"

He looked down at his hands for a moment, then looked at me. "I'm thinking about leaving Grace."

Well, so much for those big plans.

"What? Why?," I asked. "We love you at Grace!"

That had certainly been the first time I had said anything about love to Pastor Stephen, but it was the truth. He was as much a part of the church now as my father was. I couldn't fathom why he'd want to leave.

"Oh, I love Grace," he said. "It's just with my doctoral work finally done, I've been given the opportunity to teach at the seminary level."

I looked at him blankly. "Doctoral work?" This was news to me.

"And," he smiled, "this is just greater confirmation about us, isn't it? That I've been spending the last few years working towards this goal and somehow neglected to ever even mention it to you."

"No kidding," I breathed. "Well, congratulations. On finishing up. And on the possible job."

I could see him planting himself in the world of academia, teaching other pastors and leaders more about doctrine, and flourishing in a world where more time was given to studying the Bible than shepherding a large congregation.

He sighed. "I'm still praying about it, but I would start in January. That way, I can finish out the summer and the holiday season at Grace. It all depends on… well, on your father, actually." Concern passed over his face. "Actually, that's another thing I wanted to talk to you about. Have you… have you noticed that he's having some trouble remembering things?"

And there it was. Confirmation from someone else, someone else who spent more time with him than I did, who had more occasion to see him forget than I did. I wasn't sure I was ready to hear what Stephen had to say, even though I knew I had to.

"Well, um…" I began. "I think it's just probably his age, you know? We've noticed… you know, just what's normal for his age."

This wasn't entirely true, but Stephen didn't pick up on my omission, obviously more concerned by what he had seen than he had ever let on before.

"It's more than that," he said. "There have been some situations where he seems really disoriented and confused, and… Emily, it looks an awful lot like –"

"I don't think it is," I said to him, my eyes beginning to tear up at the thought of what this all would mean for us if it really was what we were all fearing, and –

"Hey," Stephen said, catching my hand in his. "It's okay. We don't have to talk about it now, if… I'm just worried about him, you know? I didn't mean to upset you." A pause. "Have you noticed it, too?"

I held his hand in both of mine and stepped closer to him, ready to tell him what I knew, when I heard my name.

"Emily?"

I turned around, surprised to find Josh standing there.

"Hey!," I said to him, blinking past my tears, trying to smile. "I wondered if I would see you here!" I knew he had taken his own youth group to camp during the same week as Grace but figured the odds of actually running into him were slim to none, given the size of the camp. I was glad to see him but confused by the crestfallen look on his face as his eyes traveled between Stephen and me, holding hands in this dark corner of the camp.

"Stephen!"

Another voice this time. Wow, were we popular or what? We let go of one another's hands as Sara came into view.

"Stephen! We just had a kid fall into the creek! I told him not to walk so close to the edge, but he wouldn't listen to me, and –"

She stopped short when she saw Josh. My very attractive, very available Josh. "Oh, hi!," she said, looking to me for an introduction.

Did I WANT to introduce my adorable friend Sara to Josh? Did I really have a choice? Did Stephen know as much or more than I already knew about my father? Did I have to finally stop avoiding the truth and admit that my dad had a problem?

What was I even thinking?

"I'm sorry. Stephen. Josh. Sara." I blinked back my tears. "Everyone, meet everyone, I guess!"

Josh shook Stephen's hand, introducing himself as Stephen did the same. Then, he shook Sara's hand, as she smiled her brilliant smile at him.

"Sorry to drag Stephen away," she said to me, "but that kid is really scraped up. And I can't even find our first aid kit!"

"I can go to the nurse's station for you, if that would help," Josh offered, avoiding my eyes.

"Could you?," Sara said sweetly. "Oh, that would be awesome!"

"Emily?," Stephen said. "Can we talk later?"

I nodded wordlessly, glancing over to Josh, who still wouldn't look at me.

"Josh, we're in Grace's cabin. Do you know where that is?," she asked.

"Yeah, I'll go get those bandages and be over there in a bit." Finally he looked at me, resignation in his eyes but still managing a smile. "I'll see you later, Emily." Then he turned and left.

I tried to say something to him as he walked away, but Sara cut me off. "Are you staying the night?"

I saw the question in Stephen's eyes but shook my head. "No, I have to be at work early tomorrow."

"Then, have a safe trip home," she said, giving me a hug, then leading Stephen away.

What a mess.

"Is it just me, or is it REALLY hot out here?," Josh asked halfway through mile three of our morning run, two weeks later.

The question caught me off guard.

Honestly, I'd been watching him out of the corner of my eye, and while I wasn't sure how much weight he had been losing, I was beginning to see muscle groups in his shoulders and arms and legs that I hadn't recalled ever seeing on him. Maybe I just hadn't noticed before, though, because it seemed as though everything about Josh – about being near Josh – made me hyper-sensitive as of late. My thoughts had been running a little hot as a result of watching him running, and when he said what he said, I was at a loss for words.

"Helloooo?," he said, looking at me curiously.

"Yes," I said, shaking my head. "It's hot. Not as hot as it will be, though."

We had seen one another a few times since youth camp, and while he wasn't much different than he had been before, I was looking at him differently, remembering the almost cool expression in his eyes that night.

I tried not to think too much about it. Josh hadn't revisited the evening, and I hadn't either. "When are you scheduled to run that marathon?"

"October, when it will mercifully be a few degrees cooler... or more, I hope."

I fought back a yawn.

"Ouch," he said, as he watched me. "Am I boring you that much?"

I ran my hand over my already sweaty face. "No, it's not you. These June brides are just killing me. And if they don't do the job, I know the July brides will finish it for them."

"You know," he said, "I find it incredibly ironic that just as YOUR work is getting crazy, MINE is getting easy and breezy."

"Yeah, you teachers have it easy with the summer breaks," I said, then cut him off before he could say it with, "and, no, I'm not being serious. Your nine month pay is spread out over twelve months, so it's not like you're getting –"

"A paid vacation," he finished. "It's like you've been listening to me or something!"

I smiled. "I always listen to you," I said softly.

He glanced at me out of the corner of his eye, then changed the subject, like he always did. Had I imagined that there might be more here than just friendship?

With every footfall I resolved to not care, to not let myself hurt over opportunities lost, opportunities that were likely never there to begin with anyway.

I made it a priority, despite the insanity of the summer weddings, to be a part of one of Grace's Bible study groups. My epiphany in Okinawa, about making my life more about Christ and less about me, coupled with the resolutions, made it even more imperative that, for the first time in years, I sign myself up for one of the summer series studies that was beginning. I carved out time in my schedule for the Thursday lunch break study in Pinnacle's department and was looking forward to it. Of course, it meant that I would likely have to revisit the conversation about my father's health with Pastor Stephen, as he was the one leading the study and would have more time to catch me after class.

Or, you know, before class even started. Like the night before.

"Hello?," I answered my phone while fumbling with my keys, trying to get into my apartment without dropping all of the contents of my purse all over the place. It had been one thing after another at work that day. Even Evelyn was looking a little less than put together after the crowds we'd seen through our offices and had declared it enough of a day at the shockingly early hour of 6pm.

I was super thankful.

"Emily?"

"Yes," I said, recognizing his voice instantly and finally getting my door open. "How are you, Stephen?" I tossed my purse onto the couch, where all the contents spilled out everywhere.

Well, so much for holding it all together.

"I'm... well, not so great, actually," he said. "It seems your dad had a bit of an oversight."

My breath caught in my throat. This was the conversation I had been avoiding since that night at youth camp. "Oh?"

"Do you remember Elaine Templeton?," he asked.

The name instantly brought to mind a sweet widow, in her seventies, who had recently passed away. She had been a church member at Grace for as long as I could remember and was such a beloved member that we had been forced to move her funeral service from the chapel to the main auditorium in order to accommodate all who wanted to pay their last respects.

"Of course, I do," I said. "Everyone knew Mrs. Elaine."

Stephen sighed. "Yeah, they did. And those who didn't were so moved by what your dad said about her at her memorial service, about how she has no need for earthly ministry now that she's worshiping at the feet of Christ... which is why I'm alarmed that she's on schedule to teach a ladies' Bible study tomorrow."

"What?"

"Oh, yeah," he said. "I have the schedule right here – teacher assignments, room numbers, times, books, all of that. And I thought it might have been a typo or an oversight, but when I asked your dad about it... he didn't know why I had a problem with Mrs. Elaine teaching."

A pause. "Did you... did you correct him?"

A pause on his end as well. It seemed that we were both struggling with knowing how much to say and even what to do.

"I didn't," he confessed. "I... I don't correct him, honestly."

I sighed. "How long has this been going on? Things like this, I mean."

"A while. A few months, maybe."

"Have you told anyone?," I swallowed back tears.

"Emily," he said softly, "I wouldn't tell anyone."

"We... we don't know what to do at this point," I began explaining. "We don't know what to think, if he even needs a doctor, and it's... complicated, you know?"

"Well, you don't owe me any explanation," he said. "I do want you to know, though, that I love Thomas and Lydia and all of you guys. And if I can do anything at all, I want to be able to. Will you keep me in the loop on this?"

I nodded, blinking back tears. "I will. Thanks, Stephen."

"That, however," he continued, "isn't why I was calling. Well, not totally why I was calling. I mean, my reason has everything to do with this. Are you ready to make my life easier, Emily?"

After hearing that he was keeping quiet about my father, I was willing to do just about anything.

"Sure."

"I need you to teach Elaine's class."

The next day, I learned a thing or two about Elaine Templeton.

The first and most important thing was that she had been, as I had well heard about, a pillar in our church when it came to ladies' Bible studies. She had been teaching this particular class for the past twenty years, and she had taught through the entire text of Scripture more than once in all those years. This made her somewhat of an accomplished theologian as far as ladies' studies go, and she was on top of her game.

The second thing was like the first. Her class, which consisted of fifteen ladies all over the age of seventy, had emulated their mentor's example, and they were even more on top of their game than she had been. They arrived with Bibles, journals, reference books, and even one very large concordance. I'm not sure how the tiny woman who carried it managed to make it into the room as the book clearly weighed three times what she weighed, but she did so with a great deal of pride and excitement, especially as she rounded the corner with the rest of the blue-haired troops to find me sitting at the front of the class.

I'm sure half of the class had diapered and fed me in the church nursery all those years ago, as they all had stories on me and each of my siblings, which they told animatedly. It was, from the way they cheered and cooed in our first introduction class, a "real treat" to have the pastor's daughter leading the study.

I was out of my league.

I knew this from the moment I told them that we would be studying the book of Romans, only to have them suddenly bombard me with facts, insights, and extraneous information about the book that left me feeling as though I knew next to nothing in comparison to their combined, collective knowledge of so many years and such thorough discipleship.

I needed some help.

"I need your help," Josh said to me the next morning, over coffee. We had just finished up another run, and I had asked him to come with me so that I could sit down, discuss my Bible study quandary, and ask him for his help.

I looked at him, puzzled. "You need my help? My help with what?"

"My niece is turning fifteen," he said. "And she had a huge to-do scheduled and organized and all that for a quinceanera." He smiled at me. "You don't even know what that is, do you?"

I knew exactly what it was, this coming of age celebration, but I had never helped to plan one myself. "I have an idea of what it is, yes," I said, blowing on my drink.

"Well, my sister-in-law had it all planned out, with everything booked, and all the arrangements made. It was an all-inclusive deal with this venue, where they handled everything. La Bella Fiesta – you know it?"

"The Beautiful Party," I said. "Yeah, I've heard of it."

"Yeah, it burned down a few days ago."

"Oh, wow," I choked.

"Yeah, not so beautiful anymore, apparently," he laughed. "Anyhow, the party was scheduled for the middle of next month. But, as you would well imagine, it's not going to happen now. At least not there. And my sister-in-law has been trying to book it somewhere else, trying to come up with all the different services they'll need, and there just isn't anything open."

I nodded. "Summertime is a busy time for those types of vendors. It's like waiting until the week before to try and arrange a wedding. Next to impossible."

"Exactly. I've already told them we can have the whole thing at the church, but without food, music, a photographer – well, there's just no point." He shrugged. "I mean, no biggie, I guess. Except that, you know, Natalie only turns fifteen once, she has the dress, her heart will be broken if it doesn't work out…" He glanced up at me. "Is any of this making you want to help a guy out?"

I smiled at him. "Do you want me to call in some favors maybe? Pull some vendors out of my magic bag?"

"Do you have a magic bag?," he asked. "Because that would be really helpful."

"I can do that and better," I told him. "I'll get it put together. Just get me your sister-in-law's number, and she and I can get it worked out."

He sighed. "Thanks, Emily, that's a real relief."

"Of course," I said, thinking about my own need for help, "I can only do it on one condition."

"What's that?"

"How much do you know about the book of Romans?"

He studied me for a moment, a slight smile of his face. "A lot… why?"

"Meet Grace's newest senior adult ladies' Bible study teacher," I said, pointing to myself.

"Senior adults! The 50+ crowd, huh?"

"No, the 70+ crowd. And I have no idea what I'm doing."

Josh leaned back in the booth, crossed his arms over his chest, and smiled at me. "Well, I know a few things about Romans. Esteemed theologian that I am and all."

I couldn't hide a smile at this. "Could you help me out a little, then? I'm not even sure where to start with teaching through it, and I'm pretty sure those ladies are going to pick me off as a fraud early on if I show up without a refresher course myself."

"You can't be a fraud," he said. "You've been in the church your whole life, right? And you're Thomas Fisher's daughter, so YOU should probably teach ME. You know more than you think."

I looked down a little self-consciously. "It's been a while since I've... really studied, you know? I even struggle to... read the Bible at all." I grimaced at him. "That sounds pretty bad, doesn't it?"

"It sounds awful," he said, giving me an incredulous look.

I felt my face blaze as he began laughing.

"I'm just kidding, Emily," he said. "No, you're fine. And who knows? Maybe that's why God has led you right to this new responsibility."

"So I can look like an idiot in front of women who are three times my age?"

"No," he smiled again, "so you can get back to where you need to be, in God's word."

"You'll help, then?"

"Sure, I will." He looked at me for a moment, then softly asked, "Why didn't you ask your dad or, you know, his associate pastor... that Stephen guy?"

"Oh," I said, sighing, thinking about dad's condition, Stephen's scrambling to hold Grace together, the mess of it all. "They're just super busy, you know?"

He nodded, not saying anything for a moment. Then, "Well, you came to the right place, because this guy here?" Pointing to himself. "Dean's list all six semesters. MDiv WITH Biblical Languages. While teaching high school fulltime, pastoring bivocationally. Without losing my mind completely."

"With credentials like that," I kidded, "you should be charging me."

"More like I'd end up paying for the privilege," he said, smiling around his coffee cup.

"Five receptions down, and three to go," Stella high-fived me on her way out of the mid-day reception and on her way back to the kitchen to prepare for the next one. That last one had been a bit of a mess with the chocolate fountain beginning to spurt and sputter at guests halfway through the bride and groom's first dance. The catastrophe had led to an emergency call to an outside vendor, one we had never used but who was able to be there at a moment's notice and had more than enough experience with confectionary machinery to adequately assess our problem and have it fixed. I had a great conversation with the guy who came out, who turned out to be the owner of his own dessert reception business. I had taken his business card and his information, filing it away mentally for near future reference. Alyssa Star had just about determined that a dessert reception was the way to go for her own wedding, and I thought this might be the most affordable vendor I could find to help make her celebration what it needed to be.

Ah, yes. I was still doing consulting under the radar. Totally inappropriate and likely completely unethical, not to mention absolutely illogical when viewed through the lens of all that I was already swamped with as far as hotel clients went. But I did so enjoy finding deals and arranging it all for Alyssa, as her wedding plans came together for a celebration that (if I was being completely honest) would be nicer than any I had done at the hotel. The thought of this made me smile.

"That's what I like to see," Evelyn trilled as we passed one another in the hallway. "Pleasant, joyful expressions even in the midst of mayhem. And there IS mayhem. The Webb ceremony is set to go in thirty minutes, and there are groomsmen without socks, a late instrumentalist, and the flower girl just vomited in the grand ballroom." At the mention of this, she finally noticed the chocolate stains on my clothes. "And speaking of vomit, pray tell, what is that?"

I was so surprised to hear her actually say the word that it took me a moment to recover. "Oh, it's chocolate," I said. "The fountain had some problems, but it's fixed now. And I have a new contact to add to the files."

"Wonderful," Evelyn trilled. "Our little undercover, under the radar Emily, always finding secret deals," she said, giving me a knowing smile.

Did she know about Alyssa Star? Before I could obsess over the danger in this, imagine the warning in her eyes, she was moving again.

"Three prospective brides observing the Murphy wedding tonight, dear," she said over her shoulder. "Let's put our best foot forward!"

"Always," I said to her retreating back, turning towards my own list of preparations for our busy night. "Always."

The book of Romans was coming alive.

All of Scripture was coming alive, actually. I didn't know how much of it to attribute to my sweet Bible study class, who always came prepared and who always taught me so much. I didn't know how much of it could be attributed to all the mornings I spent in study and prayer these days, as I started and ended them in God's Word. And I didn't know how much of it could be attributed to Josh, who had been faithfully studying with me and teaching me as we went. All I know is that God's Word was meaning more lately than it had in quite some time.

"And that," Josh whispered to me at the end of another morning spent with him over commentaries and lexicons, "is a question likely only answered in eternity."

We had been going up to the seminary after our morning runs, studying together and discussing my class. He had been such a great teacher, and it always seemed as though our time together was so short. Too short.

"So you don't have the definitive answer on election and predestination," I whispered back in the hushed stillness of the third floor stacks.

"If I did," he smiled, "I would have explained it to you long ago. I can't believe how much you've been learning. It's incredible to watch how you've grown."

"It's amazing," I told him, "how no matter how many times I've read it before, God's Word still has something to say that's new and life-changing. You know? It's not that His Word has changed – it's that it's changing me."

He smiled at this. "And the truly incredible thing is that no matter how old we get, how many days we see, no matter what the challenges we weather and survive, it will still be fresh and new and able to change us."

"Living and active," I said.

"And sharper than any two edged sword," he finished for me.

"It makes me sorely regret all the time I've been neglecting it, you know? Why have I stayed away and not been in it when it's able to speak truth to all my circumstances?"

He shrugged. "Isn't that the question? And as we concluded today, there are a lot of questions that just aren't so easily answered right now. That's why we've got the rest of eternity to figure it out."

"Wow," I whispered, sitting back in my seat and crossing my arms over my chest. "I'll bet your preaching is amazing."

He laughed out loud at this, then moved back to a whisper after seeing the looks this earned him from the students gathered near our table. "Well, I'm no Thomas Fisher."

"Well, he's got a few years on you," I managed through my own hushed laughter. "I can't tell you how much I appreciate what you've done to help me. What you're still doing, actually." A pause. "This has been, very literally, life-changing for me. Your church is very lucky to get to sit under your teaching."

He studied his hands for a moment. "I appreciate that," he said softly. "You know, I know you're really involved at Grace and all, but if you ever get a free Sunday or something, you should visit Redeemer. I have it on good authority that there would be a place for you."

"That's really tempting," I said, looking at his hands as they continued to fidget. "But I'm pretty sure I wouldn't understand half of it, would I? Me no habloing espanol and all, right?"

"No habloing for sure," he said with a playful grimace. "But I would totally translate it all for you later. From up here," he tapped his head, "right to you."

"Well, then," I said. "I'll definitely have to."

She had, in her words, BIG news.

Unfortunately, Sara's big news meant that we would all three have to meet up. Not that I was opposed to meeting up with my friends, but lately, Melissa and I had been having enough meetings to endanger any good will we had between the two of us. Trish Thibideaux must have had a million frequent flyer miles to use because she flew from New Orleans to DFW every weekend to help with wedding plans. This far out, there weren't enough wedding plans to necessitate so many meetings. Melissa had made the big decisions – the date and the venue – already, and the rest could stand to wait at least another month. Her mother-in-law –to-be, though, was on the ball, so to speak, which meant she was in town every weekend, which meant that I had an arranged meeting with the two of them every weekend. I was the unofficial wedding coordinator, which was (in Melissa's code) another word for "mediator."

Trish was, in my opinion, just an energetic mother-in-law who was trying very desperately to be a team player and to win Melissa's favor from the beginning. The saying "a daughter is a daughter for life; a son is a son until he gets a wife" is an apt one – I've seen the truth of it more times than I can count in my line of work. I can only guess that Trish felt winning over Melissa early on meant that she wouldn't lose Beau in the long run, and she was working at it with gusto. Unfortunately, her son was marrying a woman who was the polar opposite of his mother, and her efforts, though admirable, were stifling Melissa to death.

This is just exactly what she wanted to talk about as we met up at my apartment and waited for Sara to arrive with the pizza and her BIG news.

"She's coming into town next week," Melissa droned from the couch, where she had laid herself out with her hand draped across her forehead dramatically. It was like she was the patient and I was the therapist. "I tried to tell her not to, but she knows someone who owns a bridal boutique. Something about sorority sisters or something. I don't know. I tried to tell her that it was too early to try on dresses –"

"Well, it's not really that early," I said. "It's actually a great time to find a dress."

She glowered at me from lowered eyelids. "Are you on my side or not?"

"Your side, of course," I sighed.

"Anyway," she said, throwing her hand back over her eyes, her eternity band winking at me, "she said that it was a great time to find a dress and that this friend who owned this shop could shut down for a day so I could come in and have the whole place to myself, staff and all. Trish arranged it all, along with pedicures and spa treatments, for this weekend. ANOTHER weekend gone."

"What a witch," I said.

"Tell me about it!," she exclaimed.

Before I could point out the obvious – that she was getting a mother-in-law most women would kill to have, Sara breezed through the front door, pizza box in hand.

"Hey, girls!," she shouted. "It's hot out there!"

"It's hot in here," Melissa continued to complain. "Emily, does your AC even work?"

"It does," I said, checking the thermostat on my way to help Sara with the pizza. "But unfortunately, this is a crappy apartment, and it doesn't retain cool air quite like your exquisite mansion does."

"It's not a mansion," Melissa said.

"Compared to this?," Sara asked. "It so is. And no offense, Emily."

"None taken," I said. "Hey, you got cheese!"

"That's all that was 'hot and ready,'" she said.

"It works," I said. "Melissa, do you want a piece?"

"Sure," she came over to the table as I began putting down plates and Sara began pulling drinks out of the fridge.

"How are wedding plans coming along?," Sara asked Melissa, and I shot her a look.

"Oh, I don't want to talk about it," Melissa muttered.

"Hallelujah," I mouthed to Sara, who smirked behind the Coke bottle she was placing on the table.

"It's just Trish is driving me crazy!," Melissa exclaimed.

"Too many pedicures and spa treatments," I said.

"Oh, well I can see how that would be... rough?" Sara looked at me, confused.

"You just wait," Melissa cried, pointing her finger at us. "You just wait until you both have crazy mothers-in-law who monopolize all your time and expect YOU to be a bridezilla."

I wanted to point out that her attitude made her the very worst kind of bridezilla out there and that the only crazy person in the relationship was her (and maybe Beau for wanting to hitch his wagon up to hers), but Sara interrupted me, mercifully, before I could get the words out.

"Well, like I told you, I have some really big news."

We sat at the table and looked at her with anticipation.

"I didn't sign a teaching contract for next year."

Melissa and I looked at one another. "You're not going to teach anymore? Or just not at the same school?"

"I'll still be teaching," Sara smiled, "just not at the school. And not in Fort Worth."

Melissa's face paled. "You're moving away?"

"Not until after the new year," she reassured her, "so, I'll be there for the wedding."

"I don't give two flips about the wedding," Melissa said. "I'm upset that you're moving! Why? Where are you going?"

Sara couldn't stop smiling. "Remember a few weeks ago, after youth camp, when I went out of town? Well, it was for an interview with the mission board."

The pieces began falling together in our minds with a certain sense of finality. I sat back in my chair, stunned.

"You're... moving to Costa Rica?"

"Yes," Sara said. "They've offered me a position, teaching at a mission school in San Juan. My contract will be for three years. Initially, at least."

"Initially?," Melissa asked. "Holy cow."

We sat in silence for a moment. Melissa and I exchanged looks, then glanced over to Sara mournfully, as she continued beaming.

"Guys, this is a GOOD thing," she said. "I have skills that are really in demand there. And with this appointment, I can be in Costa Rica, not only teaching but helping with short term groups that come through, building relationships with nationals there on the field, and really being a part of the team already there that I worked with when I went. It's like a dream come true!"

Melissa looked at me helplessly. We had all been apart during college, of course, but something about this seemed more permanent, more definitive. With Melissa getting married and now Sara leaving the country, I began to feel as though the world was shifting beneath me, tumbling relationships about as it did so, leaving me wondering what would be left.

But this? This WAS a good thing. We had known Sara wasn't the same, that she had left part of her heart there in Costa Rica, and that her decision was one that hadn't been taken lightly.

"I'm sad, of course," I told her. "But I'm happy that you've gotten this position and that you're going to be able to do exactly what you've been wanting to do."

"Yeah," Melissa said. "We're going to miss you!"

"I'm going to miss you guys," she said. "I still have to raise my support money, though, so it's not entirely a done deal. But I have a feeling that it'll all work out." A pause. "Why don't we eat before our pizza gets any colder, okay?"

We ate quietly, processing this all, as I thought about what it meant. I had a feeling it would all work out like Sara had said... and I wondered what that meant for the three of us.

8 JULY

It was going to be a month of... well, stretching. For some of us, at least.

"I don't even think I know someone in need," Melissa muttered to herself. "Unless I can count helping Beau's mother to butt her nose out of my business?" She looked at us hopefully.

We were having lunch together and discussing what we were going to do for our resolutions for the month.

Some of us were obviously having more trouble than others.

"I don't think that's in the spirit of the resolution," Sara offered. She glanced over at me before taking another bite. "How about you?"

I shrugged. "I'm not really sure either." My father was doing well – better than he had been in a long while. My constant need to be so involved with him and my mother, helping out where I was needed and even where I wasn't, had all but diminished.

Sara regarded us both as we munched through our salads, clear exasperation on her face. "This is one that you should be super eager to do!," she pleaded with us, appealing to our charitable sides. "So many needs out there, and you two can't even –"

"So many needs out there FOR YOU, maybe," Melissa said, unaffected completely by where she was coming from. "Yes, since you're surrounded by needs from the field, communicating back and forth all the time and preparing to leave. For us? We're not face to face with poverty and need every day. Give us a little room here to figure things out, okay?"

Sara clamped her lips together tightly. Her exuberance for Costa Rica was admirable, but ever since she had returned home, there was little else she discussed, shared, or (apparently) thought about. After a moment of silence, she seemed to guess my thoughts and said, "Well, as a matter of fact, I found a need right here – a local need – that has nothing to do with Costa Rica."

"Oh, yeah?," Melissa asked.

"Yes," she said, then cast a shy glance in my direction. "I got to know a friend of Emily's at youth camp, and there's a need in his church, working with the youth choir as they go on tour this summer."

My head snapped up as I fought to keep my expression neutral. I could guess which "friend" she meant but couldn't begin to explain why the thought of beautiful, sweet Sara spending a good portion of the summer with MY Josh left me feeling a little nauseated. Laughing over the antics of teenagers, spending late nights in rehearsals, experiencing those spiritual highs that came with ministering together, falling helplessly in love...

Wait. MY Josh? What was I even thinking?

Melissa, oblivious to my internal strife gave a laugh. "Youth choir? That'll be a beating." Sara frowned at her. "What church?"

"Iglesia Redeemer," she said, confirming my fears. Iglesia Redeemer, Pastor Joshua Morales. How many times had I driven by their sign and smiled to myself, thinking of his face?

"Ah-ha!," Melissa shouted, causing me to drop my fork. "A bi-LINGUAL church! Trying to work on your Spanish. This is so totally about Costa Rica."

"Not about it," Sara said defensively, "but, yes, that's a definite benefit." She shrugged as she speared another leaf of lettuce. "Besides, Josh is a really nice guy, and I have the time to help out. It'll be fun!"

I cautiously studied her face for signs that "really nice guy" meant something more, chiding myself for caring either way. Josh wasn't mine. He had never made a move to be anything more than a friend to me, and... well, that was that.

Wasn't it?

Seth was still "cooking," as Jessica described it. She was thirty-two weeks along, and as she told me, would likely require the standard pitocin induction at forty-two weeks, which is when she had delivered all four of my nephews. Those inductions had been torment for the rest of the family, as Jess refused any pain medication each and every time, choosing to manage her discomfort "naturally" by screeching at everyone within a ten mile radius of the delivery room, up until the moment when she would inevitably yell, "Get the freakin' doctor in here, because I've got a HEAD coming out of my –"

Oh, how I was dreading Part Five of this drama.

"I'll be TEN MONTHS pregnant," she told me in the McDonald's PlayPlace. I had taken an extended lunch break after she called me at work in a tiffy, obviously irritated by the July heat and needing to vent. "Ten months!," she exclaimed, her eyes trailing over to my four nephews. "Stuie! Do NOT lick that!" She looked at me, a disgusted expression on her face. "Do you think they sanitize this thing daily?"

I was fairly certain that McDonald's didn't sanitize every inch of their playground equipment, but my increasingly terrifying pregnant sister didn't need to hear that. "Sure they do," I said, popping another McNugget into my mouth.

"Wow, it's hot," she said, having forgotten the germs all over Stuart's tongue. "I always tell Nick that I'm NEVER going to have another summer baby, and it just keeps happening. It's like I can only give birth when it's over 110 degrees outside or something. Which would be great if I would JUST GIVE BIRTH ON TIME!" She stuffed a french fry in her mouth. "You know what the worst thing is?," she asked around the mouthful. "The OB says I'm not dilated. Not even a peep."

I cringed at her loud use of the word "dilated" and looked around to see if anyone was listening. The PlayPlace was full of mommies, though, who likely were having conversations of their own about dilation, cervical mucus, tearing in unmentionable places –

"Hemorrhoids!," Jessica shouted at me. "My cervix won't budge an inch, but I've got hemorrhoids already! How is that FAIR?!"

"Good grief, Jess," I hissed at her. "Could you keep it down a little?"

She smirked at me. "Are you embarrassed?"

Duh. "Well, yeah," I said, making a face at her. "Besides, you're not far enough along to even WANT to be... dilated. Ugh, I can't believe you've gotten me to say that word or to even KNOW what it means!"

She leaned back in her seat, then jerked forward. "SCOTT! Do NOT kick your brother!" She slid back again. "You know, that's the great thing about motherhood. After a whole delivery room full of people has watched you poop while you push – not to mention ALL of your business – you really have no shame left. I think my OB has seen more of my body than Nick has. Probably more than even I have! No shame, I tell you." She leaned back in her chair, folding her hands over her bump. "Which is good, you know, since breastfeeding opens up a whole new world of opportunities that would shame the average person. But not me. Not now. Not after four children."

I took a drink. "What an enlightening treatise on the gift of motherhood."

She smiled. "I'm just saying, is all." Sam came toddling over for another sip of juice, and she put her hands gently on his face, wiping away the remnants of ketchup, smiling at him adoringly, and kissing him all in the same moment. We watched him take his drink then run back over to the equipment.

"I just know this will be another induction," she said.

"Maybe he'll come on his own," I said to her, hope in my voice. "For ALL of our sakes maybe he'll come completely on his own."

Jessica rolled her eyes. "Highly unlikely, Em. Highly unlikely."

Alyssa Star and I continued to meet on the sly. Undercover, if you will.

Well, not really. I met with her in my free time, never at the hotel, and never at my office. Over the weeks we had become friends, so it wasn't even like I was stealing clients. I was chatting with a friend over lunch, discussing the details of her wedding.

A wedding that I had turned away from my company, of course. I tried to push these thoughts aside when we met, though.

We met at Alyssa's venue of choice – a lovely landscaped garden on the grounds of a very quaint bed and breakfast. The B&B owners, an elderly little couple who had inherited the large plantation-style home, had never had a wedding there. But after going over some details with me and meeting the lovely bride, they were extremely accommodating and, more importantly, eager to make this event a huge success. They were working with us to house the reception and dance in the house, and I was working with them to guarantee full bookings for a solid week during an off-season.

This meant that I would be doing more weddings independently. I had gone into it knowing the implications, knowing what I was doing… yet, still feeling torn, conflicted, and most of all incredulous that I was doing it. I couldn't help myself, though. As Alyssa described in detail what she envisioned, and as I turned those details into her future reality, I felt as though I was finally doing what I was created to do.

And that was worth it all.

Natalie's quinceanera was scheduled for the last Friday of the month. Her mother, Josh's sister-in-law Debbie, had been so wonderful to work with, and she was so pleased by the setup I had done that she was able to really enjoy being there for her daughter's big night. Evelyn was taking the small rehearsal dinner scheduled for the evening at the hotel, freeing me up to be part of the celebration as well. The party was underway by the time I was finally able to leave the kitchen (where a miscommunication in catering had caused some unexpected work for anyone – me – who had free hands to prep buffet servers), and I was pleased to see that people were already dancing and having a great time.

Rubbing my hands together, afraid that the food smell would remain for days despite the washing and scrubbing, I scanned the crowd for Josh. He had been gone for two weeks with the youth choir, and I had missed being with him. Our mornings of running and studying Scripture together this past month had done nothing to diminish the feelings I was having towards him, and I had counted down the days of the youth tour, eagerly waiting for him to come home.

"Great party." The very welcome voice came from over my left shoulder. I turned around with a smile on my face, taking in Josh's own glowing expression as he looked at me.

"Hey!," I said, touching his shoulder briefly, awkwardly, stopping just short of the hug that I wanted to give him. "I'm glad to see you survived the tour."

"Narrowly survived," he said, laughing. "I think it's going to take a whole week to catch up on the sleep I've missed. What a trip!"

"Mrs. Fisher?" A worker from the kitchen turned my attention away from Josh and the million questions I wanted to ask, the first and most important being *can we ditch this party and go somewhere alone together*?

"It's Miss Fisher... actually, just Emily," I told the worker, flustered. "What do you need?"

He wrung his hands. "More help. We've run into a problem with some of the desserts."

Oy, what a night. I turned to Josh. "I'll be back in a bit. Just a minor emergency."

A whole hour later, my hands now also smelled like chocolate and strawberries as I made a mental note to remember to triple check orders with this particular caterer in the future. My hair was a sweaty mess, my dress had flour all over it, and I probably smelled awful. I came back to the party to see that everything was progressing just fine without me when my eyes found Josh, laughing and smiling with... some other woman.

My heart sank as he caught my eye and motioned me over. I walked to him numbly, telling myself that I had no claim on him anyway, when the mystery woman turned around.

"Oh my gosh, Emily!"

I blinked. "Sara! What are you doing here?"

Besides looking so beautiful and adorable, the exact opposite of everything I was even at my best, not to mention at my worst after fighting the desserts for an hour.

She smiled. "Well, Natalie invited me, of course!" She laid a hand tenderly on Josh's forearm. I could feel a vein in my neck begin to bulge. "We had SUCH a great time on the choir tour, and even though she put in the guest list a whole month ago, she begged me to come. And Josh totally agreed."

Josh smiled at her, then glanced at me, "Well, we HAD to have Sara here!"

She giggled... and I wanted to kill her. My best friend, Sara. What was wrong with me?

"Oh my gosh!," she shrieked. Could she read my mind? "That kid's hat!" She pointed animatedly to a kid all the way across the room. "Do you see that hat? Do you REMEMBER the story about Caleb and that hat?," she asked Josh, giggling between syllables.

He started laughing as well. "Oh, that was hilarious!"

Great. An inside joke. That I totally didn't get. Between my best friend and my... running buddy. Hmm, that didn't seem to really capture Josh at all, but —

My phone began ringing, saving me from the blush that crept up my neck. I indicated that I needed to take the call, and pressed the talk button.

"Hello?"

"Emily?" My mother answered, panic in her voice.

"Mom, is something wrong?"

"Your sister is in labor, but there are some complications. I think you should come to the hospital right now."

"I'm on my way."

The hospital was only about a fifteen minute drive from the party. I had been able to rush out quickly, after making my apologies to the Morales family and checking to make sure that Josh could handle the rest of the festivities. He had offered to take me to the hospital himself, but I told him that it wasn't that big of an emergency.

I second-guessed that assessment as soon as I found my way into the labor and delivery wing and saw my mother consoling Nick.

"Oh, Emily," she said, relief apparent on her face, "you're here."

"Is she still in labor?," I asked, worry weighing heavier and heavier on me by the moment.

"No," Mom said, shaking her head. "Seth was born about twenty minutes ago. It went fast… so fast. Jess wasn't even in labor for an hour hardly."

"She said it was a backache," Nick said softly. "Just a really bad backache. The doctor said sometimes women feel labor back there. But we didn't realize…"

"By the time they got here, they couldn't stop her. They would have ideally put her on bedrest for the next few weeks, to give him some more time, but it was too late when they got here."

"Well, still," I said, "thirty-four weeks… that's far enough along, right?"

Nick and Mom exchanged a glance.

"Geez, is he okay?," I practically shouted at them.

"No, he's in the NICU. He… he's not breathing right. His lungs weren't ready, and he's just… just really small," she managed, beginning to cry.

"Is Jess okay?," I asked, looking to Nick.

He nodded. "She's upset, but the labor wasn't hard. She did great." He looked over to the delivery room. "I should probably get back in there to check on her, to let her know what I know about Seth... which isn't a lot at this point." He put his hand on my mother's back reassuringly.

"Are your parents here?," I asked.

"On their way," he said.

"Where are the boys? Who's watching the boys?," I asked.

"Your father. I dropped him off with the boys at Jess's house," my mother choked out. My eyes widened a little at this, which she picked up on. "Honestly, Emily, the best thing you can do right now is go and help him. Take care of the boys, until we can figure out what's going on and what we're going to need to do, okay?"

"I'm on it."

"Dad?," I asked, cautiously opening up Nick and Jess's front door, alarmed when the boys met me. It had taken me longer to get there than planned, as I fielded calls from Nick in the NICU, then my mother in delivery, finally turning off my phone completely so as to get there faster.

It wasn't fast enough, though, as evidenced by the look on Sean's face.

"Aunt Emmy," he said, "Grandpa's playing a MEAN game."

"He... what?," I asked. "What kind of game?"

"He's pretendin' like he doesn't know our names!"

"Aunt Emmy, where's Mommy? Is da baby here?," Sam asked me, sucking on his thumb.

"Okay, guys," I said, taking a shaky breath. Where to start? "Where are your brothers?"

"Scott's in the playroom, but I don't know where Stuie is," Sean said, turning to go towards his room.

Oh, no. I began walking briskly towards the kitchen, looking for Stuart, praying that he hadn't gotten himself into anything dangerous. No Stuart in the kitchen. No Stuart in the living room. Then, I heard my father's voice.

"And then, David took that smooth stone, put it into his slingshot, and knocked that giant Goliath right off his feet!"

I hurried towards Nick and Jessica's bedroom to find him sitting in the rocker, Stuart sleeping peacefully in his arms. He looked up as soon as I entered the room and smiled.

"Lydia," he said, holding Stuart even tighter, "I told you I could get Matthew to sleep. See?"

My breath caught in my throat. The problem was too big to ignore now, wasn't it? We had crossed a line, my father and I had.

"Yeah... I see," I said softly.

"He's a lot harder than the girls were, isn't he?," he murmured, kissing the top of Stuie's head.

"I've always thought so," I said, swallowing past the lump in my throat. I walked over to him, laid a hand on his arm, and said, "Could you just... just sit there with him and rest for a minute?"

"Of course," he said, smiling at me. "You should get some rest while you can, you know."

I made my way back into the hallway, fumbled over to the television, and put a DVD into the player. It was way past the boys' bedtime, but that was the least of my concerns. I hustled them back into the living room, started their movie, and left them to fall asleep on their own.

Who to call? What to do? I was running out of options here.

I turned my cell phone back on, ignoring the list of missed calls I had gotten in the meantime. I punched in my mother's number and held my breath, waiting for her to pick up.

"Hello?"

"Mom, praise God," I said.

"Oh, you heard then?," she sighed. "Jess is already back on her feet and has been up to see Seth. That's good news. They've set up his feeding tube, and she's already pumping. She's so determined already to get him through this NICU thing, and the doctors have said he's stronger than most, so –"

"Mom," I cut her off. "We have a problem with Dad."

A moment of silence. Then, "What's going on?"

"It's bad," I said, tears beginning to roll down my cheeks. "Really bad. You need to… we need to get him home."

"Okay," she said, her voice all business, hiding the shaky emotion I knew was behind it. "I can come out that way and get him, just as soon as –"

"Why don't you just go straight to the house as soon as Nick's parents get to the hospital? That'll save some time. I'll call Pastor Stephen to see if he can come out to help, or –"

"Great idea," Mom said. Then, "It'll be okay. We'll figure this out."

I had just finished moving all the boys, now asleep, to their rooms when Stephen arrived.

"Stephen! Wasn't expecting you this late!," Dad said, smiling at him.

"Hey, Thomas," he managed, finding my eyes quickly. "Just in the neighborhood and thought I'd drop in to see if you guys needed any help."

"Well, Emily and I are managing just fine." I breathed a sigh of relief to hear my own name, after an evening of being called Lydia.

"Hey, Dad," I said, "I think I've got it covered here. Maybe Stephen can give you a lift back home, huh?"

"Yeah," Stephen said, picking up on my cues. "I'd love the chance to get to talk through some church business with you." I smiled my thanks to him.

"Well, okay," Dad said. "I just need to get my wallet... and I'm not sure where I put it. Lydia? Do you know where that wallet is?"

I saw Stephen's eyebrows go up as my heart sank.

"Umm... I can help you find it," I managed. We began searching the kitchen as my cell phone rang from its post by the front door.

"Stephen, can you get that for me?," I asked, too far to grab it myself.

"Sure," he said, picking it up. "This is Stephen," he answered, listening for a moment. "She's not available right now. Can I take a message?" He nodded. "Okay. Will do."

"Oh, here it is!," Dad exclaimed loudly. "Right in my pocket. Don't know why I didn't look there first."

"Me neither," I said. "You go on home with Stephen, okay?"

"Sure thing, Em," Dad said, patting me on the arm.

"Hey, Emily," Stephen said, as my dad made his way out the front door. "I'll call you later. Oh, and someone named Josh just called to say he was praying for your sister. And for you."

We needed all the prayers we could get. "Thanks, Stephen."

Good days and bad days. Good days and bad days. The next few weeks were full of them, both for Seth and for my father. They were lung issues, even heart concerns, with my preemie nephew, and the doctors weren't positive with their assessments. Common problems? Yes. Insignificant things that would clear up with time? Maybe. Either way, only time would tell, and a combination of good days and bad days were the only way to get through it. They had told Jess that she couldn't do much beside help with feeding while he was in the NICU, a task that made her even more of a zombie than she had been with her other children. She carried her pump with her constantly like a good luck charm, back and forth from the hospital to her home, where Nick's mother moved in temporarily to help out.

I did what I could to help out as well, relieving Nick's mother, driving my sister, and taking the boys to visit Seth one by one through the NICU during visiting hours. Evelyn had been surprisingly gracious and more than generous when it came to my schedule, somehow sympathizing with my sister's challenges and worries. For the first time ever, I wondered if perhaps there was more to the story of why Evelyn, who could certainly have been a mother to teenagers by now, remained childless. In any event, I was thankful for her understanding.

My mother was struggling. Seth's birthday had finally given her enough definitive evidence of a problem greater than any we had feared regarding my father's health.

"Still, though," she told me one afternoon, as we passed one another in the hospital's waiting room, "we've got to get through Seth's homecoming first. Soon. Soon, he'll come home, and we'll deal with all the rest."

All the rest. My father's diminishing capacity to comprehend reality had been reduced to this. He needed help, real help, but my mother was too stressed and too afraid to get it. Instead, she never left him alone, going with him everywhere to protect him, to keep his mix-ups from being detected by anyone, and to preserve his dignity. As much as we both disagreed with her methods, Stephen and I enabled her behavior, making ourselves available to do whatever she thought best.

I reached my limit the Sunday that Dad got to church and told my mother that this wasn't Grace, then went on to describe the Grace we had known some twenty years earlier. Mom took him home without even discussing it with anyone, leaving Stephen only thirty minutes to put together a sermon and leaving me so disgusted, tired, and emotionally spent that I got in my car before the service started and drove away.

I wasn't even sure what my plan was until my car was in a parking space at Iglesia Redeemer.

I had called Josh back the night of Natalie's quinceanera. He had so patiently listed to me explain what was going on with my sister, and in tears, I had shared everything that was going on with my dad. In the weeks that followed, as my nephews and my family consumed more and more of my time, he had been so understanding, changing his schedule to fit our runs in, helping me even more with preparations for my ladies' Bible study, and praying for me, praying together with me, every chance he got.

I needed a break from life, and I wanted it to be with Josh.

I entered the sanctuary timidly, scanning the gathering crowd for Sara, who was nowhere in sight. She was splitting her time on Sundays and Wednesdays between Redeemer and Grace, helping out with the youth here, then meeting up with her Costa Rica spring trip teammates at Grace on other weeks.

This must have been a Grace week for her, because she was nowhere in sight.

Just as I began to get anxious about not really knowing anyone there except for the pastor, Natalie spotted me and came over enthusiastically, giving me a huge hug.

"Emily!," she shouted. "I didn't know you were coming!"

Natalie and I had spent considerably less time together than I had spent with her mother, Debbie, while we were planning the party, but as Josh had shared with me earlier, I had quickly become one of her favorite people after all of her friends had gone on and on about how great her party had been.

"Didn't know I was coming until just a little while ago," I told her, catching Debbie's eye as I did so, as she walked over to where I was standing. As Natalie continued gushing on about her party all these weeks later, more of Josh's relatives, most of whom I had met briefly at the party, began making their way towards me with hugs and hellos.

It had been a long time since I had been a visitor at any church, but so far, this church? Was potentially the most welcoming church I had ever been to. Before I knew it, I was being moved along in the sea of Morales family members from the back of the church where I planned on inconspicuously sitting up to the very front.

"Josh is usually already out here," Debbie whispered to me as we sat down together, "but there was some issue with plumbing in one of the bathrooms." She shrugged. "Not that he knows much about plumbing, of course, but he's always doing odd jobs around here. Putting out fires and all, you know."

As a pastor's daughter, I knew all about it. Lately, though, the only fires being put out at Grace were the fires my dad seemed to be causing in his confusion. A lump formed in my throat as I thought about how confused he must be to be at home on a Sunday morning and how stressed out poor Stephen must be, trying to clean up the mess left behind.

Before my eyes could fill up with tears for the hundredth time this week alone, an elderly gentleman made his way to the front for announcements. A small praise team, mostly made up of teenagers I'm sure Sara had spent all summer working with, sang a few songs, and another gentleman came to the front to pray.

It was entirely in Spanish. All of it – the singing, the praying, the announcements. So much for being a bilingual church.

I was beginning to doubt the wisdom of being here, at a service that I wouldn't be able to understand at all, when a side door opened and Josh stepped into the room, his Bible in his hands as the ushers began taking up the offering.

After another song, he took to the pulpit, making a joke about the plumbing and apologizing for the messy way he looked.

I only knew this because Debbie was whispering the English translation, to which I responded, in a whisper back to her, "He looks good to me."

Before I could wish the words back into my mouth, she smiled knowingly and patted my hand.

As the laughter from the congregation subsided, Josh opened up his Bible, glancing over at his family and freezing as his eyes met mine. He stared for a moment, smiled back down at his passage, and began reading.

Debbie patted my hand again, softly laughing to herself.

"Come to lunch with us," Debbie said as the service ended. "Grandma cooks about two tons of food every Sunday, so there's more than enough. It's amazing that none of our guys have fallen over dead from heart attacks yet after all these years of her stuffing them full, you know?"

I paused for a moment on the familiarity and camaraderie behind "our guys," then responded with, "I'm sure it's great, but..." I hesitated, not wanting to barge in on Josh's family time.

"Hey!" Suddenly, Josh was standing right with us, smiling at me.

"Well, that's the fastest you've ever made it down here," Debbie smirked at him. "And the only time I can remember you coming down to see your family before greeting the rest of the church as they left."

Josh glanced at her with a warning in his eyes. "Have to greet the visitors, right?" He extended his hand, taking mine in his, and formally said, "Welcome to Iglesia Redeemer. So glad you could visit with us today."

I smiled at his formality. "Thanks. I really enjoyed the sermon."

"Didn't understand a word of it, did you?," he grinned.

"It was about Jesus, right?"

"You got the gist of it," Debbie said, patting me on the shoulder affectionately. "You," she pointed her finger right into Josh's chest, "can tell her all about it at lunch. She's coming with us to Grandma's." I opened my mouth to protest, but she hugged me close to her before I could say anything. "Josh will tell you how to get there. See you in a few!"

And with that, she was on her way back down the aisle. My mouth was still hanging open, wordless.

"You don't have to come if you don't want to," Josh said. "Debbie is really pushy, I know."

"She made me feel right at home here. All of your family did, actually."

He smiled. "I'm glad to hear it. And I'm glad you're here... but I can assume that something's not right if you're not at Grace this morning.

Are you okay?"

I shook my head. "Bad day for my dad. Really bad." I glanced at my watch. "I should probably call and check on him, but I'm just so... exhausted."

He ran his hands along the back of the pew, thinking. "If you'll give me just fifteen minutes to say good bye to everyone and close the place up, we can talk," he said. Then after a slight hesitation, "And maybe you'd let me take you to lunch with the family?"

"Are you sure I won't be in the way?," I asked, wanting very much to be with him.

"No, you'd be right where you belong," he smiled at me.

Josh's grandmother didn't speak any English. Josh seemed relieved by this when upon meeting me, she smiled broadly, kissed me, and began exclaiming many things, much to the amusement of everyone else, my confusion, and Josh's embarrassment.

"Natalie," I asked, when Josh made no move to explain, "what did she say?"

Natalie was all too happy to let me know. "She just said –"

"Oh, no, you don't!," Josh told her, ushering me over to a seat at the table. This only made the rest of the family members gathered there roar louder with their laughter.

"Grandma loves you, Emily," Debbie managed. "As do we all. And I do mean ALL of us." She shot another furtive glance at Josh, but I hardly noticed since all of my attention was quickly and fully focused on the spread set before me. Grandma Morales had gone above and beyond the call of duty. Debbie's estimation of two tons of food fell woefully short of the outstanding amount that loaded down the table we all crowded around.

"It looks great," I whispered to Josh, as everyone settled into their seats.

"Oh, it's better than great," he smiled, taking my hand as we all bowed our heads and he prayed.

After I had helped him shut down the church, Josh had driven me over to his grandmother's house. I had updated him on my dad's condition on the way over, detailing this most recent episode for him as he listened. Much to my horrified surprise, the caring concern on his face made me cry. Josh said nothing for a while, just reached over and held my hand as he drove and I wiped away my tears.

"You know," he said, as we neared the house, "we don't have to stay here. I can take you anywhere you want to go. Wherever you can relax and just escape from what's going on."

"No," I said, drying my eyes. "It will do me a world of good to hang out with you and get my mind off of everything while we're with your family. Honestly."

And, as we sat around the table, eating, talking, and laughing together with Josh's huge family, I knew it was true. For a few wonderful hours, I was able to distance myself from it all.

Then, as we were saying our goodbyes, my phone rang.

"It's Stephen," I said, when Josh leaned over to check my phone with me. After a moment's hesitation, he looked at me, his expression somehow changed. "Everything okay?"

"Probably just calling to check on my dad," I sighed. "I should probably get back."

He nodded shortly. "No problem."

The drive back was much quieter, as we intermittently came up with an amended schedule for our running and Bible study for the week. We pulled into the church lot, right next to my car, and he got out quickly enough to open my door for me, as he had done every other time that morning.

"Thanks," I said, taking the hand he offered to help me down.

"Can I pray for you before you leave?," he asked, holding onto my hand still.

I nodded, and he prayed such soothing, calm words over me, over my family, over all that we were facing in the days ahead.

As he finished his prayer, I reached my arms around his neck and pulled him in tightly for an embrace. He hesitated only a moment before putting his arms around me and holding me close.

"Call me if I can do anything to help, okay?," he whispered in my ear before releasing his hold on me.

"Okay," I said, not wanting to let go of him, but doing so anyway, as I moved away from his side to go back to my life as I now knew it.

We were on our thirty-fourth game of Candyland. Yes, I had been counting.

"Oh, boys," I said, "how many times can we play this game?"

Sean clapped his hands. "I can play it ALL DAY, Aunt Emmy!"

All day AND all night, it seemed, as I looked out the front window, noticing that the sun had gone down as we had been Candyland marathon-ing it. I had been with the boys since lunch, after fitting all my meetings at the hotel into a busy morning.

Just as we were about to start a new round of the game, Nick came in the front door, starting a chorus of loud cheers from the boys and silent praises from my own heart. It wasn't that I didn't love spending time here – I was just worn completely out.

"Emily," Nick said, in between giving hugs to all four boys, "thanks for staying so late."

"No problem," I managed around a yawn. "Do you want me to help get them ready for bed?"

"Aren't you... well, weren't you supposed to be up at work tonight? Jess told me that I needed to be back by six so that you could –"

"Could be there by eight!," I shouted, suddenly remembering the very late ceremony that we had scheduled. It was so out of the ordinary – a ten o'clock ceremony – that it would have escaped my attention on a good day, much less a day like today. "Oh, no, what time is it anyway?," I said, searching for my purse in the pile of toys the boys had stacked up in the corner of the living room.

"Eight thirty."

"Just what I needed," I said. "Just exactly the kind of stress that I needed right now, you know?"

"I'm so sorry, Emily, I should have –"

"No, it was my problem. I should have remembered and called you," I said, finding my phone and seeing the unanswered calls from Evelyn. Great.

"I've got to go," I told him. "Kisses from Aunt Emmy," I said, kissing tiny faces as quickly as I could.

"One more game!," Scott cheered.

"Next time, buddy," I told him, patting Nick's shoulder as I made my way out the door. "Next time."

Evelyn wasn't nearly as upset as I had expected. Which wasn't to say that she was cheerful. Just that she wasn't as upset as I had expected. And I had expected the worst.

"I know it's been rough, Emily dear," she said to me. "But you really need to be more on task."

"Yes, Evelyn," I said. "I'm so sorry. It won't happen again."

"The garden room is already set up. The groom is in the side room, and the bride is on the fifth floor suite. Go time is in…" She looked at her watch. "Well, five minutes. Time to hustle."

And hustle I did. It was a small wedding, thankfully, just beautiful in the twilight of the garden room, with candlelight and soft touches everywhere. As the bride and groom said their vows then moved on to a reception set up in the same room, I was so soothed by the harpist and flutist they had performing that I found myself nodding off as I stood by the wall.

I needed a break.

The event was over by one o'clock, and I was in my car on the way home thirty minutes later. Just as I was contemplating how late Evelyn meant when she told me to sleep in and come in late, I felt my car slow to a screeching halt, then start dragging itself.

"What in the world," I muttered, getting out and moving to inspect the offending part… which quickly showed itself as a blown out tire.

"Great." I put my head in my hands, considering just lying down on the road next to the car and getting some sleep already. A quick glance over the neighborhood, though, had me rethinking that decision, as I got back in and locked the doors behind me.

I was stuck.

Stuck only a few blocks from Iglesia Redeemer. There was a bright spot in even this most recent chapter of calamity in the drama that was my life. Without considering the hour, I went to my recent call list and touched Josh's name.

He answered on the third ring, grogginess in his voice.

"Emily?," he asked. "Are you okay?"

"I'm sorry to bother you," I began calmly, as though I was just calling him to chat. "But I've had a tire blow out. By your church."

"What? Are you there now? At the church?"

"No, I'm about three blocks SOUTH of the church."

"Oh, man," I could hear him getting out of bed. "That's a bad part of town. The church is in a bad enough part of town, but it just gets worse the farther south you get."

I had noticed. "Yeah, I've noticed."

"Stay in your car, keep your doors locked, and I'll be right there," he said. "I'm getting dressed right now, and as soon as I find my own keys, I'll be there. Okay?"

Thankful tears filled my eyes. "Thanks, Josh."

"No problem."

Ten minutes later, his truck pulled up behind my car, and I got out, meeting him.

"You're still dressed for work," he said, looking at me appreciatively.

"And you still have bed head," I said, reaching up and touching his hair before thinking better of it.

He shifted his weight as he laughed uncomfortably. "Well, yeah, I was asleep, you know." He looked at me again. "You've got to be cold."

"Well, it's July. In Texas."

"And it's one o'clock in the morning, and you have that... that tiny dress on. Here," he handed me his keys. "Get in my truck and stay warm. I'll get the tire changed and get you out of here, okay?"

"Are you sure I can't help?"

"Do you know anything about changing a tire?"

Regrettably, I did not. I looked at him blankly.

"Yeah, that's what I thought," he managed through his laughter. "Get in the truck. It'll take me ten minutes. Time me."

I watched him as he worked, appreciating what he was doing... appreciating the way he looked doing it, as his muscles stretched and worked under his T-shirt...

He seemed to sense my eyes on him at one point and looked over to where I sat, staring at him. I waved rather lamely. He waved back, looking more than a little self-conscious, and went back to work.

Ten minutes later, he was done. "Okay," he said, opening the truck door for me, then shutting it after I had stepped down. "It's just a spare, so don't go trying to break any speed records, okay?"

"I wouldn't do that with a good tire," I said, leaning back against the door.

"When you go in and get that tire changed tomorrow morning – and please do it tomorrow morning and not a moment later – have them change all four tires. You're riding on nearly bald tires."

"They're so expensive," I whined, "and I've been so busy –"

"Emily, I'll take the car and pay to have them changed myself if you don't," he said, putting his hands on either side of my shoulders, in an effort to look me more closely in the eyes. "It's not safe."

"I know, I know. I'll get it done," I managed, my breath catching in my throat as I realized how close he was. Suddenly, I was no longer exhausted but completely and fully alert, conscious of every move he made.

"Good," he breathed out, moving away.

My heart continued to race, even as he wiped the sweat off of his face with the bottom of his shirt. "I should probably go. Thank you for coming out here and helping me. I… I really appreciate it."

"Can I follow you home?," he asked. "Just to make sure that spare makes it?"

"Sure," I managed.

I took care to drive slower than normal with Josh following me, my mind racing over all these feelings that he was bringing out in me. When had things gone from complicated to a whole lot clearer? Why was I just now able to admit that I felt a lot more for him than I had been willing to confess before?

These things were at the forefront of my mind when I pulled into my parking space, took a deep breath, and got out of my car, making my way over to where Josh was waiting in his truck with the window rolled down.

"Tomorrow morning, right?," he said.

"Yeah, I'll get it done. First thing tomorrow morning."

"Good."

"Do you… do you want to come in?"

He looked at me as though I was crazy. "Emily, it's two o'clock in the morning."

Of course it was. Stupid, stupid, stupid...

"Which wouldn't matter, you know," he said diplomatically, "if you didn't look so tired. But you need to get some sleep."

"You're right," I said. "That's what I've been saying all night."

"Okay," he said softly. "Have a good night."

"You, too, Josh. And thanks."

I made my way to my front door, noticing that he waited in the parking lot until I was safely inside.

Trish Thibideaux, in a very generous gesture, gifted Melissa a girls' weekend trip for her birthday. She arranged for flights to Florida, for a hotel suite, for a rental car, and for spa treatments for all three of us at the end of July. I could almost picture Melissa rolling her eyes at the mention of yet ANOTHER spa treatment ("how many times can I be exfoliated, really?!") as she told me about it over the phone, but by the time her birthday rolled around and we were in our swanky suite that overlooked the beach, she had come around on her thinking.

"To Trish," Sara declared, toasting us with her Coke as we lay around the pool.

"No kidding," I said. "Does Trish have any more sons? Because I would be willing to marry anyone if it meant getting gifts like this."

"Nope," Melissa said. "Beau is only the lonely as far as sons go. What do we have on the schedule for today?"

"I think," Sara said, checking the schedule Trish had the concierge give to us on arrival, "today is an off day for pampering. Just a relax by the pool day."

"Hallelujah," Melissa said. "My skin is all but rubbed completely off."

"How are you doing, Em?," Sara asked, glancing at me out of the corner of her eye.

"Awesome," I breathed out. It had been a rough month, to say the least. During the weeks, I had been a surrogate mother for my nephews while Jess spent the majority of her time at the NICU with Seth when Nick was forced to go back to work. The business couldn't run without him, and thanks to Evelyn's generosity and surprising level of understanding in the situation, I had been able to pick up the slack. Evelyn's generosity had extended to this trip, when she had allowed me some time off to be with my friends. Well, provided I work like a maniac to cover BOTH of our work the next week so that SHE could go out of town.

It was a fair trade, though.

"Well," Melissa said, sitting up in her chair to get a better look at us, "I suppose since there's nothing on the schedule that this is as good a time as any to talk about the resolutions. How did this month go for you guys?"

I closed my eyes. "Seeing as how I practically became a mother this month? I think I did an okay job of helping someone who was really in need."

"Have they given Jess any idea when Seth will be out of the NICU?," Sara asked.

"Another week or two, I hope," I answered.

"That would be so hard," Melissa said. "Makes me wonder if I ever even want to have kids, knowing that something like that could happen."

I shrugged. "I guess it's always a risk, but look at the other four boys. All past due, with no problems. God has His reasons for allowing something like this to happen, and I think, once we're all past it, we'll see that it wasn't just some random chance but that God used it for good."

"You know, that's exactly what we've been talking about in our Bible study," Sara said. "About how God uses all things for His good. And I really believe it. I think about how different it would be if Jon and I were still together, about how there's no way I would've even gone to Costa Rica, and now? Now I'm going to be moving there!" She shook her head. "I mean, God even went further than that and worked it all out so that I have the financial support to go and do this thing. I still don't know who made the donation, or how that all worked out, but wow. God just totally provided. He made something good out of all that I thought was bad. Isn't that incredible?"

I thought back to the day that Melissa and I had gone over some of the particulars on her wedding list. Her flower budget was rather astronomical, with all the Christmas trees and poinsettias Trish had suggested on the expense list.

"That's a lot of money," Melissa had said, looking at the sum.

"Worth it, though," I had agreed, "if it's something that's really important to you."

"How can plants in a sanctuary be really important?," Melissa asked, incredulously. "I mean, let's really think about this. That much money... for plants? Plants that we'll use once, for one day, that will just die."

"Well, they can be left to decorate the church."

"AFTER Christmas? Christmas trees after Christmas?"

I nodded, seeing her point. It was a conclusion I had already reached myself. "You're probably right. It's a one day expense."

She shook her head. "You know how much I could do with that money? How much better that money could be spent?" She paused for a moment, then lowered her voice. "Beau and I were talking about... well, about Sara and Costa Rica. And you can't breathe A WORD of this to her, right?"

"Absolutely not," I said, holding up my hand in an "I swear" motion.

"Well, we'd like to... sponsor her, you know. Support her on the field this first year."

I was surprised by the generosity of this.

"I think that's awesome," I offered. "But why wouldn't you want her to know about it?"

Melissa shook her head. "I don't want her thinking she owes me anything, owes us anything. And Beau and I are really convicted that we don't invest more of ourselves – our time, our talents, our money – into more eternal things, you know? This is just the first step."

"Sounds amazing," I said. "And I truly mean that. I know Sara would definitely be blessed by it. And God would be honored through it."

She nodded, silently looking at the budget for the Christmas finery. "You know what?," she said. "Cut out the crap, and I'll send the money to the mission board in Sara's name."

And we had. And she had. And Sara came to me in tears just a couple of days later, after she had been notified that her expenses had been anonymously covered for that first year.

I couldn't help but smile as I thought about this in the Florida sun.

"It IS pretty incredible," Melissa conceded. "How about you? How have you been doing with helping out someone in need?"

Sara smiled and reclined in her seat. "Awesome," she said.

"Redeemer's youth choir is just awesome. I thought it would all end with the tour, you know, that they wouldn't really need me anymore, but I've been able to help out with the youth a lot since then. It's been so great, loving on those teenagers, learning more Spanish, and, of course, being around Josh."

I shifted uncomfortably at the mention of Sara and Josh together. Life had continued on as normal for Josh and me, fitting times to run and study together around all the changes in my own schedule, and I just assumed, wrongly so, that most of his life was spent with me. But he was a teacher, with a freer schedule during the summer, and so was Sara. And it just made sense that the two of them, seeing as how they had gotten to know one another so much better, could have become closer without me ever picking up on it...

"Josh, huh?," Melissa said. "Are you guys..."

Sara glanced over at me. "No, but, y'all... he is so sweet and funny and passionate and... well, he's hot."

I was certain my own face must have been turning a deep shade of red as Sara continued on, listing Josh's "hot" features, one by one, meticulously detailing all about him that I had noticed long, long ago, until I thought I would scream. I had no claim to him, right? This wild jealousy I felt every time I imagined Sara and Josh working alongside one another was completely unjustifiable, as was the rage slowly building in me as I listened to her talk about him as though he was someone she had been thinking about entirely more than was absolutely necessary and –

"Helloooo? Emily?"

I looked over to see Melissa staring at me and Sara smirking in my direction.

"I'm sorry. What was the question?"

"There's no question, but geez, you look like you want to kill someone!"

I made an effort to smile.

"Oh, sorry," I said. "I'm just... thinking of work, I guess. July brides, you know."

Sara studied me for a moment longer, then directed her attention to Melissa. "What did you do this month to help someone out?"

"Well, I didn't kill my future mother-in-law," she said. "And I helped the two of you to this fabulous vacation, didn't I?"

9 AUGUST

I needed a distraction. A really great distraction.

Since my sister's children had become my children for the better part of July and since any sanity I had left after the deluge of summer brides had dealt so severely with me was instantaneously zapped away by four screaming, rambunctious nephews, I needed a break. That, coupled with all the thoughts running through my head regarding my father, regarding one of my best friends moving to the jungle, regarding my other best friend getting married, and regarding my own complicated, unrequited feelings for my running buddy/accountability partner/who knows what he is... well, I needed a good distraction.

"I'm thinking of making a change," I told Melissa, as we surveyed my cramped apartment bathroom.

She looked at me out of the corner of her eye. "Oh, I think we're well past the stage of just thinking about it," she said, twirling a wrench in her hand. "I'm ready for some demolition."

Back in January, when we had come up with the resolution to improve our homes, I had honestly thought I might own my own home by this point. But life hadn't gone as expected, and I was still in my apartment.

I hadn't figured I could do much of any improvement, but after looking over my lease and double checking it with my landlord, I had discovered that there were some cosmetic enhancements and changes I could make, DIY fashion. Sara, who had moved home to save money for Costa Rica over the summer, had no interest in helping out, but Melissa had been quite enthusiastic about drawing up some plans, going over the schematics, and helping me to pick out all the new pieces of my dream bathroom.

Well, as close to a dream as I could get without rendering the space completely unusable for the next month.

I studied Melissa carefully, as she knelt in front of the pipes underneath my bathroom sink. "You DO know what you're doing, right?," I asked.

"Please," she waved away my concern. "I have degrees in engineering. I think I can figure out a few simple plumbing issues. That new sink is going to make all the work worth it. Just watch." She began working with the wrench.

"Okay," I told her, looking once again over to the box that held the new cabinet, the boxes that held all the new fixtures, and the literal sink that was sitting there waiting to be put in the old sink's place. "It's just that –"

And with that, water began shooting from the pipes, all over my bathroom.

Two estimates later, I was looking at the most expensive bathroom remodel to ever hit a crummy apartment in the history of mankind.

I decided I wasn't going to pay someone to do it, though. Hadn't I learned my lesson about DIY projects? No. However, I had learned my lesson about letting friends with engineering degrees use wrenches on your pipes without properly researching it beforehand. I had a whole long list of DIY demonstrations I could watch online to help guide me through the process, and I had a feeling I was going to be on a first name basis with the entire staff of Home Depot before too long.

I told Melissa about it over dinner – her treat – the next day. "Oh, man, Emily," she moaned. "I feel so bad about this. I mean, I'm sure that I was changing out the right pipe, and I don't know why it all went down like it did, but –"

"What's done is done," I told her. "I just want to get it fixed."

I was in the midst of "getting it fixed" later on that night when my phone rang. Thankful for the distraction from my distraction, which had turned into a session of me yelling unintelligible exasperations at the mess left by the torrents of water Melissa had allowed to spew all over my personal space, I picked up the phone.

"Hello?," I barked unceremoniously at the unsuspecting person on the other end of the line.

"Oh, hey," Josh managed. "Did I catch you at a bad time?"

I looked at the water we hadn't been able to see and clean up. Apart from changing out everything – which would take time – and replacing pipes (again, more time), I hadn't counted on finding such filth. I was wondering what water, standing water, could do to make the problem worse.

"No," I told him, not convinced myself. "Do you know how long black mold takes to form?"

"Black mold?"

"Yes. Isn't that the kind that can kill you?"

He didn't say anything for a moment. "Well, I don't think it's a good kind of mold. I'm not sure there ARE any good kinds of mold." A pause. "Are you having apartment problems?"

"THAT would be an understatement," I told him. "I've got all kinds of problems with a bathroom renovation."

"Call your landlord," he offered. "You're just a renter. Black mold is really someone else's problem."

"Well, it would be, but since I've undertaken this project, I've assumed the responsibility for myself. Which means that I get to deal with the fallout from the flood that happened yesterday."

Another pause. Then, he began laughing.

"Yeah, this is hilarious, isn't it?," I said, throwing the clump of paper towels I had been working with in the middle of the floor. "I can really see the humor in me dying from black mold exposure."

He managed a breath in between laughs. "No humor in that, but... how did your apartment flood? What did you do?"

I sighed. "I didn't do much of anything except watch while Melissa did it. It's a long story. And it's going to be a longer fix."

"Do you have a contractor coming out to look at it?"

"Done and done. But they're too expensive. I'm going to fix it myself."

"Hmm," he said. "Do you know what you're doing?"

"No idea!," I exclaimed, "which is why I'm in such a great mood." A pause. "Did you telepathically sense that I would be this annoyed and call to cheer me up somehow?"

"Oh, no, I called to tell you that I'm not going to be able to run at the same time tomorrow. Teacher in-service starts earlier than I thought. Can you meet me an hour earlier?"

I thought about how late I'd be up with this mess. Would I even sleep at all?

"Sure," I said. "The extra hour will get me away from my home improvement. Might improve my mood."

"Hey," he said, tentatively. "Do you... do you mind if I come by tonight and try to help you?"

This made me perk up considerably. "Would you? Do you know anything about this stuff?" I irrationally began to hope that he had some plumbing skills that I knew nothing about. Maybe that incident with the restroom at Redeemer, on the Sunday I had visited, had given him some special insight...

"Oh, I have no idea what I'm doing, but since it doesn't seem like you do either, maybe we can figure it out together."

This sounded infinitely better than doing it alone and second-guessing myself all night long.

"That's a great plan."

I hung up with him and waited, more than a little anxious, for his arrival.

Four hours later, we were no closer to a solution than we had been.

"This is a mess!," Josh had exclaimed when he saw what we had done to the bathroom.

"You see why I'm worried about black mold?"

He smiled up at me from where he was cleaning behind the pipes with some paper towels and a whole lot of bleach. "Well, that's probably not going to be a problem now, now that you've so graciously allowed me to scrub it all up for you, but..."

"I do appreciate it," I told him, handing him another wad of paper towels.

"The only thing is," he concluded, "I have no idea how to move out these cabinets and this sink and redo it all. You know, this is why I bought a house that was already move-in ready. I'm out of my element here."

I had shown him the list of DIY videos online and told him what my plan was. As he threw down the last of the wadded up paper towels, I held out my hand to help him up off the floor.

"Do you have a few minutes to watch the first video? I think it's called 'Welcome to your new bathroom!'"

He brushed his hands off on his shorts and smiled at me. "Now's as good a time as any."

"I thought we were just going to have a string quartet?" Lauren Evans was panicking.

I had never, in all of my years of doing this work, seen a bride panic as much and as often as Lauren. When I considered how inexhaustible the funds she was drawing from were, I was dumbfounded as to why she could be anything but stress free and easygoing. I thought about brides who probably had reason to be stressed out, like Alyssa Star, whose own wedding was just around the corner and would just barely be paid for enough to pull it off. I saw the stress on her own face every time we talked about dollars and cents – and there was no profit being made on anyone's side in her case.

This was not Lauren's problem.

"Laurie," Dorothy said calmly, "we WERE going to do that, but William and Pamela," she looked to me, "they're our friends from the club, Emily," then back to Lauren, "are big donors to the symphony, and they so WANT to gift you with this for your wedding."

"A whole orchestra, Mom? Really?" Lauren looked like she was about to hyperventilate.

"Lauren," I interjected, "I'm not sure it will make any difference to you personally. There's nothing you need to do any differently than you would have had we stuck with just the quartet. And I've seen the church – there's plenty of room to put in as many instrumentalists as you have available. Your mother and Evelyn have already drawn up the plans for how they can all fit, and it's going to be –"

"Just peachy, dear," Stan smiled in her direction.

Lauren visibly continued to tense up, but she pursed her lips together tightly and didn't say another word for the entire meeting.

"Will and Pam just LOVE our Laurie," Dorothy continued on. "Isn't it wonderful how everyone just wants to give her the best?"

Before I could think of an adequate response to this, my phone rang. I let it go to voice mail, going back to the plans laid out on my desk, ready to initiate a conversation regarding some MORE upgrades that the Evans family had for the reception, when the phone began to ring again.

"I'm so sorry," I said, excusing myself. "I probably need to see if that's an emergency."

Seth had finally gone home the week before, and while I thought this would reduce the level of crazy surrounding my sister, the transition to five children all in one place was ratcheting up her insanity levels more than having a baby in the NICU had. I had been fielding her calls all week.

Sure enough, it was Jessica's number that lit up the screen. I was about to silence the phone for good, when I saw there was a text message from Jess as well. Opening it up, I read…

"Dad had car accident. Mom needs you."

My breath caught in my throat. I looked up at the Evans family, all three of whom were watching me with concern. "Can I..." I began, swallowing hard. "Can I reschedule with you guys for another day? My dad isn't well."

I had called Jess back, trying to get more details. Because my mother had chosen to leave so many people in the dark about Dad's condition, Jess thought my concern was overkill.

"Geez, Emily, it's just a fender bender. Mom needed you to go up there to help out because I can't leave since, you know, I have FIVE children now who I can't get out of the house at the same time because I'm losing all my marbles over here –"

"I'll talk to you later," I had said, hanging up on her.

I had tried my mother's number next, but she wasn't picking up her phone. Left with no other choice, I called Stephen on his cell phone.

"This is Stephen," he responded.

"It's Emily," I said. "Is my mother—"

"She's right here," he said. "She called me when she couldn't get a hold of you. They're talking to the police right now."

"Oh, wow, was it a bad accident? Where are you guys?"

Stephen took a deep breath. "Well, it wasn't that bad, actually. We're just a few blocks from the church. It... well, it's okay, and he's okay. But he's... not sure where he is. Or how he got here. And he told the police that."

"Great. Just great," I said.

"You know," Stephen lowered his voice, "it might actually be great. Maybe this will help your mother. Maybe this will force her to finally get help."

I recalled his words as the four of us -- Mom, Dad, Stephen, and I – stood in his office at the church.

"Why was he even driving?!," I yelled at my mother, finally fed up enough to have the nerve.

The hurt and anguish on her face as I yelled at her didn't seem to be helping much at all, and the stress of the morning was clear on her face as she cast guilty eyes downward.

"Emily, it's not her fault. Lydia has been really good about taking him everywhere, and she hasn't been letting him drive at all," Stephen spoke softly.

"Yeah," my mother managed to spit out at me. "Do you think I just handed him the car keys and told him, 'Go on, Tommy! Go out there and get yourself killed!'"

"No, but I can't believe... I can't believe we even have to stand here and have this conversation! Either you're going to take care of him so that things like this don't happen or you're going to get him help. I'm tired of the three of us carrying this around by ourselves!"

My mother took a quick breath. "I was just taking a shower. Just five minutes to myself, and when I got out, he was gone. The keys were gone. The car was gone. I had no idea WHERE he was, and it..." She put her hand on her mouth, holding back a sob.

Stephen put a hand on her shoulder. "It's okay. He's okay now. The damage to the other car wasn't even that bad, and he's here. And safe."

"He needs help, Mom," I said again, softer this time. "Please, take him to the doctor and –"

"She's right, Lydia," Dad spoke up from where he had been sitting behind his desk.

"Thomas, are you feeling better?," Mom asked him brightly.

He shook his head. "Was I in a car accident?"

"Yeah," Stephen told him. "Just a small one."

"I don't even remember driving anywhere," Dad mumbled. "Am I... is something wrong with me?"

None of us said anything for a moment, watching realization dawn in his eyes.

"Lydia, I think Emily is right."

"But, Thomas —"

"I think I need some help."

She was able to get him to his primary care physician that same day. His doctor, a longtime church member, was so disturbed by what he heard and what he observed after asking my father some simple questions that he had him referred to a neurologist that same afternoon. More tests were done, results were promised in a few days, but by the time my parents left the office, the doctors' combined best guesses were in agreement and were clearly a foregone conclusion already.

Alzheimer's.

The word had been brutal. Honest. Unforgiving. My mother had seemed relieved to tell me the news on the phone, to finally have a word to put to the problem. There would be help now, a way to adapt with what they now knew, and she and Dad both felt like today had been a victory.

I did not.

He was too young. As I thought about this, driving back home after a very distracted afternoon in the office and brushing away the tears that wouldn't stop coming, I did the math. Sixty-three. My father was sixty-three years old. Clearly not too young to have this disease.

But I was too young. There was the truth of it. I was too young to have a father suffering from this, to deal with sick and aging parents, and to make sense of what their life changes meant for me. It was selfish, but it was honest. What was I going to do? How was this going to change my life? Where could I even begin in trying to sort through it all?

I pulled into my parking space, still wiping tears away, and made my way to the door, fumbling with my keys as I cried. I needed to talk to someone. I wouldn't call Jessica. I needed someone who could be level-headed, not someone so emotionally tied into the situation, and I was sure that after my mother called her, she would be in no condition to talk to anyone intelligibly for quite some time. I wouldn't call Matthew. That was for my mother to do, when she could call him at a decent hour in Okinawa and explain the whole thing to him. Sara was out of town. Melissa was busy with work.

And suddenly, I knew that there was only one person I wanted to call anyway. I picked up my phone, dialed the number, and said a silent prayer of thanks when he picked up the line.

Fifteen minutes later, he was knocking on the front door. I peeked through the peephole and saw him, running his hand through his hair and shifting from one foot to the next, concern for me etched all over his face. I was so thankful for him.

"Josh," I said, opening the door. The tender way he looked at me caused me to burst into tears again, as I ran into his arms.

Once he got me inside, got me to calm down, and had listened to what the doctor had said, he leaned back on my couch, taking a deep breath. I was still nestled in comfortably underneath his arm, and he pulled me closer as he began talking.

"Emily, you know about my mother, right?"

We had talked about her more than a few times during all the days we had spent together. She had been diagnosed with breast cancer when he was fifteen, after being healthy her entire young adult life. The doctors had given her six months. She only lived two.

"Yeah," I said, then shook my head at my own silliness. "Wow, this seems like nothing in comparison. You were just a baby when you lost your mom. And I'm a grown woman who isn't really even losing a parent. Not yet at least."

"Well, that's not why I'm bringing it up," he said. "An ailing parent at ANY age is a big deal. Don't discount what you're going through just because you're an adult."

I nodded.

He spoke softly. "It was about what we learned in the whole process. Mom wasn't even through the first round of chemo when she started talking like, we thought, she had given up. Made us all so mad, how she kept talking about heaven and what it was going to be like and how she WANTED to be there." He smiled at the memory now, all these years later. "At one point, I even told her that I wasn't okay with just seeing her again in heaven one day. I wanted to see her when I got my first recording deal, when I was rich enough to buy her a really nice Cadillac Escalade."

"You were going to buy her a Cadillac?"

"Well, duh," he said. "I was going to be a famous rapper!"

I smiled at this as he continued. "I may have been a hoodlum in my younger years, but I was still a good son," he said, prim and proper. "Anyway, I told her that there was too much living left for her to do and that I was NOT looking forward to seeing her in heaven. That I wouldn't even look for her if she left us now, when we still needed her." His voice grew even softer. "And she said, 'Joshua, by the time you get to heaven, I'll still be on my face in front of Jesus. I won't have even had enough time with Him to get past the glory of His feet.' "

I began to cry silently at the truth of this. Hadn't he and I, just this summer, gone over passages in Scripture that spoke of the glory of Christ in eternity that made life here all the more insignificant and temporal? "Wow," I told him.

"Yeah," he said. "I thought, at that point, that she had totally lost it. She had basically told me that she didn't give two hoots who she saw in heaven – not even her own son. She was so ready to worship Christ in the fullness of His glory that nothing else mattered. The more her words kept swimming through my head, the more I wondered about how she could feel that way, how any mother could feel that way, how she wasn't at all angry about the circumstances, and... well, why she could almost look forward to death. Eagerly!"

I looked up at him at just the same moment that he looked down at me. He smiled. "She had just started going to church a few months earlier. She tried to share her faith with us before the cancer, but we wouldn't listen. When she started saying all these platitudes about the feet of Jesus, though, we all took note. A dying woman will give some credibility to theories on eternity, you know."

"I can imagine," I said.

"And finally," he said, "after the Gospel made sense to me, and God made Himself known to me through His Word.... I saw that wanting more painful years for my mom here on earth was selfish when it would be infinitely better for her to be worshipping at the feet of Christ. Would be infinitely better for us all, actually. So, I didn't fear death – not hers, not mine."

I considered this, my heart breaking even more resolutely, as I thought of my father forgetting even the Scriptures as he preached. The words of life, slipping from his mind, the security of Christ alone, becoming a mystery to him in this worn-out earth suit. How wishing for more time was selfish, as it robbed him of a longer piece of eternity worshiping at the feet of His Lord in glory.

I didn't realize I had closed my eyes and that I was crying again until Josh lifted my chin with his hand, wiping my tears away with his thumbs. "Hey," he said softly, "I'm not saying it's wrong to mourn. But Scripture tells us that we are not among those who mourn without hope. And not because we'll get to see our loved ones on the other side. But because our loved ones will be so enthralled and enraptured by the presence of God in all of His glory that they won't even notice us when we get there. And we won't even notice them. Why would we want to keep them from that? Why would we wish them back here when they're going to be perfect and complete?"

I nodded. "I know it's true," I cried, "but... what are we going to do now? What is my mom going to do? And the church?"

Josh gathered me up into his arms again, letting me cry against his chest. "I don't know any of those answers," he said. "But I know that if God used your father as much as He did while he was healthy, that He'll use him all the more during this trial, too. God knows what He's doing."

We sat like that for another hour, talking at some points, then sitting in comfortable silence at other moments. I didn't even realize how late it was until my clock chimed one.

"It's late," I told him. "You have school tomorrow morning."

"I'm okay," he said. "I can sit here as long as you need me."

I nodded. "Thanks... but I think I'm okay now." I paused, struggling for the words. "I... it... you really helped." I looked at him. "Thank you."

He squeezed my hand. "No problem. You just call me again if you need to, okay?"

I nodded silently, then walked him to the door.

"Good night, Emily," he whispered.

"Good night, Josh," I whispered back, giving him a hug before he turned to leave.

I had never been more thankful for a wedding.

There were two reasons for that on that particular Saturday, though. For one, I was in need of some time away from all the issues my family was plodding through, awkwardly and clumsily. My sister had been beside herself at Dad's news, and Matthew was stuck trying to find any time in his schedule that he could take leave to come home for us all to talk face-to-face. My parents, for their own part, were doing better than we were, which still wasn't saying much. A wedding, this wedding in particular, would be a great way for me to escape, if only for a little while.

The second reason for my thankfulness was because, for the first time, I was getting to see my own skills and talents put to the test. I wasn't making a dime from all of my work on Alyssa Star's wedding, but it was, astonishingly enough, shaping up to be the best work I had ever done. The plantation home hosting the event had been completely transformed after a full day of facilitating all the many vendors through the area, directing them and helping them out, along with the help of Sara, who was my trusty (and free) assistant for the day.

"Oh, it's beautiful," she breathed, as we took in the ground floor, which had been set up for the reception.

"She did great, didn't she?," I said, crediting Alyssa with so many excellent choices.

"She? YOU did great, Emily," Sara said. "You are SO doing my wedding when the day comes, okay?"

"I wouldn't miss it for anything." I smiled to myself, then turned to go and check the garden, all set up for the ceremony, just as I had ten times already that morning.

"Emily?," Alyssa's father approached me, somewhat timidly.

"Yes, sir," I said. "Is everything okay?"

"It's perfect," he said, looking around and smiling. "You did better than I could have expected. I was just wondering where Alyssa was getting ready."

"She's in the cottage out back," I said, leading him that direction. "I figured that would give her the most privacy and keep her from being seen by anyone until the perfect moment, you know?"

"This place is... well, I can't believe they're not charging us more," he said, dumbfounded.

I had been a bit surprised myself, but the couple who had inherited the home were new to this as well. We were the first big event they had ever hosted, and while I knew their prices would increase, I was confident that they would stay low for a while, as they kept building their client base and word-of-mouth publicity kept getting out.

"Okay," I said, my hand on the doorknob of the cottage. "Take a deep breath."

"Why?," he asked.

"Because," I said with a smile. "You're going to be amazed by how she looks."

I opened the door, where Alyssa stood, smoothing out her dress as she looked at herself in the mirror. She turned to face her father, who I was watching intently. This was almost as good as the moment when the groom sees his bride.

"Alyssa," he breathed out. "You look… "

"Dad," she said. "Look at you in your tuxedo!" She walked over to him with a smile, smoothing the lapels of his jacket, lightly fingering the boutonniere that I had helped pin on him earlier that morning. "I told you that this cut was the way to –" She stopped, watching him closely, her eyes tearing up. "Dad, are you crying?"

"You look… you look just like your mother," he managed through tears. "She would've given anything to see you like this, right here, right now."

Alyssa fell into his arms as I discreetly handed her a tissue. I turned away from their special moment, thinking of my own father, in need of a tissue myself.

Matthew had been able to take leave, and he and Shoko arrived in the US within a couple of weeks of Dad's diagnosis. Jessica and Nick found a sitter for the four older boys and arrived at my parents' house with Seth in tow. I completed the group, as we all came together to discuss what was going to happen.

Despite the stress of the situation, my mother had managed to fix a meal that rivaled any Thanksgiving feast we had ever enjoyed growing up. She so rarely had all three of her children home at once that the temptation to celebrate, even at a time like this, was too much to resist.

"Welcome to America, Shoko," Nick said out of the side of his mouth as we gathered around the table and my mother continued to heft large platter after large platter of food before us. Shoko, whose eyes had been perpetually three times their normal size from the moment the food parade began until now, glanced over to me.

"These portions… are larger than I expected," she whispered to me.

"Larger than we all expected, my dear," my father said congenially. "Lydia, I really think you've outdone yourself. Are you trying to medicate me with meat and potatoes?"

"And how," Matthew said around a mouthful of steak, not even bothering to wait for the mealtime prayer.

"Are we wanting to talk about medication already?," Jessica blurted out, clearly frustrated by the giant elephant in the room. "I mean, seriously, is no one going to talk about it?"

We all turned to look at her, as she continued to rub Seth's back, scowling at the rest of us. It was true – my parents hadn't said much of anything to us about the diagnosis. They were spending more time talking about our lives, getting to know Shoko, playing with the grandsons, and successfully evading the subject of what they planned to do next.

"Well, that's why we're here," my mother sighed, finally taking her seat. "Thomas, I think we're ready."

We joined hands, prayed, and loaded up our plates in silence. Before the atmosphere could grow any more awkward, my father cleared his throat.

"You should all know that I'm leaving Grace."

I dropped my fork, the clanking echoing through the silent dining room.

"Is it... is it that bad?," Jessica managed to choke out.

"Um, yeah, I think so, since they had us come all the way back here," Matthew spat out, exasperated, indicating himself and Shoko.

"Well, excuse me for living, I just –"

My mother held up a hand. "Please. Can the two of you just let us explain it all?"

My eyes never left my father's. "Dad, when are you leaving Grace?"

He reached over and took my mother's hand. "This will be my last week to preach."

"Daddy!," Jessica practically shouted at him, tears beginning to make their way down her cheeks. "This is too fast!"

I glanced over at Matthew, who sat silently, irritation etched all over his face. The news was affecting us all in our typical, temperamental ways. Jessica was emotional, Matthew was angry, and I was, in true middle child fashion, somewhere between the two extremes.

"It's not too fast," he said, calmly. "We've known the diagnosis for two weeks now. I've made the elders and deacons at the church aware, discussed this with the staff, and made preparations to have supply preaching in place until the church can find a new pastor."

Silence, for a moment, then Matthew clipped out, "So, that's it? You're just going to quit, after a lifetime of ministry? You seem fine to me, like you could keep on preaching until it gets too bad to go on."

My mother opened her mouth to say something, but my father stopped her with his words. "It's already gotten to that point, Matt." He looked over to my mother, then leaned forward to address the five of us. "I promised myself a long time ago that I wouldn't compromise what went on in the pulpit for my own pride. If... if I was starting to falter up there, starting to speak things that weren't right on theologically, that I was going to stop. And I'm pretty sure I've already gotten to that point. There are days when I can't remember Scripture passages that I know I've memorized by heart several times over, and I don't want to chance having one of those days on a Sunday. Not when so many people and their understanding of the Gospel are at stake."

Jessica had handed off Seth to Nick and wiped at her eyes with her napkin. "Daddy, is it that bad already?"

I thought about the things I had seen, the slip ups he had made in front of me, the episodes Pastor Stephen had shared with me, and knew the truth. I saw it as he met my eyes across the table. I wiped away a few tears of my own.

"Yeah. It is." He managed a smile. "The good news, though, is that God is not done with me. We just..." He looked at my mother. "We're just entering a new season is all."

We finished the meal in silence, as my parents continued to tell us what would happen, as my father left our church, as arrangements were made for medication, as plans were made for long-term care, and as our lives all changed forever.

Between dinner and the time that my parents went to bed early, leaving the rest of us to ourselves, Jessica and Matthew must have duked it out and come to a peaceful agreement. I can only assume that this happened while I was on the phone with Evelyn, who called me in a tiffy and a half, insisting that I come to the hotel "immediately and with foreboding urgency" because things were all off kilter with the Gibbons reception, and it was all going to fall apart if I wasn't there to take the beating and the abuse that was sure to come my way as soon as I walked in.

As I was trying to sort out all of my parents' issues and deal with my own work issues via text to the different vendors on location at the hotel at that precise moment, my siblings cornered me, much like they had as we were growing up.

"What are we going to do?," Matthew hissed at me as he stood shoulder to shoulder with Jessica, who had crossed her arms over her chest and managed to look menacing, even while holding her tiny baby.

I sighed. "What do you mean, what are we going to do?"

"This whole mess with Dad. Leaving Grace. What are we going to do?"

"Look," I said, ignoring the likely urgent text that was coming my way from Stella, "I don't think Dad needs our permission to do what he needs to do at Grace."

Jessica rolled her eyes. "We're not saying he does, but, geez, Emily, don't you think they're rushing into this a little? I mean, he's not even... well, it's not even bad enough that any of us knew!"

I thought about all the months I had known, how I had carried this along with my mother and Stephen, and how my siblings were now pitching the weight of their own frantic emotions onto me as well. My mouth tightened in irritation as Jessica finished up her lengthy tirade on how this wasn't right.

"Yeah!," Matthew huffed, "I mean, we just got the news ourselves, and now, he's quitting the ministry and they're talking like he's going through dementia and... what are we going to do?"

"He has Alzheimer's, you moron," I managed to spit back at him. "It is EXACTLY like he's going through dementia! Except worse. Much worse."

Matthew seemed taken aback by my words, but Jessica continued to plow on forward.

"What does this mean for us? I mean, are we going to stay at Grace, or... what kind of pastor are they going to get? What's Daddy going to do now? Is Mom even THINKING about any of this, or –"

"You know what?," I finally said. "I understand that this is hard for more than just Mom and Dad. Believe me, I understand. I know that none of us have any idea how to handle any of this or how to really be there for them. I don't know what this means for our future, at Grace or just life in general. But I do know this much – Mom and Dad know what they're doing. Dad is more than old enough and prepared enough to retire comfortably, and we need to let him do what he needs to do. And just because Dad is doing what he needs to do professionally, for the sake of his ministry at Grace, doesn't mean he's quit on life. And just because they're thinking through what the future looks like doesn't mean we need to panic and act crazy –"

Jessica opened her mouth to speak and likely reinforce my predictions on acting crazy, but I stopped her with an upheld hand.

"All I know is that he IS sick. I've seen it. I've heard it. And I know it. And surely, SURELY, if we've trusted him to be our pastor, if Grace has trusted him to be their pastor, all these years, then we can trust him to do what's right now. And if we can't even do that, then surely we can shut our mouths, stop acting like overgrown children, and trust God to take care of him, to take care of our church, and to take care of us. Because, that?"

I looked at their shocked faces.

"That's what we're really asking here, isn't it? What's going to happen to us now that our father is sick? What's going to happen to us now that we're becoming the adults that they're going to need us to be, right? It isn't about HIM or about Mom. It's about us, isn't it? And I know because, y'all, I've been asking myself these very same questions and have come to the very same conclusion – I'm more worried about what this means for ME than I am about what it means for THEM."

Neither Matthew nor Jessica said a word.

"I have to go to work," I muttered. "I'll see you guys tomorrow."

For the first time in a long time, I didn't want to leave work that night.

Evelyn had been thrilled to see me and had been more than happy to have me close out the evening receptions, even telling me to keep the tips as I did so. The money had been somewhat of an unexpected bonus on an otherwise dreary evening, what with my mind preoccupied by all that was going on back in my childhood home. As soon as my own job was done, I helped the other crews get their work done, lingering in each room longer than necessary.

Stella and her crew left a piece of one of the cakes on my desk, and when I got back, I kicked off my shoes, curled my legs up into the chair underneath me, and dug into it. Finally. Rest and peace, even as my mind raced and I wondered what I was going to do –

"Knock, knock!"

I very nearly jumped out of my own skin at the sound of her voice from the doorway.

"Oh my gosh, Emily," Sara gasped, her own hand to her mouth. "Did I scare you?"

"No, not at all," I muttered sarcastically, sweeping up the crumbs of cake that had gone flying when she popped up so unexpectedly. "Because I was totally expecting you to just randomly show up at –" I glanced at my watch, "—midnight. What are you doing here?"

She sat down across from my desk. "The team was meeting up at the coffeehouse down the street. I drove by on my way home and figured I'd come in and see if you were still in. Which, of course, you are. Because what else would you be doing on a Saturday night, right?"

I shrugged. "Well, that's true. I can't believe you're keeping these hours!"

She smiled. "Isn't it great? I mean, it's one of the best things about NOT teaching for the first time in... well, a lot of years. I don't have to be up early in the morning, so I can afford to stay out late like this. Of course, it's ALL I can afford now that I'm not teaching."

"Spare me your economic woes," I told her. "My car is literally just a few miles from death's door, and I'm pretty sure my entire house savings is going to have to go to buying a new one unless I can figure out how to walk everywhere I need to be."

"You know," Sara said, eyeing me, "I could sell my car to you. I'm not going to need it in a few months."

I looked at her dubiously. "Your car is older than mine."

"Yeah, but mine isn't totally falling apart."

"I appreciate your charity," I told her, "but no thanks."

She smiled. "I didn't say anything about charity. I would have charged you an exorbitant amount for it, of course."

"Which I surely can't afford, thanks to my bathroom remodel," I said. "Although with Josh helping out, I haven't had to hire contractors. Praise God."

Sara was apparently still hung up on my last statement, though, as evidenced by her next question.

"Josh has been helping you a lot, huh?"

"What can I say?," I said. "He feels a burden to help the clueless."

"You two sure do spend a lot of time together," she continued, fishing for details.

"He's a good friend," I offered lamely.

"A very good friend, obviously," she confirmed.

I thought about all of the mornings we had spent together, all of the evenings he had helped me out. All the extra time spent studying Scripture together. There were even a few times I had helped him grade some of his chemistry papers, knowing that the quicker he was done, the more time we had to spend together talking.

Come to think of it, I was spending more time WITH Josh than I was spending WITHOUT Josh. It hadn't been helping me to feel better about the fact that he wasn't interested in anything more than being my friend... my best friend honestly, but still just a friend. Despite the fact that all the time spent with him wasn't helping my heart in that sense, I so enjoyed being with him that I was willing to deal with the angst that came from wanting more and the disappointment with knowing that there wasn't going to be anything more.

It was complicated, obviously.

"Is something more going on with him? With the two of you?," Sara asked quietly.

I looked up at her, watching how she studied her fingernails. I saw how she was pretending not to care, and it hit me again, not for the first time, that she was likely interested in him.

Who wouldn't be?

"Why do you ask?," I treaded carefully.

"Just wondering," she said.

Being vague was getting us nowhere in this conversation. I sighed and laid it all out. "I would love for there to be more, but honestly? I don't think he's interested in the slightest."

"Really?," she asked with a smile.

Was she happy about this?

"Really," I admitted, defeated. "Why? Are you interested in him?"

She laughed out loud. "I was. I mean, who wouldn't be?"

Exactly. Of course, this didn't keep me from wanting to kill her.

"I was totally interested," she said, looking at me. "But he's so in love with you that he never even looked twice at me."

Could this be true? "What?," I managed to just barely squeak out.

"Wow, Emily. Clueless!"

"Well, that IS what I said. But do you really think...."

"Oh, yeah. He has been from the moment I met him. Probably before then. You two just need to get on with it."

I wasn't sure how to respond to this. I opened and closed my mouth a few times, feeling rather stupid that all words had escaped me. Josh had feelings for me? Since when?

"Speaking of getting on with it," Sara began in a shaky voice. "I heard that Jon is getting married."

"No way!," I gasped. "Who is he marrying?"

"Katie."

"But they've only —"

"I know," she said. "They've only been together a handful of months, as opposed to the YEARS he spent with me."

Again, I was at a loss for words. "Well... that... sucks." That's right. So helpful.

"Yes, indeed, it does suck," she nodded her head, her eyes brimming with tears. "And the fact that he proposed so quickly to her, after refusing to propose to me for so long... well, that should tell me that this is more right for him. And I should be happy for him. And I am. Kind of."

"Hey," I said, "I think you're allowed to feel what you're feeling."

"I know," she nodded. "Here I am, about to start this exciting new chapter of my life, and it should be enough... but I think of Melissa getting married, about Jon, and... it just feels like I'm getting left behind. Even like... like I'm not as good somehow. As Katie or Melissa or even you, with Josh falling all over himself around you."

How had I missed Josh "falling all over himself"? Before I could get too sidetracked thinking about this, I focused on what she had just shared. "I think," I said, then, "and I'm learning it myself, that careers, relationships, exciting changes... well, they shouldn't be the focus, the goal. And when we say they're not enough, well they shouldn't be. Because Christ alone is enough. Only Christ, and who we are in Him, is sufficient to fill every longing of our heart. Anything else is a poor substitute. We should find our everything in Him."

As soon as my mouth closed, I found my head racing back to Josh and his wonderful smile...

"And I say this," I said, "as someone who is really struggling to do just that."

She smiled at me, wiping away tears. "I know that. But it's good to hear you say it." She looked at her watch. "Why are we even still here? What was that about careers not being everything?"

I threw away the rest of the cake. "Right you are. Early morning tomorrow, after all."

"Yes, and I sure do need to hear something big from God tomorrow at church," she sighed.

I wasn't sure about what God would be saying, but what Thomas Fisher would be delivering was plenty big enough on its own.

"You bet," I said as we made the move to finally leave.

Sunday morning came early.

I found my mother sitting on the back pew, so far from her front pew, uncharacteristically missing the Sunday school hour. She was watching the set up for the service, likely anticipating the announcement that would be made, and smiling.

"Hey," I told her as I slid in next to her, hugging her to my side. "Are you doing okay?"

She shrugged. "I'm doing as well as I thought I would." She smiled again. "Actually, I'm doing better than that."

"Really?" I thought about my father's face as he had informed us all of his decision, how his voice hadn't broken at the mention of leaving Grace, and the resigned way that both of them had accepted it, knowing more than we knew about his illness. He was farther along than we thought, farther along than he really believed, farther along than my mother had let on.

"You know," she said smiling, "I've seen a lot in our thirty plus years of ministry. And you know what I've concluded?"

I expected her answer to be something profound. About the glory of God, about the sanctifying work of Christ, about the centrality of the church...

"I've concluded," she paused dramatically, "that people are rotten."

I looked at her, a little alarmed by her attitude, worried that someone might be able to hear her.

"I don't... think they're really rot—"

"Oh, honey," she patted my knee. "You don't know the half of it. Do you know what kinds of things people have complained about over the years?"

I shook my head. I assumed that there had been times when people had complained about my father, when they had borrowed his ear for tirades, and when life hadn't been rosy in the pastorate. But I couldn't recall a single incident because my parents never let on.

This protection was apparently null and void now.

"Uh, no," I admitted, nervously.

She started ticking them off on her fingers. "There was the one time people were upset about where we put the offering in the service. Then, a group of people were all up in arms about the color of the pew cushions when we remodeled. More times than I can count, people told your father to NOT preach certain texts of Scripture. There was a lady once who asked if we could post signs about keeping nursing infants and their mothers out of worship. And another man who talked to EVERY SINGLE DEACON about having the air conditioner bumped down two degrees because it was too cold, then two degrees up because it was too hot, and on and on and on –"

"How is that rotten?," I interrupted.

"It's ROTTEN," she said forcefully, "because people were so caught up in things that had NOTHING to do with the work of the Lord and that they dragged your father through the mud and back again over and over because they were more concerned for their own comforts and preferences than they were for the lost and for seeing Christ glorified and magnified."

"Oh," I offered, dumbly.

"And I won't EVEN get into how ridiculous the shouting matches have been during business meetings over what kind of music we worship to. Worship – ha!"

This was not like my mother. Or not like the mother she had ever let me see.

"The worst EVER, and I mean EVER," she hissed, conspiratorially, "was when your father had to confront someone on an issue – was compelled by Scripture to confront them as their brother in Christ – and was told," she leaned even closer, " 'Pastor Tommy, I don't care what the Bible says.' " She looked at me, bewilderment on her face. "I mean, REALLY. And then, he spread lies about your father, ALL over the church. Lies!"

She shook her head, her lips pursed tightly together. "More than once I've prayed that the fire of God would just come right on down and consume large groups of fallen pew sitters like He did in the wilderness."

I wasn't sure how to respond to this. "That's... not good," I offered, not sure whether I meant what people had done, what my mother had prayed for, or both.

"You know," she said, not even noticing my discomfort, "there have been several times that I've had to literally hold myself back and bite my tongue, wanting so desperately to dress down, yell at, and just sucker punch people who have been rude, hurtful, and malicious to your father. Just thinking about it even now, all these years later, just makes my blood boil." She shook her head. "And what makes it even worse is knowing that with all that I DID know, your father only allowed me to see the tip of the iceberg." She sighed. "For every hurtful thing he allowed me to know about, there were likely a dozen more that he kept from me, not wanting me to be hurt like he had been hurt."

She looked at me, tears in her eyes. "He's a good man. So good, in fact, that I think he kept even this... this sickness, from me until he no longer KNEW he was keeping a secret at all. I mean, SERIOUSLY, just kept it a secret until bless his heart, he didn't even KNOW there was a secret he was keeping from me!"

I swallowed past the lump in my throat, thinking of how great my father really was, how loving, how selfless, how –

"Rotten! Just like the rest of them!," my mother practically shouted.

"Mom!," I whispered, as people began coming into the sanctuary, "he is NOT."

She couldn't keep herself from laughing. "Oh, yes, he is... silly old man, trying to protect me from everything when it would have been easier to just let me in before it got out of control. He told me one day while I was in the shower that he was leaving for work, and I remembered some curriculum I needed him to copy at the last minute, so I rushed through, dressed, and ran out to the car, only to find him sitting there in a shirt, his tie, a suit jacket, and his BOXERS. No pants!" This made her burst out laughing.

I blinked past my tears, feeling my anger rise at her insensitivity. "Mom, he's sick. He didn't know –"

"Oh, Emily," she said. "I know that. I'm only laughing because… oh, I don't know." She sighed heavily. "He was as surprised as I was, tried to pass it off as a joke, and I knew but tried not to know, and he just…" She shook her head again. "Rotten, just like everyone else…" Her voice lowered. "… just like me, actually." She looked at me again, a faint glimmer of hope in her eyes. "That's what I've concluded, though. That we're all rotten… and as such, don't deserve much of anything. Which makes it all the more incredible that God gives us grace, mercy, and fullness and life and completion and wholeness in Him." She sighed. "And that… that's something to remember right now. That's what I'm holding on to."

Our bodies fail. Our minds fail. Even when we're not sick in a physical sense, we're forever sick in a spiritual one. Yet, He healed us once and for all for all eternity when He chose the cross. Eternal glory in Christ, compared to the rotten lives we lead apart from Him. Hope, something worth holding on to, even as everything temporal is falling apart.

"Me, too, Mom," I said quietly, squeezing her hand.

I don't remember my father's first day at Grace. But I will never forget his last day at Grace.

Perhaps if the church body as a whole had been given more warning the shock wouldn't have been as great. Perhaps if they had been given time to process what was happening they wouldn't have reacted as emotionally as they did. Perhaps if my mother and I had been braver to address the problem earlier on, it wouldn't have been such a sudden change for the entire church. As it was, though, there were audible gasps, many despairing words, and no shortage of tears that morning. The thrill of seeing Matthew there, meeting his fiancée, having Seth in church for the first time, and celebrating all these things with us as their pastoral family was cut short by the news.

My parents, to their credit, were strong and composed all morning long. After my father's last sermon and the resulting hour of embraces, tears, and chats with a constant stream of people, the Fisher children were a few steps short of falling completely apart. My father, however, looked better than he had in weeks. He was leaving on a strong note.

"How about lunch?," he asked us all, acting as though it was just another normal Sunday.

"That works for us," Jessica sniffed, dabbing at her eyes with a fresh Kleenex. "Matthew, Shoko?"

Matt nodded, glancing at me out of the corner of his eye as Mom and Dad were cornered by another concerned, teary church member.

"Emily," Jessica whispered, as we began making our way to the lobby. "I'm sorry." She looked to Matthew. "We're both sorry. You were right. We need to… grow up."

Inwardly, I sighed, wanting to NOT grow up at all but to throw myself on the floor of the church and have a great, big pity party and fit all thrown into one.

"Yeah," Matt said. "We're just… not having an easy time of it." He sighed as Shoko looked at him supportively. "But he did have a great last sermon, huh?"

I smiled weakly. "Going out on a high note, I guess."

"Oh, that reminds me," Jessica began, trying for her best smile as we made our way to the front doors. "Pastor Stephen and some of the deacons came to me about doing a retirement/farewell party for Dad. Kind of a chance for everyone to say goodbye, and I'm wondering if there's a chance that we could do it before Matthew and Shoko have to get back. Do you think you could help the church put it together, Emily?"

I looked out over the parking lot and sighed. "You know, I'm swamped as it is, and –" I stopped short, startled to see someone very familiar making his way through the parked cars to the doors.

"Who's that?," Matthew asked, following my gaze.

"Excuse me," I said, pushing past them and out into the sunlight, meeting Josh halfway down the sidewalk.

He was dressed for Sunday. Not in a suit like my dad but neat and well put together. I thought about how he must have come as soon as he had been done preaching his own service, how it hadn't been easy to get here so quickly with the distance, and how he had been thinking of me enough to make the effort, even though the worst of the day was over. Despite all that was going on, this made me feel better. Infinitely better.

"Hey," he smiled, glancing past me towards the curious stare of my sister and likely the confused gaze of my brother. "Came over as soon as our service was over to see how… " He looked back at me and crossed his arms over his chest uncomfortably. "Well, to see how you're doing."

I put my hand to my forehead. "I think this could have been one of the worst Sundays of my life, honestly. But it's a lot better now that you're here to rescue me from my siblings. "

We both looked over to where they continued to stare, Shoko clearly keeping Matthew from barging in with questions and introductions, Nick trying not to watch as Jessica's mouth flapped up and down with wild arms gesticulating towards us.

"Family reunion, huh?," he asked, looking back at me with a warm smile. "I'm glad they all could be here for your dad today."

"Do you... do you want to meet them?," I asked, not entirely sure that I wanted to subject kind and compassionate Josh to this circus. At least not in its current state of disarray.

"I would love to," he said, glancing their way again, his expression changing as another person came into view. Pastor Stephen. "But, I can't stay. And I want you all to have your time together this afternoon to decompress from this."

"Are you sure? I would love for you to finally meet my dad." And I meant this, knowing how much my father would like Josh, how much they had in common already, and how much they would have to talk about together. As much as I would have liked for it to mean more, having him meet my parents, I still wanted him to know my family. He had been such a big part of my life for the past seven months – it only seemed right to have them know all about him, even if I didn't mean that much to him after all.

He held my gaze for a moment, then glanced back to the scene in the lobby. Stephen was trying to tell my sister something, and Matthew was openly glaring at Josh. Great.

"Maybe another time, okay?"

I nodded, choked up. "It was nice of you to come and check on things. I really do appreciate it."

He nodded back. "No problem. Hey." He put his hand on my arm, and I looked up at him. "You call me if you need anything, okay?"

"Okay."

"Bye, Emily," he said softly, turning back and jogging the rest of the way to his truck.

I took a deep, long breath, then turned back to the church, where Jessica and Matt were quick with the questions.

"Who was that?"

"Emily, who was that guy?"

Pastor Stephen, seeing my discomfort and pure exhaustion, offered, "Hey, Emily, your dad asked me to come out with all of you to lunch. Will you ride with me so we can talk about the farewell party?"

My eyes met his understanding gaze, and I tried to communicate my thanks to him. "I would love to. Let's go."

The Monday after Dad's big announcement we were scheduled to try on bridesmaid dresses for Melissa's wedding.

Trish Thibideaux had arranged to have her friend's bridal shop closed down for us alone, just as she had for Melissa's trip to buy her own gown. She also booked a limo to take us all out to dinner afterwards and had gone through a lot of trouble to make it a special event for Melissa.

"I can totally cancel," Melissa said to me on the phone Sunday night, after I finally arrived home. Our lunch out with the family had been longer than anticipated, as we ran into many, many church members while eating out, all of whom wanted to tell my father what he meant to them, with such sadness and grief that it was like he was dying already.

It was exhausting.

"Cancel? Why?," I had asked Melissa as I pulled off my shoes.

"Well, the news about your dad. About Grace! Hardly seems like the time to celebrate anything," she said.

"It's the perfect time," I said with a deep breath. "Your wedding and your marriage has nothing to do with my dad's illness. You should feel more than free, more than justified, to enjoy yourself and to let me enjoy this all with you."

"I know," she said, "but, Emily," her words were choked and heavy with emotion, "he's my pastor, too."

This was the truth. As we struggled with our own emotions over this, we had been reminded that Dad didn't just belong to us and that there were more than just a few whose lives were changing with ours.

"And as your pastor," I told Melissa, "he would want you to do everything to get ready to marry Beau. As he always says," I said, smirking, "better to marry than burn, after all."

This was, regrettably, one of my father's favorite things to tell young couples that he counseled who were intent on having super long engagements. His counsel was good, that they should just get on with the business of getting married already if that was their intent, but the implications in what he said were more than a little mortifying for me as his daughter.

Ugh.

"Oh, don't remind me, " Melissa said. "He did our counseling, and I can't tell you how awkward some of those sessions were."

"Well, at least he's not a prude who won't touch the subject, I guess," I offered. "Anyway," I said, moving away from the topic, "is this great need to cancel more about my dad or about you getting out of spending another evening with Trish?"

"Trish?," Melissa asked, surprised. "Oh, I have no problem with Trish."

"You've had a problem with her from the first day you met," I accused.

"Well, not anymore," she swore. "Maybe I was being unfair, but she's won me over."

"How so?," I asked, disbelieving.

"Well, I thought she was so superficial. All fluff and no substance, you know. A few weeks ago, she found out that I had cut all of those ridiculous plants for the ceremony out of our budget. And she was just beside herself that we would do that. Like it even really matters! But she was freaking out about how bare the sanctuary was going to look. Before I could give her what for about it all, and believe me, I wanted to –"

I could believe it.

"—well, Beau explained it to her, about what we were doing with the money instead. And she just went ballistic! I mean, over the top emotional, crying, wall-eyed fit. I thought we were going to have to have her committed, honestly."

"So, you pity her now because she's unstable?," I asked, confused.

"Will you let me finish my story already?"

"Geez, sorry."

"Anyway," she said heavily, "her reaction was all because – get this – SHE had been a part of the same program years ago! After college, she went to China, with the same mission board for three years. Trish! In China! For real! She swore to us as she cried these huge, ugly tears that it had been the best time of her life and that we had done the right thing for Sara. Then, she broke out her checkbook and wrote a check to me for twice the amount we had saved and told me to get it to the board in Sara's name!"

"Oh my word," I said, astonished. "Two years' worth of support money?"

"With the promise that she would do even more if Sara needed it." A pause. "Can you even believe someone would keep that much money in their checking account?"

"Well, I don't know that that's the most incredible part of the story, but wow. I guess this means that Sara is really going."

"Yep, and she'll never know that her main benefactor is a Gucci-carrying, Prada-wearing socialite in New Orleans. Who, you know, can just randomly speak Mandarin Chinese thanks to the three years she spent backpacking through the mountains, sharing Jesus with villagers!"

"Way to go, Trish," I said.

"I know, right?"

I couldn't help but think of this as I watched Trish adjust the straps on the adorable dark red dress Sara was modeling for Melissa at the bridal boutique that Monday evening. I was wearing the same dress in green while Beau's youngest, most petite sister, Chloe, wore it in silver. They had gone with my advice to look at the same dress on a range of body types – tiny, typical, and towering – to make their decision. Melissa had picked the style of dress and was now trying to settle on the color. The style looked good on everyone, but the color –

"Geez, Emily," Mel gaped, "you look like the Jolly Green Giant."

"That I do," I said, eyeing myself in the three way mirror. "Mrs. Thibideaux, is this the only shade of green this dress comes in?"

"It's Trish, dear, and regrettably, it is." She looked to Melissa. "The choice is obvious, isn't it?," she said, looking between the two less jolly models.

"I'll say," Melissa agreed, looking to Beau. "Silver, it is." Beau put his thumb up in the air, his eyes never leaving his laptop, which he had been using to communicate with work all night long.

I could see the surprise on Trish's face as she looked longingly at Sara's dress, but she covered it quickly by saying, "Lovely choice, dear."

"If I can just get everyone's sizes," the shop owner said, "Trish and I'll take care of the arrangements."

"Trish," Melissa said, "Beau and I budgeted to handle this one ourselves."

"I would be honored to do it for you," Trish said, not being at all pushy. "Honestly honored."

"If you're sure," Melissa said hesitantly.

"Thanks, Mom," Beau said, raising his eyes and smiling at her.

"My pleasure," she said, following us back to the dressing room, where I began struggling to get my zipper down.

"May I help you, Emily?"

"Thanks... Trish," I said, practically kneeling so that she, even in her high heels, could reach halfway up my back.

"Melissa told me about your father," she said quietly to me. "I... I wasn't going to say anything to you about it, but my Daddy had Alzheimer's, you know."

"He had..." I said softly. "So, he's passed on?"

"Oh, yes," she said. "But he was seventy-five. Lived with the illness for a long time. Had more clarity for longer than we thought he would, too."

She smiled brightly at me. "Not that it wasn't hard. On my mother. On me. On my brothers. Because it was."

I nodded at the truth of this.

"I only mention it, because if you ever need to talk to someone," she said, meeting my eyes, "someone who has been there... well, I'm here."

"Thank you, Trish. That means a lot."

I was back in the groove at work and thankful for it. After so many weeks of watching my nephews, dealing with the fallout from my father's illness, Alyssa's wedding, and the impromptu remodel of my bathroom, I had been all over the place physically and emotionally. It was good to be back where the work was steady. Steadily chaotic but steady all the same.

We had done three weddings so far that day, and our final ceremony was set to start in an hour. I hadn't been too involved in Andrea and Hunter's arrangements, mainly because the bulk of their meetings had been in the past two months when I had been out and in so sporadically.

And also because Hunter had grabbed my butt after our first meeting several months earlier.

I knew his number from that day on and made doubly sure I wasn't in the same room alone with him. EVER. That was my general policy with grooms anyway (because you can never be too careful when it comes to how things look, per Evelyn's wisdom), but he was a sneaky one. After making eyes at me during that initial consult, while his fiancée went on and on without ever noticing, I had been happy to walk them out together and only mildly annoyed when he came back alone to pick up the jacket Andrea had forgotten. He had somehow managed to maneuver himself just so, backing me up against my own desk, as he told me how he'd like to get to know me better. Oh, this had happened with other grooms before, always to my horror, but he was more forward than the others had been, as evidenced by his response to my "take a hike, bozo" speech, which was to pat me on the backside and point his finger at me as if to say that we weren't done.

Well, I was done with him. Evelyn had listened to my account of the whole incident, told me there wasn't much we could do since he was a client, and said she'd take care of the little pea-brain. There was no sense of legality or morality behind her decision to just ignore it all, but that didn't matter much to Evelyn because Hunter's fiancée was rich.

And that was that.

Until, of course, it wasn't.

"Emily," Evelyn met me in the garden room, where I was helping to close out the last reception we had done that afternoon, "there's some trouble with the Collins wedding. The bride's grandmother is a diabetic and needs a snack." She rolled her eyes at me.

"Is that even our job?," I asked.

"It most certainly isn't," she huffed, "but what are we going to do? The old bag is loaded."

My eyes widened at this.

"Forgive me," Evelyn said, honestly repentant. "I shouldn't be so un-PC, but this bride! She's a horror, my dear. Sooooo over the top."

If Evelyn knew anything, she knew about over the top people. Because it took one to know one.

"Well, I'll be happy to do it. I'd rather take care of someone's ailing grandmother than a drama queen bride, that's for sure."

Evelyn nodded. "Thank you. Andrea and her bridal party are on the fifth floor, in room –"

"Andrea?," I asked. "Collins..." Realization dawned on me. "Oh, THAT one."

"Yes, the infamous Hunter," she frowned tightly. "Just let me deal with him. He wouldn't DREAM of touching me."

Not unless he had a certain death wish.

I contacted Stella on my walkie talkie, then went to the kitchen where her crew had a fruit bowl and some crackers prepared for me. I made my way onto the elevator, pressing the button for the fifth floor, wondering what drama waited for me in the flamboyant Andrea's room, when the elevator stopped on the second floor. I pasted my most professional smile on my face...

... which disappeared when Hunter walked in all by himself.

"Well, hello," he said. "Haven't seen you in a while."

I mentally reminded myself to remain calm and professional. "Only about thirty minutes until your big moment," I told him, glancing at my watch. "Andrea is going to be just beautiful."

"Yeah," he sighed, glancing over in my direction as the elevator doors closed and left us alone together.

Great.

"There's just one thing I need help with," he said, moving closer to me. "You know, help from our wedding coordinator."

"Well," I said, inching farther away from him. "I'll be sure and send Mrs. Primrose your way, then."

"Oh, not her," he said. "You're the one I want."

And before I could say another word, his arms were around me, and he had planted his lips right on mine. I did my best to push him away, just as the door dinged. Praise God for whoever was coming from the fourth floor!

I rushed off the elevator as soon as the doors were open, leaving Hunter far behind me as I hustled to the stairs. I had to find Evelyn.

Evelyn, sorry to say, was no help at all.

"Oh, I could just KILL that little —" she fumed, stopping herself just short of an expletive.

"Me, too," I said, my hands still shaking while they held the fruit bowl and crackers. "I think I should... I should TELL someone, right?"

"Why? That's not your job," Evelyn said.

"This," I said, holding up the food, "isn't my job either, but I'm doing it because it's the right thing to do. A diabetic grandmother needs it, so I'm taking it to her. And telling the bride that her husband-to-be is kissing — excuse me, ASSAULTING — someone else thirty minutes before the wedding? It's the right thing to do."

"None of our business, Emily," Evelyn said. "What's going to happen if you tell her? Do you honestly think you're going to stop this wedding?"

"Well, yeah!"

"You're not going to stop anything," she said. "I've seen it before. Trust me. That girl is getting married today, no matter what. You go in and tell her what you're telling me, and the only thing she'll believe is that you're trying to ruin her big day. And she will make our name MUD with all of her little rich friends. So, what good would it have done? What good?"

I was at a loss for words. For just a moment. "The good is that it's... it's the right thing to do. Even if it doesn't benefit US. Don't you understand that?"

"No," she said. "I really don't. But I do understand why you're upset." She gave me a sympathetic look. "Why don't you go home? Just take some time for yourself."

"But, Evelyn —"

"There's nothing we can do," she said, taking the fruit and crackers from me. "Nothing."

I numbly drove myself home, then sat down on my couch, not even bothering to change out of my clothes or take off my heels. My phone buzzed, indicating a text message, and I looked at it hopefully, thinking that Evelyn might have had a change of heart and driven that couple out of the hotel like Jesus drove the moneychangers out of the Temple.

I was comparing Evelyn to Jesus now. Clearly I was just that upset.

When r u going to be home? Picked up new mirror for bathroom. Want to bring it by if ok with u.

Josh. I quickly typed out a response. *Home early. Come over.*

He must have either been in the neighborhood or speeding when he got my text because ten minutes later, he was knocking on my door.

"Hey, don't you look nice?," he said, smiling at me, holding a huge mirror in front of himself.

"Thanks," I managed. "Just bring that on in."

"It's bigger than you were wanting, isn't it?," he said. "I was there looking for a different set of bits for the drill – oh, yeah, I just used the words 'drill' and 'bits' in their correct context – and I saw that this was marked down, and I thought I'd –"

He stopped short, when I sunk back down onto the couch.

"Hey," he said softly. "Are you okay?"

"Yeah, tough night at work."

He leaned the mirror against the wall and looked at his watch. "I thought it was pretty early for you to be done. Something go wrong?"

He sat next to me, turning to face me.

"Well, the wedding was lovely, I'm sure. But the groom is a... well, he's an awful kisser."

Josh looked at me, confused by this.

"What?," he managed. "How would you..."

"How would I know, right?," I said, nodding my head at him. "I wish I didn't, but after he grabbed my butt a long while back, I've just been all up close and personal with him."

"He grabbed your butt?" Josh looked appropriately horrified by this.

"Yes, he did. And then he cornered me tonight and kissed me."

"What?!," Josh stared at me. "Who did this? What's his name?"

"Hunter. Oh, geez. He even sounds dangerous, doesn't he? "

"When did this happen? The... the kiss?"

"Thirty minutes before his wedding. I mean, what kind of creep does that? Really? Just forces himself on someone who isn't interested at ALL, much less thirty minutes before his own wedding?"

Josh stood up, turning his phone on. "What was this guy's last name?"

"Collins. And he's marrying a Newborn. Probably is already married to a Newborn right now. And she's rich. Rich, rich, rich, though I don't think it would have made a difference to Evelyn either way, honestly, because even a little money is still money."

"Hunter Collins... Hunter Collins..." Josh began typing on his phone.

"Don't look him up," I said.

"How else am I going to track him down and kill him?" He was fuming.

I put my hands on my face. "I just want to forget all about him. I feel so dirty. Ugh."

Josh crossed his arms over his chest, gaping at me. "Well, YOU shouldn't feel that way. HE should, though." He shook his head, visibly angry, going right back to typing on his phone. "Do you have an address for this guy? I'd love to pay him a little pastoral visit, if you know what I mean."

"Oh, don't go all big brother on me," I said. "Josh, please." I reached out and touched his arm, pulling his phone away from him. "What's done is done, and now, I'm never going to have to see him again. Hallelujah."

"I'm not going all 'big brother' on you," he continued, still vey bothered. "I just don't want... I don't want you treated like that. It's wrong. You're worth more than that."

I slid my hands down my face. "What's wrong about it is that I had to stand back, after this happened, and not say anything. Do you know how hard it is to KNOW that a marriage is going to be doomed, to know that it's a sham, and to just be forced to go on with it, to not be able to intervene, to just stand there with grimy handprints on your butt —"

"Oh, geez," Josh rubbed his own face.

"—and not say a word? I hate this business. I hate it." I looked at him. "Please sit down. You're making me a nervous wreck."

He plopped down on the couch next to me. "Maybe it's not the business you hate. Maybe it's working for THIS business."

I bit my lip thoughtfully. "Yeah... I've thought that before, you know. That maybe I should just... should just go out on my own, do this independently, not have to put up with things that just aren't right or ethical."

"Then, you should," he said. "You totally should."

"It doesn't pay the bills," I said. "THIS barely pays them anyway these days."

"Well, there's got to be something you can do," Josh continued on, more bothered than I was by it all now. "We can't just sit here, and let things like this happen. You're worth more than that, and –"

"Josh," I said, leaning my head against his shoulder. "I'm just so tired. So tired."

And at some point in sitting there with him in companionable silence, I must have fallen asleep because the next thing I knew, it was morning. I was lying on the couch, a blanket draped over me, my shoes on the carpet, my hair freed from its French twist, and a note on my coffee table.

You're worth more than that to me. Josh

10 SEPTEMBER

I got over the grimy butt handprints. Or as over it as I was going to get.

Josh had just about driven me crazy, trying to make sure I was okay after it all happened, and I was still half-convinced that I'd hear of Hunter Collins's untimely demise at the hands of some sort of Ministerial Mexican Mafia. But as time went by, we both cooled off, and I tried to forget about it.

What I didn't forget about were the conversations I had with Josh later, about at least looking into doing my own consulting on the side, making it into a business, and walking away from the messed up ethics of Evelyn's business.

I was in the midst of thinking through these things when Melissa, Sara, and I met up at the beginning of the month. Our schedules were busier than they had been in the months prior – Melissa was still wedding planning and working forty plus hour weeks, Sara was trying to pack up her life for Costa Rica and sell everything that wouldn't journey with her, and I was trying to spend every free moment from work with Matthew and Shoko, who would be going back to Japan at the week's end, after our family's farewell reception at Grace.

Which I was also coordinating.

"I can't believe this is the only time we could all meet up," Sara said, after rushing into the bridal shop thirty minutes late.

"Hey," I said, giving her a hug. "We all did the best we could." I still smelled like French fries and chicken nuggets, thanks to the fine feast I had just finished taking my nephews to, courtesy of the Golden Arches.

"I would give you a hug, too, you know," Melissa said from atop her perch before the three way mirror, her arms held out perfectly perpendicular from her body, "since I'm not going to have the chance to in a few weeks. But, I don't want to – OUCH!"

The seamstress barely glanced up from where she was pinning pleats. "Sorry about that."

"Oh, it's so beautiful," Sara said, reaching up to squeeze Melissa's hand, admiring the train of the gown, touching the material delicately. Then, peering more closely, "I wonder what kind of beads these are…"

"Seed pearls," the seamstress murmured past a mouthful of pins.

"I'll have to write that down," Sara said, pulling a notepad from her purse. "I've got a million lists going on here, y'all. So much to remember."

"And now, seed pearls," I said, sitting on the couch in the fitting room, slipping my heels off. "Why do you need to remember that?"

"Well, actually," she began, "it's part of the resolutions. And bigger than that. I've been thinking about what kind of hobby I could start, you know, without adding just more nuttiness to my life."

"We could probably have foregone the whole list of resolutions anyway," Melissa said. "Life has taken a few crazy turns for all of us this year. I mean, I didn't even do the home improvement thing –"

"Neither did I," Sara confessed.

"Oh, I did," I muttered.

Melissa ignored me, "Maybe it's best to just be done with the resolutions, huh?"

"Oh, no, I've already started on this month's," Sara said. "See, that's the great thing. This resolution has given me an incredible idea for a ministry in Costa Rica. I'll be doing my teaching, of course, but I was hoping to do something with the women I met when I was there in the spring. Some of them are widows who have a hard time supporting their children, making ends meet and all. I've heard about some other ministries in other parts of the world that help to create trades and businesses, using the skills the women already have, to assist them in making a sustainable income. I know the women there do gorgeous beadwork for themselves, and I figure, as I'm learning to do what they do and finding out what kind of supplies I can take with me to Costa Rica to help them do what they're doing... well, I can take steps to promote that with people back home. Sell their products, with all of the profit going back to them." She looked up at me. "Is that crazy, or do you think it might work?"

I was at a loss for words at the creativity and genius behind this idea. I could see Sara steering this ship, creating this business, loving these women in Christ's name, and making a difference – not just in eternity but in the world, right here and now.

"It sounds amazing, actually. I could talk to some ladies at Grace about getting involved as well."

"Already done," Sara smiled. "Stephen said he'd get me in touch with the right ladies. Not like he needs anymore work right now, but..."

She stopped short, looking at me apologetically. Before I could tell her that it was okay, this reminder of my father's condition and our very changed lives, Melissa spoke up.

"Well, that's a whole lot more noble than my hobby," she said. "I've taken up tennis."

"Tennis?," I asked. "Don't you have to have someone to play that with?"

"Oh, I do," she said. "Chloe."

I thought about Beau's sister, Chloe, about how she had just moved to town to attend college on a... tennis scholarship.

"Oh, wow," I said. "You're playing with a college athlete?"

"If you can call it that," she said. "I mostly run all over the court, swinging for my life, likely looking like an idiot as I do so. Chloe is a very patient teacher, but I? I am no athlete." She looked at her dress in the mirror. "And goodness knows I need to do something to keep my weight down. I think I'm past the point of ordering another, bigger dress."

"You are," the seamstress chimed in. "And you're past the point of being able to gain any more curves in THIS dress. As it is, I'm going to have to let out these darts here, Mrs. Thibideaux," she said, pointing to Melissa's hips.

Melissa only seemed to hear what she wanted to, a smile on her face. "Mrs. Thibideaux... I do like the way that sounds."

"Speaking of," I said, pulling a huge file out of my bag, "Mrs. Thibideaux – the real time Mrs. Thibideaux, not the future one – gave me some more details on the reception meal. We need to look over it after you're done so that I can get it arranged tomorrow morning before I go to work."

"Will do," Melissa said.

"You're working as much for Melissa as you are for your hotel clients these days, aren't you?," Sara began. "And that wedding you did last month –"

"And the two I have this month," I added. "It's probably not wise, taking these extra clients on, but... well, I'm considering it a hobby."

"A time consuming hobby, at that," Melissa added.

"That it is."

"You know," Sara began, "you should really think about doing this on the side, as your own business. Full time, you know. How great would that be?"

I took a breath, daring to believe, not for the first time, that it might be possible. I opened my mouth to tell them that I had already been thinking about it, when the seamstress stepped back.

"And you're done," she said to Melissa. "Only one more fitting left. Don't eat anything, okay?"

"As if," Melissa said, admiring the back of her dress. "Hey, Emily, can you help me get out of this thing without pricking holes all over myself?"

I smiled, tucking my dreams away for now. "That's why I'm here."

We had just finished a six mile run. This was a big, huge deal to me, seeing as how I had never run that far in my life, but Josh had literally taken it in stride. He was nearing the end of his marathon training, and six miles was a short, restful run for him.

I wondered how six miles could be restful for anyone based on the amount of sweat released when I took off my baseball cap and let my hair loose outside our coffee shop.

"Ewww!," I yelled. "It's like I just took a shower... where sweat was coming out of the showerhead!"

Josh was watching me, a strange look on his face, as I continued to shake my hair loose. "Almost as refreshing as your own shower, huh?," he finally remarked.

We had moved on from the sink to the shower the week before, and in the process, we had eliminated any and all hot water from coming out. I was a week into cold showers and saw no end in sight. Sara had told me that cold showers were all she would have in Costa Rica, to which I reminded her that I wasn't living in Costa Rica… just a really ghetto apartment that I had destroyed with my own two hands.

"Don't start with me on that shower," I told Josh, giving him my best reproachful look.

"Sorry," he laughed. "Why don't I make it up to you by getting you something to drink? Something with ICE in it, perhaps?"

"That's great," I said. "I'll sit out here so my smelly self doesn't offend everyone inside."

I claimed the table we had spent the spring and summer using, propping my exhausted feet up on the chair next to me, waiting for Josh and checking my phone for messages. Everything was coming together for the farewell dinner for next weekend, the two weddings I had that same weekend, and the small ceremony I had coordinated on my own for a friend of Alyssa's. With the extra money coming in from the independent jobs, I had once again started believing that I might finish the project on my apartment bathroom and maybe, just maybe, might be able to start saving again for a house.

Maybe.

"What are you thinking about?," Josh said, walking to our table with drinks in hand.

"Houses," I said. "Houses with warm showers."

"Still on the shower thing, huh?," he said, handing me my drink. Just exactly what I would have ordered myself. "You know, I'll come over this afternoon to work on it if you want me to."

"I wish you could," I said, "but I've got a shopping trip with Sara planned. She found these hiking shoes that a missionary on the field swears by, but the only place that sells them is an hour away. Some outlet mall or something, who knows. I told her I'd go with her since I have ZERO weddings on the schedule for today."

"No weddings, no work," he said, smiling.

"I'll make up for it the rest of the month," I told him. "Don't worry about that." Then, after my first sip, "Are we still okay to meet on Monday night?"

My ladies' summer Bible study had long since ended, but I wanted to keep meeting with Josh, studying Scripture with him. It was the best part of my week, and I was hesitant to stop doing it. Josh was fine to keep on, seemed even eager to do so, even though it meant meeting up with me after a long day of school and usually before a long night of lesson planning and sermon prep for the week ahead. I should probably have felt guiltier for taking up his time like that... but the thrill of more time spent with him easily won over the guilt.

"I'm there," he said. Then, after taking another drink, "You should come to Redeemer tomorrow. Debbie keeps looking for you every week. All of them do, actually."

I noticed that he didn't include himself in the group, in the general consensus of the Morales clan. I had gone to Redeemer a couple of times and wanted to go back, but I didn't want to overcrowd him.

As if spending every waking moment with him wasn't already doing that.

I thought back to Sara's comments and wondered if there wasn't more to what he was saying, in what his eyes were saying as they met mine across the table. I was tempted to ask him, to try to define what was going on, when he asked me, "You ready to head on back to our cars? We can drink as we go, then get you on the road for your shopping trip."

I nodded, regretting just one of many lost moments. "You bet."

My parents' farewell party at Grace came with more than a few surprises.

The catering and the decorations had been a breeze to coordinate, as had all of the extra help, with those who were serving dinner, the musicians who provided background music, and Stephen, who was good to lead the celebration. Matthew, Shoko, Nick, Jessica, and I, along with my nephews, spent the evening going around to shake all the hands there, to receive and give embraces, and to present a united front as the Fisher family. We were going forward together, all of us of one mind and one spirit.

Only we had no idea what my parents had planned.

Dad was given the opportunity to say a few words of farewell at the conclusion of the reception, and as he said all that we expected – that Grace had been home, that ministry had been a joy, and that we would not be strangers as we were all one in Christ – we smiled and nodded, wiping away a few tears ourselves. Dad, however, had a whole lot more to say.

"God is doing a new thing with Lydia and with me," Dad said, smiling at Mom warmly, a gesture that she reciprocated. "Even though this illness has taken me from THIS ministry, we still don't believe that He has taken us out of ALL vocational ministry. And I'm very excited to tell you about what we're going to be doing next."

Jess looked over at me, confused. I shrugged, not sure where he was going with this either.

"We've been in touch with the mission board, explained our situation, and there's a need that we can fill. It's just a short term trip for now, with the opportunity for more short term trips in the future, my health considered, of course. We'll be leaving for a few weeks in November to go to Rwanda to train pastors in theology and church leadership."

Gasps of surprise, followed by appreciative applause, filled the room.

And the three Fisher children shared incredulous looks. Really?

It took the rest of Shoko and Matthew's time in the States for my parents to convince us that this was indeed a wise decision.

"The doctors have cleared it," my mother said to me, as I was the last one to be convinced, likely because I had seen effects of the illness more intimately than the others. "And if at any time it's NOT a good thing for your father, I'll bring him home, and we'll stop doing this."

"Mom, I just don't understand why he –"

"God is NOT done with us," she said firmly. Then, with lowered voice, "And if your father is going to pass on, to slip away from us forever, well then he wants to do it serving Christ."

How can you argue with that, really?

I couldn't. "Okay," I said. "I trust you, Mom."

It was my twenty-ninth birthday, and I was the only one who had remembered.

Work was beginning to calm down after the summer rush, and I had been blessed that day with a series of meetings with calm and mellow fall brides, all of whom seemed to dispensationally match the breezy, cool atmosphere of their nuptial season of choice. After my final meeting with the Disney couple, I left with big plans to settle in at home and order a pizza.

My sister was still dealing with the adjustment to five children. My mother was still dealing with the adjustment of retirement and medical changes. My brother was likely still dealing with jet lag. Melissa was dealing with wedding arrangements and a hectic schedule at work. Sara was dealing with the pressure of selling all of her stuff before she had to leave for a two month long training across the country.

They were busy. And it was only my twenty-ninth birthday. Not a really big one in any sense.

Still, though, the apartment was quieter than usual when I arrived home. Josh and I had managed to get parts of the bathroom back to full functionality. There was still some major cosmetic work left to do and my shower still only spit out cold water, but we had already done more than I thought we'd be able to, thanks to the DIY videos and perseverance. And many, many hours together. I smiled as I changed my clothes, thinking of those hours well spent.

Just as I was about to settle in on the couch and find something on the television, there was a knock on my front door. I went over, peeped out through the hole, and smiled to see Josh, holding a dish in his arms.

"Hey," I said, opening up the door for him. "I didn't know you were coming over!"

"Hey," he smiled back. "I'm sure you have plans for tonight, but I wanted to stop by and tell you happy birthday."

I could feel tears gathering in my eyes, something that was happening more and more lately with all the drama going on in my life. "You remembered my birthday?"

"Well, yeah," he said in his best "duh" voice. "Of course I remembered."

"I'm sorry," I said, "come on in. And I actually DON'T have any huge plans tonight. I think the rest of the family is a little preoccupied because September 16th isn't ringing any bells for any of them."

"They forgot your birthday?," he asked, setting down his dish on the kitchen counter.

"Yeah," I said, "but it's not a big one, right?"

"Just the death of your twenties," he smiled over at me.

"Well, that does make it sound important."

"Which is why I'm especially glad I came over. I have a little something you might enjoy," he said, handing the dish to me.

I lifted the lid to find —

"Cinnamon rolls! How did you —"

"Well, I can't take all the credit," he said. "It's my grandmother's recipe. And she made them. But only because they were for you."

"I can't even believe it."

"What? That my Mexican grandma can cook anything besides tamales? How very racist of you."

"No, not that," I said, hitting his arm, "that you remembered how much I love these. Better than —"

"Cake," he finished for me, imitating my voice. "All those brides, all that leftover cake, when all you want is a —"

"Cinnamon roll," I said softly.

"I do listen when you talk, Emily. I've been planning this for a while." Then, lower, in a conspiratorial voice, "Oh, and my grandma does make tamales. Cliché maybe, but she does. And they're even better than these cinnamon rolls. Hard to believe, I know. Did you try them when you had lunch with us?"

I nodded, unable to say anything else.

"Oh, and you have no idea the calamities I went through to bring it back from my grandmother's side of town," he said. "Construction both ways on the freeway, with rush hour thrown in, until I finally just got out of there and took all these crazy side roads to get here. Got lost in the middle of it all, and I was passing all kinds of cow pastures and fields, totally out in the sticks, taking way longer than I should have, so they aren't even warm anymore, but –"

And without thinking through the wisdom of it or wondering if I should, I reached over, touched his face, and brought my lips to his, my eyes blurred with tears over this very simple gift that meant so much, over this man who meant everything to me.

It was a soft, lingering kiss, simple and sweet, over as soon as I caught myself, right as Josh was just beginning to respond in kind by pulling me closer, kissing me back more deeply, clouding the very little sense of reason that I still had in my grasp.

I backed away, surprised by myself and the rush of emotion that filled me as I looked at his familiar face, the feelings more intense than they had ever been. Perhaps this kiss had been a long time coming, but judging from the shocked expression that washed over his features, I could guess that he wasn't completely prepared for it or for his own reaction.

Neither was I. I put my hand to my lips, thinking through how he had been right there in the moment with me, hoping that it meant something more...

We watched one another in silence for a moment.

"Well," he said softly. "I'll have to drive out to the sticks more often."

It was exactly what I didn't need. Josh and I had just finished another Saturday morning run, saying our quick goodbyes and heading away for a busy, on my part at least, Saturday. As I drove away from the park, my car sputtered and slowed to a crawl. The "check engine" light flashed at me repeatedly, as if to say "savings account drained," "hopes dashed," and "just scrap metal" to me again and again. Lovely. Just lovely.

And this? Was just the tip of the iceberg. After I had kissed my best friend the night before (because that was going to turn out well, right?), the two of us had a series of awkward interchanges dancing around some obvious issues we had. In my attempt to downplay the intense feelings rushing through me, I had managed to convince him to stay for pizza, a movie, and a feast of cinnamon rolls. He had agreed to stay, even though he acted as though he felt uncomfortable doing so. It was my own fault. If I had kept my lips to myself, he wouldn't have had to feel strange about spending more time with me. I had begun to wonder, as we watched our movie in silence, if I had made things weird forever. And those seeds of thoughts that Sara had placed in my mind about Josh being in love with me? Yeah, those were all but completely refuted by his reluctance to even look me in the eye the night before or as we had a very quiet run the next morning.

And now, my car was vomiting who knows what beneath the hood. Fabulous.

I pulled my phone out of my purse and clicked through my list of contacts, searching for someone – anyone – who might be available to tow me to a mechanic who would, no doubt, charge me an exorbitant fee to tell me that my car was dying a slow, painful, and expensive death. Perhaps I could bike everywhere. I would certainly save on gas that way, wouldn't I?

Just as I had concluded that my best option was Melissa, who could either haul my coupe away or just drive over and squash it with her Hummer, Josh got out of his truck and jogged up to my window. I attempted to roll it down to talk with him, and as if on cue, the window fell right off its track and started falling into the door.

"Hey, there's something you don't see every day," he said, catching the corner of the glass in between his fingers before it disappeared into the dark abyss of the car door. "Do you mind if I...?" He motioned to the window.

"Oh, by all means. What could it hurt, right?"

He smiled, and using both hands, he yanked the window back up and somehow fit it onto the track. I was impressed. "Wow! How did you do that?" I bent over to roll it all the way up, but his exclamation stopped me short.

"Whoa! I didn't fix it. Just... just pulled it back up. Don't roll it up until I can get a good look at it. Is that why you were stopped?"

I leaned my head back on the headrest. "No, unfortunately, that was just one of many ailments the old girl is having. The 'check engine' light came on. And there's probably smoke. Something broken I'm sure, beyond repair. And probably a whole family of possums living in the engine. Nothing would surprise me at this point. Just all kinds of good stuff."

He motioned to the hood. "Do you mind if I take a look?"

I peered at him skeptically. "I think this is beyond some DIY videos."

Laughing, he opened my door, and reached down near my ankles to release the hood, creating a wave of butterflies throughout my system.

I joined him as he walked to the front of the car, lifted the hood, and waved smoke away from the engine. "Hmm...," he said thoughtfully.

"Hmm... what?" I asked eagerly. "Is it bad?"

He peered a bit more closely, then looked at me solemnly. "Yes. It's very bad. And by bad, I mean that I can't see anything wrong with it."

"Fabulous," I said. "Can you haul me to the mechanic on 4th and Main?" A pause. "We're on a first name basis and all." This was not my car's first rodeo. It had been in and out of the shop over the spring, and I had paid hundreds, if not thousands of dollars, to my mechanic to keep it running. At this rate, I would single-handedly put the man's children through college.

Josh shook his head. "No. Not in good conscience, at least." He slammed the hood shut. "I *can*, however," he said, facing me, "take you to *my* mechanic."

I exhaled slowly, relieved. "Well, I do have my loyalties, you know," I said, sarcastically. "How will his children eat if I don't keep giving him my service, huh?"

Josh brushed some dirt off the hood. "Something tells me that he could feed them steak every day for a year on what you've already paid him to keep putting band-aids on this engine." True that. "Seriously, my dad's shop isn't too far from here. And if he won't do the work for free, my brothers – excuse me, his 'associates' – certainly will. They can't resist being heroes to a beautiful woman. Especially when that beautiful woman is you, who they seem to like more than they even like me, honestly." I began to protest his generosity, when he stopped me with, "But feel free to go to your own mechanic if you need to. Just offering."

"No," I said, sighing. "That would be really helpful. Are you sure you have time today?"

He wiped his hands off on his shorts. "I'm free all day."

I gave him a sheepish grin and said, "Thanks, Josh. I'm so sorry to ruin your day off. I know they're rare." I could feel a lump forming in my throat, thinking of all the times he had come to my rescue and how much I had put at risk the night before with my kiss.

His eyes never even met mine as he said, "So totally not ruined." Then, with a quick nod, he was on his phone, calling his brothers to bring a tow truck.

"Okay, so what we've done is replaced the —" And so began a ten minute dissertation from Josh's oldest brother, Mike, on what exactly he had done to my car. I didn't understand a word of it. The prognosis had been bad, veering just short of fatal, and while they had done massive repairs during the long afternoon, charging me just for the cost of parts, Josh's father and all four of his brothers had concluded that my little coupe was not going to live to see another year. Would it get me through until my Christmas bonus? Very likely... but they gave me the number for their tow service just in case.

Josh and I had spent the hours at the shop, chatting awkwardly in the break room, watching the work in the garage from our air conditioned, elevator music-wired sanctuary. More than once, I caught a brother watching us from where he worked and Josh's father glancing up often in our direction.

As I got into my car to leave, Josh offered to have me follow him back out to a stop near the highway so that I wouldn't get lost in the unfamiliar neighborhood. I trailed his truck through twists and turns for the ten mile distance before I could see the freeway up ahead. I killed the engine and stepped out of the car after following him into a McDonald's parking lot and saw slight surprise register on his face. He got out, too, and came over to where I stood. "Is something wrong with the car?"

I shook my head. "Oh, no, it's perfect... well, not perfect, obviously. But well-doctored for the moment." I bit my lip. "I just wanted to stop and again, say thank you. This was really too much."

He waved his hand at me. "It's no big deal. You would've done the same for me."

"Well, I don't know if I would have been so instantly generous. But I'm very seriously indebted to you and want to return the favor some day. So, when you need someone to plan your wedding for you, just give me a —" I stopped short, feeling suddenly embarrassed that I was talking about weddings with Josh. Not just in general but about *his* wedding, to some girl I would probably irrationally hate because she was marrying him, and… and I wasn't? Was this what it was all going to boil down to? The end of our friendship because what we had suddenly wasn't enough?

Josh must have seen the confusion on my face, because he quickly covered over my embarrassment with, "Well, no need to worry about that any time soon. But I appreciate the sentiment."

"I'm… I'm really sorry, Josh," I began, trying to explain away the night before. "About… you know."

He exhaled sharply. "It's okay. I mean…" His eyes wouldn't meet mine. "We're okay. We really are."

He was wrong. We really weren't okay. Even though he was a grownup who had kept the lines drawn without any drama, I was ruining it all by falling all over myself in love with him. I thought about all of the months we had spent together and how much I was going to miss him, knowing that we really couldn't be okay when I couldn't stop thinking of him as someone more than who he wanted to be.

"Okay," I mumbled idiotically, just as Josh closed his eyes, shook his head a little, and began with his own explanation.

"Emily, I just… well, I don't want to think that you're saying something that you're not saying, when it's clear that you've never been saying it. Do you know what I'm saying?"

He looked at the ground, confusion on his face. Not that I understood what he was saying any better than he apparently understood it, but I just wanted out of this demoralizing, sad conversation. "Yeah," I said, softly. "I know what you're saying." Then, just a flicker of disappointment on his face, mirrored by my own. I wasn't the only one upset that I had ruined our friendship.

"Well," I said, taking a breath. "Thanks again. I guess I'll see you... " I looked up at him apprehensively. Would I see him again?

He seemed to be thinking of something else entirely. "Emily," he blurted out, finally looking me in the eyes. "Are things really serious with you and Stephen?"

Me and Stephen? "Stephen who?," I asked stupidly, realizing who he meant just a moment later. "Oh, Pastor Stephen!"

And suddenly, all the pieces began clicking into place. I remembered how Josh had been last spring, the way he had watched me and the flirty things he had said. Then I remembered that night at youth camp, the disappointment that washed over his face, how my conversation with Stephen might have looked like something more, how I had been so sidetracked by everything else going on, how Josh had begun acting differently in the meantime. And I remembered all of the details of the last few months, with Stephen helping to hold my father together alongside me, and viewed all those moments through Josh's eyes.

Oh, no. This all could have worked out a whole lot earlier.

I sighed, relieved that this tension was all a misunderstanding. "No. No! I went out with him a few times in the spring. But, no, things aren't serious. They never were. We're just friends now."

"Ohhh," Josh said, clear relief written all over his face. "This whole time, I just assumed..."

"Yeah," I said. "I mean, no. About me and him. But yeah to the... I mean, yeah, I assumed, too."

"You assumed that you were almost engaged to your associate pastor?"

"No," I shook my head. "I assumed that you knew that nothing was going on. You know what I mean." Then, a gasp. "You thought I was almost ENGAGED to him?"

"What was I supposed to think? You never let on that it was anything different," he said, worked up. "He was always there, calling you, there with your family, having a moment at youth camp –"

"And then I kissed you!," I practically shouted at him, my hands flying up to cover my mouth. "What must you have thought about ME after that? Serious with one guy, kissing another –"

"Well, I didn't think badly of you," he reassured me. "I felt like I was probably the one who was wrong, knowing you were in a relationship with someone else, yet here I was, spending all of my time with you, making up excuses as to why we needed to spend even more time together, and praying at every opportunity that he'd screw up somehow and give you a reason to want me instead. And then, you're all vulnerable and emotional and you kissed me, and I didn't even care if it was because you were sad, I just wanted to REALLY kiss you, and --"

"Me, too," I said softly. "What a mess, Josh. When I think of all that you must have taken another way..." Like any of it even mattered now. "I'm so sorry. I think... I just..."

"Wish we hadn't wasted all of this time," he finished for me.

"Yeah," I said, nodding.

He took my hands, very naturally, very comfortably. There was nothing awkward or tense about it... and yet still, I could feel my pulse speed up, my heart beginning to beat so rapidly that I was sure he could hear it. I couldn't hide my smile.

"Emily, can I take you out tonight?"

"I would like that," I smiled back at him.

I didn't stop smiling the entire trip back home. My grin never left my face as I rushed through getting ready for the busy afternoon and evening schedule I had at the hotel. My giddiness didn't even falter as I fielded phone calls from my mother, Sara, and Melissa, all of them mortified that they had forgotten my birthday.

I was pulling on my shoes and listening to my mother moan about her own forgetfulness, my constant smile growing even wider as she continued on and on.

"When I think of you sitting there all alone last night, I just feel AWFUL. I mean, I know life has been crazy for us here, but still, you just don't forget your own child's birthday!"

"Mom," I interrupted. "It's okay. I wasn't alone."

"Did Sara and Melissa do something for you? Such sweet girls. Always have been, and —"

"No," I said, laughing a little, "Josh was here."

Silence for a moment. "Who?"

I had managed to keep Josh from the scrutiny and endless interrogation of my family thus far. But thinking about the way he had looked at me as we said our goodbyes, the texts he had already sent in the brief two hours we had been apart, the unabashed way we were both saying things we had never said until now... well, I figured he was going to be around for a long, long while. It was time to let them know all about him.

"It's a long story, Mom. But he's... well, he's just wonderful."

"What? What was his name? Where did you meet him?"

"Josh Morales. We run together in the mornings. He's been helping me with the ladies' Bible study. And with the bathroom. Oh, and his brothers fixed my car today, but I'll probably still need to buy a new one before the end of the year." I sighed, the sappy smile still on my face. "Isn't that great?"

"Emily, are you feeling okay? Do you have a fever?"

I laughed out loud. "I'll tell you all about him later. Soon, okay?"

The weddings that day were just lovely. Busy and frantic at different moments, mainly at the first when the bride's mother fell off the stage at the reception and at the second when the bride stepped too close to the votive candles during the ceremony and a portion of her skirt went up in flames... but beautiful still despite these frantic episodes. I was so busy that I hardly had time to think about Josh, except, of course, during every free moment, every busy moment, every random, single moment throughout the day. Evelyn was very pleased with what she called my "sunny disposition" and my ever-present smile that had nothing to do with all the calamities going on around me.

The dance at the final wedding lasted longer than planned, and I raced to my car, huge tip in hand, intent on making it home in time. I checked the clock. I was going to be cutting it close.

By the time I got through traffic and pulled up to my apartment, Josh was sitting on the steps. I saw him smile as my old clunker heaved itself into a parking space.

He looked wonderful. He had traded in his sweaty old shirts, running shorts, and battered shoes for nice jeans, a button down shirt, and boots. I had seen him so rarely dressed up, just a few occasions, and the sight produced another wave of nerves throughout my system. I got out of the car, smiled shyly, and saw him do a quick once-over of my own outfit. I was still in my "wedding gear" – a little black dress, my hair swept up into a twist, make up done, and those Japanese stilettos.

"Wow. I don't know why, but I was expecting you to show up in your workout clothes!," he smiled, echoing the very same thoughts I had about his own appearance. "Not that you aren't beautiful in those, but this... well, I've always liked this."

I smiled at him. "Work clothes, you know... though, I might be a little overdressed for tonight, huh?"

Still staring at me, he whispered, "It doesn't bother me," then smiled as he gathered me in his arms for a very different hug than those we had already shared.

The night flew by.

Every other first date I had ever been on had been awkward, had dragged on, and had been full of silences and stuttering conversations. This, though? Was something else entirely. Dinner flew by, followed by a walk through downtown to browse the stores, holding hands and sharing smiles. I had a lingering sense of doubt, as I wondered if this too-good-to-be-true situation really was too good to be true, what it meant for the future, and how we could, if he even wanted to, be a long term part of one another's lives.

Maybe I was getting ahead of myself, though. I resolved to not overthink anything and just BE with him, which was decidedly easy to do as he smiled at me and squeezed my hand reassuringly.

Back home, he walked me to my front door, where I leaned weakly against the frame, literally short of breath around my good friend, Josh, who was so familiar, so comfortable, and so much like home to me. I couldn't even sort through half of what I was thinking or feeling, looking up into his face, a face that had become so precious to me during these long months of knowing one another.

He leaned against the frame as well, with a slight sigh, and smiled at me, our faces just a few inches apart. "I had a good time tonight," he said very softly.

I thought for sure he could hear my heart about to beat out of my chest as his eyes lingered on my lips, and before I could think better of it, I blurted out, "Josh?"

"Hmm?" His eyes met mine again, coming back to reality. Oh, harsh, harsh reality, where Emily doesn't know which way is up or what her plan is or how she ended up here with all of these *feelings* threatening all of her preconceived ideas about what, when, and who is right for the life that she wants. Silly Emily, who can see how right this relationship could be, but who wonders if indulging now would ruin a really tremendously great friendship or might somehow, in the most wonderful of all twists and turns, end gloriously in a life where she's a pastor's wife, thereby horrifically becoming her own mother completely and fully and --

Sigh.

"Josh, I feel..." I began, trying to express something intelligent, to express all the conflicting, self-doubting, surprisingly sweet feelings racing through my heart, "... a lot." Brilliant.

His brow furrowed. "A lot?" Then, a smile. "Me, too," he managed through his laughter.

Comfortable, familiar Josh again... yet, still, there were the feelings, even greater, more pronounced, inching me even closer to his face, his sparkling eyes, his lips. Oh, my...

"I wonder, " I managed to breathe out, "what this all means for us. You know? I don't want to... lose us, in all of this. Because us? We're really, really great."

He watched me for a moment. "We ARE great, aren't we?"

"You know what I mean."

He nodded, his gaze travelling back down to my lips again then up to my eyes. "I do." And then, "I think it's all just going to get better. And I have no intention of losing us."

"Really?," I asked, moving closer to him.

"Really." His smile spread wider, and in my mind, I willed his lips to mine, hoping for his kiss and almost fearing for the flood that was sure to come with it. He seemed to read my thoughts as he put his arms around my waist, pulled me the last few inches to his chest, and finally covered my mouth with his own.

Oh. My.

I would totally be willing to become my own mother if it meant kissing this man every day of my life.

My own mother was at the forefront of my mind that next morning, when I arrived at Iglesia Redeemer to find her sitting with my father in the back pew.

It was a surprise that I was even there myself, actually. After more than a few kisses at my door the night before, a few more inside my apartment, then another few as I smiled against Josh's very eager lips and proclaimed that – really – it was getting late, he took a deep breath, his forehead pressed against mine.

"You should come to Redeemer tomorrow morning," he whispered. "I'm not trying to steal church members from Grace," he smiled, "but I want you to be a part of my church. If you want to."

"I think I do," I whispered back. "But, of course, this means I'll have to learn Spanish, doesn't it?"

"Oh, you'll have plenty of time, trust me," he said, kissing me again. Then, backing away with a sigh, "Okay, I'm really going to go now." One more kiss. "See you tomorrow." Another last kiss. He turned to go.

"Hey, Josh," I said, pulling him back, winding my arms around his neck, pressing myself against him as tightly as I could as he groaned, kissing him once more, longer and deeper, then releasing him reluctantly. "Okay, now you can go."

I shut the door behind him, as he left with an incredulous expression, and slid down to the floor.

Oh, my.

The memories had played through my head a thousand times as I drove to church that morning, bringing one smile after another to my lips, but they had come to a screeching halt at the shock of seeing my parents.

"Oh... um... wow," I said, standing in front of them.

"Oh, um, wow, indeed," my mother said, standing to hug me as my father waved from behind her, shrugging his shoulders with an amused expression on his face.

"Why are you here? How did you... oh, my."

"You gave me his name, you know," she said. "His name and just enough information that I was able to look him up on Facebook."

Oh, Facebook. It would be the downfall of our entire civilization with its ability to enable meddling parents to continue to be too intimately knowledgeable regarding the details of their adult children's lives.

"Oh, please tell me that you didn't friend Josh on Facebook," I said.

"Well, not yet," she said. "THAT would be awkward. But really, he needs to change some of his privacy settings because after I searched his name, found a Josh Morales that shared mutual friends with me – one of them being you, dear – and determined that he was a runner, like you mentioned... well, it was simple to figure out ALL of his information, mainly that he was Josh Morales of Iglesia Redeemer. And I told your father—"

"'Iglesia Redeemer!' she said to me," my father picked up the story.

"'Isn't that the church that Grace planted twenty years ago?' And it was."

"And it is! Who knew that your friend, Josh, has been a member of the great big Grace family all this while, and we never knew?" She narrowed her eyes at me. "Of course, we never knew about HIM either, but that seems to be the trend, what with your brother hiding Shoko from us, and you hiding Josh from us. I mean, seriously, are you kids worried that we're going to –"

"Oh, Mom, PLEASE don't get all crazy on me this morning and –"

"Good morning," a calm voice said from behind me. I turned to see Josh, a wondering smile on his face as he looked at my parents.

"Hey, Josh," I breathed softly, thinking about the night before, my cheeks turning pink as I remembered the goodbyes.

He seemed to be thinking of the same thing as he continued to stare at me, my mother indelicately clearing her throat to break our attention away from one another.

My father was standing beside her now, smiling, looking to me for an introduction.

"Josh, these are my parents."

His eyes widened in surprise. Oh, yeah, we were ALL a little surprised.

"Thomas Fisher," my dad said, extending his hand as Josh's eyes grew even wider.

"Um… wow…"

"Yes, that seems to be what everyone is saying this morning," my mother quipped. "Lydia Fisher. It's good to meet you, Josh."

Josh shook their hands, his natural warmth coming through in the brilliant smile he gave them both. "Josh Morales. Mrs. Fisher, it's a pleasure. And Dr. Fisher —"

"It's just Thomas," my dad corrected.

"Thomas," Josh nodded, "it's a real honor, sir."

"Well, we're glad to be here this morning. We knew the founding pastor of your church, Rick Martinez. He was a member of Grace, you know."

Josh shook his head. "I didn't know that, actually. The church was started long before I was even a Christian, honestly. I've only been here for fifteen years myself. Only ten as the pastor."

"Ten years!," my father exclaimed. "That would have you serving here, what? Since you were early twenties or so?"

"I started here right before seminary. Bivocational, still, all these years later, but I like it."

"That's admirable. Very admirable." He winked at me. "Good job, Emily."

Oh, geez.

"Well, we don't want to keep you," my mother told him, smiling despite herself at Josh. I could tell they both liked him a lot already. A WHOLE lot. Was it the fact that he was in ministry, too? That they knew this bivocational road was one that only the most committed men took? Or was it simply because I was, once again, staring at him with a gushy expression on my face? My mother glanced over at me in amusement. "We know how busy you must be on Sunday mornings," she said to Josh. "Trust me — we know. We wrote the book on Sunday mornings for the pastor and his wife... or, you know, sweetheart or whatever. Anyway, go on, Emily. Go ahead and go greet people with him."

Oh, geez! "Oh, Mom, I don't think I —"

"Yeah, Emily," Josh managed to keep from laughing. Just barely. "You should really come and meet some people with me."

As we turned from my parents, he took my hand in his. "Welcome to... well, pastoral ministry, I guess. Sweetheart." He raised my hand to his lips, kissing it softly, not bothering to hide his affection from the eyes of everyone in the church.

Josh's family had surrounded me a few moments before the service started, and once again, I was carried to the front in the sea of Morales brothers, sisters-in-law, nieces, nephews, and cousins. Debbie took my hand. "Are those your parents back there?," she asked, indicating the couple on the back pew.

"Yeah, those are my parents," I confirmed.

"That's what I thought," she said. "Saw you talking with them, and just assumed... you know, that all the white people in the room must be related, right?" She stopped herself. "Oh, well, that sounds horrible doesn't it?"

"Well, probably, but in this case, you're right on."

"I'm so glad, because I invited them to lunch with the family," she said.

Oh, wow. Could this day get any weirder?

"They said they had plans. But maybe next time you can talk them into it, huh?"

I nodded my affirmation as the service started, relieved by at least this stroke of good luck.

I was surrounded at the close of the service. News was spreading quickly about Josh's new "lady friend," thanks to the church grapevine.

Apparently, this was common at all churches – Spanish and English alike – this quick relay of any and all information from pew to pew. I did the best I could with the language difference, thankful when someone spoke English to me, accommodating as much as I could when people couldn't. Being a part of Josh's life was going to be exhausting in this respect, at least, but I hardly thought it worth even considering as a cost when he came to my side and gave me his smile as the congregation began leaving the building.

"I was able to thank your parents for coming," he said. "But just barely. They were hurrying out pretty quickly."

"I better go say goodbye," I told him.

"Lunch at Grandma's afterwards?," he called to me.

I gave him the thumbs up and went out the door to see my parents unlocking their car.

"Mom, Dad!," I yelled across the parking lot as I hurried out to speak with them.

"Emily," my mother said, "that was a lovely service."

"Very well preached," my dad said, giving me a hug.

"Could you understand it?," I asked.

"I've preached that same passage probably one hundred times myself, so, yes."

My mother rolled her eyes good-naturedly, then smiled at me. "We like Josh. SO much. He's a good match for you."

"I hardly think that you can tell that after just –"

"He is," my father said. "Just the kind of man we've prayed would find you one day."

I looked at them dubiously. "What?"

"I've always told your mother," my dad began, "that you'd find your way into ministry one day. Just something about you, I guess. Something that we didn't see in Jessica or Matthew the same way we saw it in you. And I've often wondered what kind of role God had in mind for you."

"And I've always suspected," my mother said, "that He had plans for you to be a pastor's wife. You have the right gifting, the right skills, the right disposition. And you definitely know what it looks like, having grown up in our home."

I shook my head. "Well, we just started, and I mean JUST started dating. Kind of early to think like that."

"Is it?," my mom asked with a twinkle in her eye. "You know, I always hoped something would work out with you and Stephen, but I've seen you around him for years, and you've NEVER looked at him the way you looked at Josh today. And the way he looked at YOU? Well, it's all over for him. A mother can tell these things."

She looked to my dad. "Thomas, why don't you drive?" She tossed him the keys, which he caught with one hand.

"I think I just might," he said. "It's a good day," he winked at me, his double meaning clear.

"Have a good afternoon, Emily," my mother said as she waved. "How about we have a family dinner soon so that you can properly introduce us to Josh, okay?"

"Sure," I said, watching them get in the car and drive away. "Sure."

I was, needless to say, in a fantastic mood that Monday. My step was so light that I was practically skipping as I went through the lobby. I noted with surprise that our office door was already open, which meant that Evelyn – shock of all shocks – had arrived early.

Sure enough, as soon as I stepped through the door, I caught her bright smile as she spoke with a hugely pregnant woman. Before I could speak, the woman turned around to face me.

"Stacy!"

I hadn't heard anything from Circus Bride since the wedding, but as she stood to give me a hug, she said, "I've been meaning to call you!"

"I'm so glad you came by!," I said, meaning it. I looked her over, obviously surprised by the baby bump.

"Lots has happened since the wedding," she said, patting herself.

Behind her Evelyn rolled her eyes. This conversation was heading in a "non-genteel" direction quickly. Stacy whirled around to look at her as she daintily cleared her throat. "Mrs. Gofdustopus," she said politely (how DID she manage to pronounce it right after all this time?), "Emily will be happy to assist you with your plans. If you ladies will excuse me, I have an appointment to get to." Code for "I'm taking a three hour lunch."

As soon as Evelyn was gone, I motioned for Stacy to sit, sat next to her, and said, "Plans? What are we planning?"

"A baby shower, of course!," Stacy trilled. "For my little honeymoon baby. Can you even believe it?"

I could believe it. Honeymoon babies happened all the time. What I couldn't quite wrap my mind around, though, was the glee that Stacy seemed to have concerning her budding figure, the responsibility of motherhood, and how this new development would change her life. After all, this was the same woman who had undergone colon cleansings to fit into her dress and had (believe it or not) actually lost her $10K wedding band in the hotel bathroom in between dances. (Our plumbing department was not at all happy when she discovered two hours into the hysteria that she had put it on the wrong finger and that it actually wasn't in the toilet they had dismantled.)

"Congratulations," I told her. "You seem so happy!"

"I am!," she smiled, clutching her hands to her chest. "This was so unexpected, but we're so thrilled. It's a girl! A girl!"

I smiled and was about to ask about names, but before I could, she threw her hands up in the air.

"Emily! I did want to talk to you about a baby shower brunch, but more than that, I wanted to talk to you about your services. For some friends."

I blinked, confused. "Do you need some information sheets on our amenities and prices?"

"No, YOUR services." She shook her head. "The hotel is GORGEOUS, don't get me wrong, but I have a few friends who are planning weddings for next summer that want outside weddings. And the garden room here just isn't big enough to accommodate their guests." She lowered her voice. "I mean, these are HUGE weddings. High dollar, if you know what I mean."

I did know what she meant... and at the same time, I had no idea what she meant. "My services?"

She nodded. "Yes, I told them all about how wonderful you are and how you could make their dreams happen, and my phone has been ringing off the hook, asking for your number." She dug around in her oversized purse for her phone. After pressing a few buttons, she looked at me expectantly. "So, can I get your number and let them know they can call you?"

I hesitated only a moment. "You sure can."

11 OCTOBER

"The bride wanted Michael Jackson... and you sent us the Beatles."

It was another wild wedding day at the hotel.

I glanced over inconspicuously at the four shaggy haired young men in suits who had arrived from Dearly Departed Karaoke. "Nothing personal," I said in their direction, as I continued talking to management over the phone.

"No offense taken," Paul (or Ringo?) said to me.

I listened to the secretary, who was desperately trying to operate beyond her own pay grade and explain away this mistake. "Oh, I'm sure they're just great," I said. "But she wanted Michael Jackson. And correct me if I'm wrong... but half of the Beatles aren't departed quite yet, are they?"

Ten minutes later, I had been connected to someone who could get Michael Jackson sent to us at the last minute. I handed my phone to John Lennon (I think), letting him speak with the man on the other end.

"Mix up," he told me. "Michael Jackson is at Beaumont Ranch for a reception... and we're supposed to be there."

"Sounds like there are some clerical issues at the office," I said.

"Yep," he muttered. "Thanks for your time," he said. "Come on boys, let's get going."

They filed out of the office, just as Evelyn was coming in. "I would ask what that's about," she said, "but I probably don't want to know, do I?"

"It'll just get more confusing when Michael Jackson arrives. But that's what the bride wanted, and –"

"That's what the bride will get," Evelyn finished for me. "And speaking of brides getting what they want, the Evans family is here. Lauren has some last minute concerns about the reception, and I told them that this evening's event is comparable to what they're going to have... of course, it isn't half as grand, obviously, but close enough. They're going to watch and observe."

"Wonderful," I said. "I've got some time before the next ceremony to go speak with them."

I found them in the lobby – Stan smiling broadly at Dorothy as she looked around, making notes, while Lauren wrung her hands. Typical, in other words.

"Dr. Evans, Mrs. Evans," I said, shaking their hands, then reaching out and giving Lauren a hug. "So glad to see you all."

"Thank you so much for letting us do this, Emily," Dorothy cooed. "Laurie just had some concerns, some jitters, you know," she smiled at me, knowingly, "and we thought this might help." She sighed contentedly. "Plus, I just can't get enough of this place!"

"It's just peachy, dear, isn't it?," Stan rocked back and forth on his heels.

"It is," she said.

"Well, you're more than welcome to go ahead and go on into the grand ballroom. The head of our catering department —"

"Stella, right? We're on a first name basis," Dorothy smiled.

"Yes, Stella's already in there, getting things set up with her crew, and I'm heading that way to make sure everything else is in place with my crew. Would you like to come with me?"

"Why don't you and Lauren head that way?," Stan said. "Dorothy and I need to talk to the front desk about a block of rooms we've secured for out-of-town guests."

"I'd be happy to handle that later on, if you'd like," I offered.

"Oh, no," he said, "You and Laurie go on." He winked at me.

As they walked away, I linked arms with Lauren and headed her towards the grand ballroom.

"You look a little stressed," I said quietly.

"Do I?," she asked, biting her fingernails.

"Yeah, and you're ruining your nails." I took her hand. "And those don't look cheap."

"Oh, I can get it fixed later," she sighed. "If I can find time, you know. This is, like, the busiest semester of my life, and I don't know why I let my mother talk me into waiting until December to get married, when I knew it would be so crazy right now."

"Tough load of classes?," I asked, sympathetically.

"Absolutely," she said. "I'm doing my student teaching next spring, so now, I'm finishing up all the classroom work, all the workshops, and I have finals right before Christmas, and I'm already trying to find a job, and... I'm in way over my head. And then, there's this WEDDING. Which was going to be simple until it turned into this living, breathing —" She put her nails right back into her mouth. "I think I'm going to lose my mind. Seriously."

"I told you we'd take care of the details," I said. "And we will. You can just relax."

She sighed. "I think you know that's not possible. Even if everything is taken care of, I'm still worried about it."

"Well, then," I offered, "get your mind off of it for a while. How's the job search going?"

"Not so great," she said. "I have no idea what I'm doing with the whole public school certification. Or how to even get a job in my field."

"High school biology, right?" We had discussed it before in one of our many phone conversations. Lauren had become a friend – not just a client.

"Yeah, and I don't know what any of the schools are like in the districts around here. I'm clueless when it comes to so many things about the whole system. About the hiring, about the benefits, about the resources available to secondary science teachers... all of it, actually."

"You know what?," I told her, as we finally made our way into the grand ballroom. "You need to meet my boyfriend. He's a teacher. High school chemistry."

"A boyfriend?," she smiled. "I haven't heard anything about a boyfriend."

"Well, probably more technically, a MAN friend, at our age," I smiled.

"When did this happen?"

"It's a long story. Why don't you and Justin meet us for dinner one night?"

"Sounds good," she said. "I'll give you a call."

I looked out over the chaos of preparations in the grand ballroom. "This isn't helping your stress levels at all, is it?," I said, as the woman putting down all the linens tripped over her own bolt of fabric, one of the musicians knocked a microphone stand over, and Stella threw her hands in the air and let out a mighty cry of exasperation over a tray of chicken wings.

"Not at all," Lauren murmured, her fingernails going right back into her mouth.

I would NOT be taking part in the Billings-Smith wedding.

The divorce was final, the baby had been born, and as Ashley had calmly informed me when she came to my office, they were ready to do this marriage legally – fancy ceremony and all.

It was at that point that I discovered something about myself. It wasn't the legality that had bothered me as much as the part I had played in so many doomed marriages. I had worked with so many couples over the years that were clearly not ready for marriage. Either because they couldn't argue without resorting to some sort of violence towards one another, because they were drawing up such elaborate pre-nups that confirmed what little faith they had in their marriages lasting, or because the grooms actually propositioned me. Rather than standing firm on my convictions about the sanctity of marriage and how it wasn't to be taken so lightly, I had been the first to usher them right into a contract and a congratulatory pat on the back. All because it was my job. It was my job to play up the wedding so much that the marriages would suffer in the long run.

I had gone along with it. But I would not be doing so with this couple. I could remember Ashley's son and the sad look in his eyes, as his mother prepared to marry for the third time in three years. What was he learning from her example? And what was I doing by becoming an accomplice in the process?

I went into Evelyn's office, knowing how this might possibly end. I put the file on her desk and said, very simply, "I won't be taking part in this wedding."

She looked up from her desk, questioningly.

"What wedding is that?," she murmured, reading over the information. A look of realization dawned on her face. "Ahh… THOSE people." She took her glasses off and studied me for a moment. "Emily, it's not like any of us like working with them. They're crude, ill-mannered, and frankly, a little low class for this venue."

"That's not it," I said. "I couldn't care less what kind of class of people they are."

She looked at me as if she really didn't believe that last part. "Well, then. Whatever in the world is your hang-up?"

I took a breath, willing myself to not be emotional. "She has children. And this is her third marriage. She leaves her husbands, refuses to be reconciled, and drags her children into quick relationships with her. It's not right. It doesn't honor God, and it doesn't honor the sanctity of marriage."

Evelyn watched me for a moment. "That may be all well and good in your church," she said evenly, "but you are no one's judge, Emily."

This was true. I wasn't one to judge at all. But I couldn't see something that was wrong and go along with it. Not anymore.

"I can't be a part of this, Evelyn."

She put the file down. "It isn't our job to teach ethics and morality. Our job is to put on weddings. And to take couples who want to get married for whatever reason, for whatever price, for whatever they want – and do it. We do what the customer wants us to do. It's called business."

"Evelyn," I said, feeling inspired. "Would you do a wedding where the bride and groom wanted to sacrifice a child as part of their ceremony?"

She looked at me, horrified. "Emily! That's awful! Of course not!"

"So, you're judging them?"

She paused, then gave me a dirty look. "No, I'm just doing what's right."

"So am I." I stood my ground, as Evelyn's face softened. She sighed and rubbed her eyes.

"Emily, don't make me do this."

"No – don't make me do this," I gestured weakly toward the file.

"You understand," she said, "that this will not be the last time you have ethical concerns about a client?"

I nodded.

"And so excusing you from this one... well, it would just lead to the inevitable. You would have another one to refuse later, and on and on and on until... until I would need a new assistant."

I nodded again. "Well, best be getting on with it, I suppose."

She shrugged, picked up the file, and looked at me again. "Are you sure?"

I felt the tears collecting in my eyes and managed a weak, "Yes." Six years, gone. All of my career plans, gone. But it needed to be done.

"I won't let you quit," she said softly, "because there's no severance with that. I'll have to fire you."

I had figured as much, and I appreciated her generosity in this.

"Good-bye, Emily. I'll expect you to have your desk cleared out by five o'clock."

"To integrity!" Josh held up a can of Diet Coke, toasting the box that held all of the personal effects from my office. Six years, gathered into a cardboard box.

"Yes, to integrity," I said. "And severance pay, thank you very much, Evelyn." I leaned back on the couch and closed my eyes.

"Hey," Josh said, sitting down and nudging my arm. "You're going to be okay."

"Oh, yeah," I said. "Just peachy." God bless Stan Evans and his cute little sayings. Hey, maybe Stan Evans could hire me to clean his house! The pay would probably be three times as much as I had been making. (But I could only imagine how big the house must be.)

"You did the right thing," Josh said, sliding an arm around my shoulders.

I looked up at him. "Did I? They're still going to get married. And they'll likely still get divorced. What good did I do apart from getting myself kicked right out of there?"

"Well, first of all," he said, "you don't know that they'll end up divorced. Maybe God is going to do something huge in their lives, and this time, it'll be forever."

"That would be great," I said, genuinely meaning it, thinking about that precious boy and his tiny little sister.

"I think you showed a lot of wisdom today in being so sensitive to God's leading. You knew what your part was supposed to be in all of it, and now, you've just got to trust Him with the results of your obedience. Of standing up for your convictions. Of—"

"Telling Evelyn, NO MORE!" I waved a fist in the air triumphantly, just like Josh did as we ran.

"Exactly." He placed a tiny kiss on my forehead. "And you've been praying about this."

"About losing my only source of income?"

"No," he said. "You've been praying about whether or not this – working for the hotel – was something that God intended for you to keep on doing. And you stood by your convictions, by godly convictions, and you were forced to leave. Is that not an answer to prayer? Is that God clearly giving you an answer?"

I sighed. "I guess so." A pause. "Now what, though? I've done the math. There's no way doing events on my own is going to be enough to cover my bills. I've grown to accept the fact that I'll be living in this apartment forever –"

"Well, probably not forever –"

"And that my car is going to have to be laid to rest very soon –"

"My brothers can keep resuscitating it –"

"But still!," I exclaimed. "Even if I'm fine with all of that, and I really think I am... I still won't be able to make ends meet." I closed my eyes. "All those years, working there... and I know this is the right move to make. But it's requiring a lot of faith at the moment, faith that God's going to provide just at the right time."

"He will," Josh answered, pulling me close to his side.

After a few days of panic and apprehension, Josh's words sunk in, as did the counsel of Scripture. And I realized that truth was truth and that God was going to make a way. I didn't stress about the job. The severance package would keep me afloat for three months. On my now immensely leisurely days, I would wake up in time for Josh to pick me up from the apartment, go run with him, and send him back home with a kiss. While he went to work like the rest of the world, I got back in my pjs and started making notes. What would it take for me to do what I had always secretly dreamt of doing? How much did I need to live on? Could I make that while coordinating weddings on my own – without the regulations, wild expenses, and blind ethics that had been the very essence of my career? I crunched the numbers, weighed the odds, and came up with a number. This, I told myself, is what I would have to make at a SECOND job in order to have my own business.

And it seemed hopeless. But God didn't leave me without help or direction when He called me to be faithful and obedient. I prayed over the plans, confirmed to Him that He already knew what I needed, and admitted that only He knew how it was all going to work out in the end. I prayed to be open to whatever possibility He had for me and trusted that He would honor and glorify Himself in the journey.

And I trusted Him.

I called up Stuart, my new accountant. Yes, Stuart of Frank's Fried Chicken Bucket. He was happy to help come up with some financial plans in exchange for some wedding planning expertise for him and his new bride-to-be. I began making calls to the lists of vendors I had in my planner, the vendors I had enjoyed working alongside, the ones who had grown to be like my own little bridal family over the past six years. Mr. and Mrs. Otto at the Lotta Love Bakery, Denis at Denis Downing photography, DJ Mike from Prime Time Entertainment, the ladies of Wedding Dreams dress shop, Kate Moore from Consider the Roses floral design... I called vendor after vendor, discussing my new business with them, making appointments to drop off the business cards I had made, and promising them referrals to any and all brides I could book.

It was a start. A small move... with big faith behind it.

"Sara, are you even there?" Melissa was losing patience. "Technology bites." She looked at me, irritated.

"Says the woman who spends her life in a technological field," I said.

"No, that's science, pure science, not any of this DSL, WiFi, idiotnet stuff. Sara, can you hear me?"

"Yeah," we heard her squeak out from the iPad. "Melissa just wouldn't shut up long enough for me to say anything. I'm here. I've been here."

We were having an unconventional girls' night in. Sara had settled into her missionary training halfway across the country, and we were doing our best to keep in touch, all three of us together, despite the schedules we were now keeping.

"Em, how's your dad doing?," she asked.

"Better," I said, squeezing close to Melissa so that she could see us both at the same time. "His episodes aren't as bad lately. I think the stress of leading then leaving Grace was doing more harm than we thought because he... well, he's acting fine." I paused, then remembered. "Well, there was the day that he was certain my mother was a telemarketer who had found his house and wouldn't leave him alone."

"A telemarketer?" Melissa looked at me with raised eyebrows.

"Yeah," I said, "he kept getting calls from a company selling vacuums, and after he hung up one day, my mom got the vacuum out to clean, and he... well, he freaked out on her. Called her Hoover Girl for a good long while until she could convinced him that she was who she said she was."

"Wow," Sara managed.

"She's actually pretty glad about it," I said, "because it's given her a reason to hire a housekeeper. Let someone else be Hoover Girl, right?"

"I guess," Melissa said. "Hey, Sara, how's it going out there?"

"Just awesome," she said with a bright smile. "I'm learning so much already. I thought I already knew all that I needed to know, what with the job being a teaching position and all, but there's SO much information to know about living cross-culturally."

"Are they keeping you too busy?"

"Not TOO busy, but I'm definitely not sitting around with nothing to do," she said. "And I'm meeting so many great people. A few of them are even going to Costa Rica for language school, so I'll be able to meet up with them on the field."

"We miss you!," Melissa shouted at her.

"I miss you guys, too! How's the wedding planning going?"

"Oh, fine," Melissa said. "When I have time for it. Which is what I wanted to tell you, especially since this month is our resolution to improve our careers and all... I got promoted."

"Really?," I asked. "Why didn't you say anything?"

"Well, I wanted to wait until I could tell you both at once. Not much has changed, just an increase of a few responsibilities, more time, more PAY, of course."

"That's great!," Sara said. "Definitely not a pay increase here with my job, but I'm really happy. How about you, Emily, what are you doing career-wise?"

"Well, I quit my job."

Neither Sara nor Melissa said anything for a moment.

"Did we get disconnected, Sara? Are you still there?," Melissa offered lamely, a few seconds later.

"Still here," Sara managed.

"Oh, it's not as bad as it sounds," I said. "I had some... well, ethical concerns with the job. I've had them for a while. You guys know this."

"Yeah, but... well, do you have something else lined up?"

I sighed. "I'm doing some weddings and events on my own, but as for a real job?" I shook my head. "Nope."

"How are you meeting your bills?," Melissa asked, concerned.

"Severance pay, praise the Lord," I said. "And after that runs out... well, something will work out. Surely. Or I can donate a lot of platelets. Or sell my body to science. Right?"

"Well, let's hope it doesn't come to that," Sara said, exchanging, through WiFi space, another worried look with Melissa.

I hadn't been gone a week before I got a call from Evelyn.

"Emily, dear," she practically purred at me. "How are you doing?"

"Fine," I said, treading carefully. "How are you, Evelyn?"

"Just wonderful," she trilled. "Though I must tell you, we've been missing you around here."

"Really?" There had to be a catch.

"Oh, yes," she murmured. "I had no idea how many of our brides had formed such close bonds with you."

There was only one that I could think of off of the top of my head. One very important bride who Evelyn did NOT want to upset.

I didn't say anything, waiting for her offer.

"You can imagine how crucial it is for our entire establishment that you… that you come back, dear."

I exhaled sharply. I hadn't been counting on this and had started to enjoy the thought of working on my own terms and using my skills as a ministry, not a cold, hard business. True, I didn't know how I was going to manage it financially, but I had already poured myself into the project. "I don't know," I told her honestly. And I didn't know how God was going to work it out, but going back to the hotel for the long term wasn't the right move. I was sure of that.

I could hear slight panic in her voice. "Will you come back on your own conditions? No more weddings that you find… unsavory? Just the ones that you want?"

"Are you saying that you'll do the –"

"Yes, dear, I'm saying that I'll do the weddings that you have moral objections to," she said, and I could hear the irritation in her voice. This would no longer be a good working relationship. She sweetened her voice. "Please, Emily?"

I could only imagine how upset Lauren had been, how upset the entire Evans family had been, when they had discovered that their personal wedding planner had left the job two months before the wedding. Evelyn was now bending over backwards to save face and win me back for them.

I wouldn't let her continue this. "Evelyn, I'll come back for the next two months. With the understanding that I won't be doing a wedding that I find objectionable. The Evans-Bennett wedding will be my last one at the hotel."

I could hear her relief. "Oh, Emily! That's just wonderful. Your pay will be the same, and you can keep your severance –"

"No," I told her, surprising myself, but feeling a calm peace about it. "I don't want to be paid. The severance will be enough."

She seemed even more pleased by the idea of free labor. "Well, if you insist. I'll expect you back then, tomorrow morning?"

"Tomorrow afternoon, actually. I have something I need to do tomorrow morning."

My "something" was a meeting with Stephen, up at the church.

As I walked into his office and saw him smile warmly at me, I wondered how we had ever been so awkward and anxious around one another. I thought back to the last few months and how he had been such a champion for my father, such an encourager for my family, and such a great support for my mother, even now as she and my father prepared for the next, very different phase of their ministry.

After all this time and all the rampant speculation by so many at our church, Stephen had become as dear to me as they had hoped he would. But in a different way.

"You wanted to see me?"

"Hey, Emily," he said, closing the book he was reading, motioning to the chairs across from his desk. "How have you been?"

I took a deep breath. "Okay, all things considered."

He nodded. "I talked to your mother earlier today. She was asking me about a way to get your father's library in a digital format so that, and I quote, he could pull up commentaries from the jungle."

I sighed. "Yes, because a man with Alzheimer's needs to be trudging through the Amazon."

He laughed. "I think it was Rwanda."

"Even better, right?"

He leaned back in his chair and smiled. "She seems better. And so does he."

Leaving Grace hadn't been an easy transition for them. But, as the doctors suggested it might, the decline in stress for my father had made his episodes less frequent, and though he would never get better in the way that we all hoped he would, he would be well enough to spend whatever time he had left ministering, even in the most remote places and situations.

They would be fine. They would be better than that.

"You didn't really answer my question, though," Stephen began again. "How are you doing?"

"Good, actually. Not just okay." I took another breath, thinking of the phone calls from church members, the visits, the worried glances cast in my direction. "People have been asking a lot of questions. I don't know how much to tell them while still protecting Dad's dignity." I shook my head. "As if he should need to feel embarrassed because of something that's out of his control."

Stephen nodded. "That's just it, though. His dignity is somewhat wrapped up in having control and being a source of stability to others. Which he has been for many years, to most of the people who are asking questions now."

"Stephen," I began, hesitantly, "I don't think any of us has adequately expressed how thankful we are for all you've done. You probably saw the worst of it."

His face was unreadable, as he clearly censored what I should know. I could see in his face all the scenarios I had only before imagined, finding Dad disoriented, looking over incomplete work, taking direction that made little sense. Seems Pastor Stephen and I were leading parallel lives, long before either of us were able to speak to the obvious.

He breathed out slowly. "He's always been my pastor. From the day I arrived here, until the moment he read his resignation... but I've found myself being his associate, *really* being his associate, this year. And it was an honor to be able to come up beside him. To keep his arms lifted up like they did for Moses, as it were."

I closed my eyes and fought back the tears as I whispered, "You knew a lot longer than we did, didn't you? You were keeping it from us." No condemnation. Just gratitude for those few extra months when life was as it should have been.

He nodded. "No. Just keeping it from him." He offered a weak smile. "I would correct things that he had gotten... not quite right. Picked up where he had forgotten to fill in. Generally made a nuisance of myself as his shadow so that he wouldn't know sooner than he needed to." He paused and looked down at his hands, his eyes aged beyond his years, clouded with concern and regret. "I probably shouldn't have. But I care about him so much and know that for men like us, so much of 'us' is preaching, ministering, being available and useful to God. I couldn't have him thinking that he was beyond useful... because every moment he's shared with me has been so completely extraordinary." He looked at me with tears in his own eyes. "He's still my mentor, whether or not he remembers my name in the months to come."

I remembered his first Sunday as associate pastor, how my father, boisterous and commanding, had embraced this shy, awkward young man onstage... and had seen him grow into a competent and effective minister of the Gospel. God had been good.

As tears spilled out of my own eyes, I put my hand on his and squeezed it softly. "You're a good man, Stephen. And an even better pastor." I paused for a moment, remembering a conversation we had shared so long ago now. "Or a professor. I guess you've got your own decisions to make now, huh?"

"Yeah," he smiled. "Funny thing about that. The pastor search committee has approached me, at your father's prompting, and has asked if they could consider me for the senior pastor position."

I gasped out loud at this. "Stephen! You'd be the perfect man to follow Dad here at Grace –"

"Well," Stephen sighed, "I'm not entirely convinced myself, because those are some big, big shoes to fill."

"Maybe it's time for Grace to get a new pair of shoes, then," I said.

He smiled at this. "I guess we'll see what God has planned."

Silence filled his office, as we both likely thought about the big transition ahead for our church. He took a deep breath and walked over to his desk. "Well, actually, that's what I wanted to talk to you about today, why I called you for a meeting. I hope you won't be a stranger, at least, even as your parents move on from the church. And," he said with a smile, "as you move on from the church. We got your letter earlier this week."

"I thought you might have," I said, knowing that Iglesia Redeemer must have notified Grace that I had joined their church.

"We're usually sad to lose members to other churches, of course," he said, "but in your case, your mother tells me that it's a very good thing."

"Did she now?" I could only imagine.

"Well, she didn't give me many details. Just told me that you're happy."

"That would be the first time she's kept something to herself," I said. "But, yes, I'm very happy." I paused for a moment. "I think being at Josh's church with him is a very good thing."

"Josh... Iglesia Redeemer... I think I've probably met him, haven't I?" He nodded as he made the connections in his head. "Well, that makes sense now." Smiling, he began shuffling through papers on his desk until he settled in on one.

"Like I said, Grace might need your help for just a while longer. The personnel committee is in the process of forming a search committee for an events coordinator."

"Really? Dad never mentioned it."

Stephen nodded. "Well, he delegated it to me a while back and has probably since forgotten about it. I'm just now really working on the whole project, what with all that's been happening lately and keeping me from it. But," he said, with a smile, "with the way the church is growing, we have events like weddings, anniversary parties, family reunions, etc booked every weekend for the facility. Sometimes more than three in one day, if you can imagine."

I could very well imagine. We received extra kickbacks and discounts (none of which we credited to the brides, simply what we took off the top of their fixed payment) for booking the same venue multiple times in the same day. It was good business if you could keep everything organized enough to pull it off. "Well, that's good business," I said dumbly, before considering that perhaps the church wasn't in it for business sake.

"It *would* be," he continued on, "if we were charging prices that would actually turn a profit. We're not, though. We're letting them book the facilities for the cost of utilities and janitorial help. Instead of it being a business venture, we're seeing it as more of an outreach venture, not just to new families in the church but to those who might become new families in the church."

A ministry. Event coordinating as a ministry. What I wouldn't give for an opportunity like this, at a church that could afford to pay what I was earning working for someone else. "That's great. It's a wonderful opportunity for an event coordinator."

He nodded. "The reason I called you in was because you, of course, have more knowledge about this field than anyone we know and probably have some valuable contacts and insights as to how we can make the position more desirable, how the position needs to fit into the authority structure of the rest of the church, and how we're going to even go about finding someone who might serve well here." He handed me the paper. "There's a preliminary description of the position, so far. Just what we've come up with as an uninformed group. The annual salary is there at the bottom. It's still negotiable, although I'm certain that we won't make it any lower than that, just higher."

My breath caught as I saw the number. It was the exact same number I had written down when I figured my budget plan... exactly what I would need to support myself as I attempted to start my own consulting business on the side. I swallowed hard.

"So," Stephen looked at me hopefully. "Can we count on you to come on board and help us find the right person for the job?"

I looked again at the number, looked at the description and duties, looked back again at the number, and said, in nearly breathless anticipation, "Would the committee consider me for the job instead?"

Surprise shown on his face. "But your job with—"

"Yeah, things have changed with that," I interrupted him, surprised that I was giving him this information. But he had been my pastor, after all. And quite possibly would soon be my boss. "Lots of things have changed actually. I'm very interested in this job for myself."

"We can't pay that much, obviously, from what you're seeing there."

"Yes, I see. It would be enough."

He smiled. "Well, you're more than qualified. Actually, over qualified." He lowered his voice, "I think the committee would disband after receiving your resume, as you're clearly more than what we were daring to hope for."

What wonderful words. "I'll send my resume to you as soon as I get to my computer."

"I keep worrying that I'm going to miss him. What was the number again?" Debbie kept looking back to her phone, where she had snapped a picture of Josh before he went to his starting corral three hours earlier. "22072... I think I'll recognize him, but maybe not. They all look alike out here!"

The two of us had camped out across the street from the hotel, right by the Mile 25 sign. We had watched Josh begin the race before dawn that morning, and as I kept a vigilant watch on the pace schedule and times he had given me, estimating a four hour finish, we went into my office where the wind chill wasn't a factor and where we could continue working through plans for the ladies' Bible study we were going to be co-leading after the new year.

I had been amazed by how quickly Redeemer had embraced me and how easily and naturally Debbie had become a good friend and confidante. She had married Mike before his mother had passed away, back when Josh was barely a teenager, and she had felt, as she began her own family, responsible for all of the Morales men when the cancer had so quickly taken her mother-in-law from them. She told me what it was like when they all came to faith within a few months of one another and how they literally doubled the congregation size at Iglesia Redeemer overnight. I was learning how important family was for Josh, and I was amazed by how much I was already a part of it all alongside him.

The whole family, all of Josh's brothers, their wives, assorted nieces and nephews, had joined Debbie and me at our spot on the corner, waiting to celebrate Josh as he ran by. Even though he still wasn't due for a while, I could tell Debbie was getting anxious, wondering if he was okay out there.

"Well, he did say four hours," I told her, pulling my jacket tighter around me and checking the pace schedule once again. "He's probably still a few miles out –"

"THERE HE IS!," Debbie began shouting, pointing to a runner just clearing the corner. Sure enough, as he came into focus, we could tell it was Josh without even checking his bib number.

I jumped up and dusted myself off. "Okay, we'll see you at the finish line," I told her.

"Good luck!," she called out as I made my way onto the course and to Josh's side.

"Hey," he smiled over at me, clearly winded and worn down. "Nice of you to finally join me."

"Mile 25, just like we planned," I said, taking his hand as I began to match his pace. "You're way ahead of your projected time. How are you feeling?"

"I hurt," he said.

"Where do you hurt?"

"Where DON'T I hurt?," he managed to laugh. "I haven't been able to feel my own butt since mile 19."

I looked behind him. "It's still there," I said.

"That's just the good news I needed to hear," he wheezed out. "How much farther?"

"Almost there," I said.

"Okay, let's finish it, then."

"To Josh, and 26.2 miles, in just over three hours," Mike toasted him at lunch a couple of hours later at Grandma's house.

"To doing crazy, stupid things," Josh echoed the sentiment, gingerly making his way back to his seat after showering and getting cleaned up. "Hey," he said, putting an arm around me, looking at the table. "I see you've already got the ibuprofen waiting for me."

"I figured you'd need it," I said.

"You figured right," he said, slipping his arm off my shoulder. "Even my arms hurt. Why do my arms hurt?"

"Full body motion out there," Debbie said. "Maybe you run like a gorilla, with your knuckles hitting the ground."

"Ouch," Josh said, taking the pills. "I thought I looked better than that."

"You looked great," I said, planting a small kiss on his lips.

"Thanks," Josh whispered, giving me a longer, deeper kiss.

"I think we all better get our food down before your PDA makes it impossible to stomach any of it," Mike chided.

"Good thinking," Debbie said, taking his hand. "Why don't you pray for us?" She winked at me before we bowed our heads.

I had to drive a little faster than my regular speed to get home after lunch. I still had to get cleaned up and ready for Melissa's first bridal shower. She was having three of them – one at Grace, one in New Orleans, and one at work. The day of the marathon was also the day Grace's shower was scheduled, and like I had been nearly every time I arrived at Grace, I was almost late and still throwing on earrings and jewelry as I hustled my way in the door.

"Emily," my mother said, as I came in the fellowship hall. "I was beginning to wonder if you'd get here on time."

"Just barely," I said. "What can I do to help?"

"We've got it handled," she said, indicating the entourage of hostesses chatting up guests. "Thanks to all the work you did setting it up last night, we have more help than we even need really."

I sighed contentedly, looking around the room, transformed by fall colors and warm earth tones. Just a few touches had changed the cafeteria look of the hall into one that felt as though we were all in a cozy, intimate room together. I looked around at the guests, milling about the refreshment table I had made arrangements for, the gift table I had set up, and the scrapbooking station, where guests could make pages of well wishes for Beau and Melissa. I recognized Trish, Melissa's mother, several ladies from my Bible study, a big group from Pinnacle, and Pastor Stephen among the fifty or so people gathered at the tables, where women were chatting and laughing with one another while eating.

Wait a minute. Pastor Stephen. At a bridal shower.

He was chatting with Patty Smith, a longtime church member, when he caught my eye. "Emily, can Patty and I talk to you?," he asked, as they made their way over to me.

"Certainly," I said. "How are you doing Mrs. Smith?"

"It's Patty, dear," she said. "I've told you that before."

She had been my sixth grade Sunday school teacher, and all these years later, I still wasn't able to call any of the ladies who had taught me over the years by their first names.

"Patty," I managed, knowing that I'd go right back to Mrs. Smith the next time we saw one another.

"Patty is on the personnel committee, and she's been approached by the committee we put together regarding the new events coordinator position for the church."

"Oh?," I asked. I had given them my resume a couple of weeks earlier and had been patiently waiting to hear back about an interview.

"Yes," she said, "and the personnel committee has given clearance to go ahead and hire you. If you're still interested in the position, that is."

"They're not even going to… interview me?," I asked, shocked.

"Oh, Emily, we've known you your whole life! And, wow," she said, looking around, "this is your work! We've seen it so many times here, and you have such great references from the hotel –"

"Really?," I asked, dumbfounded.

"Yes, Evelyn Primrose just couldn't stop herself from going on and on about how wonderful you are."

God bless Evelyn.

"Are you still interested in the job?"

"Yes, of course, thank you," I managed. "When do I start?"

"Well," Stephen said. "There are a few couples who are looking to book the church for spring weddings. I had planned to meet with them this week, if…" He trailed off, looking at me hopefully.

"I'll start right now," I smiled.

"Now it's time to say good bye to ALL our companyyyyyyy…. M-I-C…."

"See you real soon," I offered, along with all of the other guests.

"K-E-Y…"

"Why? Because we LIKE you!," we all shouted in unison.

"M-O-U-S-E!!!"

And with that, my Disney bride and groom were off in their (what else?) horse drawn carriage, heading around the block to our secret entrance where I'd usher them back in to change clothes, load up into a taxi, and head off to the airport, where a plane was waiting to take them to Orlando.

"It was PERFECT!," Dawn had squealed to me, as I helped her with her wrap, right before I sent her out the front steps to the chorus of singing Mouseketeers and Mickey-shaped confetti they were ready to toss.

"I'm so glad," I hugged her. "You guys have fun in Florida, okay?"

I had given Cliff and Dawn their dream wedding, from the Mickey and Minnie themed favors, the hidden Mickeys spread throughout the reception décor, the glass slipper atop the cake, the rather spectacular castle backdrop we had made, and – to top it all off – the firework simulation on the ceiling of the garden room.

"I'm not sure how you did that, Emily," Evelyn murmured on her brief visit to the room. ("These Disney people freak me out, honestly," she had confided to me, to explain her absence.) "But, my... it IS nice."

Cliff had thought so as well, declaring their wedding ALMOST as great as having it in the Magic Kingdom itself. I considered that a grand success indeed and tucked their tip into my purse as I made my way out to my car, only to find Josh standing there waiting for me.

"Hey, you should have come up earlier," I said. "You missed the fireworks."

"Did I?," he asked. "Wait... fireworks? How did you make that happen?"

"I'll never tell," I said, putting my finger to my lips, "but I gave Dawn her happily ever after. What are you doing here anyway?"

"Just wanted to see you," he said, giving me a hug.

"You're going to see me in," I glanced at my watch, "six hours."

"Not soon enough," he said, smiling at me.

Maybe Dawn wasn't the only one who was going to live happily ever after...

12 NOVEMBER

I had never seen Josh teach chemistry. I had only ever heard him preach in Spanish, and my comprehension in that area was still sorely lacking. So maybe I wasn't qualified to make this kind of judgment on his skills, but I had concluded, after two months of being with him, that his greatest talent was kissing.

Sigh.

We were about an hour (or two?) into another evening of long, lingering kisses when my phone rang.

"I should probably get that," I murmured, as he kept trailing kisses from my mouth to my cheek then down to my neck.

"Probably," he whispered, pulling me closer as I reached for my phone absentmindedly.

Once I managed to finally get to it (on the third ring), I recognized Lauren's number. "Hello?," I rasped out, my concentration completely fixed on what Josh's talented lips were doing beneath my ear.

"Emily? This is Lauren!"

Mmm...

"I just wanted to call and tell you that... well, I'm eloping!"

And like a bucket of cold water had been thrown on me, I came to my senses. "What?!" I sat up straight, nearly knocking Josh off my sofa. He gave me a concerned look. "Lauren," I mouthed to him. He nodded, exhaling loudly and looking decidedly distracted.

"I just... I just couldn't do it!," Lauren laughed, pulling me back towards the phone and sounding for the first time ever, like she was truly happy. "The whole thing was just too much. And I just want to be married now. It's so hard to wait all of these months for a wedding when you want the marriage to start now, you know?"

I looked over to Josh, who gave me a sneaky smile. Oh, he had no idea what Lauren was saying, but from the way I held my hand to my chapped lips and continued staring at him, I'm sure he could guess. And as he continued to give me his own smoldering gaze...

Oh, yeah. I understood how waiting could be hard.

"Your parents," I said to her, forcing my mind back to the issue, back to poor Stan and Dorothy and all their plans. "I'm happy for you, of course, but your parents had so many plans. I just can't stand to think of them missing out on the –"

"No, that's the great thing!," she assured me. "They're going to be there! Both sets of our parents! I mean, Justin's parents aren't thrilled by it, but they've all agreed that if this is what we really want, this is what we'll do. My parents had no problem at ALL with it!"

This sounded like the Dorothy and Stan I had come to love over our months of meeting. So accommodating, so generous, and so completely enthralled over their daughter – just a dream to work with through the whole process. I felt guilty that although they wouldn't lose everything, there would be deposits that wouldn't be refunded this late in the game, and so many other costs – financially, socially – would hit both families hard. Even so, they were willing to do it to give the couple what they wanted. I had to admire that. Of course, Evelyn was going to throw a fit, but that was Evelyn's problem. And no longer – glory! – mine.

"Well, congratulations," I told her, smiling at her happiness. "When is the big day?"

She laughed. "Tomorrow! Right here in my backyard. Bare feet and all!"

I laughed at this. "Are you still going to wear your dress?"

"Yes!," she said. "I love that dress, you know." Then, after a pause, "You've been so great in all of this, Emily. I want you to be there, too. Not as my coordinator but as my friend. Can you come?"

"I wouldn't miss it," I told her.

"And, I hate to ask last minute like this, but can Josh sign our license? You know, nothing fancy for the ceremony, just to help us say our vows and make it legal? Do you think he would mind?"

Josh and I had shared more than a few meals with Justin and Lauren over the past few weeks, discussing high school science and the different school districts in our area. They had fallen in love with him, which was something I could understand completely.

"I think Josh would be delighted to do that for you," I smiled over at him, and he moved closer to me, smiling again, his arms wrapping around my waist, his lips heading straight back to my neck. I snuck a kiss to his lips and gave him a mock scolding look. "Hold on," I mouthed.

"Awesome! We're thinking about six o'clock, right as the sun is setting. Is that good for you?"

"That's great for me."

"Okay! See you then!"

"Bye," I answered, but the line was already dead.

"What would I be delighted to do?," Josh asked, as I tossed my phone to the floor and put my arms back around him.

"A wedding. For Lauren and Justin."

"Do they not have a pastor lined up for next month?"

"No, they don't have a pastor lined up for tomorrow," I smiled. "They're eloping. I just lost the biggest client I've ever had."

He studied my face for a moment, grinning at me. "You don't seem all that upset about it."

"Well, no, because the loss is really Evelyn's. I think she managed to upgrade herself right out of the whole package because she never listened to what the bride really wanted. I'm sure she wouldn't have been able to believe that a bride with parents that rich would want anything simple."

"So... we're making a wedding happen?," he asked, leaning his forehead against mine.

"We're going to try our best."

And we did make it happen the very next day, right at sunset. There had been a few more calls made from Lauren to me, about some of the finer details that she hadn't considered. The first one came about five minutes after her big announcement, forcing Josh and me apart once again, just as things were getting a little intense.

"It's probably good that she keeps calling," Josh sighed after the second time she interrupted things. "Maybe I better sit on the other side of the room."

"Good plan," I murmured. "Let's keep ourselves occupied, shall we?"

Thankfully, there was no shortage of things to keep us occupied for the rest of the afternoon and into the next day. Eloping quickly turned into a simple ceremony and reception which, even though it was quite the scale down from what she had originally planned, still involved work. Dorothy and I put together some simple plans for flowers, for cake, for music, and for Josh's ten minute service. And, as Lauren's friend, first and foremost, I found myself (and Josh, who was roped in as well) there at the Evans' huge home three hours early, setting it all up so that the spur of the moment wedding would be exactly what Lauren had wanted.

I was happy to do it, happier even still when I got to stand in the circle with the few other guests, around the bride and the groom, listening to Josh as he talked about faith, marriage, and love. I had never been one to let my mind drift, during the many ceremonies I had attended in my career, to thoughts of my own future, to play with what ifs, and to imagine what my own marriage might look like.

But that was all changing now. Especially after it was all over, when Josh came up behind me, wrapped his arms around me, and whispered in my ear, "What do you think?"

"I think you did great," I whispered to him. "I think WE did great. And at the very last minute, too."

"I wasn't talking about that," he said. "I mean, what do you think about having a wedding like this? Backyard, just a few of our friends, barefoot in a really huge dress?"

I could feel my heart race. "Are you talking about... my wedding?," I smiled.

"Well, I was thinking of it as ours," he smiled at me, nearly sending my heart right out of my chest. "But since you'll probably be more involved in the planning, sure, we'll call it yours." He laughed at his own joke.

"Well," I said, taking a deep breath, "I want to wear shoes. And I can't afford a dress like that. But other than that… I don't know. It was nice, in its own way, wasn't it?"

"Oh, you know what?," he said letting go of me, "Dr. Evans gave this to me." He held up an envelope with my name on it. "Based on the warning he gave me to tell you that you weren't to refuse it, I'm guessing that you COULD afford a dress like that, if you use whatever's in this envelope."

Curious, I opened it up, took one look at the check, and gasped.

"Oh, my word, Josh," I breathed. "This is enough to… to buy myself a new car."

He looked over my shoulder, then whistled appreciatively. "A car much nicer than the one you're driving right now. Which, you know, wouldn't take much. But this is a lot of money," he offered diplomatically.

I looked at him. "I can't take this."

"That's what Dr. Evans said you would say. And he told me to tell you that it's yours, that during all of this, you were just –"

"Peachy," I finished for him.

"Exactly," he said. He touched the corner of the check. "I don't think this to him and her is nearly what it is to you. This doesn't seem as outlandish to them as it does to you. And I really, really think that they want to bless you, to thank you for being a good wedding planner for Lauren. And for being her friend."

I was struggling to process what this meant, how suddenly, everything was changing.

"What are you thinking?," Josh said, softly, noting the tears that were gathering in my eyes.

"I just wonder... you know, why everything just seems to be going... SO right, right now, you know?"

He smiled. "Sometimes that just happens."

Melissa and I met up without Sara once again.

"Doesn't it feel like she's been gone forever?," Melissa managed around the salad that she was eating.

"Why are you eating salad?," I asked. "There's steak on the menu."

"Yeah, tell me about it," she said. "That wedding dress, I've got to fit into that wedding dress. And the more I eat the less likely I will, so I'm living on this rabbit food."

"Well, you should probably cut out some of that dressing and the croutons if you're looking to lose weight, and –"

"Hey!," she shouted at me. "I'm eating SALAD, okay?!"

I let her be.

"Back to your question, though... yes, it does feel like she's been gone forever. I hardly hear from her these days, you know?"

"She's so busy," Melissa said. "She's met so many people out there, and with so many of them going to Costa Rica, too, I guess it's just to be expected that she'd be spending time getting to know them."

"She's doing a great job with the resolution for this month, isn't she?"

"Yeah," Melissa nodded. "So am I, though. And you! Who would've ever guessed this would be so easy, with me getting to know my in-laws and all of their friends, and you getting to know a whole new church full of people?"

It was true. I had met so many people at Redeemer in such a short while and honestly felt, even this early on, as though I knew most of them on more than just a superficial level.

"Are you going to judge me if I order dessert after I finish forcing this down?," Melissa asked.

"No, I'll split one with you."

She scoffed at me, then smiled. "Get your own, honey. I'm hungry."

I was having a hard time keeping up with him.

Thanksgiving was just a few days away, so Josh had the whole week off from school. I had the big dinner at Grace to put on Wednesday night and plans to celebrate the holiday with Jess and her family on Thursday for lunch. Josh was going with me, then we were heading to his family's Thanksgiving for dinner.

"Two Thanksgiving meals," he told me, patting his now non-existent belly. "I'm going to have to do a high mileage run on Wednesday to prepare myself for that."

I had moved my consults to Monday and Tuesday so that I had all of Wednesday morning, which just happened to also be his birthday, to run with him and celebrate.

His idea of high mileage and mine differed greatly, however, so we agreed to split the difference at ten miles and met up at the park to get it done.

"Josh," I panted at mile seven, "I think you're running too fast."

"I think you're running too slow," he responded, nudging me with his shoulder. "Enchiladas, fajitas – Grandma is fixing them all, and we've got to be prepared."

"Okay, okay," I grumbled, as he slowed his pace slightly for me.

Over two miles later, I was spent. "Seriously," I managed to sputter, "I've never run this far!" I stopped to put my hands on my knees.

"Oh, good grief," Josh managed around his smile. "Here," he said, lifting me up in his arms. "I'll carry you the last bit to our coffee shop, okay?"

"I'm not sure that's wise," I said. "You're going to hurt your back."

"I'm not that old," he protested.

"And I stink," I added.

"You smell like empanadas," he said.

"I... what?"

"You do," he said. "Delicious, even after nine miles."

"Wow, you really have food on the brain, don't you?"

"And how!"

"Nine and a half miles," I said, relaxing in his arms as he walked the last part of the route.

A few minutes later, he came to a stop. "And we're at ten," he declared, putting me on the ground at the door of the coffee shop.

"I ran farther than I thought," I said.

"Could have run it all," he said, "but that would have denied me the privilege of those last few steps."

I gave him a soft kiss. "Let me get the drinks for us, okay?"

"Sure," he said, handing me his debit card. "I'm going to grab that table outside."

I ordered our drinks, thinking over the consults I had earlier in the week, wondering how my parents were doing in Rwanda. It was the first Thanksgiving that the Fisher family would be spread out over three continents. I wondered if it might just be the first of many, smiling at the thought of how fulfilled my parents were, even as they dealt with my father's illness. Josh and I had done dinner with them the week before, and my father had been doing great. Clear, focused, and totally there – so much so that I marveled over his disposition as I watched him talk with Josh outside as they grilled the steaks while my mother and I made the side dishes in the kitchen.

I said a quick prayer for him and for mom both, wondering what they were doing right then.

Once our drinks were ready, I took them out to the front, where Josh was sitting at the table we always sat at, a fluffy bathrobe on the table in front of him.

"What's that?," I asked.

"That's for you," he said. "You know, since it's getting cold. And your shower is still not fixed."

"You think this will make it easier to warm back up afterwards?"

"It just might," he said. "Try it on."

"But I'm all sweaty," I said.

"You just let me carry you the last half mile. You should be spring fresh," he laughed at me.

"Fine," I said, slipping it on. "Oooohhh, that IS nice. Thank you." I smiled at him. "Where did you get this from"

"Oh, it was in my truck. I parked here before we ran and went over to meet you. Why did you think I asked to meet up here separately instead of coming together?"

"I don't know, I... wait, do you mean you've run twenty miles today?"

He nodded. "I plan on eating a whole lot of carne asada." He pulled me down to sit on his lap.

"Well, I appreciate the robe... it's just perfect. But why are you doing this? It's your birthday, not mine," I said, my hands on his face, running my fingers over his stubble. Geez, I loved the way he looked in the morning. And in the afternoon. And in the evening. All the time, actually.

He gazed at me for a moment. "Yeah, I know," he said softly. "And the best present you can give me is to say yes."

"Yes? What's the question?"

"Check your pocket."

I gave him an amused look, wondering what the joke was, and gasped when my fingers touched a little velvet box.

"Josh..."

"I had hoped to get down on one knee to do this, but... well, you're still sitting on me. And you still haven't pulled it out of your pocket."

I jumped to my feet. "Okay, I'm getting up, I'm getting up, and here's the... oh, wow!," I exclaimed as I pulled the box out and opened it up, revealing a cushion cut diamond ring. "Josh, it's a ring! It's a ring!"

"I know, I know," he said, getting down on one knee, taking the ring out of the box that I was still holding in my outstretched hand, too shocked to do much else. "Emily Fisher," he said, meeting my eyes, a smile in his own. "Will you marry me?"

It didn't take me any time at all to answer.

"Yes!," I exclaimed, snatching my ring out of his grasp and putting it on my left hand. I held it up in the sunlight, wiggling it just so.

"Look at it! LOOK at it!"

"Emily, I just ran twenty miles. Can you help me get up?," he groaned.

"Oh, Josh," I exclaimed, pulling him up, giving him a long lingering kiss… then going right back to the subject of my fabulous new ring. "Was it in your truck?"

"Yeah, why do you think I was running so fast? Scared to death to leave it out here, let me tell you. What if someone had stolen my truck?"

I laughed and hugged him again. "When did you… how…" I looked at him, still so shocked. "I can't believe this!"

"I talked to your dad last week," Josh said. "He was great with it, which was good, since I bought the ring the day after your birthday."

I gasped out loud. "That's CRAZY!"

"Yeah," he said smiling. "But when you know, you know."

I was dumbfounded by the simple logic of this. I had always thought a decision like this would be complicated and difficult to make. Not nearly this easy and natural. "So," I said, peering closely at my new ring, "when do you think we should get married?" A pause. "We're getting married! I can't believe it!"

"Well, I'd do it today, if you were willing," he said.

"How about the spring?," I asked. "Is that too early?"

"How about Christmas?"

He smiled at me, as I gave him a look.

"I think that's a little too soon to really plan anything. Not that I want a huge wedding, but let's at least give ourselves a few months to coordinate a celebration."

"Are you sure? Your dad told me he was all for a short engagement." Josh grinned.

I was horrified by what I was sure this meant. "He didn't talk to you about –"

"Oh, yes, he did," Josh laughed. "Better to marry than burn and all. He even pulled out some Song of Solomon on me."

"He wasn't thinking clearly, obviously," I said.

"Totally in his right mind," Josh said. "Because he concluded his speech by telling me that even if he did the ceremony, he did NOT want to counsel us."

"Praise God for that," I muttered.

"So... how about Christmas?"

"Not enough time, seriously." My mind began racing through the possibilities for a spring wedding. Maybe as early as March but before May, before the summer rush started in...

"I can't believe you said yes so quickly," Josh murmured, pulling me into his arms.

I looked at him, surprised. "Did you think I would say no?"

"Not really," he shook his head. "I just assumed you'd have some reservations about saying yes so quickly. I mean... we've only really been together for a couple of months, right?"

"I think," I said turning to face him head on, putting my hands on either side of his face, "I would have said yes two months ago. You know, back when YOU bought the ring. I just KNOW that this is right. And I never thought, in a million years that I would ever meet anyone who I would be so certain about. YOU are HOME for me, Josh."

"Well, that was easy," he said, taking another kiss.

"It sure was," I said, laughing out loud.

I managed an email to my parents about the good news as I rushed around that afternoon, getting ready for the Wednesday night meal I had organized at Grace. They weren't getting phone calls from their remote location, but my mother had promised me she would check email once a day at least and communicate with all three of her children that way.

My phone rang approximately five minutes after I sent the email, confirming the truth of her promise.

"What have YOU done?!"

"Good afternoon, Jessica," I managed, around my toothbrush, still brushing.

"So, I just got a funny email from the other side of the world," she said, tersely. "About this younger sister I have, who, you know, I THOUGHT I was close to. But as it turns out, we must not be very close at all, because the guy that I just met a few weeks ago for the first time? Yeah, well, she's getting MARRIED to him, and I'm left wondering why I was kept in the dark so long about how SERIOUS this relationship is and —"

"Hold on," I said, spitting. "I've got another call coming in."

I put her on hold, despite her protests against it, then clicked over. "Hey," Josh said. "Just thinking about you and wanted to call. Do you have time for me to come by before you need to be at Grace?"

I looked at my watch. "I would, but I'm on the phone with my sister. She's pretty steamed."

"That we're getting married?"

"That she didn't know about it," I sighed. "Perfectly normal, as she is my mother, only younger, you know."

"Ahh."

"And I just said goodbye to you," I looked at the clock on my bathroom counter, "about thirty minutes ago. Are you already missing me?"

"Yes," he said, sadly. "Which is the whole reason we're getting married. So I don't ever have to miss you, right?"

"I thought it was so I could live somewhere where I don't have to keep taking cold showers," I said, pulling my new bathrobe closer.

"Yeah, you've mentioned that I still need to work on that, huh? And by work on that, I mean, figure out what in the world will fix it."

"Yes, you do," I said, rinsing my toothbrush off.

"And speaking of cold showers," he cleared his throat dramatically, "have you given any more thought to a Christmas wedding?"

"Hold on, I've got another beep. Jess probably hung up and is calling back."

"Tell your sister to get back to her five children, and –"

"Hello?,"

"Geez, Emily, what's the deal?!"

"Matthew," I said. Mom had been getting the job done online, apparently.

"Mom tells me that you're getting married… to who?!"

"You're one to talk, you know."

"When I was in the States, you know, just a little while ago," he continued on, "you weren't even dating anyone, and now –"

"You are going to LOVE Josh."

A pause. "Seriously? That's all you can come up with?"

"Right now? Yeah. And I need you to look and see when, if it's at all possible, you can manage to come home in the spring for the wedding. We're waiting to set a date until we know for sure that you and Shoko can come back for it."

"Can't do it," he said. "I have no leave until next fall."

"Next FALL?"

"I just took leave, Emily," he said. "And in case you've forgotten, I have my own wedding coming up then, so my leave won't be yours, thankyouverymuch."

I thought about this for a moment, sitting on the edge of the bathtub to collect my thoughts. "Any long weekends, maybe?"

"None."

I frowned. "You don't have any days off until the fall? There are labor laws against that."

"Well, I have three days and a weekend at Christmas, but—"

"Christmas?" I sat up straighter. "Have you... did Josh put you up to this?"

"What?," he asked. "No, Emily, it would be impossible for him to put me up to anything since I don't even KNOW him and all –"

"Oh, hold on, I've got another call... hello?"

"Well, I got tired of waiting, so I hung up and called back," Jess huffed. I had figured as much already.

"Hey, Matt's on hold. Do you mind if we just table this discussion until tomorrow? Josh and I'll come over earlier than planned and help out with the meal, okay?"

She sighed. "Okay… and congratulations. I really DO like Josh. Just wish I knew him better –"

"That's what tomorrow is for. Love you!" I hung up before she could protest, then switched over to Matthew.

"Can you take leave for a Christmas wedding?," I asked, breathless, all of the pieces clicking together in my mind.

"Really? Christmas?"

Wrong person. "Josh, I thought you were my brother." I looked at my phone. "I guess he hung up… or I hung up on him. Oh, well."

"You know Christmas is only… four weeks away, right?"

"Yeah," I said. "But it looks like it'll have to work. Why don't we meet up after the dinner and figure it out, okay?"

"That sounds great," he said, obviously gleeful at the idea of both – dinner later on and a wedding sooner than hoped for. "I love you," he said.

"I love you, too," I smiled.

I floated through the dinner at Grace, stealing glances at my ring approximately every five minutes as I moved through the tables, checking that everything was going according to plan. A few people noticed my new jewelry, among them Pastor Stephen, who congratulated me warmly.

My sister, who had spent the majority of the meal back in the nursery thanks to a starving Seth ("he eats like a horse and kicks like one, too, so I'm not nursing him under a wrap, lest he kicks it off and lets the entire church check out my goods"), was able to come back into the fellowship hall afterwards, where I was busy cleaning up and counting the minutes until I would be meeting up with Josh for dinner at his house.

"Hey," she said, stepping in beside me, picking up and straightening the linens I was sliding off the tables. "I got a call from Mom a while ago."

"She's able to call out of Rwanda now?"

"No, they're actually in Germany," she said, glancing at her watch. "Well, they're probably in the air right now, on their way back home."

"Is everything okay?," I asked, worried about my father for the first time in a long while. Had the trip been too much for him?

Jess shook her head, a sad grin on her face. "No... Dad's been confused. And since they had the travel insurance to cover the cost of changing their tickets anyway, Mom decided it was best to just get him home. They should be here early tomorrow morning."

"Oh, man," I said, dropping the tablecloth I had been folding. "Is he going to be okay?"

"I think this is what 'okay' is going to look like from now on," she said calmly, transformed from her frantic, distracted state only a couple of months earlier. "Good days and bad days, you know. That's how he and Mom talk about it."

"Good days and bad days," I repeated, sadly. "Well, at least there ARE good days."

"That's right. And," she said, looking at my ring again with a smile, "there are plenty of good days up ahead, you know."

Josh fought off a yawn, as we drove into the airport's parking garage. "I feel like we just said goodnight, you know."

"Mmm-hmm," I said from where I had been dozing in his passenger seat. We had said goodnight at midnight, after eating leftovers in his kitchen from Grace's dinner.

"One of us has to learn how to cook," I had told him, noting his own inability to do much besides hit start on the microwave.

"I'll play you for it," he had said, holding up his hand for rock, paper, scissors.

"One, two, three." Then, groans from me as he had cheered, "Rock beats scissors!"

I looked over to him now, where he sat concentrating on the road and trying not to fall back asleep, smiling as I began to doze off again.

"Hey, we're here," he said, waking me from my daydreaming. I checked the clock. 4am. They should have landed by now.

We quickly made our way to the arrival lounge, where my eyes found my mother in – what else? – an outrageous African dress. My father must have been in his right mind because he was dressed in his normal, American clothes, as he pulled their suitcases behind him.

"Emily, Josh!" My mother ran the last few steps to us, embracing Josh first and kissing him on the cheek. "Congratulations," she said. "We're so happy."

She turned to me, and I met her eyes, looking for an indication of how bad Dad's most recent episode had been, finding only a peaceful resignation there. "Let me see your ring," she said after hugging me. Then, as I held it up to her, "Just beautiful. Thomas, look at this," she said, holding my hand out to him.

He looked at it and hugged me. "So happy for you, dear," he said. "When's the wedding?"

I took a breath to break the news to them, about how Josh and I had decided the night before that Christmas was the perfect time, if we could arrange to get Matthew and Shoko back in time for –

"I'm sorry," Dad said, moving past me, holding his hand out to Josh. "Have we met? I'm Thomas Fisher."

My mother's face fell slightly, as my own heart took a plunge. But Josh never missed a beat, as he took my father's hand in his own and said, "Josh Morales. It's a real honor, sir."

At some point in the drive back to their house, Dad came back to himself. And by the time we all met at Jessica and Nick's, it was as though he had never had a problem.

"A good day," Jess whispered to me, the relief clear in her voice.

I nodded, smiling, as Josh squeezed my hand in his.

We told them the news, about a Christmas wedding, and watched as Jess freaked completely out, and as my mother got Matthew on the phone, sending Nick to the computer to get online and check ticket fares from Okinawa. Josh and I watched them all, speechless at their flurry of activity, broken out of our stupor by my father, who put his hand on Josh's shoulder and proclaimed, "Well, I'm all for short engagements, you know. Better to –"

"That's right, Dad," I said, cutting him off with a smile. "You're right."

Our meeting with Evelyn, later on that week, wrapped up in record time. Perhaps that was because I already knew the business inside and out, and she didn't have much to explain. Still, though, Josh was impressed.

"Wow. THAT was Evelyn," he said, as we left her office.

"I know," I said. "Isn't she incredible?"

"If by incredible you mean incredibly scary, then yeah," he breathed a little sigh of relief. He had gotten just a preview of her business savvy, as we booked the garden room for our Christmas wedding reception. It had always been my favorite room in all of the hotel, and to my great surprise, Evelyn waived the cost of renting it entirely, offering me a price that covered just the wages for the extra set-up crew, leaving herself with no profit for her own time and work.

I nudged him. "She really scared you, huh?"

He laughed again. "I didn't know whether to bow, kiss her hand, or cross myself. She's like the evil queen of some bridal land."

I smiled at him. "You know, that's EXACTLY what I thought when I first met her." I sighed. "Well, minus the evil part. At least, at first."

"So, the wedding is planned now, right? One meeting, and we're done!"

"Oh, no," I said, as we made our way to catering to talk with Stella. "It's just starting."

"It. Is. Done."

Josh and Beau stood back surveying my crummy apartment's bathroom... which was no longer crummy. The bathroom looked amazing and was once again completely functional, thanks to Beau's talents.

"We should have called you a lot earlier," Josh told him, awed appreciation in his voice. "Maybe Emily would have been spared all those months of cold showers."

"He fixed the shower?," I asked, incredulous. "How?"

"Oh, it wasn't any big deal," he said. "I could explain what I did, but... well, you probably wouldn't understand any of my explanation."

"Probably not," I muttered, turning on the hot water in the shower and testing it with my hand. "Josh! It's hot! It's hot!"

"I feel bad about not helping out earlier," Beau said. "Work has been really busy, and with Melissa's promotion, we hardly had time to communicate about all the wedding plans, much less about the fact that the bathroom she destroyed was still in shambles."

"Ha. Ha." Melissa gave him a look from the kitchen where she was busy making dinner for all four of us.

"Don't worry," Beau whispered. "Her cooking is better than her plumbing skills."

"I can still hear you!"

"How's that dinner coming along, darling?," Beau winked at me as he made his way into the kitchen.

"Almost done," she said. "Josh, I hope you like fried chicken."

"I like food," Josh summed up concisely.

"This is, like, the only thing that Beau's mother ever made for him growing up. Because he won't eat anything else."

"Why bother when fried chicken is so great?," he asked, sneaking a piece of fried okra from the serving dish Melissa had already set out.

"Well, it hasn't hurt your figure, our your mother's, or your sisters'," she said, "but I swear, my butt has doubled in size since we've been together."

"A constant diet of fried chicken will do that," Josh nodded sagely.

We all looked at him.

"Seriously, substitute Taco Bell for fried chicken, and you have the entire reason why I gained the freshman fifty back in college."

"That's the freshman fifteen," I corrected him.

"Oh, no, it wasn't."

"Well, he's right," Melissa said. "About the chicken, at least. It will. I had to go back and order a bigger size for my wedding dress!"

"Speaking of," I said, "my parents get home next week, and we're going dress shopping if you want to come. I've already talked to Sara, and she's coming."

Melissa sighed, "It'll be good to have her back home. At least for a little while. But, yeah, I'll be there for the dress shopping."

"Isn't this all really quick?," Beau said. "Didn't you just get engaged a week ago?"

"Yeah," Josh said. "But with Emily's brother coming stateside for Christmas, he'll be able to stop over for a few days for a wedding. And with Sara leaving for Costa Rica in January…"

"And with Jess not pregnant the last time I talked to her, we need to get on the ball before she becomes pregnant again, has to wear one of those awful maternity bridesmaid dresses, and hates me for the rest of her life," I finished for him.

"Wait a minute," Melissa said. "Christmas? You're getting married THIS Christmas?"

"Yeah," I said. "We've already made arrangements for another visa for Shoko to come with Matthew, which makes for… a whole lot of bridesmaids."

"Wow," Beau remarked, sipping on his iced tea.

"Yes," I answered, "which is why I've got to get a dress… like, yesterday."

"Geez, Emily! That's only a... four week engagement!," Melissa shouted.

"I'm not complaining," Josh said to Beau.

"I wouldn't have either," Beau responded back.

"It's like Thomas told me – better to marry than to –"

"Burn. Oh, I remember that talk, and let me tell you, it –"

"Will you two shut up for a minute?," Melissa scolded them. "Can you even get everything ready by then?"

"Yeah, I think I can get it ready in half the time. We've already taken care of most of the planning this week, what with all the vendors I have on speed dial who owe me favors."

"It's not about favors," Josh chimed up. "You wouldn't believe how much these people love Emily. The guy at the bakery actually cried – I mean, totally wept – when Emily showed him her ring. It's like his first born child is getting married or something."

"They're very sweet people," I smiled.

"And Emily's lease is up at the end of the year," Josh looked to Melissa again. "Which is why we're doubly indebted to you guys for the help with the remodel. We can start moving her stuff out, and after Christmas, she'll be done with this place."

"And then, what?," Melissa asked. "You're going --"

"To Josh's house, of course."

"Well," Melissa frowned at me, unmoved. "I guess you've got it ALL figured out."

I looked at her. "Are you seriously irritated by that?"

"No," she said, clearly irritated. "It's just... all these changes! Everything's changing! Too quickly!" A pause. Then, an ear-splitting shriek. "What about MY wedding?! Are you even going to still be in town for –"

"Yes," I said, taking her by the shoulders, calmly looking into her eyes, so tickled that I was doing my patent hysterical bride intervention on the one woman who swore she didn't give two flying flips about any of this wedding planning nonsense any way. "Breathe. Just breathe."

"Don't you pull any of your hoo-doo voo-doo wedding planner stuff on me," she said. "I've heard your stories, and I'm NOT freaking out –"

"I'm going to be there for your wedding. ALL week, for ALL of the festivities and ALL of the plans. Nothing is changing."

She rolled her eyes. "Don't you see, though? That's just it! EVERYTHING is changing! Sara's running off, our church is going to completely change, my job is totally different, we're getting married, and... doesn't it feel like everything is going to be different?"

"Maybe it'll be better," I said, smiling.

13 DECEMBER

"What is this?," Melissa asked, holding up a thin scrap of black lace.

We had hit the mall just a few weeks before Christmas. While I would normally avoid the mall at all costs during this time of year, Melissa and I had gladly put ourselves in the path of homicidal holiday shoppers to help Sara celebrate her last birthday in the US. "Won't be able to go to the mall in Costa Rica," she had told us. And while she would likely find a mall of some sort in Costa Rica, the mad rush of American shoppers intent on finding the perfect Christmas gift would be missing. So, she was right.

"Seriously," Melissa shouted, still holding the black lace, "is this some fancy hair scrunchie?"

She began gathering up her hair into a ponytail to try it out when my words stopped her.

"It's a thong."

She froze, held it out from her, and asked, "Really?"

Sara glanced up from where she was thumbing through a sales paper.

"Yep, that's exactly what that is," she said. "How could you not know that?"

Melissa gave her a look. "I'm not in the habit of buying things like this. Obviously. And besides," she inspected the thong again, loudly continuing to pontificate on it, "why would anyone wear this?"

She was drawing the attention of several other shoppers in the small lingerie store. I had been surprised when she took us in there, but she had explained it away with a muttered "gift card from Beau's sister because THAT'S not awkward at all, right?"

She didn't know the meaning of awkward. Awkward was standing in the middle of this store as your friend continued flinging around flimsy underwear and shouting about it as she shook it in your face.

"How is this even comfortable?," she continued on.

"I don't think comfort is the point," I hissed, snatching it out of her hand and placing it back onto the table.

"Well, what's the point of any of these things?," she said, checking the price on a corset. "All this money for stuff that... well, frankly, I won't even be wearing for a handful of minutes."

Sara smiled and shook her head, her eyes never leaving her sales paper.

"Don't you stand over there laughing at me. I'm not stupid, and I can guarantee you that –"

"Men are visual," I said quietly, cutting off her tirade while inspecting a rack of see through numbers, my mind shifting to the most recent proof of this claim, a late night spent at Josh's house. We were there studying like we always did, and before we knew it, a few sweet kisses turned heated, there were hands everywhere, and Josh breathlessly declared that he was completely incapable of stopping himself. And then, he valiantly hightailed it to the other side of the room, as far away from me as he could get without actually leaving his own house.

Of course, at the time, I had been wearing my junkiest pair of sweats and an oversized fleece pullover that had holes in the elbows, but Josh had sworn that it wasn't taking a whole lot at this point to get him worked up. He insisted that the visual, in this case, was just me and that we would do well to limit the time we spent alone together at his house until we were married. I had agreed. But still, as I looked at the clothes around me in the lingerie store, remembering his reaction to my most unflattering clothes, my mind couldn't stop from imagining what he would do if he saw me in one of these little –

"Visual?!," Melissa spat out, holding up a bright red piece (that just about matched the blush that now likely covered my entire body) against herself. "Me in one of these things? That's a visual no one needs. Especially not Beau."

"You know," Sara offered helpfully, "maybe Beau's sister wasn't trying to get you to buy thongs with that gift card. Haven't both of his sisters been helping you pack? Maybe they caught sight of your holey drawers and thought you might appreciate some new ones. You know, since someone will actually be seeing them."

"My underwear is not holey," Melissa sniped. Then, thoughtfully, "But maybe you're right. It's not like they'll ever know if I get something more practical with their gift card, right?"

"Exactly," I said. "Forget the lingerie. Let's just replace the necessities."

Melissa moved over to the pajama section, where Sara followed her.

"How's the moving going?," she asked Melissa, as I made my way over to where they browsed.

"Great, actually, since Chloe and Sophie blew through and took care of it all. They packed up the place in no time at all!," Melissa answered. Her house had finally sold. I felt no sadness over the loss of my dream home... since Josh's house was so similar yet so much better, given who was already living there and waiting for me to move in. I had already started thinking of it as OUR house and had said more than one thankful prayer that life had kept me from buying my own house months earlier.

"One week until closing," Melissa said, "and I've just about got all of my stuff moved out. Most of it to Beau's house, then what I'll need until the wedding at Chloe's."

"Are you loving having a roommate again?," I asked, smiling to myself, knowing that Melissa had always loathed roommates in college.

"You know," she said, diplomatically, "I thought I would hate it, but Chloe is... well, never there, actually. Between her offseason training, her odd hour classes, and her social life, we just pass each other coming and going." She lowered her voice. "Beau would flip out if he knew how late she stays out at night. I mean, there are nights when I feel like going all big sister on her myself."

"How late does she stay out?," Sara asked, concern on her face.

"She came in at MIDNIGHT the other night." Melissa raised her eyebrows at us, shaking her head disapprovingly.

"I think it's been a while since you've been in college, Melissa," I said. "That's normal."

"Wasn't for me!," she bellowed. "I had classes at eight sharp. I was in bed by ten. Every night."

"Not me," Sara said. "Oh, wow, I remember how things didn't even get started until midnight most nights."

"Yeah, I think midnight was an early night for me. And then, I'd sleep in until noon," I said. "I really miss those days sometimes."

"Well," Melissa huffed, "then perhaps the two of you would like to move into sorority row and let me move to one of your places."

"Still with my parents, remember?," Sara said, smiling. "Which is weird after being on my own so long, but I think they're enjoying the extra time with me before I leave."

"Yes, well maybe they keep my hours," Melissa said.

"And my apartment is just about empty," I said to her. "The people who bought my living room furniture and Josh's bedroom furniture are picking them both up next week, then we'll move the rest of it to his place, and I'll probably just go stay with my parents."

"Geez," Melissa breathed out. "This whole combining two households into one is stressful, isn't it? We had a horrible time trying to decide what to keep, what to give away, what to sell, what would fit –"

"Tell me about it," I said.

Sara laughed at us, checking the sizes on a stack of pajamas.

"What?," we asked together, at the exact same moment.

"Nothing," she giggled. "It's just I've spent the past month packing what's left of what I own into two suitcases. Seriously – two suitcases. That's all I have left! And you guys are lamenting having two households full of stuff. How weird is it that our lives are taking such different turns?"

"You're only taking two suitcases?," Melissa asked, disbelieving. "I'm not sure two suitcases would even hold all of my shoes."

We both looked at her for a moment, confused as to why our non-fashionista friend would find a need for more than one pair of sensible shoes that she could wear with everything. She looked up at us, exasperated. "Well, I've bought a few pairs of shoes. It's Chloe. She's... she's really rubbing off on me, and she finds these deals on these incredible shoes, and I swear, Trish brings me a new pair of shoes every time she comes into town –"

"And you really, really suffer," I said, laughing at her.

"That's not what I meant, it's —"

"Hey, Sara, if you get to Costa Rica and are in need of more than just the two pairs of shoes you're packing with you, just let me know, and I'll steal some of Melissa's and bring them with me when Josh and I come to visit you next summer." We were already making plans to take a team from Redeemer to help out with summer projects that Sara would be setting up. I couldn't wait to see her in her new home.

"Duly noted," Sara smiled at me, as Melissa rolled her eyes at us.

"I'm sorry, y'all," she said. "I've been spending too much time with Beau's sisters. They've been working on overhauling my entire wardrobe. I never even knew that clothing went out of style from one year to the next until I met them."

I shrugged. "Evelyn always tried to tell me that, but I didn't really let it affect me."

"I'm glad I'm moving to Costa Rica," Sara said, gathering a pair of pajamas in her arms and heading for the cash register. "You really don't have to worry about those kinds of things there."

"No, you just have to worry about other things, probably," Melissa followed her, a few purchases in her own arms. "Who are you getting those for?"

"My mom," she said. "I still have a few more gifts to buy for Christmas."

Melissa looked over to me, my arms empty. "Aren't going to buy anything? Sara and I have ten bags between us, and you have nothing."

"Yeah, and I have to celebrate Christmas earlier than both of you," I confirmed. "I know, I know. I need to get on task. I've just been too busy to even sit down and figure out who I'm shopping for, and with everything happening over the next few weeks—"

"It hasn't been a real priority," Sara said with a smile.

"Maybe you can just do Christmas... well, AFTER Christmas," Melissa offered, handing her credit card over to the sales associate.

Yeah, that probably wasn't going to work out. I took a deep breath, my mind racing over all that still had to be accomplished in the weeks ahead. "I feel overwhelmed," I said, listing them all in my head – finishing up my last two weeks of work with Evelyn, all the holiday festivities planned at Grace, Sundays at Redeemer, Wednesdays at Redeemer, a bridal shower, all the preparations for my wedding, all the preparations for Melissa's wedding, Christmas with TWO families now, the big day—

"Isn't it great?," Sara said, smiling at me. "You know, being overwhelmed because things are so great?"

I allowed myself a smile as well. "It is."

Grandma Morales and Debbie had a surprise planned for me.

They had arranged it for a day when Josh was teaching, proclaiming that it was impossible to get me alone unless he was at work because all of the other time, to quote Debbie, "you two never leave one another alone." This was likely true enough.

"Seriously," she told me in the kitchen, as Grandma bustled around, "the two of you have become like one entity to us. Josily, we call you."

Grandma recognized the word Josily and let out a delighted laugh, muttering to herself. "Josily, Josily..."

"Well, it is biblical, you know," I said, "becoming one, right?"

"I suppose so, but... well, I'd kill Mike if I didn't get a break from him every now and then." She looked at me, grinning. "I mean, honestly. Praise God for the garage that takes him away from me and gives me a rest every now and then."

RESOLUTIONS

All of Josh's brothers were like him – wonderful, godly men – but Mike had especially been wonderful to me as of late. With Dr. Evans's check deposited in my account, right alongside the house savings that I would no longer need, Mike went with me as I went shopping for a new car, showing greater knowledge than I had on my own when it came to what kind of car I needed, what kind of upkeep and maintenance it would require, and what fair value was. I'm sure I would have been robbed blind on my own, but thanks to Mike's calm, no nonsense presence there in the dealer's office with me, I came of the deal without taking out any kind of loan on my brand new car.

"He's a good man," I said. "You're very lucky."

"Oh, I know that," she said. "But YOU – YOU'RE the lucky one today. Grandma is going to teach you how to make a few of Josh's favorite dishes."

Grandma smiled over at me, as she continued pulling ingredients out of the fridge.

"I don't know how to... well, how to cook anything," I whispered to Debbie.

"Good," she whispered back to me, "because Grandma would have told you that you were doing it wrong anyway, if you had come in with any skills of your own. Well, told ME, which I would have had to translate for you, then you'd have your feelings hurt by ME, not HER, and... well, it's easier this way. You're a blank slate."

Four hours later, my blank slate was being quickly filled, as I was hands on with three separate dishes and as Grandma Morales continued to lecture me on how to do it better. I just smiled and nodded, making notes for myself on what I was doing, having no clue what Grandma was saying, and wondering where Debbie had gone to, just as she reappeared in the kitchen doorway. "Well, Josh will be here in a few minutes. Just called to tell me that my time was up and that he was stealing you back from us."

My eyes didn't leave what I was working on. "I think he'll change his mind when he sees what could be waiting for him in... I think Grandma said forty-five minutes? For this to cook?"

"Muy bien, Emily," Debbie praised me. "You'll be speaking like the rest of us in no time at –"

"Hey!," Josh yelled as he swept into the kitchen, kissing his grandmother, nodding his head at Debbie, and stopping short as he saw me working at the counter.

"Did you speed the entire drive over here?," Debbie asked him, looking at her watch.

"I may have hustled a little more than normal," Josh said. "What are you doing?," he asked me.

"Cooking," I said. "And, yeah, I know. Wow, huh? I made everything you're going to eat later on."

Smiling, he made his way to the stove, where the enchilada sauce I'd put together was simmering. Putting a spoon in, then lifting it to his lips to taste, even as his grandmother chided him, he turned to me and said, "Well, just when I thought life couldn't get any better, my dream woman learns how to cook. Like my grandmother, no less. Best day ever!" He put his spoon down and moved to wrap his arms around me, forcing me to stop what I was working on and put my food-covered hands on him, my split-second negligence likely wrecking the last dish that Grandma was teaching me how to make.

"Ah, Josily," she sighed, elbowing past us in the tight kitchen and finishing the job herself, a smile on her face as she did so.

"Emily! Emily, let me see you!"

Stacy, my Circus bride, was nearing the end of her pregnancy and was glowing... and waddling. I had asked her earlier why she was playing such a big role in planning the baby shower her aunts were throwing for her at the hotel, especially when it was increasingly more difficult for her to get around in her condition, but she had told me, in typical Circus bride fashion, "Well, I couldn't leave it all to them! It would have been all kinds of tacky, you know?"

"Tacky," which was nothing like the pink overkill which I found myself in. Pink chairs, pink tablecloths, pink flowers, pink drinks, pink food – pink everything. Obviously, Stacy's definition of "tacky" differed from mine, but it made no difference because she was clearly over the moon, as evidenced by the look on her face as she approached me...

... and grabbed my hand. "Oh my WORD!," she screamed. Then, with alarming precision, she began reciting. "3/4 carat, cushion-cut diamond, good clarity, nearly colorless...." She peered closer. "No inclusions visible to the naked eye, on 14K white gold."

"Actually, it's platinum," I said. "But wow."

"Oh, I know diamonds," she said, without a trace of humility. Still, though, she was still so likeable in her adorable pregnant condition that I couldn't help but smile at her. "But what I don't know is how this ended up on your hand! Tell, tell!"

I told her our story in an abbreviated form – running partner, best friend, pastor, fiancé, and soon-to-be husband.

"When? When?," she trilled.

"Christmas Day."

"Really? That's so fast! I saw you just a few weeks ago, and you didn't have this little beauty yet," she said, still holding my diamond up to her face. Then, a knowing look on her face. "Are you... you know?" She indicated her own advanced gestation.

"Oh!," I exclaimed. "No, no, no. That would be... well, impossible, actually, barring immaculate conception." Confusion clouded her face, as she opened her mouth to say something else, but I cut her off with, "It's just the best time for our schedules, my brother's schedule with the Marines, all of that. Plenty of time to plan a great wedding, though. Still plenty of time."

"You know what?," she said. "You need to meet Emma and Kendall." She pointed them out from across the room, where they were helping themselves to treats from the pink table. Well, from one of the many pink tables. "They're newly engaged – to MEN, of course, not to one another – and are wanting SPRING weddings. I told them they were CRAZY for trying to pull off a wedding in four months, but would they listen to me? Nope! You've done such a great job with plans for Meredith's wedding and for Ana's wedding, and now, you're doing your own in, what, four weeks?! I just know you could help these girls out, too."

Still holding my hand with the diamond (yes, still), she led me over to them. "Hey, girls, you need to meet Emily. She's crazier than you two are!"

"Well, this WAS a walk-in closet at one time," Josh muttered, standing in front of his closet, trying to step inside past the boxes.

Or maybe I should say his "former closet."

He noticed this only a few seconds after getting in and seeing that all of my clothes were hanging up in there. "Hey, where are MY clothes?"

"I know," I said. "I'm so sorry."

He looked at me, confused. "Well, it's okay, I knew you'd need your own space, but... " He pushed aside some of my clothes, laughing. "Seriously, are they hiding back here somewhere?"

"I moved your stuff to the hall closet," I said. Then, feeling guilty, "It's not like you were even utilizing a fraction of the space in here. Your clothes literally fit on just the back bar. This was made to be a woman's closet, Josh."

"A woman who doesn't share any space with her husband," he said. "But that's fine." He took it all in again. "Wow, I thought you said you didn't have much!"

"Clearly, you grew up with nothing but brothers. This isn't much by most women's standards. Trust me."

We had been moving boxes all month, and with a week left until Christmas, I had felt free to start unpacking. In between appointments and consultations for the different events I had on the calendar for the new year and while Josh was blissfully unaware at school, I had been turning his home into our home. There were a few unpleasant surprises along the way for him, like the closet switch-out and, as Josh called it, the "alarming quantity" of products that now filled his bathroom cabinets and crowded out what little he had in there, but there had been more than a few concessions along the way as well. I had a surround sound system installed as an early wedding gift for him, keeping his xbox in its prominent place of honor, along with his ancient recliner, all of them set up in the living room and ready to greet him....

... which softened the blow of losing his closet. Kind of.

"There are thirty bags in here, Emily," he said, still gaping at my work.

"Purses," I corrected.

"Okay. Thirty PURSES. How in the world can –"

"You know what?," I said, pulling him from the closet and directing him back into the kitchen. "We really should get to unpacking in here, too. Everything else is done. And you hardly had anything in here anyway, and now, we have all of these great shower gifts, these wedding gifts, and –"

"Yeah! They keep showing up at the front door! How many people are even invited to this wedding? Do you know every person in Texas?!"

I leaned forward and kissed him. Not so much to distract him (which was an added bonus at this point) but because I had so missed him in the hectic few weeks we had spent all but passing one another as we finished up preparations for the wedding. I could feel him relax and pull me closer, as I mentally praised God that we were only a week out from the wedding now.

Breaking away from him, I whispered, "I don't know EVERY person in Texas." A pause. "But... yeah. I'm kind of a big deal around here, you know," I shrugged, smiling.

He rolled his eyes, running his hands down my arms and smiling back at me. "Well, that's what I've been saying all along." Another kiss, then a sigh. "Okay. So, the kitchen. What should go where? I don't even know where to start." He picked up a brand new pepper grinder out of one of the most recent boxes to arrive. "What is this thing anyway?"

I took a deep breath and took it from him. "Let's figure it out together," I said, already searching for a place to put it.

"Emily, if you weren't marrying Josh, I would."

Obviously, Matthew liked Josh more than any of us had anticipated. He and Shoko had arrived that morning, and less than an hour after hitting US soil, we had ushered them right over to my parents' house, where we were all enjoying an early Christmas Eve lunch. Matthew was halfway through a plate of the tamales that Grandma Morales had sent over to us, and he looked at Josh with mock adoration.

"I mean, seriously. I would marry you on the basis of these tamales alone. I love you, man."

"I appreciate the love," Josh patted him on the back. "But my grandmother made those. And, hey, she's available, you know."

Matt raised his eyebrows thoughtfully at this, and they both burst into loud laughter.

Oh, yeah. They were going to be great friends.

"Silly, silly boys," Jess said, smiling.

"Who's a silly boy?," Sam asked, looking up from the Christmas tree, where he and his brothers sat with my father, climbing all over him as he laughed, waiting for the signal that we could start opening gifts.

"Your uncles are silly boys," my mother answered.

"Uncle Matt, is Josh going to be my uncle, too?"

"Seems so. Tomorrow at this time, it'll be official," Matthew said, putting his plate down and sliding his arm around Shoko's shoulders as she yawned and rocked baby Seth in her arms.

"Shoko, would you like to take a nap?," I asked her, but she just shook her head in response, smiling at me as she curled up closer to my brother.

My mother and Jessica had been discussing the wedding non-stop, and Jess took our brief lull in conversation to jump back to the topic. "I can't believe you guys aren't even doing a rehearsal dinner," she said, clearing away our plates. "Are we going to even have any idea what to do tomorrow for the ceremony?"

"Redeemer is a lot smaller than Grace," Josh said. "It'll be easy to figure out. No need for a fancy wedding coordinator, you know," he winked at me.

"Yeah, who needs one of those, right?" I said, moving to stand behind his chair, putting my hands on his shoulders as I leaned down to kiss him. "Honestly, it was just easier NOT to have one. We've packed this month so full already, and with Matt and Shoko so exhausted, it just didn't make any sense to keep adding things to the list. Especially when Josh and I still needed to fit Christmas with his family into our schedule and tonight worked out as long as we weren't having a rehearsal dinner."

"You say Redeemer is SMALLER than Grace?," Jess said, hung up on that last detail. "How are we going to get everyone in there, Emily?!"

I looked at Josh, and Josh looked at me. Together, we looked at Jess.

And shrugged our shoulders.

It would be interesting to see how it all played out, that was for sure.

"It's Christmas," my mother said diplomatically. "How many people will really be able to come out on Christmas Day? Right?"

I nodded. "That's what I'm thinking. And if I'm wrong... well, Josh's brothers and Nick –"

"I know, I know," Nick said from his perch on the couch, where he was watching a football game, "we're going to move in chairs from somewhere and put them... somewhere."

"Exactly," Josh smiled at Jess.

"Oh, my WORD," she said, groaning and glaring at us both. "I'm exhausted just thinking about the whole ordeal!"

Matthew spoke up. "And you didn't even fly halfway across the world today... yesterday..." Confusion clouded his face. He looked at Josh. "What day is it?"

"Yesterday, man. Our today is YOUR yesterday."

Shoko smiled at this. "The longest day ever." She explained it to Matthew, who still looked confused. "We left on Christmas Eve in Japan yesterday, and today... is Christmas Eve in America. Is that right? I'm so tired."

"Shoko, why don't you go upstairs and rest for a while?," my sister asked, concerned. "I know you must be completely worn out, and –"

"And I left you a path to Jess's old bed through all of my suitcases," I added helpfully. My apartment was empty, and I was bunking my last night as a Fisher in, appropriately enough, my old room in the Fisher house.

"What about me?," Matt asked. "Why is everyone worried about Shoko but couldn't care less about me? I was on the plane, too, you know."

"We like her more than we like you. And Mom's never even touched your old room, so it's just as gross and smelly as when you left it after high school," Jess said, taking Seth from Shoko's arms. "Seriously, Shoko, go get some rest."

"Well, it will be better if I stay awake until it's dark," she said. "This is only our second trip, but I've already learned that switching to our destination's time makes it easier to get over the jet lag."

"I'm so sorry we had to do it all like this," I told them, not for the first time and certainly not for the last.

"We're glad to be here," Shoko said. "And I am very excited about being in your wedding. Lydia said there's a dress for me..."

"Already upstairs," my mother answered. "Why don't we take some time to try it on and make sure there aren't any alterations that need to be done before we start opening gifts –"

"Grammy, let's open gifts NOW!," Sean shouted gleefully.

"Well, we really need to take care of –"

"NOW!," Matt yelled along with his nephews, getting his second wind and getting us all to take up the chant with them, as my mother looked at us with scolding in her eyes, trying to hide the smile that was threatening to creep onto her face.

"NOW! NOW! NOW!"

She threw her hands into the air. "Fine! You all win! Thomas," she began, moving to the tree, "can you –"

And she stopped short, leading us all to turn and see what was wrong. Jess clutched my hand with a quiet sob and my eyes begin to fill with tears, as we watched my father weep silently, holding his grandsons close in his arms, looking up at all of us as we all watched him with concern. Slowly, he raised his eyes to my mother.

"Oh, Tommy," she said, kneeling down next to him. "What's... what's wrong, sweetheart?"

He put his hand tenderly on her face, a laugh of delight escaping his lips, despite the tears that continued to fall. Sam buried his face deeper in his Grandpa's shirt, while Scott and Stuart played with his shoelaces and Sean smiled at him, wondering at what the great joke was.

"It's just," he began, looking at the four boys, then over at the six of us, gathered around the table, watching him anxiously, "how did we get here, Lydia? With all of... with all of this?," he laughed out loud through his tears. "All of these people? How did we... you and me... end up with so much?"

She laughed with him, tears rolling down her own cheeks. "God has been so very good to us, Tommy. So very, very good."

It was my wedding day.

And it was not without drama, of course.

The drama in Josh's office (which was our makeshift bride's room) that morning had been that Dad was a little confused about exactly where I was getting married, needing Mom to explain to him, again, why I wasn't getting married at Grace. I wasn't sure if his confusion was preferable to his weepiness that had continued on the night before, but even as we prepared for the day, my mind kept going back to him, wondering at how he was showing more and more signs of drifting away from us.

"I would stay back here with you," my mother told me as we stood in Josh's office, all of us cramped together, our dresses hanging from bookshelves. I hadn't even gotten dressed in my wedding gown yet, but I hugged her, saying simply, "You need to stay with Dad, to make sure he's okay." Then, with a smile, "If anyone knows how this whole thing is supposed to go, it's me, right?" She nodded and left, as Jess and I exchanged another look.

"Okay," Jess said, in her no-nonsense voice, ready to rally the troops for my big day. "Shoko, can you help me get the dress ready for Emily?"

And so we went through the motions, all of us wondering if he was going to be able to walk me down the aisle and do the ceremony after all. I was immensely thankful that we had prepped Stephen beforehand and that he was, right now, sitting in the sanctuary with his own copy of the ceremony in his Bible, ready to go at a moment's notice.

Once I was dressed, we all headed down the hall towards the sanctuary, following the very last guests as they were ushered into their seats. One by one, all of the bridesmaids made their way down the aisle – Sara, Melissa, Debbie, Shoko, then Jess, who looked nervously at my dad, who had come to stand by me.

"How are you, Dad?," I whispered to him after she left, just as they were beginning to open the doors to Redeemer's sanctuary for my own entrance.

He looked at me, no confusion on his face at all, as he patted my hand and whispered back, "Don't worry, Emily. It's a good day."

And it was better than a good day. From the moment my eyes met Josh's, urging me to hurry down the aisle to his side, the ceremony was perfect. I didn't even notice that the pews were filled past their capacity, chairs lined up in all the overflow areas, and so many people there as witnesses as Josh and I smiled at one another, hardly seeing anyone else. Dad linked my arm through Josh's, then took his place at Josh's pulpit, where his message was clear and consistent, sincere and sweet, and most definitely one of the finest marriage ceremonies he had ever performed. We all breathed a sigh of relief as Josh and I said our vows and were declared man and wife.

From there, the day passed by in a blur. The pictures, the rush over to the hotel for the reception, and all the people, moving around us, congratulating us, and experiencing every moment with us – they all breezed by so quickly. I had heard brides say this again and again, but I didn't believe them until it was me standing in the receiving line, cutting the cake, dancing the first dance, and throwing the bouquet. I only soaked up a general celebration, no particulars standing out in my mind, only Josh's face and the words that he whispered in my ear at every opportunity he could find. "I love you so much."

The day after Christmas dawned early and bright, and for a moment, I couldn't remember, as I took in my strange surroundings, where I was or even who I was. I glanced over and saw Josh, still asleep, curled up behind me, his arms still around me.

I smiled and turned to face him, kissing him awake with slow deliberate movements. He quickly began responding, peering at me from freshly opened eyes and whispering, with a brilliant smile, "Good morning, Mrs. Morales."

Ahh. THAT'S who I was.

I held his hand out, touching his wedding band. "I didn't remember where I was this morning," I told him. "I've never stayed somewhere this swanky." Hotel management had comped us the honeymoon suite, telling me that with all the business I had given them and would likely continue to give them, that it was their pleasure to do so. Josh had chalked it up to more people who "love them some Emily," and he was probably right.

"Me neither," he said, reaching over to kiss me. "Just another perk of being married to the woman who used to run the place."

"Well, kinda used to run it, I guess." I looked over to the bedside clock, propping myself up on my elbow. "I have the entire day, just for you. Nothing planned." Josh had gotten an old classmate from seminary to fill the pulpit at Redeemer for him this morning and for the next Sunday, which is when we would finally leave for a week-delayed honeymoon. Getting married that weekend had been a smart move in terms of who could be there, but because it fell right before Beau and Melissa's wedding, which I had more than just a small part in making happen, we'd have to wait to go away together.

"No wedding planning today?," he asked, lightly brushing my hair from my eyes. "No big events at Grace? No competition for your time?"

"None. Today is all yours."

"Then, I think," he said, "I'd like to take you home."

"That sounds great."

"But first," he said, gently laying me on my back, smiling as his lips touched my neck, "maybe we could spend a little more time enjoying this swanky, swanky room."

"Mmm-hmm…"

"So, the hostess for this bachelorette party is married," Chloe, Beau's sister, sighed. "What a drag!"

Sara nodded towards her as she continued to pass out desserts – Melissa's choice – to the ladies in the room. "And so newly married, too," she said, looking to me with a wink. "Already gone off and left her husband for a night of partying with the girls."

"You sound like Josh," I said, scooting past her to uncover more of the desserts. "I don't know how we're all eating this stuff after that rehearsal dinner. I've never seen so much food!"

"Trish didn't want to be cheap," Melissa piped up, halfway into a giant slice of strawberry cake.

"Mom's never cheap, Mel. Haven't you figured that out by now?" This from Sophie, Beau's other sister.

"I have," Melissa said, putting down her cake, defeated. "I don't think I can do it. I've got to fit into that dress tomorrow. AND I have to make it up those stairs in the sanctuary without falling over, because if I do, all the seams are busting out." She looked at her sisters-in-law-to-be. "Seriously. Isn't that what the seamstress said?"

"She did," Chloe affirmed. "Told you all your business would be hanging out if you gained another ounce."

"I'll finish that off for you, then," I said, picking up the remnants of Melissa's dessert. "I don't have to fit into a wedding dress ever again. I can rip all the seams I want to."

"This is really good," Sara murmured. "Did this come from –"

"The same bakery that did our New Year's Eve cake, yes," I finished for her. "I have them booked for ten more weddings in the next three weeks."

Business was good. Very, very good. I had been fielding referrals from so many sources now that I couldn't trace them all, and my calendar was quickly booking up completely with weddings, receptions, anniversary parties, showers, and church events. Just two weeks ago, I had to turn a bride down for the first week in June because I was already out of availability. Of course, the past week had been reserved entirely for Melissa and Beau, at a time when the rush was down because of the holidays and which I had rejoiced over greatly, knowing that every second I wasn't spending in a consultation, meeting, or an event was one that I was spending at home with Josh.

At home. With Josh. Would the thrill of having a home with Josh ever wear off?

"What's that smile about?," Melissa asked, eyeing me.

I shook my head clear of thoughts of home and who waited there for me. "Just thinking about tomorrow," I told her. "And New Year's." I smiled over at her and Sara.

"Tomorrow night at this time, we'll be toasting to another year," Sara said, a smile on her own face. "A little more exciting than last year, huh?"

Melissa nodded. "Let's hope I don't fall on my face and make it REALLY exciting."

Melissa managed to keep from falling during the ceremony, so her dress was mercifully spared. With direction from Dad and Stephen both, who did the ceremony together, Beau and Melissa recited their vows with almost scientific precision, as though they had, after thorough processes and methods, concluded that this decision was the correct one.

The sterile manner with which they did this didn't stop Trish Thibideaux from weeping as though it was the most romantic moment she had ever witnessed.

After pictures with the wedding party, I joined Josh from where he stood in the fellowship hall, surveying the surroundings.

"Hey," I said, taking his hand.

"Hey," he smiled at me, trailing his eyes down to my heels then back up again. "Geez, you're tall!"

"You know, you've said that a few times already," I said, distracted by a familiar face near the punch bowl. The scowl over the fact that we were serving just punch was hard to miss. She caught my eye as well and smiled beautifully, if not a bit tersely.

"Evelyn," I said, as Josh and I crossed the few feet over to her. She and I did our standard hug and air kisses, just like we had done for the past six years at occasions like this. Old habits die hard.

"Emily, dear," she cooed. "You look lovely."

"You, too, Evelyn," I noticed the man at her side, whom she didn't introduce us to, even though we were all obviously expecting it. An awkward silence lingered until I asked, "How do you know the couple?"

She smiled, touching the lapel of her (what else?) pink suit, where her quatrefoil badge was proudly displayed, as it had been in all of the days I had worked with her. "Trishy... well, I guess YOU would know her as Mrs. Thibideaux ... she and I were sorority sisters at LSU. Phi Mu sisterhood never ends, you know."

Oh, I did know. She had told me this time and time again, every time a bride and her sorority sisters all gathered together for a picture at the end of their receptions. "Sisterhood never ends," she would say, wiping away a tear.

Apparently not. But... was Evelyn even old enough to be Trish's sorority sister? Could she honestly be old enough to be not only MY mother but BEAU'S mother? I glanced again over at the silent man at her side. Mr. Primrose, perhaps. And older than Evelyn looked certainly.

I risked it. "Mr. Primrose, I presume?," I asked, extending my hand.

He seemed surprised to be included in the conversation. "Dr. Primrose actually. How do you do?"

His last name was actually Primrose. Well, color me surprised. And he was a doctor!

"Fine, thank you." I shook my head. "Please forgive my rudeness. Dr. Primrose, I'm Emily Fish—uh, Morales. And this is Josh Morales, my husband."

"Pleasure," he said. "It's so nice to finally meet the best assistant my wife has ever had."

This was news to me, as I looked to Evelyn, who shrugged in response, a begrudging smile on her face. I was about to respond with praises of Evelyn myself, but Josh was moving us away from the topic.

"What's your specialty, Doctor?," he asked. "I hope it's sports medicine because I sure could use some advice about an injury I have from running the marathon last October. I mean, running it in just over three hours is bound to cause injuries, right?"

He couldn't resist telling people about the marathon and his finishing time. Any and all people. I had a hard time not laughing out loud.

"Oh, heavens, no," Dr. Primrose replied gleefully. "I'm a plastic surgeon."

And I couldn't stop myself from swiveling my eyes right back to Evelyn, who gave me a cold stare. A cold stare that still didn't flaw the fine work her husband had done in taking about twenty years off of her face.

Wow. Good work.

I was about to ask him if he did tummy tucks (Jessica was STILL carrying on about how five children was the breaking point as far as skin elasticity went and that her skin would NEVER shrink back to tautness), but Evelyn cut me off, obviously wanting a change of subject.

"I take it that... you planned this event?"

I looked around at the decorations, the flowers, the atmosphere of the room, all just a step above the simplicity that Melissa wanted, all just a step below the formality that Trish wanted. Rather than each party being irritated that they didn't get what they wanted, they had (very maturely, I might add, which bodes well for the future of their somewhat antagonistic relationship) enjoyed that a middle ground could be found.

"Yes," I said, perfectly content. It had been a joy to do this wedding, had been a joy to do things my way, and had been a joy to see it all come together without all of the unnecessary stress.

"Well," she said, looking it over and managing to look almost... appreciative of some of the more subtly understated but elegant effects. "You do lovely work."

I knew what this cost her to admit. So, I said, as sincerely as possible, "Thank you, Evelyn. That means a lot coming from you."

She gave me a short smile, then took a breath. "You know, Trishy and I were going to plan this wedding. We were going to make it a HUGE event at the hotel. Grand ballroom, you know. Flowers from Bali, gold-rimmed china, a full-sized band, the works." Her eyes sparkled. "It was going to be lovely. And then," she cut her eyes at me, "the bride told us that she had other plans, a friend who coordinated weddings in-de-pen-dent-ly," she spat out, annunciating every syllable. "Well, never in my wildest dreams did I think that she meant YOU. Until, of course, last week when I saw her at YOUR wedding, and then, I just put two and two together and figured out that you were the friend, which just baffled me, honestly." She softened a bit, as she whispered, "I mean, the one time I met her last summer, she wasn't wearing any makeup AT ALL, and I just can't believe that you associate with such inelegant people."

Oh, Evelyn. I was going to miss this, believe it or not.

"But anyway," she said, her voice again trilling, "I suppose this means that you and I are now... competitors." She smiled a smug little grin, likely sizing up the vast differences between her operation and my new little business.

I thought about pointing out these differences to her, praising her awesomeness (as I had done on numerous occasions, unfortunately), and laying to rest the "utterly ridiculous," as Evelyn would say, notion that I could ever be as successful as she was. The truth of the matter was that it didn't matter to me how much money I made, how many clients I won, or how successful I became in the world's eyes. It only mattered that I used my skills and talents to bring others closer to Christ, even in the midst of wedding mayhem.

I thought about telling her all of this, but instead I said, quite simply, "It appears so."

"Well," she said, her eyes twinkling a little too brightly, her voice dipping a little too deeply, "what FUN!" I half expected her head to revolve an entire 360 degrees, but before it could, she snapped out of it and took Mr., I mean Doctor, Primrose's arm.

"You keep well, dear. I see some more Phi Mu sisters over there, so if you'll excuse us."

She was already dragging him away, as Dr. Primrose said his good-byes and hurried after her.

Josh watched them walk away, then turned to me with a laugh. "Still crazy scary," he affirmed.

"Still crazy scary," I echoed, leading him to the dance floor.

"Now, this," he said, pulling me close to him, "seems very familiar. Weren't we just doing this very same thing... last week at this time?"

"Less than that," I said. "Six days ago."

"Ahh," he murmured, "back when we were young newlyweds."

I grinned at him mischievously. "Aren't newlyweds supposed to... you know..."

"No," he said with a smile, "I don't know. Why don't you tell me?"

"Supposed to STOP planning a wedding already? Supposed to run away from wedding planning and life for just a little while? Because, wow. This girl right here?" I pointed to myself. "NEEDS to run away for a while."

He nodded. "Well, that's what I've heard. And I've got it on good authority that in approximately –" he glanced at his watch "—two hours, we're going to toast this new year, blow this joint, and leave. Just leave. I've already packed our bags, put them in the car, and –"

"Really?," I interrupted. "Already packed up and everything?"

"Yep. And we're going to run away for a while. Just you and me."

I closed my eyes and leaned my forehead against his. "Sounds good. Happy New Year, Josh."

"Happy New Year, Emily."

ABOUT THE AUTHOR

Jenn Faulk is a full-time mom and pastor's wife in Pasadena, Texas. She has a BA in English-Creative Writing from the University of Houston and an MA in Missiology from Southwestern Baptist Theological Seminary. She loves talking about Jesus, running marathons, listening to her daughters' stories, serving alongside her husband in ministry, and playing with her larger than life German Shepherd. You can contact her through her blog – www.jennfaulk.com

Made in the USA
Charleston, SC
26 March 2013